To the politically i
an airplane; who l
and thought

Thank you for believing that this had potential.

✠

And to Emma, the winner of the 2nd Edition contest.

Thank you for your wonderful creations.

PRONUNCIATIONS

Luc: *Loose*

Søren: as it is in Norwegian, as *Seuh-ren*

Sør: *Soar*

Thanatos: *Than-a-tos*

Pruinae: *Prue-ee-neh*

Horkos: *Hore-kos*

Págos: *Pah-goh-ss*

Sych: *Sick*

Kóri: *Core-ree*

DAUGHTER

OF

FIRE

STACEY WILLIS

THE DAUGHTER OF FIRE SAGA

Daughter of Fire
Son of Death
Mark of Kóri
Heir of Bones

✠

OTHER BOOKS IN THE SERIES

Reaper of Gods
Tempting of Fate

PART I

THE

DEATH

CHAPTER I

SAVANNAH

WHEN I WAS a little girl, my mother would braid my hair with the wild chrysanthemums we would find in the forest, while my father prepared turkey sandwiches for lunch. A few stray petals were nestled in my hair now, even though we had not been to the forest in eleven years. The chrysanthemums in my hair were tame; they grew uniformed and orderly in my mother's back garden. They swayed gently in the breeze and seemed to beckon, like they were asking to be freed. Sometimes I had half a mind to dig up the earth and throw them outside of our fence, into the street.

I knew they would get trampled, but it did not seem to matter to me.

It would still be the same if I were one of the chrysanthemums. I would be free for only a moment; before the reality of life outside of the protection of a small house ran over me like a car tyre.

I stared out to the stream that ran past our house and the neighbour's, squinting at its murky waters in hopes of spotting a fish. I had found a golden koi fish the last time we had ever went upriver to the nature reserve, and I had named it Goldie —very creative.

There were no fish as far as I could see in the stream. My legs ached to leave this place; to run back to the river and just escape the loop that was my life. *But routines are comfortable*, my mother insisted. And she was right. They were extremely comfortable —dangerously comfortable.

I sighed and glanced up, just in time to catch the sight of a man holding a briefcase who was walking down the street. My heartbeat accelerated and I breathed shallowly —but I knew it was not him.

It could not be him.

My father had left long ago, but his tall form and black suit still flashed in my subconscious in fuzzy static images, like an old television with bad signal. It was as though he was trying to send me a message. Which I would be very open to receive, because it would establish some kind of connection between him and me.

I missed being part of a three-person family, but my mother's attempts to appease the issue with another one of her *boyfriends*, did not put her down in my good books.

Phoebe Green did not like me talking about him —my father. I could not even ask about him. She tried her best to erase the proof of him from everywhere: there were no photographs, no postcards, no text messages, and certainly no birthday and Christmas presents.

In her perfect world, he did not exist, and they had never met.

I would tell her that it was rather weird to tell me that she wished she had never met him. It was a notion that offended me enormously. Did she not realise that she was implying that *I* should not have been born?

"Savannah!"

I turned around at the sound of my name, and automatically cringed at the scowl on my mother's face.

"What are you doing outside?" she asked, throwing a dish towel over her shoulder. Our ginger tomcat, Ron Weasley II, padded past her and walked up to my legs to rub his warm body against me affectionately.

I could not tell her the truth. "…Thinking," I settled for, fiddling with my fingers and leaning against the doorframe.

She stiffened but to her credit, kept a level expression. "I certainly hope that it's not what I think it's about."

"Nope," I said quickly, shaking my head, before blowing upwards to get my hair out of my eyes. "I was thinking about…nature." I glanced back at her army of chrysanthemums. "The stream, the trees, the flowers —"

"That's nice dear," she cut me off, "But can you please put on some warm clothes? It's freezing outside."

She then glanced down the length of me; in a short-sleeved t-shirt and swimming shorts. She turned her nose up in a huff as her gaze landed on my purple nail-polished bare feet. I offered her a sheepish grin.

"It is?" I asked stupidly, blinking. "I couldn't feel it."

Ron purred and flicked his ringed tail against my shin as though he understood and agreed with me. I bent down and picked him up off the ground, before holding him in my arms like a little baby.

Phoebe stopped doing what she was doing and froze, as if what I was saying unnerved her. It had been just over a year now, but little instances like these still seemed to spook her. It was nothing medical or even explicable —I had simply become immune to the weather; my body was always burning with its own heat; and certain plants with an aversion to sunlight seemed to wilt in my wake. We kept it to ourselves, still finding the means to function and hope that things would straighten themselves out.

Phoebe pointed adamantly towards down the hall. "Just do it, Savannah."

I trudged off in that direction, in no mood to argue. It had been a really long day, and I did not need her attitude at the moment.

Ron jumped down and walked ahead of me, then insistent on his regal and entitled independence.

I unlocked the door to my room and picked up the first pair of jeans my hands reached out for, before grabbing my favourite hooded jersey and pulling it over my head. I then caught sight of my reflection in the mirror on my way out, and nearly jumped a foot into the air, causing Ron to mewl.

I wondered if I had even brushed my hair that morning.

I rummaged through the mess I called a dressing table, looking for my hairbrush. I cursed as soon as I found my efforts unfruitful and stomped out to head to my mother's room instead. She must have lost hers this morning and so, snatched mine, before conveniently forgetting to return it.

Her room was off limits at all hours of the day —but I could usually get away

3

with sneaking in and out in five-minute intervals if I needed something.

And I knew that Phoebe would not willingly give me back anything she had taken in her haste.

Even if she would have given me the hairbrush, she would have also taken offence at my assumption; concluding that I was accusing her without proof. She was stubborn that way.

You hardly ever use it anyway, she would end up defending herself, too proud to say she had just borrowed it. Her pride was a really big brick wall that I wished I could sledgehammer to the ground.

I scattered everything that was on her dressing table and scanned it before spotting my black plastic hairbrush and snatching it up triumphantly. I was about to turn away and leave, when I spotted something shining in the sunlight underneath the bed.

Hesitantly, I knelt down and felt around for it with one hand balled up into my jersey's sleeve —since I did not know what to expect. I pulled out a solid black box, decorated with beautifully three-dimensional intricate silver flowers. I wondered why I had never seen it before. Phoebe and I had always gone shopping together, so I would have known.

Ron was suddenly next to me, staring at the box too.

"…Hey there, Weasley," I whispered, scratching underneath his chin. "Looks suspicious, right? I wonder what's inside."

Ron looked at me and then back at the box. He slowly extended a hesitant paw, before scratching rhythmically at the box's surface. I chuckled softly and ran my hand across his arched back, telling him to relax. Curiosity got the better of me and I moved to lift the lid up with my bare hand.

"*Ow*…What the —?" I hissed, recoiling as my fingers stung horribly. I sucked on them, hoping to cool down the sensation of burning flesh. Ron yelped and leaped backwards, startled. I sighed and stroked him again, needing him to calm down. Then I got back to that box. Besides the strange security, the lid itself was extremely heavy. "What is this *made* of…?" I wondered out loud. It was as if I would need a crowbar to even lift a measly inch. My gaze then travelled

4

downward and narrowed at a strangely shaped keyhole. The shape of the hole was unlike any key I had ever seen, yet it looked a little familiar. My hand instinctively flew to my chest, clutching the necklace that always hung there underneath my clothes. I took it out and it sparkled in the sunlight; its sleek glass finish glinting mesmerisingly. It was a pair of black angel wings —beautifully intricate, and it seemed to radiate something so other-worldly.

It had been my father's last gift to me before he had left. He had said that he had wanted to wait to give it to me until I was older, but feared that he might not be around when that time came.

It was almost like a religious symbol to me, and I never took if off unless necessary.

Still filled with trepidation, I carefully leaned down and placed the necklace by the keyhole. It looked like a perfect fit. I then stuck the pendant lengthwise; holding onto the other wing; into the hole and turned it, satisfied to hear a click. The lid opened up by itself —and inside, its treasures were revealed to me. Ron peered in too, as curious as I was.

Paper.

Stacked in tight piles and held together by thick string, were squares of paper. Then I looked a little more closely and found that they were actually letters. They were all addressed to our house, and to my mother. I wondered why she had not yet opened them —or possibly why she would keep unpaid bill notices under lock and key —before I lifted up a bundle and found that their stamps looked nothing like a postage stamp should.

I glanced towards the door, my heartbeat accelerating, but no footsteps approached, and the distant singing stayed in the kitchen. Ron padded around the box once, before sticking his nose up and stalking off towards the door and disappearing around the corner. It seemed as though I would have to uncover this mystery alone. I breathed a shaky exhale, before sliding out a single letter from a stack and examining it.

It smelled like something had died inside of it.

I made a face, holding it out at arm's length. But then I noticed how the black envelope shimmered, even without the sunlight. I tore the flap open, in one swift movement. Then came the letter —crisp white paper overwritten by beautiful black typewriter print.

My Dearest Phoebe,

I know that you never want me to see her again, but
if she is really behaving the way of which I have been
informed, then I really need to see her. This may have something
to do with my...nature; and if this is the case, then it is
imperative that we take immediate action. I
fear for her life — her immortal life. And I know that
I ask for this every time...but may I see her? Just once?
Only for a minute — or even a glimpse, Phoebe. I just
want to know how my daughter is doing.

H.

My eyes widened as I scanned the letter. I focused on the word '*daughter*' and frowned. It was from my father —the man whom I had been told to consider as dead. He was still alive and well —and seemed to be...concerned about me. I was unsure of how that made me feel.

Did he know about what was happening to me? It was not an issue if so —he was my father after all. What unnerved me was my parents' discussion about it and me, behind my back. Did I not have the right to know?

I was tempted to grow angry, but I knew deep down that it would yield nothing. My head had to remain levelled. I could not let my mother anger me without uncovering all of the facts, and considering her thought process. She only would have done it to protect us —to protect me.

Unable to resist, I grabbed another letter and hurriedly tore it open.

My Dearest Phoebe,

I am truly sorry about all that has happened. Please forgive me. Memory is a tricky thing when you are as old as me. But do not get the wrong impression — I wanted to come and attend her thirteenth birthday. But Charon will not let me cross without permission. I found it rather ridiculous that he meant that I should get approval from someone below me, but I cannot argue with Charon. He is the only one who can brave the waves. But enough about me. I regret not being present for Savannah becoming a teenager, but I hope to see her soon — if you are willing. Please, Phoebe.

H.

I blinked and a tear spilled and travelled down my cheek, before landing on the letter. Even if my parents were conspiring, it would have been good to know that my father was still around —and that he wanted to see me.

How could Phoebe have kept these from me all this time?

To my surprise, the salty tear water that had dripped then began to bubble on the surface of the paper, before it evaporated completely. I consequently dropped the letter, and accidentally knocked over the box, spilling the other bundles of letters onto the floor.

"Savannah, honey! Dinner's ready," my mother's voice then suddenly carried down the hallway. I froze.

"Eh…coming, Mom!"

I began to panic. I quickly grabbed the fallen stacks of letters and turned back to the box. My hands hovered there in hesitation —and before I could stop myself, I stuffed them up the front of my jersey instead. The paper of the envelope unnaturally warmed my stomach, but I did not have the time to think about that.

After lowering the lid back down with jersey-covered hands and hearing a satisfying click, I slid the box back underneath the bed and stumbled to my feet, clutching at my midsection in an effort not to drop the letters. I hobbled over to the door, closed it quietly, before tumbling into my own room.

I let out a relieved sigh and quickly stuffed the letters into my pillow cover; out of sight.

My cellphone then vibrated four times, and my rattled nerves caused me to jump. I unlocked it to find that all of the messages were from my best friend Luca Georgette, and they were all in caps lock. She was demanding to know why I was not answering any of her messages. And under that, was a prompt to take a look at Francesca Minetti's Snapchat story.

I smiled a little at the typical behaviour that could only be described as Luca being Luca; but I cringed at the last couple of messages. There was no doubt that Francesca's Snapchat Story would be filled with bright lights and blurred images, as her iPhone camera tried to keep up with her intoxicated jerky filming. Anyone would get nauseous just from watching it.

I typed a reply —a short, curt response to properly illustrate my thorough distaste for anything to do with Francesca. I knew that Luca was only gauging for a reaction because she wanted to make me laugh, but I could not even bring myself to be in the mood to cooperate.

I pressed *send* and sighed in exasperation. I could not understand why Luca even entertained the idea of Francesca in the first place. All of my other friends tolerated her, but her and I just could not seem to get along.

Francesca Minetti was a carbon copy high school rich-girl-first-world-problems-drama-queen; and all of her equally fake girly hangers-on worshipped her like an Egyptian god.

Her smile was as flashy and misleading in authenticity as her bright purple bedazzled Porsche; and while people thought that the Devil wore Prada, I could testify that she wore Louis Vuitton and Gucci, bought using her daddy's apparently limitless credit card.

I did rather enjoy our little passive aggressive banter every now and again though. Her petty and internet-stolen insults were always amusing and mood lightening —even on dismal weekdays.

Deciding not to dwell on it any further, I set my cellphone down beside my bed and headed towards the door and out of my bedroom.

✠

"Don't you *like* mac and cheese?" my mother said through a mouthful, eyeing me suspiciously.

I had been poking around my plate with a fork; my mind drifting away to the letters clumped up in my pillowcase and how my fingers itched to open all of them and try to read them in the voice I had imagined my father to have. Ron weaved his way amongst the legs of the table and the legs of the humans, providing a strangely comforting feeling when his fur brushed against them.

"No, no. It's fine," I mumbled, bringing a forkful to my mouth to prove it. Then I paused, the fork in mid-air. "...Do you ever receive any...mail about me?" I put tactfully, careful to leave out '*he*' and '*still in contact with*'.

My mother's fork stopped scratching at porcelain. I looked up, but her gaze would not meet mine. Phoebe Green was not a shy or reserved woman. If she had something on her mind, offending someone by voicing it was always the last factor which she took into consideration.

"...What? You mean besides reports from school?" she almost forcefully chuckled, as though she were trying to laugh it off.

I did not elaborate. If she wanted to be that way, then fine. I looked down, twisting my fork in the pasta and sticky cheese sauce.

"Savannah, if you're asking about...*you know what*," she growled slightly for emphasis, "I can assure you that there has been no such activity. No contact; no mention —got it?" She pointed her fork at me.

That was her mantra. *No contact; no mention.* She did not limit the use of it to my father —it seemed to satisfy and dismiss every problem she faced.

I had to admit, I was a little crushed to hear her deny it —but also a little disappointed. Not in her, but in myself, for actually knowing that she would never admit to something like a weird occult box hiding underneath her bed.

9

So, I tried to play if off normally and nodded, bringing the same forkful of mac and cheese to my open mouth again.

"…Got it."

✠

I lazily collapsed onto my bed, ready to sleep dressed in my t-shirt and pyjama shorts. Ron was past that stage and was already curled up on the far side of my bed, purring softly.

"Sav, don't give me that look," Phoebe said sternly from where she stood in the doorway. I looked up at her properly with my pitiful pout. "I think you know very well where I stand. And I also think you know that there is no way any mail would have ever been sent about you."

I frowned at her use of the passive voice. Why was she feeling the need to remove herself from that sentence and not just say that she had never received anything —as untrue as it may be?

"…Sure." I shook my head, trying to show that I agreed with her. I had no energy at that moment to push the issue.

She sighed, and her expression softened. "I love you. Very much."

I smiled sadly and nodded. "…I love you too."

I watched her leave and close the door. Once I was sure that she was gone, I grabbed my cellphone and sent a distressed message to Luca. She was the only one I trusted with this kind of information.

I thought about how much I should give away. Luca knew about the situation regarding my father, but she did not know everything. While in reality my contact with him was a dismal zero, I had told her that I hardly saw him though he was still very present.

I started to feel a little guilty for bending the truth to my best friend —but then I remembered that I refrained from getting too attached to someone.

Not enough to share family secrets; especially ones of which even I had not been aware. So, I only told her about the secret stash of letters, and that they were

10

from my father. They also shared the same sent date —the twelfth of April. And Luca was pretty sharp.

She immediately caught on that the letters probably come routinely. And that the date was also my birthday.

I froze as I read her next messages. Yes, that date was my birthday. But to Phoebe and me, it was simply the day Savannah Ivy Green had started *existing*. Luca's shock was only a result of intentional amnesia —but even she could not resist connecting the dots.

Today was the eleventh of April. I did not like remembering the fact that it was my birthday tomorrow, but I could not resist the feeling of hope for another letter coming. A more recent letter would make him feel a little more real; make him feel a little closer, and reachable.

If this was to be my only contact with my father, then I was sure as hell going to take it. I rolled over onto my stomach, reached for my charging cable and plugged my cellphone in, before turning onto my side and pulling up the covers —which was a little difficult with an adult sized cat laying on them but I succeeded without waking him up. I then shivered, thinking about tomorrow's date. The letters crackled as I moved my head, making me sit up again. I slid some of them out and spread them on the sheets.

My alarm clock said that it was 21:04.

I had time. So, I settled down onto my stomach again before I opened one and began to read.

CHAPTER 2

SAVANNAH

BIRTHDAYS WERE NOT things that were celebrated in my household. They meant cake; presents; cards; and the expected absence of my father. They were supposed to be happy and spent with your family —so how were mine supposed to be celebrated, if my family had been torn in two and my wish would always be to have been born on purpose?

Phoebe did not want to put me through that. That was why she treated it like any other day and made no effort to treat me any differently.

That was why I told my friends not to make a fuss. Though thankfully even they knew that the topic was taboo, and had stopped sending me Happy Birthday messages and presents willingly. No one else really inquired as to how old I was; because I made it a touchy subject.

Except Aaron Carter; my boyfriend of three years. He was making it his personal mission to make my eighteenth birthday, a birthday. It was so typical of him —since we had met, he had gone out of his way to see me smile; to hear me laugh; or to just get a reaction from me. I had called it picking on an innocent soul. He liked to recall it as flirting.

"Happy birthday!" Aaron exclaimed, holding a cake out to me at seven in the morning.

Ron whined in protest, and remained curled up, his back turned to us. I stumbled backwards in surprise whilst lacing up my left sneaker; not having expected anything of the sort. Aaron was wearing his usual ripped jeans and plaid, sporting an ebony leather jacket. His messy brown hair was unusually well kept this morning and he had made the effort to fill in every single piercing in his ears; but a *Disney Princess* party hat sat on top of his head, looking very out of place.

Once I had gotten over my heart attack, I looked at the cake and blinked in bewilderment at the crazily scrawled iced words.

welcome to adulthood ♡

congratulations on not being dead yet!

"...Wow, Carter. Just wow," I deadpanned, turning away from the cake. "Where did you even get that from? And how did my Mom even let you in?"

"I made it," he said, shrugging innocently. "And your Mom loves me, Green, you know that."

I looked between him and the cake, cringing uncomfortably. "...Hard pass."

"Aw come on, I slaved on it for like, *forever*," he reasoned, pouting. I gave him a look. "What, are you not even going to try it?"

I clicked my tongue but swiped a finger across the cake, ruining the message. I smiled at him triumphantly, before sucking on my finger. His face fell a mile, but I was too busy concentrating on cake.

"Mm...buttercream," I hummed, before patting his shoulder.
Aaron shook his head, disappointment written all over his face as he put the cake down on my bedside table. "What is wrong with you, Green?"

"You're my boyfriend. Aren't you supposed to know that?" I quipped, standing up on my tiptoes to plant a kiss on his cheek.

He frowned. "I would have thought you would loosen up for your sixteenth at least, but you proved me wrong, as usual. Why can't you just be a normal teenage girl for once and enjoy your eighteenth birthday?"

I paused, grabbing my backpack and slinging it over my shoulder. I did not answer him straight away. His question made me think.

It made me break.

I had never disclosed the true reasons why I never celebrated my birthday with anyone besides Luca —not even Aaron knew. I felt that no one else *deserved* to know. And I certainly was not ready to share the information I had found in Phoebe's room with anyone else but Luca, either.

"None of my birthdays are *enjoyable* anymore," I whispered, turning my back on him and wiping my face hurriedly.

"Hey," his voice grew gentle, "I saw that."

"You want a prize, then?" I whipped around and clipped. I abruptly clenched my fists and growled, before turning back around. Then I gasped, feeling the tears stream down my cheeks in a fulminating burst.

I was crying…properly. Ardently. I stood there at a loss, my chest compressing and my lungs burning.

I had not cried like this in twelve years; since my father left.

"Savannah —" Aaron tried.

"No. Leave me alone," I sobbed, beginning to wipe the tears away as soon as they escaped with the back of my maroon top's sleeve. "I don't need to tell you *anything*."

He backed off immediately at that, and slowly lowered himself down to sit on my bed as I sobbed by my bedroom door. This was one of the reasons why birthdays were not celebrated. There was simply nothing to celebrate.

At least my father had not left *on* my birthday. That would have banished the word from my vocabulary entirely.

"…Hey, you should take what you get as it comes," Aaron sighed eventually, dropping one of my snow globes with which he had been playing onto the carpet suddenly, "Being alive is something to look forward to more than when you won't be, or choose not to."

I frowned and looked up, not believing him. I then gestured being sick by shoving a finger in my mouth. "Yolo," I deadpanned.

"That's the spirit," he encouraged sarcastically, jumping up and setting the snow globe by my bedside.

I lidded my eyes and wiped my face dry one last time. "You're not very good at comforting people, are you, Carter?" I snorted, folding my arms.

"The only person I need to comfort is you, Green," he smirked, circling my waist. I reached up and took the party hat off of his head, before putting it on mine and sticking out my tongue.

"*That*, is so alarmingly cheesy," I chuckled weakly, hugging him closer to me and pressing my lips against his. That did not seem to satisfy him —he took the irreverent liberty of deepening it. Though I did hum in satisfaction, so he tilted my head back and ran his hands down to my black denim skirt; his body enveloping mine. I loved the way he smelled —a subtle mixture of *Axe* and rained-on wood. His scent always put me at ease.

He had this needy heated habit that came and went —but it did not throw me off or make me want to resist. I would not admit it aloud, but I loved the insatiable side of him as much as the solicitous.

I could easily stay in his embrace indefinitely.

"…You did your hair. Kind of," he then commented when we reluctantly broke apart, remembering what time it was.

I absentmindedly twirled a lock of my curled dark red hair, smiling slightly. He had noticed. "Why not," I quipped, before tugging off the party hat and shoving it back on his head.

"You are unbelievably lucky to get away with that, Green," he chuckled. "It's a good thing you're so cute —and mine."

"I'll let that one slide," I giggled as he grabbed the cake from my bedside and followed me out of the door. "Since you're pretty cute too."

We then made our way downstairs and quickly headed for the front —only to be stopped by my mother in the kitchen.

"Savannah, there's someone I'd like you to meet before you go," she smiled, moving aside to reveal a large man doing something that might have been washing the dishes, at the sink. "Don, this is Savannah."

15

My skin crawled and I remained still as Aaron stood behind me. I blinked, still processing the meaning of the situation.

Ron emerged and jumped down the stairs two at a time, before staring at the strange out-of-place giant man in our house too.

"Hello, Savannah," he greeted, turning around. I was a little surprised to hear the slight Korean lilt to his accent; and to see that part of his ancestry shine through in his warm grin. He resembled a lumberjack —the murderous kind. "I'm Don. I'll be hanging around for a bit," he beamed.

I glanced from his untamed dark hair and five o'clock shave; to the greying hair on his arms and legs; and to his wild green eyes.

Big, gruff and hairy was not what I had imagined to be a turn on for my mother. But I supposed that I was in no position to be too quick to turn my nose up at him considering Phoebe Green's past experimenting with different types of men, in all various shapes and sizes.

I then looked at her. "Another one?" I scoffed before I could stop myself.

Ron arched his back threateningly before turning on his heels and walking into the living room.

"Savannah," my mother warned, "be nice."

I failed to see what obligation I was under in order to obey that. "I don't have the time to deal with this, Mom," I said truthfully. "We're going to be late for school." I then turned sharply to leave.

"No, we're not —" Aaron started.

"*Late*," I insisted, pushing him out of the door, with him spewing out more protests as he nearly dropped the cake. I growled as I stomped over to my car, before forcefully opening the driver's door.

"Savannah," Aaron chuckled, shaking his head, "Sooner or later you're going to have to deal with a boyfriend of your Mom's —one who you're not going to be pissed off with."

He slid in and balanced the cake precariously on his lap.

I gave him a look as I turned the ignition. "That's some really helpful advice, Carter. But I will never be happy with any of her boyfriends," I sighed as I put the car into reverse gear. "…Especially not one that looks like a grizzly bear." I gave him a tired and knowing smile.

Aaron cracked a smile. "Happy birthday, Savannah Green," he chuckled. He knew that saying that would get on my nerves.

"I don't *know* you," I sang begrudgingly, reversing out of the driveway.

✠

School was in a strange and unexpected louder buzz than usual for a Friday. Students were littered around the main building, engaged in suspiciously excited conversations, and holding pieces of paper. I frowned, wondering what on Earth could have gotten them into such a zealous mood. Perhaps the Environmental Club was finally resorting to bribery.

Holy Reed was a plain, and sadly not desolate high school which cared more about our basketball team than the students' grade point averages —the only enriching thing left was probably being part of the physics club.

I parked the car a good distance away from the entrance before Aaron and I then made our way there. Several pairs of eyes glanced in our direction; with wide smiles still glued onto faces. We must have looked a sight —a bad boy and his girl. I used to laugh at couples like that; now I was part of one of them. It certainly was not his delinquent charm for which I had fallen.

I quickly spotted Luca in all of her puffy, dark curly-haired and honey-skinned glory passing out what appeared to be flyers.

I made a beeline for her.

"Hey lovebirds." She winked as she saw us approach. "Here —take these."

She gave us a colourful flyer each and then grinned expectantly as we skimmed over them.

"…A private party?" Aaron commented, raising an eyebrow. "At a nightclub the next town over? Aren't we legally underage?"

"It's hosted by Francesca Minetti," I muttered. "I'm not surprised."

I then spotted the words, '*in honour of Savannah Green's birthday*'.

17

I tensed up as Aaron and Luca both glanced at me. So that was what all of the commotion was about. I bit my lip to prevent myself from saying anything I would regret, before letting out a sigh and shaking my head.

"...I think the *hell* not," I said calmly, folding my arms.

"She promised me ten bucks if I handed the flyers out," Luca confessed, offering me a sympathetic smile. "Besides —maybe it's time you loosened up a little. It's your special day; it only comes once a year. And it's your *eighteenth*." Then she paused, noticing how I fidgeted. "...I know you hate birthdays. But...we just wanted to do something special." She then gave me a small smile. "We were kind of hoping you'd say yes?" she said hopefully.

"I don't hate birthdays," I grumbled. "They're just...hard," I whispered, my gaze flickering downwards.

"Don't let this get to you," Aaron murmured as he put a strong arm around me, "Francesca has always been a little...difficult. But I think she's honestly just trying to help."

He was right —she never had been good at understanding and considering other people's feelings. I took a deep breath and exhaled noisily, letting out my frustration. "Maybe you're right. But we should get to class before we're late."

I dismissed further discussion with a wave of my hand and started walking that way anyway.

"What about this cake?" Aaron called after me.

I turned around to walk backwards through the crowd, shrugging. "Put it in your locker or something. I mean, I kind of ruined it, so maybe just toss it."

He gave me a disappointed look, which I returned, before turning around again. School was manageable on a day like this. As long as everyone kept their mouths shut and averted their gazes as they usually did, I could survive and file another twelfth of April under unquantified success. But unfortunately for today, Fate had other plans.

"Happy birthday, Savannah!" someone said to me in the hallway, which only caused a ripple effect for others to blurt out the same. "It's awesome that you're celebrating it again!"

...*Right*. I smiled nervously in response and picked up the pace, fighting the feeling of bile rising up in my throat.

"Hey, if you weren't taken, I could have given you the best birthday present you've ever experienced, babe." Some weirdo winked at me, just as Aaron steered me to the other side of him and kept his arm on my waist.

"*Disgusting*," Luca spat.

We agreed, ignoring all the cat calls that entailed.

When I had started dating Aaron —who had been the designated *bad news* when he transferred —it had taken me to centre stage in the scandal theatre. Growing up in a small town made it difficult to hide anything from prying eyes and ears. I had been relatively quiet and uninterested in high school politics prior to Aaron. Time had now tainted that claim, but before, rumours had circled and suggested that we had been getting it on after someone found us making out in one of the bedrooms of Jessica Harris' house at the junior prom after party. It had inevitably further ruined my reputation.

I had worked hard to somewhat restore my dignity. But sometimes people made it difficult maintaining my composure.

We gathered around Luca's desk before class was supposed to start and chatted, though I could not bring myself to join in. My focus kept shifting to the letters, and the prospect of my father possibly sending another letter today. I hoped that my mother would not receive it first and immediately stuff it into that box underneath her bed.

"Hey, you okay?" Aaron's voice brought me back to the classroom, causing me to sigh and rest my head on his shoulder.

"Yeah, I'm fine," I whispered.

✠

Throughout the day, I kept repeating a phrase inside my head, hoping that I would start to believe it if I said it enough.

I am fine.

19

"Who said that you were going to get ready with us?" I scoffed and raised an eyebrow.

"You're a guy," Luca snorted, "It would take you fifty-five minutes less time than us to get ready, then you'd be sitting there twiddling your thumbs."

I burst out laughing, poking Aaron's cheek when he pouted and looked wounded. "Don't take it personally, Carter —it's just gender-based stereotypes," I comforted him. "We won't really take an hour to get ready," I said, much to his suspicious relief. "…We'll take two."

✠

When we arrived, *Riddley's* was already infested with school kids and working adults who were on lunch break. After waving hello to Joe Riddley Jr, the owner, we slid into our favourite booth and settled down with the menus, eager to eat something different to the usual burger and curly fries.

But as we browsed the options, I found myself turning around and glancing behind us. Someone had their eyes on me, or at least that was what the chill that ran up my spine told me. I breathed in and out deeply in an effort to clear my head, before dismissing my suspicion and trying to decide on a snack. I was scoping the menu, when my gaze happened to flicker upwards. My eyes locked with a pair of light grey ones across the diner; with the look in them hard and intense. They belonged to a tall figure from what I could see, since the rest of their face was obscured by a menu card, but other than that I could not tell anything else about them. They were dressed in black —leather, upon inspection —and looked deathly pale. Their dark eyebrows furrowed as we maintained eye contact, before the person glared at me. The air suddenly felt a lot colder, making me consequently shiver and suddenly wish for a jacket.

"I'm going to order some cheese fries this time," Luca announced, bringing me back to Earth, as she leaned back against the weathered seat across from me and Aaron. The atmosphere loosened, and the air returned to its normal balmy temperature. I blinked, shook my head and glanced back in the direction of the stranger. They were looking down, eyeing their menu.

"Cheese fries?" Aaron raised an eyebrow. "You know, I never understood the concept of them. That's just reconstituted discarded milk solids on fried potato sticks."

My best friend pulled a horridly disgusted face. "Oh my God. Well, when you put it like *that* —"

"Let the girl eat," I said, elbowing him. "What she puts in her mouth is none of your business."

Luca stared at me as Aaron then burst out laughing. "…That's what she said," she muttered —which made my boyfriend choke.

I laughed harder, feeling drawn back into the conversation —and away from the creepy twenty seconds of my life that I would never get back.

"…Have you decided yet?" Aaron then wheezed as I drummed my fingertips on the laminated card thoughtfully.

"Mm," I hummed, nodding, "I'll have a chocolate milkshake."

"*Just* a chocolate milkshake?" he questioned.

"*Just* a chocolate milkshake. I'm…not very hungry," I sheepishly admitted.

"Hey, let the girl have a milkshake," Luca came to my defence. "What she puts in her mouth —"

"All right!" I cut her off after seeing her smile grow wide. "Thank you for that. Now," I turned to Aaron, "have you decided, Carter?"

"A slice of gooseberry pie, Green," he sighed, getting a far-away look that made Luca and me share a wary one. "I've been craving some lately," he said in a matter-of-fact way. There was a pause.

"…I know that we're supposed to be ordering things that are out of the ordinary, but you don't even know what a gooseberry is, do you?" I raised an eyebrow, becoming increasingly amused.

"Of course not," he admitted, lidding his eyes.

More laughter held up the now pleasant atmosphere, before it settled down as Aaron motioned for a waitress. I glanced at the stranger again to see that they had then stood up. I could then see that they were a teenager, with messy raven hair

23

and heavy-looking black buckled boots. I watched as he picked something up from the seat next to him before walking towards the door.

A *crossbow*. I started, startled by the discovery.

"Green? You good?" Aaron put an arm around my shoulders.
I jumped again, surprised by the sound of his voice. I glanced between him and the person with the crossbow, who was now leaving.

"Yeah…" I said uncertainly. "Tell me something. Is it legal to carry around a crossbow in public?"

"What?" Luca blinked, confusion furrowing her eyebrows.

"That guy over there," I jerked my head in the direction of the door. "He's got one —can't you see?"

There he still stood, doing something with the crossbow. I then noticed a quiver of arrows strapped to his back, and instinctively shrank back against the blue leather seat. Aaron and Luca looked at each other before looking back at me. I shrugged, in a way of saying *what?*

Aaron then put a hand on my forehead, causing me to flinch.
"Are you sure that you're okay?" he asked.

"Savannah —there's no one there," Luca frowned. "Are you high? You're seriously hallucinating."

"I'm not high," I deadpanned, rather offended. I paused, and glanced back at the stranger, only to find that he was now gone. I blinked, but nothing materialised there. "…I think that I might be going crazy though," I sighed, running a hand through my hair. "It's all this party nonsense —it's getting me worked up," I groaned. They laughed, to my relief, and agreed with me. But I glared at the door. I knew what had transpired —there was no way that I was just seeing things.

CHAPTER 3

SAVANNAH

LOUD ROCK MUSIC was blaring through the car speakers; the discretion of the volume being Luca's. She was shrieking along to the lyrics at the top of her lungs —and on the outside, it appeared as though I too had entered into the spirit of things. My car was stuffed with her, a few of our other friends and me; all dressed up and ready for a night out. I had not realised that driving with a whole lot of screaming in one's ears was that difficult. I sang along politely, hitting all the notes, but my voice was drowned out by the off-pitch hysteria.

So, I gave up after a while and just concentrated on getting to *Twilight* in Saratoga Springs —where the party was supposed to be held. Francesca had sent directions on the group chat, so I could rule out the possibility of this all being an elaborate prank. Unfortunately, the unironic Homer Simpson voice on my GPS could not be heard over my ironically annoying passengers.

"*Guys*! I'm trying to drive here," I whined, finally snagging their attention — but only momentarily.

"Are we being too loud?" Luca asked.

"But it fits the occasion, doesn't it?" Samantha Gordon scoffed. Out of all of the cheerleaders I knew, she was the most down to Earth —the most genuinely invested in her craft, and not for the popularity. She tossed her wavy golden hair over her shoulder and grinned stupidly, showing off her dimples, before daring to stick out her tongue at me.

"Do you want us to arrive in one piece or not?" I responded, coming to a stop at a traffic light.

"It all depends," Olive Buhrnam —the self-proclaimed vegan witch and cynic of the group —stuck her freckled nose in the air. "Is it wise to get into a cat fight before, or after you die?"

"*Ha ha*," I scoffed.

"It's literally around the block now, Sav," Lauren Miller then sighed heavily. Lauren was an honour student and aspiring prima ballerina —she was the one who reined us all in and aimed to instil good moral values and habits —yet she knew full well that if she could not beat them, join them.

Everyone laughed at my written-off worry, while I was obligated to chuckle. It was then not even a minute before they started shrieking again. I gave up trying to reason with them —and by some damn miracle, we arrived at *Twilight* unscathed. It was a relief to spill out of the car after nearly an hour, and head for the entrance. We could hear the pop music and see the colourful flashing lights from outside, which got my friends squealing in anticipation again. I only added to their impatience by having to give our names and waiting for the bouncer to check them on the list.

"…The birthday girl, huh?" he grunted, tapping the clipboard with a pencil. "Happy twenty-first," he smiled in a sly, knowing way.

So, Francesca had lied about my age…not that it surprised me.

"That's me," I said unenthusiastically.

The bouncer unhooked the rope from the stand and gestured for us to be his guest. We scuttled through the entrance, before beholding the interior. I had snuck into a club before, but it now seemed mellow compared to that by which we were now surrounded. The ultraviolet lights shone through the hazy darkness from the ceiling and walls, bathing the atmosphere in neon purple. Everyone was wearing white, as was customary here, which made them and the whole room glow. It was all very overwhelming and immediately made me want to go back outside.

"She's here!" someone shouted before I could make my escape and grabbed me by the arm to pull me to one of the standing platforms in the middle of the room, before catapulting me upwards. I stumbled to halt before standing there

26

awkwardly and giving a small wave, causing an eruption of cheers. I supposed that was what came with popularity. My gaze narrowed as I scanned the faces; I could not care less about who was who so long as I vaguely recognised them from my grade, but my eyes searched for one person in particular.

"Happy birthday, Savannah!" the distinct voice of Francesca Minetti trilled, and I turned to find her standing on the platform next to me, before she hooked an arm around my neck. "This is all for you, babes, now that you're officially an adult. Though let's not kid ourselves —little Savannah has been a woman for a while now."

"Slut shaming is a bit of a low blow," I growled in annoyance while trying to pry her long, manicured matte black nails away from my throat.

"Right. Everybody enjoy yourselves," she then went on addressing the crowd, "The drinks on offer are already paid for, so go crazy!"

She suddenly raised her glass of God-knows-what and it splashed a little over my chest. I growled but she did not take any notice. She was then about to turn and climb down to the floor, when she dug her fingers into my shoulder and brought her lips to my ear. "…Enjoy this party, but never forget where you came from. You know very well why you're so popular —you wouldn't be here without Aaron Carter. Keep him close. We both know that this is a *much* more preferable rung on the social ladder," she whispered, before adding a soft chuckle. I frowned as she let me go and flittered her fingers in my face. "Ta ta, then!"

I shivered and watched her model-walk away. I wanted to believe that Francesca's words did not faze me. Unfortunately they rung with unsaid truth. She was not wrong about Aaron being my ticket to a greater social circle —but I had never once imposed myself on Francesca and her minions. I had never tried to rival her. I did not ever want to *be* like her, yet she saw me as nothing but a threat to her title. Even today, when it was supposedly about me, she had not resisted to tear me down further than I already felt. That was how she controlled people, I realised. She never hesitated to upstage; to remind those elevated in status by association that they would be nothing without the school's so called '*noble born*'. I wrote it off as teenage and capitalistic nonsense, though it was difficult to ignore how awkward it felt being around Aaron's friends. Like I was a corner puzzle piece from a finger painting that defiled their *Mona Lisa*.

I then blinked dejectedly, thrown off by Francesca's best attempt at the equivalent of a happy birthday wish, before turning around to see Aaron standing by my platform. My irritation melted away. None of what Francesca had told me mattered now that I was with him. He loved me just as I was —just as I had been. I smiled and crouched down as he held his arms out. He wrapped them around my waist before gently lifting me up and putting me down on the floor. Just him and me —that was what mattered.

He did not understand why I then clung to him more than usual; why I wanted to hold him close for just another moment longer. But he returned my smile, and he let me suggestively wrap my arms around his neck. That must have set him off, because he took hold of them and laced our fingers together, before leaning in to give me what I wanted —right there in the middle of the nightclub and in front of fifty other people.

I did not care. *Let them think what they want.*

"You want to dance?!" Aaron then raised his voice above the music when we pulled apart. Our audience immediately scattered, fearing his glare.

"Let's get some drinks first!" I replied, tugging him towards the bar. If Francesca was rich enough to bypass the law just for this, then I might as well enjoy it. We settled down on the stools before ordering cocktails, happy to see familiar and friendly faces as Luca and the girls waltzed over.

"Francesca is definitely already drunk," Luca sighed as she sat on the other stool beside me. I was inclined to believe her.

She fluffed up her halo of dark frizzy curls, before slumping in frustration as the volume flattened out to its usual size.

"She has pre-drinks before everything," Sam scoffed.

"Let's not be so quick to judge," Aaron frowned at us, in complete seriousness. "You guys arrived an hour late."

"He's got a point," Lauren pouted.

"I hate it when people have a point," Olive muttered, sipping her cocktail.

"I can't help it if I'm always right," Aaron smirked. I gently shoved him.

"You are not," I laughed. "*I'm* the one who's always right."

Luca raised her glass triumphantly. "I'll drink to that."

"You'd drink to anything," Aaron quipped, swiftly sipping on his own cocktail that then arrived.

"Hey." Luca reached over to smack his leathered arm. "What I put in my mouth is none of your —"

It was at that point that I zoned out and glanced around the room. I saw the general scenery of sweating grinding teenagers; nothing out of the ordinary. But as my gaze shifted towards the bathrooms, I locked eyes with a familiar set of grey irises. Though in the dark and under ultraviolet lights, the eyes glowed a luminescent silver. The male from the diner was leaning against the wall, swinging his crossbow, and not looking as tough as he had earlier: I could see that he was wearing a warm navy blue turtleneck sweater underneath the leather jacket. But the same sinister feeling returned and increased the longer his eyes stayed on me. My fists clenched. I decided that I needed to confront him, and demand to know why he was stalking me.

"I'm going to the bathroom," I announced, still eyeing the stranger. My friends waved me off absentmindedly and did not seem all too concerned.

I made a beeline for him, marching purposefully through the crowd of people. His eyebrows raised slightly in what appeared to be acknowledgment of my plans, and all of a sudden; I blinked, and he disappeared.

Just…gone.

I shook my head in confusion, before actually heading to the bathroom to splash some water in my face. Whatever tricks my mind and or eyes were playing on me, I was not particularly amused.

Breathe, Savannah. Relax. You are not crazy. This is obviously some kind of prank for your birthday.

I calmly breathed out. It was either that, or someone thought that April Fools lasted all month. As I then re-emerged from the bathroom, wringing my hands, Luca popped up out of nowhere and caused me to jump. She blinked, before I sighed in relief and raked a damp hand through my hair. "Don't sneak up on me like that, Luc."

"What's got you all jumpy?" she laughed and raised an eyebrow. "Come on, you're missing out."

She then linked arms with me, before dragging me to the dance floor, where we started dancing along to the beat. Aaron decided to join us and wrap his arms around me, pulling me closer. And when I kissed him, he murmured that he loved me against my lips. I grinned, knowing exactly what was coming when we eventually made it out of here.

For a second, I forgot about the letters in my pillow. I forgot about my father. For a second, I forgot who Savannah Ivy Green *really* was —her real sense of self was clouded by alcohol and the lack of paranoia about the future. The Savannah in *Twilight* on this twelfth of April did not know the meaning of responsibility and completely embraced that you only live once.

✠

"Give it to me," I commanded the bartender, "—vodka. Straight."
A tray of six shots slid in front of me, and I eagerly reached out for the first shot glass. Out of the corner of my eye I saw Francesca, cackling with laughter in my direction with her cellphone poised. The girls beside her pointed and whispered. *Damn nosy busybodies.*

I snorted and waved my middle finger in their direction.

"Savannah!" Olive snatched my vodka out of my hand. "You've had enough. Leave some for the rest of us."

She then downed the shot herself, much to my dismay.
"*No!*" I cried, before pouting. I grabbed her abandoned cocktail and started gulping that. It burned all the way down, but I *liked* the pain. "…Woo!" I shook my head and waved my arms in the air.

"Savannah," Aaron put a hand on my shoulder. "Steady on."

"Who's Savannah?" I frowned.

30

"She's too far gone," Lauren muttered, sipping a margarita.

"No, I'm *Too-Good-For-You*," I slurred, poking Aaron in the ribs. He agreed and chuckled as he affectionately ruffled my hair.

I grumbled lazily, nuzzling against his chest before a strange heaviness began to lull me under and I closed my eyes.

"She might pass out soon," Luca said worriedly, noticing. "Maybe you should take her to my house, Aar."

"That, I should," Aaron seized me by the shoulders and pulled me off of my stool. I protested but my friends just waved me off sweetly and watched my boyfriend drag me away towards the exit.

We stumbled onto the sidewalk and the cold air jarred me awake, alert. I clutched my midsection, feeling a growling complaint of digesting alcohol, and its putrid stench rising up my throat. I trembled, and managed to make my way to the gutter, before upping the contents of my stomach. Aaron parted my hair as I straightened up and looked into my eyes with concern.

"...Okay?" he asked in a gentle voice.

I frowned and tucked my hair behind my ears, before wriggling out of his grasp. "I'm perfectly capable of walking by myself," I scoffed, and walked forward in a wobbly line. My shoe then caught a loose stone and I tripped, but I landed in Aaron's swift moving arms instead of cutting my forehead on the sidewalk. After the sound of my heartbeat in my ears grew louder as I breathed shallowly, I reluctantly let him lead me to his car.

He buckled me in and adjusted my seat so that I could lay back. I closed my eyes and sighed as he turned on the ignition, before reversing out of the parking spot. "Hey, how come you're driving?" I asked, playfully glaring at him. "You drank *too*," I added childishly.

Aaron simply chuckled and turned on the car's GPS. "I'm the designated driver for me and the guys," he explained.

Luca was ours, and I suddenly began to wonder if I had given her the keys to my car before leaving. Then I shrugged, realising that the consequences did not really bother me. I leaned against the window as Aaron drove, vaguely listening to the female GPS voice and mouthing inappropriate responses to her commands.

"Hey Sav, you mind checking what the estimated time of arrival is? The guys weren't planning to stay too long. I might have time to make a pit stop at a gas station after I drop you off," Aaron inquired, patting me on the shoulder to get my attention. I grumbled but squinted at the central console.

"Half *past*…" I groaned.

"Half past what?"

"*Ugh…*" I glanced at the screen, but the little white figures just danced around in a blur. Remembering that I had my cellphone, I slipped it out of my pocket and unlocked it. "…It's midnight thirty-nine," I giggled. "So, we'll get there at half past…uh…that number after zero." There was a pause. "…I *think*," I added uncertainly.

"Let me see." Aaron suddenly turned towards me to lean over and look at my screen.

"What, don't you trust me?" I snapped, shrinking away from him.

"Just give me the phone, Green," he sighed.

"*No*," I pouted. "I licked it —it's mine."

"Wha —that doesn't even make sense. It's the wrong context."

"Your *face* doesn't even make sense."

We bickered on for a few more seconds, before a loud hoot grabbed our attention. My eyes widened as a bright pair of lights shone right at us, before I let out a scream and everything was engulfed by white light.

☨

It was a jarring cacophony of metal and shattering glass. The overturning momentum ensnared us on a horrifying, deadly carnival ride; crushing everything beneath a force like hydraulic pressure. My throat burned and ripped apart but all sound from it was silent. There was pain —unfathomable and searing, and with no end. But then suddenly…nothing.

Everything turned quiet and still; no longer disturbed —like the quiet after the storm. And eerily so, until the smell of gasoline filled my nostrils and I gasped, as though I had just jolted awake from a nightmare. I opened my eyes. Blurry images of smoke and glass filled my vision. Numbness was the only sensation which I could feel.

We had crashed. I could see the other car smoking across from us through the windshield. A body lay draped over through the broken glass, mostly dry and not drenched; likely not impaled. I then turned —and saw Aaron, unconscious against the steering wheel. And on his lap…was me. I frowned in confusion and sat up slowly. Sure enough, there my body was, embedded with giant shards of glass and bleeding out. I had admittedly never seen my own blood in such a quantity —and there was something strange about the colour.

I was bleeding red and silver; the colours dripping and marbling. I started and rubbed my eyes, wondering if they were being deceived.

They were not.

The blood that had initially bled out was as red as normal blood —but the more it seeped the more metallic the red became, until it was all a stark silvery liquid that resembled mercury.

I glanced downwards. I was perfectly fine —except my clothes had changed. I had put on my favourite white jeans; white tucked-in t-shirt and sneakers that afternoon. Now, I was sporting a short tan leather jacket; a black tank top; black skinny jeans and shiny black combat boots. I started even more violently, before feeling disoriented and having to wince at the dull ache of a concussion.

"…Carter?" I whispered uncertainly.

He did not respond. He still lay there, motionless. "*Aaron.* Oh God."

The silence was deafening. Cursing, I scrambled to my haunches and tried to hit out at him. But it did not make contact —my hand went right through his shoulder. I gasped and sat up completely, expecting to hit the roof of the car. But my head went up and through that too, causing me to scream.

I then scrambled to get out of the car through my side where the door had completely come off from the hinge, before the sound of sirens filled my ears. I looked to the left and spotted red and blue lights in the distance.

Perfect. Maybe emergency services could tell me what was going on. I stood a little distance from the wreckage, still bewildered at the fact that I was in two places at once, before the rustle of leaves caught my attention.

My gaze shifted to my right —the direction from which the noise was coming. But then it came from the left; and then from behind me. I was glancing all around me; fear and panic filling my senses, even though I could not feel an acceleration of a heartbeat.

"…Uh…who's there?" I stammered, whipping around sharply as I thought that the sound of rustling was growing closer.

Still nothing materialised, and I stumbled backwards, tripping over a rock. I squealed and landed on my backside, before letting out a groan. I winced and sympathised with myself for a few moments, before I heard the sound of a click. Jumping to conclusions and thinking the worst, I scrambled to my feet and held my hands up in the air, surrendering.

"Please don't shoot me!" I wailed in a terrified rush. Then I blinked, surprised, when nothing happened. One eye opened cautiously.

I came face to face with an arrow. It never fired though.

The arrow lowered, and my wide eyes met a familiar set of silver ones, glaring into mine begrudgingly. I gasped and lowered my arms to my sides. My jaw dropped in disbelief. "…*You*."

CHAPTER 4

SAVANNAH

"UNBELIEVABLE," HE BREATHED, his eyes wide and glinting in the moonlight, "I'm late. Your soul has already separated." He looked me up and down, as stunned as I was.

His gaze then lingered on mine.

"Can you tell me what is going on here?" I spoke. "Who are you. Why are you stalking me. And why am I here as well as *there*?" I gestured downwards to myself and to my body in the car.

He paused and pressed his lips into a tight line, pondering something. "…That is a lot of questions," was the next thing to come out of his mouth that did not aid the situation.

"That *you* don't seem to want to answer," I retorted.

He swung his crossbow over his shoulder and let it balance there. His sharp silver eyes studied my form again, before narrowing curiously at my torso.

"What?" I asked defensively; insecurity gnawing at my muscles as I felt them tense in self-consciousness.

He pointed at my upper arms. "The badges on your sleeves," he sighed, prompting me to look. "That's why your soul is detached," he said all of this more to himself, like an audible observation. And for a moment, my presence was forgotten. "You're one of us."

One of…us? One of what?

The red badges to which he was referring were sewn-on embroidered patches like

35

the ones from *NASA*. The logo was a small silver Grim Reaper scythe in front of a pair of golden angel wings.

I frowned and looked closer, before realising the wings looked identical to the pendant on my necklace, albeit they were different colours.

My hand flew to my chest out of habit but now mostly panic, before the familiar feel of my necklace allowed me to relax and breathe out in relief. I was not sure what I would do if I ever lost it.

The silver-eyed Stalker suddenly walked past me and headed for the car crash. "Hey," I called after him, marching there.

He lowered down onto his haunches before looking inside Aaron's car.

"…He's not dead," he declared.

"What?"

He ignored me again and wandered around to the other car. "…Not dead either. *Critical*," he said in an offhand manner, "but still alive."

He then walked around again, dragging his feet as though he were disappointed, before jumping as he suddenly came face to face with me.

"Do you mind explaining to me what is going on?" I growled. "Nothing makes sense. This entire day has been one disappointment after the next —the only thing I had to look forward to a few minutes ago was getting laid."

"Once upon a time, you and me both," he scoffed.

"What?"

He coldly offered no explanation. "…You know, you're acting strangely calm," I pressed. "Do you come to crime scenes often?"

The male clenched his jaw, swinging the crossbow again and making the effort to ignore me. As though I bored him. "…What were you doing in my favourite diner?" I sceptically demanded instead.

This time, he did not even hesitate. "Watching you."

That was very straightforward. I had expected a more evasive answer.

I blinked rapidly, before a frown settled on my face. "Uh…why? You creep. Were you planning on killing me?" I then gasped. "I bet you were. But then the car crash must have stopped you." I smacked my fist into my palm. "Well, *ha*!

I'm still alive," I smirked, folding my arms triumphantly.

His expression did not change.

"If I had planned to kill you," he said carefully, "I wouldn't have been so obvious and careless enough for you to see me."

I frowned again. Wait —he had definitely just implied that he had experience in assassination. Though I then shook my head, deciding to focus on the present problem. "Okay. So, why then?"

"You were on my list for today," he shrugged. "And it was also your birthday. So, I was wondering what could possibly go wrong for this girl."

A hint of a smile tugged at his lips, which annoyed me more than I thought it would. "Surprisingly, a lot."

"List for what?" I asked.

"List for the souls that I have to collect," he answered. My eyes widened and I gawked at him, speechless.

A list of souls…

Slowly, it began to seep in. The fact that I was still somewhat alive; the fact that I could not touch Aaron or the roof of the car; the fact that I was laying unconscious in the wreckage, and simultaneously walking around in the cold early hours of the morning. I glanced down at the badges on my sleeves —and found an identical set on the upper arms of his jacket. My eyes darted from his crossbow to his face; to the arrows and to the smoking car; before I grabbed my head and shook it, overwhelmed by all of the thoughts that were running through my mind.

"You're dead," the Stalker summed up bluntly.

I screwed my face up and tried to block him out. I had not wanted to hear him say it —to have him confirm a suspicion. "*No*," I hissed, "No way." I shook my head harder, wondering why I had not yet woken up from this nightmare. "…No, no —wake up, wake up, *wake up*."

I heard him sigh wearily, which caused me to lash out. I grabbed him by the collar —which was not easy due to him being almost a head and a half taller than me —and glared into his set eyes. "Tell me that I'm dreaming," I ordered. He reluctantly fulfilled my request. "No —be *serious*!" I demanded, roughly pushing him away from me by thumping his chest and shoulder.

"*Hey*," he protested, nursing the hurt. "Fine. You want me to be serious? Savannah Ivy Green; you no longer exist. You've passed on; ascended to a higher plane; or whatever bullshit that you want to believe. But you're not going to Purgatory or the Underworld —you're dead, not *dying*. Because of your new form and uniform, you have been selected to help carry out Death's mission and take up arms to —"

I glared at him in disbelief the entire time. "Do you have like, an entire speech planned?" I snappily interrupted, raising an eyebrow.

"Let me finish," he growled as though it really was rehearsed, "—take up arms to reap the souls that pass on every day. It is now your solemn duty, to carry on, with the task…of being a Grim Reaper."

He then had the nerve to smirk self-righteously as he concluded his verbal propaganda. I clenched my fists as anger bubbled up inside of me.

"That's it," I sneered, turning sharply on my heel, "I'm out." And I started marching in the direction of my house.

"Where are you going?" he called after me.

"Home," I hissed, quickly increasing my pace, "and as far away from *you* as possible —you psychopath."

After a few metres I paused and glanced backwards. He was not there anymore. I frowned in confusion and looked around, before turning to my left and meeting his gaze again. I jumped.

"Would you stop *doing* that?" I snapped, before groaning loudly in annoyance. "Appearing out of nowhere is considered creepy, and has been a proven factor in leading to murder," I said haughtily.

He was not amused by my attempt at sarcastic humour.

"…How do you do that by the way? Disappearing?" I then asked.

"I don't disappear," he answered. "You just stop wanting to see me —it's a subconscious thing. I just happen to use that to my advantage."

Not wanting to appear sheepish, I glared at him and turned to carry on walking, before realising that he had fallen in step with me. "Would you stop following

38

me?" I growled, whipping around before I skidded to a halt.

"But I have to," he flatly insisted, "I am your superior now."

I started. "Excuse me?"

"You're just a Turned Reaper and it's my job now as a Reaper with *experience*, to train and guide you until you can handle your own part of a district," he explained.

"Oh, really...?" I commented, nodding as though I believed every word. "Look, your prank might have been really entertaining at first, but now you're trying too hard," I then abruptly cut in. "So, give it up and let me go back to my normal life —the one I led before that stupid party."

He grabbed my arm as soon as I tried to leave. His grip was more of a vice than I would have liked to admit. I opened my mouth to say something as he slid out an arrow from his quiver and held the pointed head in front of my face.

I wondered what on Earth he was doing, until I saw my reflection in the glinting black tip.

I started violently and jerked out of his grasp; my eyes wide as I gasped for air that would not be breathed. After a few moments of calming down, I looked again, but nothing had changed. There, my formerly dark brown eyes stared back at me —my irises now glowing bright gold. I turned sharply to the side, to see if it was just a trick of the light. Yet no matter from which angle I looked, my eyes remained pure *gold*.

"Jesus Christ —what the hell?" I blurted, holding my face in my hands. "Did you put contact lenses on me while I was unconscious or something?"

"Why would I do that?" he asked, frowning. "This is a divine occurrence. All Reapers' eye colours change when they Turn. They can be the colour of any precious stones or metals."

I blinked. It did not feel as though I had contacts in my eyes. It felt normal, as though they had been that way since birth. So, I wondered if that was it —if the mystery had been solved. Was I really meant to believe this stranger so completely and blindly? I hated to consider the consequence.

I awkwardly rubbed up and down my arm, lightly reproaching myself.

"Listen. If…if what you're saying is true, then does that mean that everything I know and love…is gone?" I stammered, feeling the prick of tears in the corners of my eyes.

His expression softened a little, and he stopped looking so offended. Instead, he reclaimed his arrow and stood in front of me awkwardly, unsure of exactly what to do. I growled lowly, growing increasingly pissed off.

"Listen Stalker, I've just come to the realisation that I am apparently dead, and you've got nothing else to say for once —"

"—Søren," he cut me off.

"What?"

"My name. It's not *Stalker*," he said firmly. "It's Søren. *S*; a slashed *o*; *r*; *e*; *n*. Søren. Nice to meet you."

I knew that an '*o*' with a stroke was a vowel not found in the English language —but I had never even heard of his name before.

"It's Norwegian," he elaborated when I just gave him a blank stare. He did not have an accent. It must have been a result of being in the United States for however long he had been.

"…I see." I suddenly felt bad for calling him '*Stalker*'.

I then slowly attempted to say his name, but he ended up bursting out laughing as I stumbled over the unfamiliar vowel. Frustrated, I turned again and proceeded to resume my walk.

"…Hey —now where are you going?" he called after me again.

"Still home," I answered. "I want to see my Mom."

"You're really going to walk all that way? I know a faster way."

"What do you mean?"

I turned back to face him, but I was then distracted by the emergency vehicles finally showing up before I could say anything more. A little burst of hope ignited inside of me, and before Søren could stop me, I ran over to the crash and stood there patiently as ambulances and fire trucks pulled up in front of me.

I darted forward, waiting for them to come rushing towards me and wrap me up in a shock blanket.

40

But my smile wavered when all of the paramedics prioritised the cars.

"You don't believe me?" the sudden sound of Søren's voice by my ear made me flinch. "Just watch."

And I did. I watched them strap Aaron's body onto a stretcher. I watched them do the same with the other driver. I watched them identify everybody using their wallets and IDs.

I watched them check the pulse on Savannah Ivy Green and attempt to revive her. But it was too late.

I watched them declare her to be dead.

I was numb, and at a loss for words as a plastic sheet was placed over my bloody body. I watched it all happen —like a disturbingly realistic horror film from which I could not look away. I was half expecting Søren to say that he had told me so, but he stood beside me and listened to the sirens grow fainter as the Ambulances drove away. I stared blankly at my body on the ground; stripped emotionless.

I was dead. Truly.

The word '*dead*' tasted bitter in my mouth as I whispered the sentence under my breath. It was a word that I probably should be used to since Phoebe was always insistent on my father being so. But when I said it aloud, there was no trace of assurance. It was doubtful, even with the evidence in front of me. I had always thought that death was for old people —people who had lived enough of their lives and did not regret as much as a younger person would. I had believed that death would not dare to touch me.

"…I hadn't been ready to die," I whispered, my lips barely moving.

"People rarely are," Søren whispered back.

When all the commotion had died down, my feet decided to walk down the road, towards the only place that I felt I needed to go. I wiped my face dry and glared straight ahead, determined not to look soft.

Søren followed me in silence; so carefully and noiselessly it was as if he was not even there. I did not have the energy to tell him to get lost this time, so I let him walk with me. It was still a lot to digest, but I was not completely ready to accept it just yet. I needed Phoebe —and her opinion. I did not care if I was dead

41

or not. She was my *mother*.

The journey should have taken ten hours on foot. Yet we seemed to bend the distance and turn it into one hour; shifting through air itself as easily as a misted curtain. I gasped when we stepped into town centre, disorientated, but Søren only offered a wink as an explanation. *Okay. A perk, then*.

Though when we actually stopped in front of my house, I found myself hesitating with my hand reaching for the doorknob, unsure of whether or not I would even be able to touch it.

"Your form prevents you from getting hurt, not from opening doors," Søren sighed in an annoyingly sarcastic tone. I huffed and gripped the doorknob, before slowly turning it. Then I paused again, as a thought then occurred to me. "Will she…see me?" I whispered.

"Yeah —kind of."

I gave him a look. "What'd you mean, *kind of*?"

"She…won't exactly know that it's you," he explained, "People who you knew when you were alive can still see you. But they can never recognise you. You will look different to them."

"So, I knew you?" I guessed.

He chuckled softly. "Not necessarily. I am much older than you think. And everyone sees their own death when it approaches."

I glanced at the window and saw Phoebe sitting on the sofa with Don's arms around her. It was then that I realised that she was crying, and had probably just been informed that I was dead. Ron was yowling, probably wondering why I was not yet home. I gripped the doorknob tighter. I could not say goodbye. There were so many things left unspoken, and all of my chances had blown away in the wind. Phoebe Green had always been there for me. And now I could not even see her.

I frowned and ran the scenario of opening the door through my head. They would probably think that I was a burglar.

"…Goodbye," I whispered. "I hope that you don't count on me being in a better place, 'cause I'm definitely not."

I took my hand off of the doorknob. It hurt in a way I never could have imagined. Instead, I walked around to the wall behind the house where my room was. Thankful that it was single storey, I pushed my window open further than I had left it that morning and hoisted myself up to climb inside.

"Why are you breaking and entering into your own house?" Søren asked as he watched me struggle.

"I didn't…break anything," I panted, succeeding in getting half of my body through, "and there's something I need…from my room."

He did not say anything more. So, I continued to wriggle my way inside, before collapsing onto the floor. "…Hey," I groaned, sitting up, "am I not indestructible or something?"

"*You* made that choice to squeeze through a window," Søren pointed out. "The magic does not compensate for idiocy."

I stuck my tongue out and turned back around, taking in my bedroom for what would probably the last time. Photographs decorated my walls, and my eyes widened as I remembered my friends. I wondered if they knew that I was dead yet. I felt a sharp stab of guilt —though apparently, I did not have time to dwell on it. I just needed to get what I came for and disappear.

I grabbed a backpack that was draped over my desk chair and started stuffing it with the letters that were still inside my pillowcase.

Once every last one was inside, I zipped it up and slung it over both shoulders. I turned around and paused as I stared at the photographs again. I was never going to see them again. I was never going to be *normal* again.

"…You have to let go," Søren broke the silence, sticking his head through the window.

"I'm not really ready to let go," I admitted. "This…this is all I've ever known. I just died —now I'm being forced into some job. Where is the afterlife? Do I not get to rest in peace?"

I felt a sting in my eyes, before I blinked the feeling away. *What is the matter with me?* I had never been so incessantly teary before.

"No one asks for this," Søren sighed, "It's just Death's way of trying to get out of *his* job. He does not select at random, though. There is a reason that you

43

were chosen to be a Reaper." He then paused, letting me digest his words. "…What special skills do you have?"

I frowned. "The ability to punch the living daylights out of you," I said thickly, glaring at him.

He shrugged, unfazed. "Good start."

"What about you?" I asked.

He thought for a moment. "…Apathy," was what he settled for.

"I wouldn't classify that as a skill," I scoffed.

"But it *is* a skill —you know how much you need not to feel when you reap a soul?" he shot back. "Do you think that it's easy to separate souls from bodies? It isn't. And nothing is allowed to stop you from doing so."

I softened as I saw a glimmer of something regretful in his eyes. "…Did you have to reap someone close to you?" I asked gently.

He froze —only for a second. That was all the answer that I needed. Then whatever anguish that had been there was then suddenly gone as quickly as it had appeared, and he looked up at me as his expression neutralised. "We should go," he sighed, "—before your parents find you in here."

I frowned as I climbed back out through the window. "That man is not my Dad," I growled. I expected him to retort with something that mocked the statement, or pried, but he did not respond at all. It was as though he understood my feelings of resentment.

Either that, or he just did not care.

CHAPTER 5

SAVANNAH

"TO BE HONEST, I thought you would be an ancient skeleton guy in a black robe lugging around a two-ton weapon of mass harvesting," I said as we walked through the woods. We had already shifted across a majority of the distance, but Søren wanted me to learn the route from a certain point. It did bother me that he lived all the way in Manhattan —if it were not for the ability to shift, it would be a *long* trek home in Fulton.

I had been struggling with a one-sided conversation with the Trainer up until then, but I was desperate to keep the atmosphere light, not dreary. To bring a slither of normalcy to the unfamiliar that was now raging around me. The sound of talking calmed my nerves and distracted me from the darkness of the once inviting, but now unsettling woods around us.

"Of course, you did," Søren sighed in response to my remark, "—it's a rather common belief. I believed it myself until I died."

I then perked up, glad to receive somewhat of a reaction. "Does Death himself look like that?" I asked.

He shrugged. "I wouldn't know. I've never met him. All he seems to do is sit on his ass all day in his *Fortress of Solitude*," he muttered. "The only form of contact we have with him is through letters; daily reports of who we reaped, so he can compare them with his copy of the list. If you miss a certain amount of the quota, you will be reaped —and you will die. Again."

I raised an eyebrow. "Seriously?"

This boss was surpassing everything I had expected for someone who was in charge of something as important as people's souls —that was if he felt the need to kill his employees for unfortunate mistakes.

"Seriously," Søren said flatly.

I coughed and hugged my leather jacket tightly against me.

Some of the buds of flowers were beginning to turn their predisposed colours as they grew closer to blossoming. I puzzled over how noticeable this was to me in the darkness of a new moon night, before figuring that it probably had something to do with my new powers —or something to that effect.

We then walked on for a few minutes in silence, before emerging on the other side of the woods into the gloriously urban, Downtown Manhattan.

"Sweet civilisation!" I gasped, walking with an increased amount of vigour. Søren turned to me to give me a confused look.

"I thought that you liked the woods and suburbs."

I frowned and returned the expression. He was not entirely wrong. Yes, I liked the woods; keyword being '*liked*'. It was a past tense form of affection. Just like the affection of my father that lingered, even after he had left.

"…How would you know that?" I asked suspiciously.

Søren paused and for a second I could have sworn that something along the lines of shame passed across his face. "…Long story."

I snorted, not in the mood to egg him on about a clear answer, and instead embraced the nightly noise of the city. I had not been to New York often, but I had certainly loved it on the occasion. It was comforting to hear something so ordinary. A few cars and taxis thundered past us; and the sound of screeching tyres mingled with the early morning sounds of clubs and partygoing. My mood instantly dampened further as I thought of how I easily I had gotten swept up in all of the excitement.

"Hey —you're slowing down," Søren's voice brought me out of my thoughts. I sighed and picked up the pace again.

He had said that we were heading to his apartment —in a building with other Grim Reapers that existed in the shadows of a regular one, rendering them undetectable to mortals.

We walked down endless streets and I recognised a few of them from my previous Spring Break escapades; but my feet were beginning to tire from all of it. I had hardly walked so far in my life —especially not in the cold and darkness of the night. That trip back home was not helping.

"Uh, how come I can get tired?" I spoke up, "…I'm dead, right? So…"

"Reapers exist in between the state of living and the state of death," Søren answered, lazily swinging his crossbow from side to side. "Your heart doesn't beat, and you don't need to breathe. But since you Turned just a few hours ago, you'll still feel rather human for a while."

I grumbled at this information and decided to refrain from asking any more questions; in case I did not really want to hear the answer. But the whole still feeling human phenomenon was beginning to seep in deeper, and frustration started to overlap with my impatience.

"…Seriously, how much further?" I finally huffed.

He chuckled softly and assured me that it was not that long to go. I failed to see how walking this much of the route was really that beneficial to me, but he was the Trainer after all. I tried not to argue.

We had then been walking for half an hour or so when we stopped outside of a normal brick block of flats, that rose up high into the low laying clouds.

"How inviting," I said sarcastically, rocking back on my heels.

"That's not where I live," Søren smirked. He went around to the side of the building and pressed a small silver button. A little blue screen popped up on the wall and asked for a face scan, before approving.

"Stand back," he then warned, waving his hand in a shooing gesture. I took a few steps backwards and then gasped as each brick on the wall took its turn to turn over and transform into white slates. The entire exterior of the building changed in one rapid movement. What I was looking at now, was the exterior of a luxury five-star hotel.

"*This* is where I live —along with the others who also reap in the city," Søren said smugly, slinging his crossbow back over his shoulder. He then made his way to the entrance, prompting me to follow; still in awe of what had just occurred. The very extravagant marble lobby was fairly empty; contrary to what I had anticipated. A few people dressed in all shades of colour and yet still with copious amounts of dark leather milled around, weaving in and out of the flow of light foot traffic. They all had intimidating, glinting black weapons and little to no friendly expressions, making me uneasy.

I took a shaky breath and tried to stay close to Søren.

My gaze flickered from one pair of eyes to another as we made our way to the elevator on the far side of the room. Some eyes widened at the sight of mine, and some glared. I was a little put off by a few of the eye colours, but the staring unnerved me the most. A sharp pair of garnet eyes belonging to a tall gel-groomed blond male with a black-toothed chainsaw held mine for the longest time, and I had the feeling that they remained that way even after I had turned away. He was visibly inscribed with tattoos on the exposed surface of his arms, as well as on his neck. A sudden shiver ran down my spine, and I cringed at the thought that making eye contact with another Reaper might always rattle me. I barged in ahead of Søren into the elevator and shrunk in one corner. He eyed me with concern as he calmly strode in after me and pressed the button for the second floor.

"Are you okay?" he muttered. "You look like you've seen a ghost."

He then smiled lightly at his own joke, and I frowned, righting myself and folding my arms.

"I'm fine," I grumbled, moving towards the doors as they opened up. "What number do you live in?"

"Eight."

I marched off purposefully down the hall and stopped at number eight, taking note of the door's beautiful silver finish as well as a silver number eight.

"Is the door supposed to match your eyes?" I quipped as Søren came up next to me with a key in his hand.

"Is your fiery attitude supposed to match your hair?" he shot back, turning the key in the lock.

I pouted and trudged in after him. He switched on the lights and I blinked at

48

the brightness. My jaw then dropped slightly as I walked in further and was immediately hit with the coldness of what I assumed to be air conditioning. An old dusty rowboat sat up against one corner next to a very inviting sofa. Bookshelves lined every wall and overflowed with classic, mystery and crime investigation titles, and some books were also piled onto side tables. A desk gave the closest wall a break, and scrolls littered it instead, along with an out-of-place vintage computer and printer. There was very little furniture otherwise, but it did not feel particularly empty.

Or maybe that was just a way of trying to distract myself from realising that I felt entirely alone and vacant.

"So, do you have a bedroom? Or a bathroom?"

I glanced around for other doors. There was only one besides the entrance, and my fingers itched to go open it and see what was there.

Søren sighed and put his crossbow on the sofa. "No, I don't. Reapers don't need to sleep, nor do they ordinarily require bathing. And, in case of emergencies," he quipped, reaching over above the sofa and pulling open a white metal box mounted to the wall, "I also own a First Aid Kit."

I smirked half-heartedly. I sank down onto the sofa, before I shuffled away from the crossbow that I then realised was beside me.

Søren gave me a look and folded his arms. "It doesn't bite."

"You nearly shot me with an arrow," I snapped back, removing my backpack. "You were *this* close."

I gestured by putting my forefinger and my thumb together. He simply scoffed and shook his head, before eyeing my bag.

"So, what was so important that you had to go back for it?"

I sighed and slowly unzipped the backpack, before tipping out its contents beside me onto the sofa. "…Letters," I mumbled. Søren came over and kneeled in front of them, before picking one up and eyeing it closely. His eyes widened when he gasped, obviously figuring something out. "What?" I asked as I sat up attentively, "What is it?"

He looked up at me with a stern expression; but his eyes gleamed with uneasiness. "Where did you *get* these?" he whispered.

"They were…sent to my house. Why?" I frowned, feeling the need to withhold the fact they were from my father. It was only because Søren did not have any business in it.

He pressed his lips into a thin line and seemed to be thinking deeply about something. "Those stamps…they're from the Underworld."

"The what?" I deadpanned.

"The Underworld," he repeated, like I was simple. "In Greek Mythology? You know, where souls spend eternity?" He looked at me expectantly as I remained quiet. I nodded slowly for his benefit; not having the slightest clue. "…What I don't understand, is why you have them. When were they mailed to you?" he asked gravely.

I dithered.

"Do you have any idea who sent them?" he pressed.

I paused and narrowed my eyes at him. "Do *you*?"

He did not seem to have an answer for me then. His motivation dwindled and that far-off brooding look settled back onto his features.

I was about to open my mouth and repeat my question, when a loud piercing alarm rang out and made me wince.

"…You'll get used that eventually," Søren sighed as he got up and walked over to a desk. "It's the signal for us to report back to the '*Big Boss*'."

He emphasised his obvious distaste by making air quotations as he drawled out the title.

I then observed as he grumbled his way through typing a summary and printing it out, before rolling it up and sealing it. He pressed a button on a clear tube next to the desk, and I started as I watched the letter disintegrate in the burning golden orange flames that ignited within the tube.

"Phoenix fire," Søren smirked in a way of explanation. "Transports it straight to Purgatory."

I nodded, then picked up a letter. The black paper still warmed my skin; and this time even more so than it had in my mother's room.

50

"Did you write about me?" I asked timidly.

Surely since my name had been on the list, he would have had to report that I was now a Grim Reaper.

"Yes, I did," Søren answered. "I said that I never managed to reap your soul," he spat in irritation, and then turned to walk towards the other door.

I was about to inquire what he meant by that, but the curiosity from earlier resurfaced and I jumped at the chance to ask what was behind the door. "…Hey, what's behind that door?"

He turned around and motioned for me to come over. I gingerly climbed off the sofa and went to stand beside him, an excited shiver now running through me. Søren looked at me and his eyes gleamed with an eerie darkness. He then slowly pressed down on the handle and pushed the door open —though nothing was visible in the darkness of the space. I gulped nervously. His other hand nudged me forward encouragingly, even though my feet now refused to obey. His voice suddenly came out as a whisper next to me.

"It's time for a little…orientation."

CHAPTER 6

SAVANNAH

"YOU," I BREATHED, "are a sadistic psychopath."

I had caught sight of the gleaming weapons that decorated the walls. It screamed *assassin* and made me stiffen. Otherwise, it resembled like a regular high-rise office. One wall was lined with computer screens of various sizes, with a sleek modern computer monitor glowing an alarming electric blue sitting on the floor beside them. A cold breeze blew through the room, causing me to shudder beneath my layers.

Søren glared at me, offended. "No I'm not."

I nodded a little mockingly before I asked, "…So, what do you have all of these weapons for, then?" I started properly looking around. "Don't you just use the crossbow?"

"They're backups," he explained, "I rarely use them since my crossbow is my chosen reaping tool."

"So, does everyone have a stash of murder weapons, or…?" I muttered under my breath.

"Only Trainers," Søren answered smugly, folding his arms, evidently having heard me. "I was promoted ten years ago, entitling me to a bigger arsenal. The Boss sent all of them through the mail."

"Okay. So," I then continued, "this orientation. What's on the list?"

Søren smiled slightly, before taking off his leather jacket and rolling up the sleeves of his royal blue turtleneck sweater. "First, we need to get you a Reaper weapon. Then you can be registered."

I shrugged. "And how does that work?"

"Like this."

He beckoned me over to what seemed to be the main computer screen and sat down in the chair in front of it. I stood beside him and watched with half-hearted interest; minimally curious about what he was going to do.

"*Computer service online. Welcome to Obsidian Carrier Corp Online Shipping Service. How may I help you today, Søren?*" an automated female voice unexpectedly announced, in a very bad Eastern European accent. I stifled a laugh and covered my mouth with my hand. Søren still turned and glared at me, before clearing his throat.

"Computer, I would like to order a Reaper weapon for my newest trainee," he answered.

"*Certainly sir*," the computer responded. "*Please upload their credentials into the spaces provided.*"

He then proceeded to type in my birth date; full name; height; weight; and overall personality —without even asking me. And he did not look remotely guilty when I hit his arm and glared at him accusingly.

I was all set to lecture him. "How —"

"We have backgrounds on every single human being on the planet; young and old; dead or alive; past, present or future. We know *everything*," he cut me off. "You will understand when you're fully fledged."

I cringed and shivered, still very put off. "You mean that you're all *trained* stalkers. And I'll have to join you," I hissed.

He did not respond, and pressed enter on the keyboard.

"*Processing…*" said the computer. She repeated the word for a few moments, before a bell sounded. "*Complete. Order sent for: a one-meter double-edged obsidian plated iron core longsword with a gilt diamond handle. Strength Quotient: nine point three out of ten. Obsidian Reaping Efficiency Status: instant.*"

"Wow," I whispered, suddenly impressed.

53

I had not imagined that I would end up with a sword. I thought maybe a dagger —or even an old-fashioned *scythe*, would suit me.

"Wait, Computer," Søren said, frowning as though something were wrong. "Are you absolutely certain that that's a match? That combination sounds like…too much to handle. Even for a Grim Reaper with years of experience. State all possible matches."

"The match is at…exactly one hundred percent. There are no other possible matches detected."

"For a trainee?" The Trainer swivelled to another computer screen. "Unlikely. Display all stats for the order."

A list of statistics then popped up on that screen. Søren jumped as his eyes skimmed over the figures.

I was not as quick, so I did not know what the issue was.

"Holy…" he whistled, running a hand through his hair. He leaned back in the chair, looking distraught.

"Overall Weapon Efficiency Status is averaged at…ninety-eight point three five percent," the computer summed up.

"Holy *shit*," Søren breathed, shaking his head. "These numbers are off the charts —I have never seen an OWES that high. Or an ORES. Jesus!" he exclaimed, before whipping around to face me. "Are you even *human*?"

Something within me flinched at that question. "Last time I checked, yes," I frowned. "Look. I don't understand what any of this means. I didn't ask for a sword; efficient or not. So, if there's any way I could switch —"

"Did you not hear what Angelina said?" he interrupted me again and pointed at the main screen.

I raised an eyebrow. "Angelina?"

His eyes widened slightly before a dusty pink tainted his cheeks. "The Computer," he clarified sternly. "…Your match is at one hundred percent. That means there's nothing for you to switch *to*. You're not getting out of this one." He then leaned back and sighed, putting his hands behind his head.

I snarled. He could not be serious. I pondered the idea of carrying a sword with me everywhere I went —and it did not seem like a good one.

I opened my mouth to say something more, when Angelina then decided to announce, "*You have mail.*"

"Ah," Søren breathed as he snapped his fingers, "that would be your already infamous sword."

I blinked stupidly. "It's here already? That was fast. Just how efficient *is* this shipping service —?"

"—Hold that thought."

Søren raised a finger in front of my face and swivelled over to another tube identical to the one in the other room. Fire shot up through it, and within the flames, a large object wrapped in brown paper materialised. Søren took hold of it, unscathed. He then turned around and unwrapped it carefully, as if it were the Crown Jewels. A gold glowing black sword sat on the paper packaging; its gold handle gleaming. I flinched at the sight of an engraved '*S*' where the blade met the hilt, and I wondered if it was coincidence of shape or if it meant that it was actually marked as mine. My eyes then widened as I glanced up to see Søren gesture for me to take it.

"Oh, no way," I backed up quickly, thoroughly overwhelmed, "there is no way that I can accept that."

The Trainer sighed and stood up, still holding the sword. "Well fortunately for you, it's not a gift. It's actually your possession now, and you have to take it. There are no alternatives."

I gulped and reached out for the handle with a shaky hand. The first feeling I had…was freezing. The handle was colder than the meat locker in which I had accidentally found myself stuck once when I was thirteen —and the sensation made me flinch as soon as my fingers made contact with it. I glanced up at Søren to see if that was normal, and he nodded encouragingly. So, I tried again. I wrapped my hand around it, and winced.

But I slowly relaxed the longer I held my grip there. My skin then tingled, and my eyes narrowed on the steam coming from my hand where it was in contact with the handle.

"Is your hand...*smoking*?" Søren murmured, raising an eyebrow.

I scoffed, before lifting the sword off the packaging and holding it up. It was heavier than it looked. Suddenly the glowing intensified —I had to turn away and shield my eye as a strong light shone out from the double-edged blade along with a wave of heat; before it dissipated and I squinted back at the sword. I watched on in awe as a misty electric blue *0* was etched into at the base of the blade, before it fulminated in a small plume.

"That's a count of how many souls it has reaped," Søren explained. "It will show up every time that you reap."

I nodded slowly, before swinging the sword experimentally. "What was that bright light?" I asked, surprised by how easily I was able to swing it.

"Claiming," he huffed. "You have now officially claimed it as your weapon, and it has claimed you. By the way," he continued as I reached up to touch the blade, "I wouldn't do that."

"Why not?" I frowned, but I was past the point of no return. As though I had been electrocuted, my finger instantly flinched back; stinging with pain. I cursed aloud and screamed with my mouth closed; the familiar sensation of burning flesh registering in my nerves.

"...*That's* why," Søren sighed.

"What *was* that?" I hissed, examining my finger. It was bright red and rapidly blistering. It would seem that I preferred learning the hard way.

"All Reaper weapons are plated in obsidian," scoffed the Trainer. "Obsidian burns all divine entities. In most cases, it kills too."

I pouted guiltily. I then thought of the glossy black box underneath Phoebe's bed. I wondered if it was made of obsidian too. It would explain why my finger had burned that time.

But if so, then why had it burned me while I had still been alive?

"So," Søren vaguely regained my attention, "Let's talk about the rules that come with this sword..."

I then stopped listening. I swung the sword back and forth, enjoying how wonderfully it handled, and admiring my reflection in the obsidian. My golden irises would take more time to get used to, but otherwise I looked like my normal self. And seeing the old Savannah in me sparked memories too —all of my friends; all of the shenanigans up to which we had gotten; and, for the first time after the car crash, I thought of Aaron. My chest tightened. Was it out of guilt, or sorrow? I could not *believe* that my parting thoughts on him were that we would not be able to sleep together. I really did love him. But what did it count for now? The person whom I said that I loved; the person I had considered settling down for, was going to live on without me. Death had done us part.

As I felt myself getting choked up with tears, it hit me that I was not anywhere close to ready to move on.

"Are you...crying?" Søren asked, halting in his instructional discourse and made me look up at him.

It took me a few seconds to figure out that he had asked me a question, and I hurriedly wiped my eyes and frowned. "...No."

He mirrored my expression and sighed. Maybe he was not as apathetic as he would like to think. "That's all for now. You...can go sit on the sofa."

I turned and walked towards the door, deciding to leave the sword leaning against the wall by the doorframe.

✠

I had been staring at the wall for a straight hour, unblinking.

I knew that it had been that long because of the silver ticking clock hanging above the door. Every single tick sounded so much louder than it really was — along with the cooing of a pigeon outside and the squeak of the window as it blew back and forth in the wind. I could have ignored the clock; shooed away the pigeon; and closed the window —but those were the noises of the living; the signs that time was progressing, and life was going on.

Without me.

Søren's apartment was cold. It reminded me of the pebbly English seaside — dismal and grey and lacking. Some people preferred it that way, like faded or washed out jeans. But it only made me feel like that clouded sky —wispy, without a clear sense of direction, and the disappointment of someone's day. There was no colour in the living room, or the computer room for that matter; and there was no warmth. The speckles of variation were from the books on his shelves, since he had no choice in the colour of them. Yet even with those he had appeared to coordinate their hues, and arrange them in such a way that saturation had no place in his desolate sanctuary. Otherwise, everything was washed in an ice blue.

I wondered if that was how he felt, on the inside —like an abandoned fishing port. And more curiously, why it somewhat resonated with me.

Had I been living a lie for ten years, fooling myself into believing that I was consequential to the lives of people I knew and to the universe; when in reality, my absence for the most part went unnoticed?

"...Savannah?"

I glanced in the direction of where my name had come from to find Søren leaning in the doorway, glaring at me. It was the first time he had said my name aloud. It caused me to feel even more homesick. I continued to sulk and turned back to stare at the wall.

"You can't sit there forever."

"Oh, yeah?" I scoffed. "Watch me."

He murmured something that I could not make out, before walking over and sitting on the other end of the sofa. He was heavier than he looked, and actually caused his half of the sofa to dip and make me slide to the middle.

"...Look," he started off, "I know that it's still weird, but I honestly thought that we were making progress here. You seemed to be more excited than you had been a few hours ago. Yes, it's not easy to move on so quickly —I understand. But you can't sit here and stare into space. You can't...give up. You might as well actually be dead then."

I blinked, feeling rather offended. But I still did not face him. I snorted and folded my arms. "Stop acting like you know what I'm going through. Sure, you died at some point and it sucked, I guess," I scoffed, throwing my hands up in the air, "but nobody has the same experience. Nobody scars the same way. You certainly seem to be over it."

Once I had said that out loud a deathly silence fell over us and I stiffened. I slowly glanced in his direction to find him glancing at me at the same time. We held each other's gaze for a moment, before he stood up and walked back to the computer room. A strange wave of guilt washed over me. If Søren was as apathetic as he believed, then maybe I was just as selfish and emotionally insensitive. I blinked the tears out of my eyes again and groaned aloud, burying my face in my hands. I was not the best at this —basic human relation. Having been surrounded by selfishness and no impulse control, it was no wonder I never thought about anyone else.

Now I was formulating excuses. Aaron had been right. There *was* something wrong with me. I did not know yet if it could be fixed.

I then thought that apologising to Søren might be a step in the right direction. Maybe someone else had died in the same way as I had. Maybe they had been thrown into a world that they did not think concerned them —and *maybe*, they felt as hollow and alone as I did.

And…maybe they had healed.

I gingerly climbed off of the sofa and padded to the computer room door. It was ajar, and from what I could see Søren was typing away between keyboards, analysing multiple displays at once. He did not notice me at first. But then he seemed to recognise the presence of someone, and he glanced over his shoulder. I gave a weak smile and hesitantly lifted my hand to give a stiff wave. His expression did not change. My gaze fell and I sighed, clicking my heels together and shoving my hands into the pockets of my leather jacket.

"…So, she lives," Søren quipped sarcastically, turning his attention back to the screens.

"Hey, listen," I said as I hesitantly strode in, "…I'm sorry if I stepped on any toes —"

"—*If*," he scoffed, typing with an exaggerated vigour.

"Okay, okay," I relented. "I said some things without thinking about anyone but myself. I'm sorry. I think I might get it from my Mom if I'm honest; because like her, I've been selfish all of my life and I've never thought about how it effects other people." I felt myself turning pink as I said all of that, before pausing. "…Not even my own boyfriend."

Søren stopped what he was doing at that moment. I glanced up at the sound of silence and did not try to hide my hopeful look.

"…I know that people hurt differently," he said quietly. "And…I think I might have an idea for you. For your homesickness."

"Really?"

I bit my lip in thought as it occurred to me that I did not have much to offer in return. But I then realised it would probably mean a lot if I gave my cooperation. I looked over to my sword that still leaned by the door. The ominous glow invited me to wield it again. And this time, I obeyed.

CHAPTER 7

SAVANNAH

I WENT TO my funeral in a stolen car.

Søren promised we would return it afterwards. It was an inconspicuous, weathered little black Volkswagen Beatle that had been parked across the road outside the apartments. It had also been conveniently left unlocked —the poor owner must have forgotten to do so —making it less work for us. I asked why we did not simply walk, but unfortunately we were running late.

As it turned out, getting to Fulton from Downtown Manhattan was not as quick as Saratoga, even after shifting.

Søren assured that we would not need the car for long anyway. That it would just be an in and out operation.

It was all a part of his anti-homesickness plan —that I had not liked initially. In fact, I had wondered how it could even help.

It turned out, in a weird way, it was an important and pivotal experience.

It was the still, humid Tuesday after the accident; the sky grey and full of fat dark clouds that refused to rain. Maybe they too felt the need to bottle up the tears. It took a lot of will to attend my funeral, and before I had even set foot in the church yard, tears were already blurring my vision. I had grown up in that church; going there every Sunday in a clean white lace dress. If I was completely honest, I had not really liked it. The songs were as old and boring and stiff as the pastor; and the bathrooms smelled of something awful. Through my early teens my friends and I had dared each other to go in there and stay for a whole two minutes; trying to size each other up and see who had the strongest lungs.

But when I returned to Trinity Church, I noticed how the plants at the front were browning and dying, and how the main building was in dire need of a new coat of paint. The beautiful silver painted cross that had sat on top of the bell tower was slowly revealing its wooden underneath and was leaning to one side. It looked as though it was barely holding itself together.

That was exactly how I felt.

I ultimately scolded myself for even being there. What sort of person mourns *themselves*? I felt sick with the weight and frustration of being pathetic; in the way of not knowing how I would handle seeing my own dead body. Only at the moment of truth would I be able to tell.

I was a little late for the ceremony, so I only caught the end of a few speeches; Phoebe's sister Aunt Sophia, and her husband Derek's; and one from Luca. Hers made me reflect and ponder the most.

"…If I had known that Friday would be the last day that I would get to see Savannah Green alive, I would have told her how much she meant to me. I would have hugged her more. I would have laughed with her more. But, no one can predict these sorts of things," she was saying, with tears profusely rolling down her golden-brown cheeks. "The least that we can do is to tell the people who matter to us just how much they do, all the time. Everyday. Because you never know when it will be the last. I never dreamed that I would get to witness that '*last*' with someone at this age —someone who was *my* age. And it's so difficult not to feel completely guilty. What if I hadn't pushed for her to go to that party —what if I hadn't insisted? Would she still be here, by our side? I don't…I don't know the answer. But to make up for it, I can start with an apology, and a hug and some time.

"You know, Savannah was always teaching me new things —changing my perspective. This weekend, I think she taught me the most important lesson of all. If something is too good to be true, it won't last very long. And that's it — Savannah Green was too good to be true. She —" she then choked and paused, gasping for air, "…She was too wonderful for Earth itself —life couldn't contain her. We can't just concentrate on the fact that she's gone. We have to remember all of the good. We have to remember that all good things come to an end. That her end...came a little early."

She walked back to her seat as the respectful clapping entailed, wiping her face and sobbing. It made me want to comfort her and tell her that it was okay, that I was not entirely gone. But I could not do that —there was a risk of her asking who I was.

I then played a scenario through my head, pretending to be my own unknown identical sibling.

"Oh...I'm her long-lost twin sister. I didn't know about her until now, but I'm really sad that I never got to meet her."

"I...I'm surprised. What about her Mom? Wouldn't she have mentioned you? You would think you'd remember shoving two heads out of you."

"Oh —she's not my *Mom —"*

And then that was where I would stop short, because that is exactly the kind of stupid thing that I would end up saying.

All light-heartedness then dissipated once we went around the chapel to where my grave would be in the yard.

My mother could not stop crying. Don just stood there like a jerk with his arms around her, appearing grief stricken. What a damn faker —he had only just met me. At least, he did not cry.

I wandered around my friends and few relatives; some eyes solemnly —or begrudgingly —dry, while some leaked like a broken faucet.

Aaron Carter was not there. His parents were, though. Maybe he felt guilty for the crash. Or maybe he was still in hospital.

Whatever the reason or excuse, it hurt that he had not shown up. I had expected to see him here, mourning me no matter his condition. Because I would have done the same for him.

Lauren, Sam, Olive and Luca could not even face my coffin. Luca could not stop crying either, and buried her face in her mother's embrace; and her wild hair seemed flatter than its usual fluffy bounce. A tear found its way out of the corner of my own eye at the thought of just how much I was going to be missed. That was what was so therapeutic about this whole '*attending your own funeral*' idea. Realising the impact my life actually had had on others. That people *would* remember me after death, even if we could no longer interact. And that they could see me, yet that was as far as it went.

They all saw me alright —but they ignored my presence like a stray cat. I wondered exactly what it was they saw. When I looked at my reflection, I still looked the same —albeit the change in colour to my eyes. But to them, I suppose the rest of my appearance had to alter slightly. I could not go off scaring the living daylights out of humans by acting like the *Walking Dead*. Even though it would have been rather fun to do so.

I smiled momentarily at the thought, blinking back my tears.

The humorous idea that Søren might have done so then crossed my mind — and I nearly snorted. He seemed far too serious and uptight for something like that. He was keeping a safe distance away, hands clasped behind his back in an official soldier-like fashion. He looked like he had witnessed this all countless times before, and had developed an apathetic mask to wear at every such occasion; just as he had claimed.

But I appreciated it. I did not need sympathy.

Phoebe let everyone put roses inside of my coffin for the burial. I picked one up —the one with the most faded-out colour —and stood at the back of the line. I told myself to calm down; that I had to do this. It would be my way of saying goodbye to my old life and my mortal existence.

I shivered when I saw the casket. It was almost indescribable —to see my own dead body there in front of me. My hair had been parted neatly and my skin was deathly pale; my eyes sunken and my lips cracked dry underneath a thin layer of dark rose lipstick.

I looked like a nightmare.

But I leaned over shakily and snapped the rose in half, before fiddling with the bud to nestle in my hair. It was as good as a chrysanthemum; which Phoebe had not known was my favourite flower. I then silently watched as my coffin was lowered into the ground, before being piled with shovelled dirt. I watched myself disappear into the earth, lying next to will-be-forgotten breathless strangers. Savannah Ivy Green no longer existed.

It was simply Savannah now; a Grim Reaper in training.

It would take some time to embrace that fully. I then turned away as another round of speeches started, unable to bear any more, and walked back over dead vegetation to where Søren had been standing. He looked a little solemn; not so uncaring, but he wisely refrained from saying even one word.

"…Let's go," I rasped, choking up towards the end. I picked up the pace and wiped my face furiously, heading for the car. I got into the front passenger's seat and buckled the seatbelt, before leaning against the window. I had asked Angelina for the 5 Stages of Grief and figured that I was now at acceptance, even though I had raced through the other four. It did not mean that everything was now happy-clappy —more like super-*crappy*.

"You're brave. Most people don't actually look at themselves in the coffin," my Trainer murmured as he tried to restart the engine. "Probably because it's way too weird."

I did not respond but a part of me agreed.

I then watched him do what he had done earlier —instead of hot wiring, he concentrated and stared to see right through the car and into its mechanisms, before physically poking around in the ignition with a pin. It was a relief when the car engine finally spluttered to life after coughing worryingly for a minute. Søren then winced and grabbed the side of his head again, as if he had just come down with a strong headache. Using the X-ray vision did that apparently —it was a lot of strain on the retinas.

"It's a wonder that you're not blind yet," I spoke up; the ghost of a smirk lingering on my lips.

Søren glared at me and sighed, running his fingers through his dark hair. "I don't do this enough to be so," he grumbled.

"So, how *does* this work?" I jumped to ask, sitting up properly. "Do all Reapers have X-ray vision?"

"Yes. It's an additional compensation for not being able to pass through solid things at will," he answered, shifting the car into first gear. "The ability to pass through matter is more for safety. Since we are comparable to ghosts, albeit with solid forms, Death must have thought it would be considerate and generous to give us this power."

A sly grin then broke out on my face. "…To steal cars?"

The Reaper did not bother to correct me this time, and silently turned onto the main road. I turned to the window again and wondered if I could start using my special gift right away.

"Don't even think about it," Søren suddenly said, eyes still on the road.

"…What?" I frowned, surprised that he seemed to be responding to my thoughts. Was mind reading on the list now?

"I can tell you want to try it out," he went on, "but you can't. Not yet. Your eyes are still pretty human, and way too fragile. If you try it now as a trainee, you might rupture your retinas."

I started, paling rapidly. I squeaked and sat bolt upright, shaken. As we drove on, I slowly let myself relax and the tension in my muscles ease. "…Thanks for this. For bringing me here, I mean," I said softly, glancing out of the window. "I think that I needed it."

There was a pause, where I saw Søren raise an eyebrow at me in the corner of my vision. I think that it was the first time I had ever expressed gratitude towards him. "…No problem."

✠

When we arrived at the apartment back in Manhattan, Søren seemed to be constantly tense and jumpy —his eyes flittering back and forth between whatever was occupying his attention at that time, and the windows.

We were supposed to be training, but instead of the pupil being distracted, it was the teacher. I figured that it might be a defence mechanism, but when I tried to catch him off guard, he did not even react.

There his silver eyes stayed —at the window.

"Okay, what the hell?" I huffed, having had enough. I swung my sword over my head and let it rest on my covered shoulder. "What's so fascinating about the window?"

"…What?" he muttered, not turning to face me.

"You're not paying attention to me," I informed, marching up to him and grabbing him by the collar his turtleneck. "Your focus should be undivided. You're supposed to be *teaching* me."

He seemed to snap out of it then, and he quickly shook his head. I released my grip on him and frowned, standing with one hand on my hip.

"What's the matter?"

He sighed and shook his head again. "It's…it's nothing. Sorry, I'll try not to be so absentminded."

I hummed in response, swinging my sword forward again.

To my delight, I was becoming quite the sword master —albeit with a tendency to set fire to Søren's hair and slice cushions in half.

We started again, with a parry and attack exercise. My Trainer used a weaker and more temperamental obsidian sword than mine from his hoard of glorified murder weapons, and was finding it hard to keep up with my sword's strength as they clanged against each other.

"…Out of curiosity," I panted, stepping back for a moment, "What would happen if I accidentally reaped your soul?"

He chuckled and took the opportunity to make me back up further by pushing his sword against mine. "I would die again," he said simply. "…We're not completely immortal, you know."

"I…see," I breathed heavily, pushing back against him. "You're quite casual about that fact," I smirked, took a step backwards, before pivoting sharply on my heel and ending up being side-to-chest with him; my sword an inch from resting on the base of his neck. He scoffed, seemingly unfazed, and then ducked, moving out from underneath. I turned around too slowly and found myself with the tip of his sword to my chest.

"I think that I can handle myself pretty well, don't you think?" he quipped, smirking. "That was pretty advanced by the way. We're supposed to be practising parry and attack —not *Dancing with the Stars*."

I growled and pushed his sword downward with my clothed arm, away from me. "I'm over that now. Can't we do something more challenging? Doing the same dodge and block, *over* and over again is demeaning," I drawled. "I want to try something more complicated."

As soon as the words left my mouth Søren grabbed my waist, pulled my back towards him and held me by the neck against him; the edge of his sword's blade hovering just above my skin.

My sword lay on the floor to the left of me, out of my reach. I flushed and breathed shallowly, feeling sheepish.

"…You were saying?" Søren chuckled, which shamed me even further.

"You just caught me off guard," I quipped haughtily. "But fine —we'll go back to dodging and blocking."

"Oh, *no*, no," he went on; his grip on me tightening, "First, you're going to have to find a way to get out of this. As defence practice. Think of it as a real-life situation."

I drew a breath, reaching up to grip his forearm that was around my neck. I felt the tension in his muscles ease, which gave me the perfect opportunity to pull him. He did not expect the action, and stumbled forward, aiding my plan to throw him up and over me.

He landed on his front with a thud at my feet; and the sword clanged hard against the floor, letting out an echo. I dusted my hands and smirked, pleased with myself. I picked up my sword and waited for Søren to stand up.

He did; painfully slowly, before he turned to me with a trickle of blood dripping out of one nostril. "…Nice one," he coughed weakly.

My eyes widened as he simply wiped the blood away with the back of his hand and picked up his sword again. I hesitated —whether it was from shock or something else —and my mind instantly went back to the crash; back to the sight of silver blood. For some reason, I was apprehensive about asking if all Reapers' blood looked like mine. So, I refocused.

"…Oh my *God* —I didn't mean to break your nose," I gushed, rushing over to examine the extent of the damage.

I grabbed Søren's face and brought it down closer to me. Nothing appeared to be bent out of shape, which was a relief. I then breathed out a sigh and glanced upwards into his silver eyes. The light caught and danced within them, making them luminous and sort of beautiful.

I likely stared for a couple of seconds too long.

Then I blurted, "Are you sure that you're okay?"

He nodded convincingly. "It's really not a big deal," he insisted. "Seriously —that was very clever."

He then winced, holding the bridge of his nose.

"I shouldn't have been so rough," I mumbled.

The Reaper shook his head. "I asked you to treat it like a real situation, and you did. Well done. There is absolutely no need to apologise. I should probably go and stop the bleeding though."

He then sidestepped me and headed for the main room. I still felt guilty, but I was grateful for how well he was taking it.

A sudden bright light then shone in the corner of my vision.

I whipped around —before stumbling backwards into the desk. Sitting on the windowsill, in all its shining glory, was a fully-grown turkey-sized fiery orange and golden bird with a long, curled tail.

I gasped and clutched at my chest, feeling as though I had gone into cardiac arrest. I shakily stood up straight and squinted at the creature in front of me. It was a little too bright to look at head-on, but I did not miss its beady little red eyes boring into mine as it turned its head to look at me.

It was a *Phoenix*.

The stuff of mythology and legends, was sitting right there a few meters away from me, poking its curved beak around underneath its wings. It then stretched its

69

wings out and flapped them, before letting out a shrill squawk.

I did not even register the slight ringing in my ears.

I was too mesmerised by the flames that flickered at the ends of its feathers. I wondered if it would hurt if I stroked them; and so, I took several steps forward...only to stop about a meter away.

It radiated such a tremendous amount of heat that I had to back up, shielding my face with my arms.

"Uh...Søren," I called out worriedly, eyes glued to the flaming fowl. "We have a...visitor."

Søren poked his head around the doorframe to see what the problem was. He flinched and his eyes widened at the sight of the Phoenix, before he shrunk back in the doorway.

"Oh no —I was afraid of this."

CHAPTER 8

SAVANNAH

HAVING A PHOENIX visit was not a good thing —in fact, it was on par with being fired. Such a visit was one of the highest forms of a severe warning at best; otherwise it brought ominous news.

"It's likely here because of *that*," Søren continued, pointing at my sword on the floor. I immediately went to pick it up, very aware of the Phoenix's stare. "...Don't make any other sudden movements," Søren warned, narrowing his steely eyes at the magnificent creature.

It squawked indifferently and poked at its feathers again.

"It's so beautiful," I sighed. "I didn't know they existed until you mentioned their fire. It's amazing to see one with my own eyes."

"It's a bad omen," Søren corrected me, before walking in slowly; putting one hesitant foot in front of the other. Once he had reached the spot where I was, the Phoenix's red eyes glowed and it tilted its head back.

It breathed fire, a meter into the air —along with something dark that then landed on the windowsill —before sounding as though it were choking. It *did* cough up a few sparks and dying embers, but it recovered soon after and went back to preening itself. It reminded me so much of Ron —which sparked a small aching pang in my chest.

I glanced up at Søren, but he was making a move for the thing on the windowsill beside the Phoenix. I squinted and made out a small black envelope. I gasped, recognising the stamp.

71

"What is that?" I murmured suspiciously as Søren carefully tore the envelope open before disregarding it and keeping the letter. The paper was dark red instead of white; unlike the letters from my father.

"An inquiry," he murmured, his eyes darting from side to side as he quickly skim-read the letter. "…And a pretty damn serious one if it had to be delivered via a Phoenix."

"What's an inquiry?" I frowned, glancing back at the bird. It was now less bright than before, and staring at us. At this distance I could now see little flecks of molten gold streaking in its crimson irises.

```
                            URGENT

    Based on the request made from your traced account, there is
  reason to believe that there may have been a system glitch, or
  it may have been intercepted and altered. In order to eradicate
        such suspicions, the owner of the request must prove a
  legitimate connection by reaping one mortal soul. This must be
      done by sunset. If the task is not fulfilled, further and
                  undesirable action will be taken.

              Signed, Obsidian Carrier Corp HQ
```

"It's from Obsidian Carrier Corp headquarters. They're asking about your sword," Søren grumbled, before his eyes widened as he then read the letter properly, "—they want to see if the order wasn't a glitch in the system. You have to prove the sword is indeed a match of yours. They want you to reap one soul by sunset."

He turned to me and I blinked, mildly shaken.
I shook my head. "I can't do that —I'm not ready. All I know is how to dodge and parry. I haven't had any training for that yet," I protested.

"The best way to learn is on the job," Søren quipped, winking at me as he

72

went to grab a set of arrows from the wall. "Relax. Reaping is not as hard as you might think. I'll teach you how to do it with a sword on the way." He then tossed me a leather sheath roughly the length of my sword. "Here. So that you don't have to carry it around in your hands."

I scoffed, bewildered, before grabbing the sheath and fastening it to my hips. I limply slotted my sword into it by my side, before swinging it lazily and getting used to the heavy feeling. Then I looked back at the Phoenix. It stared back at me, cooing softly. "…What's going to happen to the bird?"

Søren glanced in its direction and clicked his tongue. "It'll turn to ash when it's ready to leave and go back to the Hell out of which it flew. It'll hopefully be gone by the time we get back."

"Oh," I mumbled, a little disappointed. It looked like my time with a magical creature would be drawing to a close before it really had the chance to begin. I then gasped as my Trainer proceeded to shoo the Phoenix away with a broomstick.

"Hey!" I rushed over to grab it from him. "Just what the hell do you think you're doing?"

"It's *vermin*, Savannah," Søren said firmly. "It's not staying here."

"But if it's going to be gone by the time that we get back then why can't it stay in the meantime?" I reasoned.

"Because it will turn to ash all over the floor. *My* floor," he hissed, his face contorting into a frown, "Are you volunteering to clean up afterwards?"

I dithered, weighing out my options. "…Yes," I decided. "I'll do it. Just don't treat it the same way as everyone else does," I said, hoping that my big pleading doe eyes would work on him. His frown deepened and narrowed into a glare — probably scrutinising my expression for any ulterior motives —before he finally relented and dropped the broom. "…You had *better* clean up," he grumbled. "Or there will be hell to pay."

"Yes sir," I grinned, even adding a salute.
He smirked, indicating that he quite liked the display of obedience. "Indeed. Now come on. Sunset isn't very far from now."

"So, you'll really let Phee-Phee stay?" I paused, looking back at the Phoenix.

It had resumed its self-grooming session, now going at it with increased vigour; littering the air with luminescent feathers that disintegrated into embers before they could land on the floor and set it alight.

Søren turned to glare at me. "…You named it *Phee-Phee*?"

"Yes," I pouted, sticking my nose up in the air. "It deserved a name. The poor thing has probably been called '*it*' for all of its life." I looked at Phee-Phee sympathetically.

"*For* a good reason," Søren clipped, throwing his hands in the air. "It's a giant bloody rat with wings. On *fire*," he emphasised. "And why Phee-Phee? What made you assume that it was female?"

"What made *you* assume that Phee-Phee was a female name?" I shot back, raising an eyebrow. He blinked and sheepishly hesitated, which gave me time to continue. "…I suppose that it *could* be classified as a female name," I admitted, "But I didn't name it because of its gender. It's spelled *p*; *h*; *e*; *e* —as in, referencing the pronunciation of the name of its kind. It will not be raised to conform to such binary confines. It's going to be Phee-Phee whether it's male or female."

Søren gave me a look before stomping over to the Phoenix and standing next to it. Phee-Phee edged away from him rapidly as though he smelled bad.

"…It's a male," Søren stated.

"How do you know?" I frowned. "You didn't look underneath." I then blushed as I said this, hearing my words aloud.

"No need to," he dismissed. "All that you have to do is look at the pattern of its feathers. Males' flow left, and females' flow right."

A sly grin spread across my face. "…That wouldn't happen to have anything to do with the fact that females are always right —would it?"

Søren frowned in annoyance as I chuckled at my own joke.
"Okay, okay, let's go." I moved towards the door. Then I paused again. "…You wouldn't happen to have any birdseed, would you?"

"Even if I did, for whatever odd reason, we're not feeding it," Søren sang, walking out of the door. I drooped but heeded to his words.

"Bye, Phee-Phee," I sighed, trudging away. The bird turned his head to the side and seemed to look at me sadly, like he did not want me to leave. That, or my imagination was playing up again.

In a few minutes we were then heading out, but not before Søren made sure to snap at me to double check the door was locked.

"Do I look like the one who owns this apartment?" I snapped back, mustering all the attitude I could.

He looked me up and down before meeting my gaze again.

"...Temporarily," he muttered, shrugging as we headed for the elevator.

I scoffed and kicked at the hallway carpet. "What is the big deal?" I spoke up again, lifting my head to meet his eye. "Do people steal old newspapers?"

To my surprise, Søren chuckled softly in response as the elevator opened up for us. I stiffened as the male with the chainsaw from Saturday morning came into view. I hesitantly pressed the ground floor button before shuffling past him to stand on the other side, as far away from him as possible. His red gaze followed me and did not waver.

"Mel," Søren then said, noticing the Reaper. A slight flush appeared in the Trainer's cheeks, startling me. He looked at the stranger with a strained nonchalance —as though he wanted to seem indifferent, but he was doing it very ostentatiously. The Chainsaw Guy's glare finally left me and turned to Søren in one smooth fluid movement, but his lips remained clamped shut. "Haven't seen you in a while," Søren continued, decidedly oblivious to the poisonous atmosphere. His gaze challenged the other Reaper's, as though the smaller male believed himself to be far superior.

There was a dangerous, unnerving air in the elevator. Whatever petty resentment it was that was between the two Reapers beside me ran deep, and it ran cold. Rivalry did not quite encapsulate it. There was painful regret in Søren's gaze. Shameful and begrudged guilt in the other's.

They towered at almost the same height —but that was where the similarities ended. Søren had the physique of a toothpick. I could see that this 'Mel' was built like a fortified tank; his limbs thickly corded with muscle and straining against the confines of his clothes.

The Chainsaw Guy snorted in response to Søren's taunt, his arms folded and expression hard. "...Mel*chior*," he said, and his deep, even voice resonated in my chest. I shivered, and I might have reflected my discomfort outwardly, because he then shot me a look. "Who is she?"

Søren opened his mouth to answer, and I gasped, outraged that he would just share that information without a second thought.

"Oh. It's not your place to know, but this is —"
He did not manage to finish, because I sharply elbowed his side before my name could be said, making him wince.

"It most certainly *is* none of your business," I quipped, turning my nose up at the Chainsaw Guy.

I may have caught his name, but it did not mean that I needed to use it. He raised his eyebrows at me, and his garnet eyes travelled down to my sword.

"Is that yours?" he murmured, a surprising look of intrigue etching in his stony, flawless features.

I panicked, thinking about what he would say if I confessed. "...No. It's not mine. That would be...*weird*, right?" I scoffed dubiously, making more of an effort to hide it behind my back.

"It's weirder if it's not yours," he countered. I lowered my head slightly in shame. He then turned back to Søren. "...She's painfully and obviously just a Turned Reaper. You certainly have your work cut out."

"Actually, she's a fast learner," Søren surprised me with a compliment. "And despite the rather advanced weapon that she has, I think that she will be ready to handle herself in due time."

The Chainsaw Guy sucked on his teeth before turning to the doors as they opened. I glanced at the buttons before realising that we were on the second top floor. I internally groaned and slumped against the elevator wall as the Chainsaw Guy looked back at us with a smug expression on his face.
He picked up his weapon and swung it over his shoulder, before pausing.

"Such a pity that the elevator was going up when you decided to enter it," he smirked. Then he walked down the hallway, just as the doors began to close. "…Good luck or whatever!" he called, flippantly raising his hand in a way of saying farewell.

I scowled, folded my arms and tapped my foot rhythmically against the diamond patterned metal flooring in newfound irritation.

"I'm sorry that you had to witness that. He's not usually…so rude," Søren said a little knowingly, and a little dejectedly. "Just…hot headed."

I snorted and shook my head. "Sure —seemed that way," I muttered as I closed my eyes to neutralise the sinking feeling. "Did you train him, too?" I asked out of curiosity, then opening cautiously one eye as the elevator stopped and the doors opened.

"No," Søren quipped and shook his head as we then walked out into the lobby. "We, uh…used to date."

My eyes widened and I nearly choked on my saliva as I moved to walk out after him and fall in step beside him. I was in no way weirded out; I was simply genuinely surprised. "Wait —are you being serious or are you just pulling my leg?" I demanded.

He glanced down at me with an expression that would not give anything away, his lustrous eyes eerily dark. "No."

✠

"So," I breathed as we walked out into the pleasant warmth of the late afternoon, "Where are we off to?"

"65 Walter Place, Terrence Centre," Søren answered. "It should be nice and easy for you. It's a man called Martin Smith. He's eighty-two and has a prolonged history of smoking, as well as some nasty back problems. Lives with his care-worker, Nancy King."

"Wait, but what about showing me the ropes? You can't really expect me to just waltz in through his front door and stick a sword in him with this Nancy being right there," I reasoned.

My Trainer chuckled and turned to face me; his silver irises now twinkling. "I'd fucking pay to see that."

"I'm *serious*," I said firmly. "I need some practical demonstrations."

"All right," he sighed, stretching his arms up over his head. "Let's see who else needs to die today."

Louise Hansen's time was also up. She was going to die of a trauma induced seizure, in the later hours of a Tuesday evening when she needed to work extra shifts to pay the bills for her and her alcoholic unemployed boyfriend. She was scheduled to die in a fight with him.

"I can't believe that you're reaping the soul of a victim of domestic violence," I rasped after Søren had finished briefing me. He did not say anything straight away, which kept us in a brief silence.

"…It happens," he eventually sighed. "It's a sick, sad world full of sick, sad people who aren't mature enough to get their shit together."

"I'm with you there," I agreed. "I hope that her death will teach him something," I murmured.

"If not, *I* certainly will," he growled, clenching his fists. I doubted that he actually could, but I let him have the moment.

Once we had reached Louise's apartment building Søren decided to use the fire escape to enter. He replied that it was the stealthiest way to get inside when I had asked why. I shrugged and nodded, intent on just observing. The window to the bathroom was open, so we squeezed inside. Søren expertly landed on his haunches on the tiled floor.

I landed on my face on the closed toilet lid.

It did not hurt as much as I thought it would, but I still managed to bend my nose in an unnatural direction. I whimpered, panic rising up inside me.

"…*Son* of a —!"

"Seriously?" Søren groaned, eyeing my face. "Right now? You're going to be a walking disaster, aren't you?"

I screamed with my mouth closed and widened my eyes in an imploring way. "…Hold *still*." He grabbed hold of my nose and jerked it the other way, straightening it out. I yelped and covered my nose with my hands, with tears collecting in my eyes. I mumbled profanity under my breath as he told me to shut it and hold a wad of toilet paper over my nose to minimise the bleeding. I reluctantly did as he said and tried to focus on the task at hand.

We made our way across the hallway, heading to where the screaming match was in full swing. "Aren't they going to see us?" I whispered, my voice sounding horribly nasally.

"She will. He won't," Søren hissed back.

I nodded slightly and walked into the living room after him. Louise was crying, hunching over as her boyfriend screamed at her. Her short summer dress was torn at the seam on the side, making me flinch at the thought that he had already recently done something to her. I looked at Søren as he looked at me, and we exchanged the same look of fear and disapproval.

"…You never *listen* to me!" Louise screamed, straightening up slightly. Her eyes were bloodshot, and she could not stop shaking as she backed away from her boyfriend. "I'm trying to keep a damn roof over our heads but all you want is for me to stay in bed all day. *Well*, news flash, Tucker. We won't *have* a bed to fuck in if I don't go to work!"

My eyes widened and I turned my head to the side, suddenly uncomfortable with the feeling of intruding —in more ways than one. My Trainer glanced over his shoulder at me and frowned, but he did not look all too comfortable either.

Tucker-The-Girlfriend-Abuser turned red and opened his mouth to scream again. "I don't give a rat's ass about your jobs, Louise! It's your damn job to keep me satisfied and that's it!"

He then raised his fist, causing Louise to start violently. Having seen enough, Søren growled and stood next to the Walking-Pile-Of-Garbage. Louise let out a strangled gasp as her gaze landed on the Grim Reaper. But no words came out of her agape mouth.

Søren reached for an arrow behind him and slotted it into his crossbow. I needlessly held my breath as I prepared myself to watch from the safety of the doorway. He poised his crossbow, and took aim, before releasing the trigger. The arrow whistled through the air, before hitting Louise right in the chest in the same instant that Trash-Head's punch struck her face. My jaw and wad of tissues dropped as Louise fell to the ground and landed on her side; he hair obscuring what was obviously a bloodied face. Then she began convulsing. Tucker-The-Jackass froze and seemed paralysed as he watched his girlfriend shake as though she was being electrocuted.

Søren lowered his crossbow and stepped back; not a glimpse of regret or remorse showing in his frown. I had always had a pretty clear picture in my mind as to how a Grim Reaper would reap a soul. But seeing Søren do it, nullified almost every shred of innocence I had had left. Seeing the soul *rip* its way out of the body was enough to make me want to gag. It was because Søren's weapon was semi instant in efficiency —that meant that the lapse between hitting a target and the soul being reaped was as long as ten seconds, minimum.

After that, the soul would be experiencing so much pain, that it would have no choice but to *claw* its way out.

Gruesome.

"Louise? Louise —oh my God, I'm going to call an ambulance. *Louise!*"
A-Disgrace-To-Humanity then panicked, tripping over his own feet as he stumbled to the telephone. I looked on as Louise in spirit form stood up and glanced at her body. She looked the same, but she was now a transparent white wispy entity; her eyes ablaze with white light and her body faintly aglow.

The soul looked at us, and then down at herself again, before hanging her head solemnly. Sudden-Remorse looked up in mid-dialling and glanced over at Louise's body.

The convulsing was coming to a gradual tremble. "...Louise?"
My eyes flickered to her, as sympathy welled up inside of me. My Trainer met her gaze and nodded importantly.

"...Rest in peace, Louise Hansen," Søren said.

Louise nodded, before she closed her eyes and her form faded before us, dissipating in the stale air like magic. A glow then came from Søren's crossbow —what I assumed to be his count of reaped souls. From the angle at which I was standing, I made out *MXCIX*.

I blinked, but before I could say anything I was interrupted by the sound of wails. Ugly, borderline showy cries that made me stiffen and want to rip off my own ears. The bastard was crying. He knelt down, bent over Louise's dead body, and held her shoulders against him and howling out apologies. I wanted to scream at him. I could not understand why he suddenly felt bad. Then I realised something. Maybe he had not *wanted* her to die —the weight of his actions had only been pinned on him now that he had gone irrevocably too far.

And there was no taking it back.

I looked at Søren, shock paralysing my face. He sighed and swung his crossbow, "…Always aim for the heart," he murmured, before walking towards the door, back to the bathroom window.

CHAPTER 9

SAVANNAH

IT TURNED OUT that Grim Reapers who reap in the same area live in a fairly get-along community —because if someone missed out on a few souls, another Reaper could complete the district's greater quota for them. The chances of letting a person live over their carefully measured out days were slim to none; and as a Trainer, Søren was partly exempted from collecting his usual daily amount of souls if he had a trainee at the time.

Which meant that part of his souls were mine to reap.

Not so lucky for me.

Terrence Centre seemed to be the hub of night life even in the afternoon, which made me wonder how Martin Smith could have possibly dealt with all of the noise and traffic for all of that time. Perhaps he had lived here since he had been in college and had gradually grown accustomed to it.

Søren stayed quiet for a long time after reaping Louise Hansen. I was not sure if I should say anything, so I left the subject alone. He flaunted his apparent apathy, but deep down, I think that it affected him —especially in this specific case. I did not really want to bring it up since it looked like it had been quite the ordeal —but it got me curious. What was it about Louise's situation that had resonated with him? It scared me a little to think that maybe his parents had been like them; like Tucker and Louise.

That was when it occurred to me that I knew almost nothing about Søren —I only knew his name. The more I tried to understand about him, the less I really got. And whenever his walls showed any signs of lowering down, his mouth then shut as some kind of a secondary defence mechanism.

I glanced up at Søren and for a moment, it was as though I was noticing him for the first time. His tousled dark tangled hair and the dark circles beneath his eyes made his skin look snowy white. The only colour came from the light pink of his thin lips and the deep blue of his sweater. The silver of his irises only added to the frigidity of his haunted demeanour. His legs were stiff in his drainpipe trousers and he walked like an old-fashioned sailor; he trudged more than walked. But he was a fast trudger.

Even with that speed, his gait reflected a certain brooding undertone. He was always thinking; always calculating. About what, I was unable to tell. His clothes matched his personality —depressing. It was nearly all black, and I knew that most of it was not a fashion choice, but he seemed to have used the dress code to his advantage. If it was a pitch black and moonless night, one might have mistaken him for a dead tree.

I on the other hand had my brown leather jacket to contrast against the black. I did not mind the lack of colour all that much —but there was so much of that darkness that it looked like one solid mass.

I shoved my hands into my pockets and sighed, before realising that I had not even noticed I had not been breathing all this time. It surprised me because after living eighteen years and having had breathing as second nature, I was now fully accustomed to no longer needing my lungs. The strenuous walk though, would not let me forget about fatigue just yet.

Søren seemed to be handling it just fine, so I did not want to complain. He still remained withdrawn, and I did not know how I was going to get around that. He was so unlike the friends I had had before, and it made me wonder if we even *could* be friends after my training was complete.

After a while, a question that had been biting me then desperately needed an answer, so I just decided to come out with it.

"Søren, what does *MXCIX* mean?" I asked.

The Reaper started at the sound of my voice but would not look in my direction.

83

"…One thousand and ninety-nine."

So, the numbers that appeared after reaping were indeed in Roman numerals. That would mean I would need to do some research when we got back to the apartment if I was ever going to understand them.

My eyes then widened as the realisation of the meaning of the number dawned on me. "You've reaped one thousand and ninety-nine *souls*?" I gasped.

He took a deep and shaky breath before exhaling, the air whistling out of his lungs. "…It's my job."

The way he said that —so flatly and devoid of feeling —it sent an ice cold chill down my spine. I nodded, before glancing away at the street.

Duty, above all, was the saying. "*And nothing is allowed to stop you*," I recalled Søren saying. I figured that it would have to become something I that needed to adopt. It would not be easy. I was more a pacifist when it came to resolving conflict, though I was not afraid to swing a punch. As a Grim Reaper, the notion of avoiding violence would have to be put to an end.

I then wondered how long it had taken Søren to become so unfeeling. I glanced up at him. Even without looking into his eyes I would have been able to tell that he was dead inside.

Was that what this job was going to do to me?

I did not want to think about it anymore. I folded my arms and walked on determinedly, decidedly pushing away the thoughts which scared me.

✠

I gulped as I stood in front of 65 Walter place —a run-down apartment building that was a little smaller than the one Søren pretended to live in. The sun was now dipping its way below the horizon, giving the sky a husky orange and fuchsia glow.

"…First floor, right?" I whispered.

My Trainer nodded.

I swung my clasped my hands and rocked on my heels, intent on stalling for as long as possible. "So, I just…march right in there, huh?"

"*Yes*," Søren answered, with an annoyed edge to his voice. I bit my lip and nodded slowly, but did not move, even when he nudged me forward.

Could I really do this? Could I really reap an old man's soul? My mind reasoned that he was old, so it was not such a big deal —but my heart screamed that it was practically murder.

"…I *told* you that apathy was a necessary skill," Søren sighed, folding his arms. I whipped around to face him and frowned; I was so not in the mood for that conversation right now.

Sunset was upon us, and here I was, dithering about needlessly. I needed to put my morality aside for the sake of my job. I took a deep head-clearing breath and exhaled, composing myself.

"Well," I sighed, shrugging. "It's now or never." I huffed and marched purposefully towards the back entrance.

"That's the spirit," Søren mocked, following after me.

I took lead and climbed in through the open window of a bedroom. It was plain and well kept, but little strong-smelling lavender fragrance candles burned in corners, inclining me to think it was likely Nancy King's room.

I jumped over the windowsill and landed on my haunches —to my absolute relief —and Søren landed after me, before straightening his jacket and quickly checking his reflection in the gilt mirror on the wall.

"*Oi* —what are you doing? This is no time to preen yourself," I snapped as I grabbed his arm and dragged him to the door, "We're here to focus."

"Sorry. I just…wanted to see how I had looked earlier in front of…" he trailed off, his expression becoming even more downtrodden.

After a brief pause, I understood what he meant. "You can worry about that later," I said gently. "Right now, we have a job to do."

"Okay," Søren breathed out and held his hands up in mock surrender. He then stepped aside and gestured for me to be his guest. I nervously held my own breath and walked down the hallway.

Martin Smith was not a shaky leaf of an old man. He looked solid and sturdy;

more rugged than fragile and brittle. He was sitting in an armchair and staring at the television but watching nothing. As soon as I set foot in the small living room his gaze found mine and fear struck every muscle in his body. He froze, flexed and almost looked like a hunter who had suddenly become the hunted. But he held my gaze and did not look away, before a knowing frown wrinkled in his features.

He was not afraid to look death in the eyes.

I opened my mouth to say something, but Nancy King decided to waltz in with a tray of what appeared to be dinner. She smiled cheerfully and was blissfully unaware of the staring contest behind her.

"Mashed potatoes and roast chicken just as you like it, Mr Smith," she beamed in a heavy Southern accent, before moving aside to go back to the kitchen. He stayed still and careful, and barely registered Nancy's presence. "…Yes…yes. Thank you, Nancy."

Nancy raised an eyebrow and paused, something evidently bothering her. "You all right, Mr Smith? You usually correct me and tell me to call you Martin every chance you get."

Martin did not respond, so Nancy followed his gaze and met mine. I stiffened at the prospect of flunking this assignment before I had even really started, but her eyes shifted slightly as though searching for something.

She looked straight through me.

After a moment, I remembered that I was invisible to her. "…*All right*, Mr Smith," Nancy said nervously and edged her way to the kitchen doorway, "I'll, uh…I'll go check if you took your medicine this afternoon."

She disappeared into the kitchen and left me a window of opportunity. Martin was still frowning at me; but it was probably now out of confusion as to why I was taking so long.

"What are you waiting for, an invitation?" Søren hissed behind me.

"Be quiet —I know what I'm doing," I hissed back, reaching for my sword. I unsheathed it, displaying its sleek shine to Martin Smith, whose eyes then widened. I walked right in, and Martin's gaze followed me until I was right in front of him. He opened his mouth, but just like speechless Louise, he did not

86

seem like he could say anything. My gaze flickered down to his plate and back to his dark eyes, before an idea popped into my head.

Death by choking.

It seemed fitting given his smoking background.

I hesitated as Martin slowly reached out as though to check if I was a part of his imagination, but what I really needed him to do was bite into that chicken. I took a step backwards and held my sword in a neutral position, with its blade faced downward. Martin paused before looking as though he got the idea, and shakily reached out for the drumstick. I waited like the evil queen in *Snow White* when she had given the princess the poisoned apple.

Martin's teeth sunk into the meat, before tearing it off the bone and beginning to chew. Then he spluttered, as though the air was suddenly not coming into his lungs fast enough. That was my cue.

I raised my sword, and in one smooth movement I swung it down, so the tip just touched his knitted sweater.

"...Mr Smith?" Nancy called, having heard something irregular. "Mr Smith, are you all right?"

I then heard her footsteps quicken.

Martin started, unprepared for the briskness of the situation.

He still gasped for air. I winced.

I want to make this as fast and pain free as I can for the both of us.

Nancy came in and gasped as she saw Martin choking. She rushed over and began to help by leaning him forward, then gently clapping him on the back.

I glanced back at Søren nervously and he gave me an encouraging nod. I looked down at Martin with his hands around his neck. I looked into his eyes and found a warmth in them, and for a flicker of a moment, I saw something of my late grandfather in him.

So, I froze. "I...can't do this," I whispered, my hands beginning to shake. "...I can't reap this soul."

"Well, you're going to have to," Søren spoke up. "...*Sunset*, Savannah," he reminded me, pointing towards the window.

I gulped as the sun appeared to be teasingly peeking over the horizon. But it only offered me a few minutes. I looked back at Martin. He looked up at me, and something forlorn shone in his eyes.

I pursed my lips and gripped my sword more securely. "...I'm sorry," I whispered, before I pierced his chest and swung in an upward motion.

I gasped as Martin's soul was cleaved with the motion my sword and floated on top of his body; now slumped over and lifeless. Nancy cried out and shook him, promising to call an ambulance.

I looked up at Martin and offered a sad smile. My sword then glowed, and I looked to find a lone *I* appear where the zero had been before it.

"...Rest in peace, Martin Smith," I said softly, and it was a relief to see him nod slightly, before his form dissipated into the air as Louise's had done.

I let out a shaky breath and turned around. Søren gave me a thumbs up and beckoned me over, signalling that it was time to leave. I followed after him but paused at the doorway and looked back at the scene before me.

My heart wrenched for Nancy, but it was nothing which I could help.

I turned away, and felt as though I understood why Søren had been so removed earlier. I had done it. I now had a reaping track record.

CHAPTER 10

SAVANNAH

SØREN KEPT QUIET as we made our way back to the apartments.
I suppose that he had been thankful for my silence after he had reaped earlier, and
so he decided to return the favour.

It felt like I was filled to the brim with tears —but I was too traumatised to
cry them. I felt a little numb, but mostly cold, and I shivered in my thin clothes. I
wanted to brood in the apartment too, sitting cross-legged on the sofa and
fingering my necklace thoughtfully.

It had begun to glow gold like my sword after we had left Martin's apartment,
and I had no idea what it meant, or if it was meant to do that.

At least the dilemma of me proving the sword was mine was now solved. I
hoped that the people who had written to us were satisfied now.

Unfortunately, I could not dwell on my necklace when we got back, because
apparently Phee-Phee had opted to overstay his welcome.

"He's still...*here*?" I said excitedly, opening the computer room door.
My Trainer's anger flared, having festered since that afternoon. "That's it," he
growled and pushed past me into the doorway, "I'm shooting it."

"Søren!" I gasped —and I was too preoccupied to realise that it was first time
that I had said his name correctly —as I stumbled in after him. "Don't you *dare*
do anything to that innocent creature!"

I caught up and pulled his crossbow away from him, before moving to defend
Phee-Phee. Søren huffed and folded his spindly arms.

"Move out of the way, Savannah," he ordered firmly.

"No," I defied somewhat haughtily. "You're not getting rid of him. And I'll keep my promise. I'll clean up after him when he decides to leave. Until then, he's staying *right here*."

"Excuse me? Here, as in, *here* here? In my office?"

"No," I frowned, "—he can be wherever I go. In the living room, I guess."

Søren tugged a hand through his hair and exhaled, expelling some stress.

"…Look, that cat of yours doesn't really count as experience, because Phoebe usually took care of him. I know —I saw. And don't even try to deny it," he added before I could argue that I *had* taken care of him once upon a time. "…Taking care of a magical creature is not the same as an average dog or cat. Phoenixes have special needs and dietary requirements of their own. And I just don't have the patience to let it settle here long enough for you to find out," he ended, folding his arms.

He reminded me of a father in that moment —and upon realising that, I shuddered and took a step backwards.

"I want to take care of Phee-Phee," I insisted.

"Naming it leads to emotional attachment."

"Well, at least then he would have felt some sort of attachment in his life," I snapped, frowning up at him. "It disappoints me that you treat him as vermin when all you should do is show him that maybe he's not what people think of him. That maybe he deserves a chance."

I glanced behind me at Phee-Phee and smiled. Phee-Phee stared back at me and cooed, hopping around on the windowsill.

"…You really want to do this?" Søren whispered, dropping the Dad Act and softening his expression.

"Yes," I said, turning back around. "I promise he won't be a nuisance. *Right*, Phee-Phee?" I asked him, nodding vigorously. He squawked enthusiastically, flapping his gorgeous wings.

Søren sighed and shook his head. "I hope that was Phoenix for '*sir, yes, sir*'. And, he better not be." He glared at the Phoenix, before glancing back at me and his crossbow. "...Can I have that back now?"

I tossed it to him and sidestepped him, heading for the living room. "Come on Phee-Phee —let's go to the other room and leave Mr Grumpy alone with his *precious* Angelina," I drawled, rolling my eyes.

Søren suddenly moved to block my path. I blinked, wondering what had gotten into him. His silver eyes were ablaze with rage. It was the first time that I had seen any kind of raw emotion from him. "Don't you dare call her that," he said in a careful, low voice. "She is *Computer* to you, and you are not to say that name —in my presence or otherwise."

My eyes widened but I nodded, taking a step backwards.

"Okay," I said carefully, moving to the side. The Reaper breathed heavily for a moment, as he dragged a hand over his face. He did not offer me an explanation or even another word —simply anguish.

He needed time to himself. So, I turned away.

"...Come, Phee-Phee," I beckoned. The Phoenix jumped down and stalked its way after me, taking note to strut proudly. On my way out I noticed a list of names on one of the desks. I scanned them and did not find one that I recognised. I believed that it was a good thing.

I sank down on the sofa and reached for a letter as Phee-Phee settled down on the side table beside me, curling his tail and wrapping it around him. I smiled and wished that I could stroke his feathers like I used to stroke Ron's fur, but I did not need to add burns to my list of injuries.

My nose was slightly tender, but it would be all right. Grim Reapers had a knack for healing speedily —another gift from Death.

I ripped open the envelope and took out the letter, ready to read when the sound of a *ting* distracted me. It sounded just like my cellphone. I frowned, trying to figure out where it had come from. The sound then repeated, and I crawled over to my discarded backpack. The inside was empty, albeit for a few letters nestled inside. So, I checked the pockets.

My cellphone fell out onto the floor, and I let out a surprised, "Oh."

I picked it up and unlocked the screen. The notifications came in —all two hundred and forty-three of them.

My SIM card was still inside and had picked up on the network. I opened the app and found that a majority of the notifications had come from an old group chat. I opened the conversation and scrolled through outdated messages, before coming to ones dating back to Sunday morning.

It was long comforting texts from my friends to each other; telling them that they were not alone, and they were all there for each other. It was so sweet —and saddening. It sounded as though Sam was not getting enough sleep due to non-stop crying. I could not help but to feel a little guilty about that. I did not want her to *deteriorate* because of me. I was glad that my friends were missing me but if something awful was happening to them because of it, I would rather they did not miss me at all.

I scrolled through the rest of the messages as my guilt grew and the ache in my chest harshened —until I reached a part where Francesca Minetti began to talk, which happened to be a few hours ago.

My eyes widened as I read her messages —some stupid half-assed excuse for why she had been so quiet. My thankfully smart friends did not seem to buy it. But when I saw a certain reply, I froze.

Aaron had agreed to go out to a night club with her —to *'take the edge off'*. He was supposed to be bedridden. I frowned and checked the time. It was now just after seven. I jumped up off the sofa and slid the cellphone into my back pocket. I did not like where this was going.

"Søren!" I called, straightening my jacket. "We've got some stalking to do."

✠

Francesca Minetti was not going to die today.

Her name was not on the list, as far as I could tell from the glimpse I had stolen earlier. But I had never wished for someone to be on that list as much as I did until now. With my obsidian sword in hand, I stomped out of Søren's apartment and into the cool night. There was a slight breeze, and the air smelled of something stale; it felt like the perfect reaping atmosphere.

With the great distance between Saratoga Springs and Manhattan, Søren had to shift us to the location of the accident. From there, I marched off purposefully to the nightclub with the guidance of street signs.

Francesca was obliviously living it up at *Saucy Red* —and as the rumours would go, she had probably already passed out and carted off by some sweet stranger. But this time as I watched her stumble out of the foggy club in precariously high silver heels, it was different.

This time, the sweet stranger was not a stranger.

Francesca's make up was running and she had a lit cigarette between her lips. Her usually styled charcoal black hair hung limply in wet strands beside her face, and her clothes stuck to her skin, making her underwear visible underneath her thin clothing. It was as if she had been dunked in a tank of water.

I growled in what I decided I would call annoyance as she whimpered and feebly tried to cover herself up.

"Do you hate her or something?" Søren interrupted my train of thought. I was watching from a fire escape, hanging onto the railing.

I turned to glare at him.

"*Hate* is an understatement," I grumbled, and refocused my attention on Francesca. I then gasped as the person with her took off their jacket and wrapped it around Francesca's shoulders.

"Remind me why we're spying on her again?" Søren hissed.

"*Shut up*," I hissed back, "I never told you, and I don't need to."

He actually seemed a little offended, but I was too busy glaring at the unfolding scene before me to retaliate.

"I was invited to the funeral too!" Francesca gasped, nudging her *sweet stranger* —Aaron Carter. He was limping slightly and holding one arm against his front. So much for being fine, as he had texted.

"...I didn't even bother going, though —she was such a freaking spoilt brat anyway," Francesca continued. "...Sorry that you killed her though. That must suck balls," she clicked her tongue, exhaling smoke.

I frowned. Why *had* she been invited?

"…I didn't *mean* for her to throw herself over me like that," Aaron sighed, "But she was kind of doing me a favour. I couldn't bring myself to break up with her before. Three years started to feel too…real."

I flinched, and then felt Søren's gaze flicker to me. I shook my head, and every little sound around me amplified. I heard the piercing screech of police car sirens; the deep roll of far-off thunder; and the struggling gasps of my own rapid breathing. I covered my ears, wincing. It felt like I could not breathe; even with the lack of needing to.

How could Aaron *say* something like that?

"Why the hell did you date her in the first place?" Francesca's poisonous voice then tore through all of the noise.

She wobbled a little and stumbled into her companion.

"Status, I guess," Aaron answered, "She was the school's most hidden potential, and I knew that dating her would get me noticed. She wasn't all that bad though. We *did* share some good times —"

"Oh my God, you are so *pathetic*," Francesca cut him off with the witch-like shrieking she referred to as laughing. "You didn't actually *fall in love with her* —did you?"

"…No," he chuckled lightly. "I just…feel kind of sad that she's gone, you know. She was kind of gullible —but she didn't deserve to die."

Francesca did not say anything to that and took a long drag. I stared, and a single tear escaped my eye and slid down my cheek, instantly growing cold in the breeze of the night. It was obvious: Aaron was confessing that he had never loved me; no matter how many times he had said it before. No matter how many times I had *believed* it. And Francesca was eating it right out of his hand, storing it in her gossip vault for future use. She might have been a witch, but she was not that insensitive to a grieving person. She would not dare to spread the truth when my death was still a fresh wound.

"My Dad is going bankrupt," Francesca then sighed, flicking ash off the end of the cigarette. "We've only got so much income from my Mom's business, so they both suggested that I get my fucking act together and start working part time."

Aaron raised his eyebrows. "The high and mighty finally crumble? What's this world coming to?" he laughed, turning it into a joke. I ground my teeth together, feeling a low growl rise from my throat.

"It's not funny —I'm being serious," Francesca, for once, spoke what was on my mind. "I'm going to sell my car, maybe half my wardrobe, and then help out at home. It's like a bloody *Cinderella* story," she whined, wiping her face and smudging her ruined mascara even more.

"It's not that bad, Francesca," Aaron sighed, putting an arm around her. "I think your Mom just wanted you to take more responsibility for yourself. I don't think she was being serious about the working part. I mean, didn't you tell me that your Mom earns twice as much as my family's income?"

Francesca pouted. "…I guess."

The blood in my veins began to boil, and when the rage surfaced, I was completely prepared to drive my sword into a chest.

The only question was, whose?

Søren turned to me and his eyes widened with worry. "Savannah —"

I turned away and closed out all background noise.

All that I wanted was vengeance.

I jumped up and off of the edge of the railing, down to the tarred road.

"Savannah, wait!" Søren called after me. I ignored him and focused on what my heart was screaming for me to do. The ground cracked from the force of my landing, but I scrambled up and swung my sword, before breaking into a run.

"*Savannah!*" Søren yelled more urgently.

I screamed at the top of my lungs, holding my sword up above my head. Aaron turned around in surprise and started. I looked into his eyes, knowing that he could see me, and charged for him.

"Aaron *Finnick* Carter. You *backstabbing* sad-carcass excuse for a human being!" I screamed, swinging at him drunkenly. I missed him, even though he was frozen to the spot. "How could you!" I cried, burning tears like liquid fire pouring down my face. "How could you do this to me?"

"What...?" he rasped in confusion.

Francesca, who was unusually the more awake and sober of the two, screamed and grabbed Aaron's shoulder, trying to pull him away. I had forgotten that she would be able to see me too.

"Get away from us, you psycho!"

"Savannah don't you *dare* —!" Søren yelled.

He had jumped off after me and was now running to catch up. I continued to ignore him, burning with rage in every fibre of my being.

Instead of aiding in their escape, Francesca managed to make them stumble backwards and fall in front of me, laying out a perfect opportunity on a silver platter. I stepped up to them, my limbs shaking uncontrollably from either raw anger or devastation. *Kill him.*

He deserves it, I assured myself. *He deserves to die.*

All of those years —had they really meant nothing to him? How had he lived with himself, watching me fall deeper and deeper in love with him yet knowing that he would one day break my heart? It was as though he possessed no heart —like a mindless popularity obsessed machine.

That guilt which I had carried —he was nullifying it now. Suddenly, I realised something very important. I no longer had to carry that burden. I no longer had to worry about leaving him behind. He had done it to me already. There was relief there, somewhere. I did not have to *feel* anymore.

I had felt so much that I had blinded myself to reality. Maybe I could have seen this coming. Life was not like a fairytale, and I was not the princess to get swept off of her feet. I could feel real life slapping me in the face. Mostly, I felt stupid. I felt so stupid and blind for having loved him.

For believing him when he had said it to me.

Die die die. I now wanted him gone.

I wanted to wipe him off of the face of the Earth —to erase every trace of him, just as he had planned to do with my feelings.

"...Go to Hell," I told Aaron as I held up my sword, "and rest in pieces." I lunged forward and stabbed him repeatedly, before slicing his soul out of his body. He writhed in pain, and Francesca started screaming for help.

Aaron's soul shrieked as it was separated, and it oddly shone a bright red instead of wispy white. I started and was about to open my mouth to say the phrase to dismiss him, but the entity shrieked again before flashing into nothingness in a horrific burst of red dust.

I blinked, and a shiver ran down my spine. That was different. Perhaps the colour of the soul reflected the person's personality; their level of goodness and morality —which would not surprise me in the slightest. I shrugged, and glanced down at my sword, watching as it glowed with the symbol of *II*. It glowed crimson, like Aaron's soul. I frowned, but ultimately thought nothing of it, and turned on my heel to strut away triumphantly.

"Why would you *do* this?" Francesca cried.

I sighed and chose to ignore her, walking faster. But I then bumped into Søren. He glared at me, with his nostrils flaring as though he might start breathing fire. I marvelled for a moment at the expression, noting how uncharacteristic it was. And then I stared him down, refusing to believe there was possibly something I had done outrageously wrong.

"...You *disobedient* little shit," he started, his veins stark and visible underneath his semi translucent skin. "You just reaped a soul that wasn't supposed to die yet!"

CHAPTER II

THANATOS

THE GOD OF DEATH knew what the glowing meant.

The iridescent golden light pierced through the musty darkness of his office; the burgundy velvet curtains drawn and stifling the room into a claustrophobic atmosphere. They were never opened when he was present, due to his homey comfort in the dark. He twirled the necklace between his fingers and frowned, eyeing the pulsing dance of light in and around the intricate pieces of glass plated obsidian, moulded into the shape of an angel's wings. At a young age, Thanatos had understood the relationship between the mundane world and the divine world —and he understood that what he was seeing was the worst possible thing that could ever happen. He was however, slightly impressed by how well it had all been kept hidden until now. This beginning of uncovering the truth had been the result of a careless misplacement, most likely. It also annoyed him that this problem would most likely be his to solve. It annoyed him even more that the one he would have to answer to would probably be absolutely no help whatsoever.

But what annoyed Thanatos the most, was that he had been enjoying a lovely glass of wine when it happened —that damned pendant on the necklace that he had been told to keep an eye on, had started glowing.

Cursing, he stood up and grabbed his blazer, before straightening his tie as an afterthought. He stomped out of his office and down the hall, his footsteps echoing on the polished marble. "I'm going out, Nina," he vaguely addressed the violet haired secretary who was typing away at the front desk, "Postpone any meetings that I have scheduled any time within the next two hours —this may run...*overtime*," he warned, his jaw setting.

"Yes, sir," Nina answered, instantly rescheduling his planner.
She raised a dark brown eyebrow at him as he stalked past her, very obviously pissed off, but obviously thought better about prying into the urgent matter since she did not say anything more.

Thanatos opened the doors dramatically to find Charon's boat already docked at the bottom of the marble steps; gently bobbing up and down on the dark storm clouds that covered the endless black abyss.

Charon himself was sitting on the edge of the steps, poking a stick around in the swirl of storm clouds. He did not turn around immediately, but Death knew that he was aware of his presence. As soon as Thanatos had finished grooming himself, the old greying ferryman turned around and looked at his tensed figure with what seemed like genuine sympathy. The immortal had always appeared the same, as far as Thanatos could remember —resembling a stooping, skeletal withered version of the mundane world's St Nicholas. Charon's molten mercury eyes narrowed at the necklace in Death's hand.

"...That was sooner than planned," were the ferryman's first words of greeting. "What is your father going to say?"

Thanatos clicked his tongue and climbed into the boat; his arms folded like an infant denied dessert. "That is what I am going to find out," he sighed. "The Underworld; let us go," he ordered.

Charon sighed and shrugged, grabbed his oar and made a long stroke into the black clouds, carrying the boat forward. Purgatory, where Thanatos resided and where Obsidian Carrier Corp headquarters were, was as busy as it always was. Souls drifted around the kiosk desks; some with identification tags and others sipping a relaxing mocha latte. After a pit stop here, Charon would ferry all of the day's casualties down to the Underworld. There, they would be judged at the hand of the god of the dead himself —Hades. Many souls attempted to stay longer than the allotted twenty-four hours in Purgatory. Unfortunately for them, Death had

had a new security system added a millennium before to prevent that from happening. It had not occurred to him that the same barcode and tag system humans used for their stores actually had some sort of value here.

"Did you bring him a gift?" Charon then suddenly rasped.

The god frowned. "What?"

"Your father," the ferryman clarified, "—did you bring him a *gift*?"

Death glared at him. "No, of course not. Why would I do that?"

"Do you not want his help? Remember what happened the last time you came empty handed and asked for a raise. He does like to be sweet-talked and bribed, as I recall."

"Not that it is any of your business," Death hissed. "He does not need to be buttered up," he sighed, clutching the necklace tighter and holding it up, "…Not for this."

☩

The Underworld was cold and devastating —and the waters of the River Styx so still and alluringly misleading. Contrary to mortal belief, there was no fire in the greater part of Hades' domain. There was blizzard and frost; vast planes of cracked blackened desert and darkness. The guard dog Cerberus was chewing a large dry dinosaur bone at the gates, looking rather bored.

Thanatos did not blame him.

"Out of the way; Thanatos coming through," he announced to the souls who were already lined up. He strode past them and offered Cerberus a pat on the right shoulder, and then walked in as though he owned the place.

It frustrated him that Hades' palace was so far away from the gates; and it was not as though he could whip out a portal and be there in a flash. He might be a god, but he unfortunately did not possess the power of instantaneous travel. But the exercise would do him good, so he walked on with increased vigour. The mortal Hell part of the Underworld —The Fields of Punishment —was the part which he had to walk past first.

In his human form, the Demons could not tell him apart from any other soul and had thus tried to grab at him on several occasions. Death shivered at the memory of being fished out of a pit of fire; and remembered how it had cost a fortune to replace a beloved grey suit.

Before he knew it, he had arrived at the side fringes of Elysium and the Isles of the Blessed —and the marble steps of Hades' looming black castle. He shivered and relaxed his shoulders and went up to the steps. The entrance; as was anything Hades did, was extravagant and over the top.

Giant marble statues acted as pillars and load bearers in odd corners, each displaying the badge which Thanatos' Grim Reapers used. Death snarled at this and stuck his nose up in the air. Hades always tried to be more involved in his son's life, and his son tried harder to ignore it —there was just nothing that Hades could do anymore that would not agitate Thanatos. He had tried to stop Thanatos from moving to Purgatory all of those eons ago, but Death had put his foot down and thrown his scythe on the floor, telling his father that he was a grown man for the gods' sakes, and that it was time to move out of the house. Hades had never been good at letting things go.

Fortunately, that quality finally had its time to shine today.

As Thanatos roamed the dark halls, shadowed pale servants of shimmering frost as tall as the ceiling drifted along the walls. The *Pruinae* had always unnerved him, even when he was a young immortal.

The throne room doors were closed, which was a little unusual. Hades was almost as desperate for attention as the Olympian god Apollo was, and therefore his doors remained open. But as Death strode inside and closed the doors after him, he soon found out why the throne room had been restricted.

"How could you possibly live in such a *mess*?" the voice of Demeter shrieked. Thanatos sighed, rather disappointed to have been foiled in his plan for a grand entrance.

"It is not my *problem*," Hades drawled in his theatrical English accent, which his son had always found irritating. "I never clean up around here. Ask Persephone."

"She's in the mortal world!" Demeter threw her hands up, her emerald eyes momentarily flashing a glow in her anger. "And what sort of man are you, making your wife in charge of all the housework?"

Hades paused and widened his eyes at the question. He was not that sort of male, and he prided himself in that.

"...A misogynistic one —is *that* what you wanted to hear?" he snapped sarcastically, before his jasper eyes shifted and landed on Death. "Thanatos!" he exclaimed, jumping to his feet. He quickly walked up to him and straightened his tieless suit. "...You are a very...*welcome*, distraction, trust me," he lowered his voice and raised his dark brows suggestively.

Demeter scoffed and picked up her skirts, all set to storm off. "Typical!"
Both males then winced as the door slammed.

"Well, there the wheat goddess goes," Hades chuckled lightly. "...Or, the world's first demonic mother-in-law, as I like to call her," he added, grinning. Thanatos did not entertain the joke, and gave the god an expectant look. His father had always had an oddly bright sense of humour, and for the life of him, he could not understand it. Being the god of the dead, one would think that Hades would be incapable of such pleasantries.

His appearance did somehow make up for it —his eyes were shadowed; his jaw strong and stubbled; his skin a dark olive but dull in the actual colour; and his black suits severe. Some might describe him as handsome, but the whole *Lord of the Damned* mien did get in the way.

"...Right," the older god frowned, growing serious again, "What is the matter? You never come to visit just to say hello."

Thanatos held up the necklace and twirled it in his father's face. "This," he sighed. Hades gasped dramatically and his eyes widened proportionately.

"Why, that means..."

"Yes," Thanatos said as he nodded, "—she is dead."

Hades lowered his gaze, a look of deep sadness wrinkling his face. He ran his hands through his tangle of dark umber hair and let out a sound that was like a strangled growl, before he turned around and fell into a pace.

102

"It was going to happen eventually." Thanatos shrugged, unsure if it was his intention to aid the situation or not.

"She was eighteen," Hades looked up and glared at him. His eyes glowed and the jasper colour saturated, warning Death of his anger. "*Eighteen*, Thanatos. Her life had barely begun and now she is dead." Then he paused, the sadness seeming to dissipate, and he frowned thoughtfully. "…Now she can find out who I am."

"You know very well that she can do no such thing," Thanatos said firmly. "You know that what you did was wrong to begin with and being present in her afterlife is not on the agenda."

"Yes, but she is my *daughter*." Hades pointed a black painted fingernail at him. "I have legal obligations attached to her."

Thanatos frowned and clenched his fists. "…Not down here you don't," he growled. Hades gave him a pained expression, before turning away and pacing again. As though Death could not possibly understand.

"…Do you think that Phoebe read any of my letters?"
His son scoffed. "I would not be surprised if that mortal wanted nothing to do with you. You are currently a disgrace to the Olympian gods. I don't think that she wanted that on her conscience."

Hades' eyes pulsed a glow in warning, before he glared at the floor. It honestly no longer fazed Thanatos. He had stopped fearing his father's anger centuries prior. Death's own bronze eyes however, still struck fear in both mortal and immortal hearts alike.

Perhaps it was the miniature working clock in each of his irises.

"Where is her soul?" Hades then asked, raising an eyebrow. He seemed to struggle to say her name, before whispering, "…Savannah's?"

Death opened his mouth, and then closed it again, realising that he in fact, had no idea. He clicked his fingers and a plume of Phoenix fire ignited in the air. An image from the security footage room appeared, before he enlarged the image and zoomed in on the list for the day, subcategory being the name of her hometown.

And then he frowned. "…That's odd," he murmured.

"What's odd?"

"Her name is not on today's list for reaped souls in that area."

Thanatos clicked his fingers again and his office materialised in the fire. He zoomed in on the summaries that he was yet to file away and scanned those for matches. Nothing came up. "She did not die today," Death concluded, his eyes widening. "But the necklace…"

He looked down at it. It still glowed just as brightly as it had before.

Hades narrowed his eyes at his son and tilted his head to the side. "You don't think —" he started, pouting.

"—she Turned into a Grim Reaper?" Thanatos finished, unfazed. "Maybe. I will need to run a system check."

Hades blinked rapidly and gave Thanatos a confused look. "Do you understand the implications of her being a Reaper, Thanatos? Phoebe used to write to me telling me of strange unexplainable occurrences linked to Savannah. Do you not get it. Do you not see? Your sister —"

"*Half*," Death growled.

Hades scoffed. "…Whether you think of her of your own blood or not, she is still very much of mine," he huffed, pacing again. "And with that, comes power. Dangerous power." Then he paused. "…*Untamed* power."

Diluted power, Thanatos thought.

He then clicked his tongue. "Regardless, she is still half mortal —whether she is a Grim Reaper now or not. Human blood still runs through her veins and god blood does too. But I am sorry, father…" Death frowned as he let the title slip, "Your *Grand Plan* doesn't sound as if it will work now."

His eyes met Thanatos' and they clouded with a fearful look. "…Thanatos. I need you to do something. Something, very important."

"What?" he sighed.

"Watch over her —keep an eye on her. If she has indeed Turned, that is. If not, please fast track her application to the Underworld. She cannot do much damage as a soul."

Death frowned. "Do not underestimate the dead," he warned his father, "for it is because of them that we even exist."

104

"…Indeed," Hades breathed, relaxing his shoulders. "Well, if that is all, then farewell. I have a serious matter to deal with," he clipped.

Thanatos snorted. "You mean, arguing with Demeter?"

"Good*bye*, Thanatos," Hades sighed, turning away. "*And*," he then drawled as he turned around in a dramatic sweep, "I expect a result of that systems check in an hour." He pointed at him for emphasis.

"Yes, yes," Death grumbled bitterly, turning on his heel. "…Old fool," he added under his breath.

"I heard that, you ingrate," Hades called after him.

Thanatos groaned, bursting out of the throne room. He stormed his way back towards the entrance where Charon would be waiting for him.

The Demons eyed Death with interest; their liquid sulphur eyes studying his suit and upward turned nose.

But he shot them all a steely look and they cowered away as soon as they saw those glowing eyes; raging and intense like wildfire. Thanatos then kicked up stray pebbles and stuffed his hands into his pockets, stomping.

Why was that stupid bastard child always *his* problem to deal with? All she did was share a quarter of his lineage and that was it.

Savannah was nothing like him. He had heard tales of her, and her mother's lives when Hades still lived with them. Savannah's mother, Phoebe, had always seemed like a bit of a limp noodle, and if Thanatos had to be harsh, he wished that he could bring her death date forward.

He shook his head, dismissing the thought, and tried not to feel guilty for it. Instead he thought about his instructions to watch over Savannah. She was a sweet, innocent little girl who could not say *boo* to a ghost —or rather, she used to be. He was not sure what she was like now, but he supposed that due to his new mission, he would find out. But there was one thing that he counted on, no matter how much he might come to tolerate her. No one was anything like Death.

He guessed that was why he had wanted to move. Maybe it was not because he had had enough of his father. Maybe it was because he thought they were better off without him. Without the odd one out.

✠

Charon whistled as the god of death climbed onto the boat again.

"How did it go?" he inquired.

Thanatos scoffed and crossed one of his legs over the other. "…*Peachy.*"

Charon smiled. "Delightful."

"*Older* fool," Death hissed.

"Do not take your anger out on *me*," the ferryman said firmly. "Your father is the one who deserves your wrath."

Thanatos frowned and digested his words. He no longer tolerated Hades, but that did not mean that he hated him. It did not mean that he desired to kill him or bring him any harm. In fact, he was almost one hundred percent sure that if anyone ever made war against his father that they would meet the brunt of Death's wrath at full force. And that applied to Persephone as well. *Maybe* even Demeter…though he was not going to make any promises.

"…No," Thanatos finally responded, surprising Charon. "No, he doesn't." He realised that perhaps his anger had been misdirected all of this time. The person that he should really be angry with was Savannah —or better yet her mother — for ruining his life and family.

The conversation dwindled after that and they arrived in Purgatory. Thanatos bowed to him respectfully after climbing out and stepping onto the marble steps and Charon did the same, with a sad but understanding look etched on his sunken face. Thanatos took a deep breath and exhaled, before ascending to the front entrance. He turned to the right and headed for the Security division, set on finding some answers.

"Um…Thanatos, sir," Nina then spoke up and stopped him in his tracks. He turned to her and she looked unsure of what to say. "How are you?"

Death paused and glared at his secretary in a way of saying '*what?*'.

"Well," she began, dropping her gaze slightly, "It's just that…you went over time, including dilations. It must have been a really important meeting."

It was at that point that Thanatos figured out that the grudge that he had against Hades was in fact old news, and common knowledge. Death sighed and shook his head, a tired smile returning her amused chuckle. "Thank you for the concern, Nina. But I'm fine."

"Always a pleasure, sir," she quipped.

His smile however, faded as he neared the Security door. He considered putting it off until maybe next month, but then he realised that this was important to his father. Hades would not let it go.

"Philipe, please double check the data base for all Reapers who Turned in the last 72 hours," Thanatos ordered.

"Yes sir."

"Who are you looking for?" Argon asked, swivelling in his chair.

"Savannah Ivy Green. I have reason to believe she died recently, but not *today* recently," Thanatos hissed, digging his fingernails into his palms. "Trace her and find out where she is."

He then turned to leave when all of a sudden, the security alarm rang out, startling everyone. The security alarm was perhaps the most annoying —it rang like an ambulance siren and fire bell at full blast.

They all paused, wondering what was going on, before a stick-thin technical assistant ran into the room.

"There's been a breach!" he shouted above the alarm. "A soul has been reaped that wasn't yet supposed to be!"

Thanatos growled, pushed past him and headed for Technical Support himself. "Just what in the names of the gods is going on here!" he thundered, making everyone whimper.

Another employee took off her headset and looked at Death earnestly. "Well, we just received a notification from a kiosk that a soul identified as Aaron Finnick Carter was reaped a few minutes ago."

"And his due date is actually September the twenty-third, 2091," someone else finished.

Death growled and could tell that his eyes had begun to glow since everyone else's eyes widened in fear. "Bring his soul directly to me," he said in a low voice, "…And find the Reaper responsible for this!"

They all nodded and turned back to their computers, hurriedly typing away. Thanatos cursed under his breath and glared into space, wondering what he was going to do once he had found that Reaper.

They would pay with much more than just their pathetic life.

"Thanatos, sir!" Argon burst in, causing Death to jump. He stared at his employee expectantly. "…We found her. Indeed, she has Turned."

"*And?*" Death snapped. "Where is she?"

"Well —" he started.

"Sir, there's something else," a technical assistant interrupted, though Argon looked all too relieved. "You need to look at this."

Thanatos went over to her computer and she pressed play on a video.

He was utterly floored.

On screen, was a young woman with deep red hair flying behind her; her clothes new and her face flushed; an impressive sword in her hands and her eyes ablaze with rage. Not metaphorically —they were literally aflame. Streaks of orange flames danced outward, rooted in her glowing irises. Her obsidian sword shone gold —but something else shone underneath her tank top. And Thanatos' eyes widened as he recognised it.

"Oh, for the love of —" he started, but cut himself off. He had no time for wallowing in rage. "…*Security!*" he called instead.

CHAPTER 12

SØREN

"WAIT…WHAT?" SAVANNAH whispered —and in retrospect, she was understandably confused as she sheathed her sword.

The Trainer growled and raised his fist —causing her to flinch —before he lowered it hesitantly. He needed to contain himself; he did not want her to see what his rage truly resembled. After drawing a sharp breath, Søren felt the frustration dissipate minimally. "I can't *actually* believe you," he said in a low voice. "I tell you to stop, and you don't. You go and carry on screaming like a banshee and *kill* your boyfriend out of a jealous *fit* —"

"Stop," the redhead murmured. Søren paused, frowning at her. How dare she interrupt him. "He is *not* my boyfriend. Not anymore."

"You still murdered him, dumbass."

For a moment the two stared at each other as though time had frozen. The word '*murdered*' hung heavy overhead in the air, threatening to crush them as the next thought ensued.

That made her a *murderer*.

Savannah finally seemed to catch on, because her self-pity diminished, and worry flickered in her eyes.

That dark haired human girl's screaming and crying faded into the background as the air stilled and all motion stopped. Søren's jaw set, his eyes boring into his trainee's, which had returned to their normal golden state.

He had noticed that something strange had happened when she jumped from the railing. Pure anger and fire had manifested, flickering out from her eyes — engulfing every part of what made her human.

Something had snapped.

Søren grunted, reached up to hold the bridge of his nose. "You have *no* fucking idea of the implications of what you've just done," he hissed.

Savannah blinked, then frowned, and shook her head slightly. "I...*murdered* him?" she choked out.

"You reaped a soul before its time," Søren reiterated more delicately, realising that the news would take a while to settle.

Then something more important occurred to the Trainer. He quickly surveyed the surrounding area, searching for any shadowy figures.

"What are you looking for?" Savannah asked.

He raised a mocking eyebrow. "...Your demise," he said in an ironically sarcastic clip. She gave him a look, but he was not joking.

"We need to get out of here. Right now." He then grabbed her hand and pulled her into a run, before immediately shifting back to Manhattan. Shifting had been a strange concept to him for a while after he had Turned —he could almost feel every molecule in his body breaking up and speeding through the air, before rearranging on the other side. It had taken a while to accustom to, so he was reluctant to let Savannah try it out on her own as of yet. He let out a weary breath when they stumbled along the sidewalk in Manhattan.

After a brief pause to reorientate themselves, they began making their way back towards the apartment building.

The trainee Reaper struggled to keep up with Søren. "What is it? Did someone see us?" she panted. As expected, she would have close to zero energy after the fiery display. He begrudgingly let go of her.

"You would've triggered the alarm," he informed, exhaling forcefully, "Word will reach that you've broken the rules. And guess who's going to come for us?" the older Reaper hinted.

The trainee did not answer; only stared at him blankly.

"The *Boss*," Søren said, glancing left and right before crossing the street.

Savannah sighed and then abruptly stopped walking. Søren skidded to a halt and looked at her curiously.

"What the fuck are you stopping for?" demanded the Trainer.

She frowned at him and straightened her leather jacket. "Personally, I don't see why you're so afraid of a man who sits on his ass all day and does nothing," she huffed, sticking her nose up in the air.

Søren was startled by her passivity. "Wha...*what*?"

"Your words, not mine," she murmured, shrugging. "Anyway," she sighed as he stared at her, bewildered, "What's the worst that he can do?"

He tugged at his hair before turning away from her so that he could think. "You have essentially robbed someone of their life, and you have the audacity to ask what's the worst that can happen? He could *kill* you," Søren warned. "It's *the* worst thing you can do as a Reaper and you've just done it. Why does it not bother you?"

He turned around and asked her earnestly, looking for some kind of remorse in her eyes. But they remained clouded and aloof, not giving anything away. "...It just doesn't," she said quietly, wholly serious. "I'm not sure why, but it feels like we're getting worked up over nothing."

She shrugged and moved to sidestep him. Søren was baffled.

Why was she taking it so lightly? Maybe she had no concept of consequence. She had never met the Boss. She had no idea of what he was capable. The Trainer had heard stories; rumours were always circulating amongst the Reapers. Some were wilder than others. Some rung with chilling truth —eye witness accounts. He still shivered to this day of the tales of Death incarnate, swooping from the sky like a shadow in a flurry of ebony wings. The stench of rot felled anything within a ten mile radius, and nothing escaped that scythe, that damned weapon. Human, god and Reaper soul and flesh alike.

It was not that Søren particularly cared about Savannah, but he knew that it would continue to bother him if he let her go in such a way without having done a thing to prevent it.

The Reaper clenched his fists in frustration, before an idea struck him. What if…they could undo it? Or what if there was a way to disguise or hide the event before the news even reached the Boss?

Time was governed by Kronos —and to Søren's knowledge, he was in Tartarus, having been imprisoned by his children. Kronos had not reversed time, however; had not tampered with it. How to summon a Titan was not part of Søren's skillset, anyway. Instead, he considered the gods.

The Trainer did not think that there was a Greek god of time —even if there was, he doubted they would be willing to warp reality, especially for one stupid teenage girl and her flaring emotions. But he had heard that there was a god who was very versatile in his responsibilities. A god known for his cunning and rule bending. If anyone could aid the Reapers in amending Savannah's mistake, it was the Winged Messenger, Hermes.

Søren did not tell Savannah about planning to summon Hermes —not yet. He did not wish to get her hopes up just in case it was not a feasible option. So, they made their way back in silence and quiet contemplation.

Søren would like to think of himself as a man of few words; he communicated with the world through observation. He did not like that he had let his anger flare earlier —his apathetic mask had momentarily slipped, revealing something human about him. He would not deny that he was human —or had been, once — however, he preferred to maintain some sort of distance from others. He did not want her to get too close.

Savannah then suddenly gasped and grabbed at his sleeve, nudging him in the direction across the street. A squadron of Reapers in what resembled SWAT team uniform with glowing red badges were gathered by an alleyway; their built forms rigid and tense, and their tall obsidian scythes glistening in the hazy glow of the streetlights. They were Grim Reapers, yes —but not like Søren and Savannah. It was as though these males and females had been bred for war; forged and hammered like creations of Ares or Hephaestus.

112

"Shit," stated the Trainer, tugging on Savannah's arm to pull her behind him. She did not fight this time, and actually cooperated by ducking behind him. "Walk in step with me," he ordered, shuffling along the sidewalk. Her feet matched his rhythm and they slowly inched further and further out of Security's field of view. Then Søren accidentally tripped on a loose brick and flailed, teetering on the edge of the road before Savannah managed to push him back upright. "*God*, you're heavy," she hissed, digging her elbows into his back as she pushed him with her side. The older Trainer huffed and glanced at the officers —noticing that they were all looking in their direction.

He cursed under his breath but kept his expression neutral.

"Oh hello, guys," he said in a levelled, unwavering greeting. Savannah stayed still; her hair gathered up in what the Trainer assumed to be her hands and not flowing in the breeze. "Long-time no see."

Søren then sighed as he realised what he had just implied. He hoped that the officers would overlook the unfortunate choice of words. The burly Reapers all gave him a once-over and raised their eyebrows.

"…Oh. It's just Søren," one female said. The others then chuckled lowly, and the Trainer almost opened his mouth again to ask what was funny about it, when Savannah yanked him by his leather jacket, and pulled him in the direction in which they had been heading.

"Keep an eye out for any suspicious activity, won't you?" the tallest Reaper nodded at Søren, his skin riddled with mauling scars. "We're looking for a female Reaper who untimely reaped a human soul. She's about average height; slim; has long dark red hair; and glowing golden eyes."

"Really?" Søren drawled with disinterest, mocking shock and slowly walking away. "That's unbelievably disappointing." He emphasised the word by kicking Savannah's shin with his heel, making her squeak. "Punishable by the *worst* judgement."

"Indeed, Trainer," another female agreed. Søren almost smirked at the title, feeling like he could get used to receiving respect from the most fearsome Reapers in the organisation. "So, stay vigilant."

113

"Certainly," he replied, walking a little faster, before ducking behind the building to which Savannah had led them. He breathed out a sigh of relief as she re-emerged, tying her hair up in a crude ponytail with stray strands.

"Who were they?" she asked as they resumed their getaway. "And how come they knew you?" She narrowed her eyes suspiciously.

"Security," the Trainer frowned, "they know all high ranking Reapers." Then he paused, realising that he needed to remind her of the severity of the situation. "…Your worst nightmare."

✠

It was raining when Søren decided to go back outside to complete the list for the day. He had barely managed to sneak Savannah into the apartment building, but luckily for them, there had not been many Reapers in the lobby. Regardless, Savannah had borrowed his leather jacket and pulled it over her bowed head so that no one could see her strikingly recognisable hair.

It was important regardless of their plans to alter the past that he continued reaping the souls which his trainee would have to miss —so as to not rouse suspicion. "I'm leaving now," he informed Savannah.

She was sitting cross-legged on the sofa, staring at Phee-Phee, her lips moving slightly as though she were murmuring to herself. "Those souls aren't going reap themselves."

She then looked up at him hopefully. "Could I…possibly come too?" she whispered. "I'll be *super* careful —I could even wear a disguise and borrow something from your closet. The more practice the better, right?" she suggested, a small smile forming on her face.

Søren frowned and shook his head. Even though Savannah was obediently deathly quiet and self-isolated —not to mention that she was still in disgrace — she still wanted to help. So, he told her there was no way in Hell that he was going to let her out of the apartment. Not yet.

"And don't you *dare* do anything without my permission either," he warned,

114

without turning to face her. "I need to complete at least half of my quota for the night," he grumbled, slipping an arrow out of his quiver and slotting it into his crossbow. "Hopefully, they won't find you here."

"What if they do?"

He shrugged. "It was nice knowing you."

"*Søren*," she whined, appalled.

"I'm joking," he sighed, turning around momentarily. Søren looked at her; seeming so small and shameful that he almost felt bad for teasing her. Perhaps what he felt was more along the lines of pity, but he shook his head and promised something that was out of his control.

"...I won't let them find you."

He then nodded goodbye and locked the door behind him. If he was honest, Søren preferred leaving her alone and going out solo. She was perky and annoying, as far as he had established. But she was also strong —*head*-strong to be specific — smart, and vulnerably kind. Her heart reflected itself in her eyes, and Søren's own heart ached every time that he looked into them.

There was no way around it.

Savannah was almost the spitting image of Angelina. The Trainer frowned at the realisation. He had not thought about her in a while, even though he had named his computer system after her and referred to her by that name. Angelina, though he had nothing good to think of her anymore, was not someone he was ready to talk about —with anyone. He had not even talked about her with Melchior.

He was not sure if he ever would, even if he was somehow close to the blond Reaper again.

Søren's chest then constricted and twisted at the thought, as though his heart were attempting to break free and escape his ribcage.

There was such a raw pain about the two, that even thinking about him caused Søren to ache. He could pretend that they managed to get along around other people. It was easier to put on a show when it was not just the two of them and their exposed feelings.

It was difficult to hear that the person one had considered spending the rest of eternity with no longer saw one that way. It was wrenching, and it made Søren feel nauseatingly pathetic for caring so much.

It was an unimaginable relief to walk into an empty elevator. The Reaper would not have been able to face Melchior alone. He was too unstable; too raw with anger and too distracted with Savannah's predicament. If he and Melchior ever did find themselves alone, all Hell would break loose. There was just too much that they had left unsaid; words which they had no right to exchange now that they had broken up. However, it was not as though Søren would indulge any chance of the sort.

A lot of words had already been said and the damage had been done.

Everything would just be simpler if they kept hating each other.

It certainly made it hurt less.

CHAPTER 13

SØREN

"REST IN PEACE, Annabella Rays," Søren said, lowering his crossbow. The soul nodded, before dissipating into the air in a trail of white mist; leaving the body of a middle-aged woman in the pile of a wreckage.

He sighed and mentally checked off soul number three of the night, before reaching into his pocket for the list and looking through the remaining ten. He was grateful for a small workload —especially given the circumstances —and that the rain had finally ceased falling; however, it rendered him itchy and damp. He readjusted his jacket with lazy tugs, while he memorised the rest of the names.

He frowned at the last one.

It was a seven-year-old girl named Yolanda Russel; fated to die from concentrated exhaust fumes inhalation. It would not take a moron to figure out exactly what that meant. It was like Louise Hansen —and Søren's chest lurched at the realisation.

Apathy be damned; it was just a *child.*

"So many car accidents this week, huh?" a voice then said from behind him.

Søren turned to find a short, feminine figure half obscured by the shadow beside a streetlight. A silver and black semi-automatic pistol twirled around her pale forefinger; the silver embellished swirls glinting and matching the luminous glow of white teeth in a maniacal grin. Light blonde hair then flew in her face; and she then emerged, spluttering as she swatted her hair out of her mouth. Søren sighed, a smile of his own forming at the sight of a familiar face.

"...Abby, I thought that I told you that I'm not fazed by your disappearing-and-reappearing act."

Abigail was a Grim Reaper and friend of the Trainer who lived in an apartment block across the city; working towards the Trainer title in his footsteps. Even though Søren had given her the benefit of the doubt, he had seriously stubborn reservations about her being Trainer material.

He had not seen her in two and a half years, but when one has eternity, it could feel like two months. Her aventurine-eyed gaze flickered upward at his taunt. "Søren," she smirked, "—long-time no see. And, I was going for a *cinematic* entrance," she explained sheepishly. Then she straightened up and eyed the male up and down. "...You're not usually out this late. Are you training again?" She tilted her head to the side and let the gun continue to gently swing on her finger.

"Yeah..." Søren answered a little vaguely, scratching the back of his head. "They're currently grounded for disobedience."

Abigail snorted. "Maybe you're taking this Trainer business too seriously," she suggested, smirking, "The trainee is meant to learn as they go —not get babied by you. You're not a Dad."

He flinched as though she had slapped him. Once upon a time, he had wanted to be. Once upon a time, that was all he had thought that he was good for. Søren paused, digesting Abigail's words. They had no consequence in Savannah's case but maybe she had a point in other circumstances.

"...Their offence is worse than you think," he put delicately. He did not need to give the situation away, and he most certainly did not trust someone like Abigail to keep a secret. He had concluded that the hard way.

"How bad can it really be?" she scoffed, folding her arms. The leather of her jacket stretched too unnaturally, indicating her jacket was too small.

"...Hey, what exactly are *you* doing here, anyway?" the Trainer steered the conversation away from Savannah and narrowed his eyes at Abigail. "Did your list really bring you this far?"

"Oh, you know me," she breathed, flicking her hair back over her shoulder dramatically, "Being in the same place for too long bores me. I need to broaden my horizons. I like to reap around."

She shrugged, as if to say *what are you going to do?*

Søren rolled his eyes and held his crossbow more securely.

"*This* is why you're never going to be a Trainer, Abby."

Her eyes narrowed as she stuck out her tongue, offended —before darting after him as he turned to walk away. "Hey wait! Come on Søren, I wasn't serious," she whined, falling in step with him. "Why don't you tell me about your current student. What's he like?"

"It's a girl," Søren corrected her.

Abigail seemed surprised. "I thought a Trainer with your experience would be able to choose who he trained."

"Then why did you assume it was a he?"

The Trainer raised an eyebrow. Abigail shrugged innocently and mumbled something under her breath, suddenly avoiding his gaze. "…Pardon me?" he asked, cupping a hand around his ear.

"Because that's your *sexual inclination*," she said a little louder, though still whispering. "I didn't want to say anything before, since you vaguely mentioned that Angelina girl; but I always thought so."

Søren did not react to that besides tensing up at Angelina's name. The assumption that he was gay was something which he heard often, and it no longer fazed him or rendered him speechless. His sexuality was a natural part of him, so he stopped trying to hide it —not that he had been very successful in that either. Melchior on the other hand, had not managed to stick so much as a *fingernail* out of the closet, publicly.

He smiled slightly and stared at Abigail, expecting her to say more. And when she did not, a chuckle escaped his lips.

"For your information," Søren started, "I'm *pan*sexual. But, it's beside the point because I don't mix relationships with work. As a *responsible* Trainer," he emphasised the word and the blonde Reaper groaned lowly, "I cannot allow myself to interact in any way that isn't platonically interact with any of them.

119

Also, no, we don't get to pick our trainees," he added, much to her disappointment.

"Well, that blows," she pouted, clicking the safety on her gun on and off out of habit. "I was hoping to train a super hunky newbie."

Søren shook his head, amused by the fact that she had not changed in the recent past years. She had always been teasing and flirtatious; the kind of woman who brought men to their knees, or sent them running for the hills. Everything was in excess with her: aspirations, expectations and her hourglass curves. Not that she had dated anyone thus far —the gun and how she handled it probably warded off any potential boyfriends.

"So, you never *like* like any of your trainees?" Abigail asked, catching the Trainer off guard. He paused, suddenly feeling squeamish.

"No. It's too weird. I'm essentially their *teacher*. That's weird in itself. I'd be *years* older than them," he cringed.

She snorted and kicked at the sidewalk, scuffing her shiny black boots. "You know as a Grim Reaper that age is a mortal construct," she chuckled. "So that's an invalid excuse."

Søren thought of another one. "I don't want to get attached more than I already do. As a trainee, they'll eventually leave and venture out elsewhere, so I ask myself what's the point of getting used to the idea of them staying." His voice grew softer towards the end, which was unplanned but seemed to do the trick of drawing empathy out of Abigail.

"…Okay. I get it," she sighed, rolling her eyes.
"This will be something that you will deal with too," he reminded her. "It's not a rule that's set in stone, but I would suggest you refrain from seducing your trainees. It should go without saying."

"All right," she grumbled. She was stropping, but Søren knew that she would not put up a fight. "So…what *is* your current trainee like?" she then eventually asked, thankfully changing the subject. "…I mean, besides an apparent troublemaker."

"Oh, you don't know the half of it," he grumbled, suddenly finding the energy

120

to continue speaking. "She is probably one of the most annoying people I have ever encountered. Did you know, she wanted to keep a Phoenix in the apartment as a pet?"

Abigail gawked at him, her jaw dropping open. "You're kidding," she snorted. "Who would want that as a pet? I'd rather have a snake."

"She died on the 13th," Søren sighed. "Barely just Turned."

"Well then, no wonder she thinks Phoenixes are pet material. She's never had any experience with one," Abigail sang, taking hold of and then spinning around a tree. "Hang on," she paused, her eyes narrowing, "…What was a Phoenix doing at your place anyway?"

He should have seen that question coming. he wondered if it was really something that he could tell her —without her getting the wrong idea. "Well…" he started, "She, uh…her reaping tool," he blurted out, before deciding to roll with it. "It's an anomaly."

Abigail raised an eyebrow. "How so?"

"Her weapon's OWES and ORES are so abnormally high —for a trainee and an average Grim Reaper, anyway —that OCC headquarters sent us a letter of concern about the probability of the match, with the attached requirement that she reap a soul before sunset," Søren explained. "And a Phoenix was the thing to deliver it."

Abigail frowned thoughtfully before responding. "…High enough to get the OCC's attention?" She nodded slowly, looking impressed. "*How* high?"

"Instant; and *ninety-eight point three*, high," he murmured.

Abigail inhaled sharply. "Holy gods —how is that even *possible*? She's barely a Reaper and she's already got power comparable to that of the Boss?"

Søren could tell that they then had the same thought, because she looked at him suspiciously as he met her gaze, their expressions mirrored. "…Do you think that he'll want to hear about this?" she whispered.

"I'm pretty sure that he already knows," Søren frowned.

"What age did she die at? Don't tell me she's barely a teen. I'm not sure if I'd be comfortable working for a boss who hires young kids to kill people.

Well…reap souls."

She shuddered, and rightly so, because he completely agreed.

"You're in luck," Søren huffed, stepping over a crack in the pavement. "She's eighteen. She died the night of her birthday, in fact."

"Aw, shame," Abigail pouted, and he could not tell if she was being genuine or not. "What a birthday present, though; bound to this job for eternity." She did a dramatic swoon, and he nudged her to get back on topic.

"She's unlike anyone I've trained before," the Trainer then admitted. "She's so emotionally indecisive and hyperactive —somewhat the opposite of me. She's stubborn and compulsive and won't take no for an answer. It's like looking after a *child*," he clipped in irritation.

Abigail giggled and her light green eyes shimmered in amusement. "Well, she *is* eighteen. She's not exactly fully mature."

"*I* was sixteen when I died and I was nothing like her," Søren said firmly.

"No one was anything like you, Søren," Abigail put a hand on his arm comfortingly. "You died when the world was more of a horror show."

He frowned and glared at the ground, muttering incoherently under his breath. He breathed out and it misted in the air. Søren had seen the world descend into total doom since being Turned, and he knew history better than the books in libraries and museums. The broader internet still escaped him, so he had not touched any of that. It seemed as though most wars were about land or people, and whose it rightly was, and the victor hardly ever flourished thereafter. The weak, small and insignificant always rose up to the challenge, and were usually underestimated.

It was all nonsense to him —even though a certain someone had told him that in order to better understand the hostility of the outside world, they had to look on the inside world: what it was that drove mortals, pushed them and motivated them to keep doing what they were doing.

"…This is my turn," Abigail then spoke up as the two Reapers approached a set of traffic lights. She stood in front of Søren and gave him a sideways smile, before a salute. "We should talk more often," she said in a matter-of-fact tone, lightly punching his arm.

"Yeah," he agreed, nodding, before softly punching her in return. "Reap around more often. Broaden your horizons."

"Get bored?" she added, chuckling softly.

The Trainer shook his head and sighed, mildly saddened by the fact that it was unlikely she would ever take anything seriously.

"All *right*, Abby," he raised his voice. "I have ten more souls to reap, so let's call it a day on this conversation."

She paused, and a mischievous grin spread across her face. "Shouldn't you rather say…" she began.

"Don't you say it —" Søren hissed, moving to put a hand over her mouth. But she was a little faster than him.

"—*Call it a night*!" she shrieked triumphantly, dodging his advances easily. His entire body recoiled in cringe-worthy distaste.

Søren sighed and massaged his temples as she laughed at her own joke, before he gave her a glare as warning. She quietened down like a disgraced toddler and pocketed her gun.

"Let's just say, that the conversation, ends *here*."
"Yes, your Trainer-ship sir," she quipped, and before he could retaliate, she was already running. "*Bye*, Søren!" she called over her shoulder.

Søren shouted it in return and stood there until she disappeared around the corner. He then turned down the left road towards the house of his next soul, who thankfully, was going to die from the natural cause of old age.

✠

Søren trudged all the way back to the apartment; his shoulder stiff and inflexible as though he had been out of practice; ready to lay down on the sofa and stare at the ceiling, thinking about nothing.

Getting through the souls had taken him all night and drained all of his energy. It was enough to make Søren feel human again.

123

He wondered if Savannah had really stayed put and heeded to his warnings and instructions. It would not look all too good for him if she was found wandering around alone as though he had abandoned her. Regret then washed over the Reaper like a tidal wave, and he suddenly stumbled as he came to a halt in front of a streetlight pole. He probably would have hit it, seeing as he had not been paying attention. He shook his head and walked around it, trying to figure out what was wrong.

If he was honest, he had been a little out of it since April Dawn; soul number six. Her tragic and untimely suicide had rendered him numb and more unfeeling than usual —simply to compensate for the feeling of empathy welling up inside. It hurt to know that he could not have done anything.

Feeling things when reaping was the worst thing that could happen, in Søren's opinion. Feel too much pity, and things take longer than necessary. Feel too much empathy, and the soul could end up being left to live —which was almost as monumentally catastrophic as taking a life ahead of its time.

Søren had only done it once; long ago when he had been younger and naïve.

And when he came for soul number ten, all of those memories came back to haunt him.

Reaping Yolanda Russel was even worse than he had prepared himself for — the look in her big brown eyes when she looked at him was vaguely unnerving and it made him hesitate. Her coarse toffee curls bobbed up and down as she tried to get out by banging her little fists against the windows. The Reaper cursed her father —soul number nine, to whom he had not said '*rest in peace*' politely in the slightest —and he had been in two minds about getting her out of the car. Her at least; *she* deserved to live.

But he was in no position to mess with death and become a wanted Reaper. It would be far easier to find him than to track down Savannah.

So, he shot an arrow, through the closed window.

The girl was crying; relentless, desperate tears streaming down her face as she was not only struggling to breathe but she was now burning on the inside. That was his doing —Søren knew that he was causing that agony. It was something with which all Grim Reapers had to come to terms; they caused souls unimaginable and unavoidable pain as they passed on.

Søren had to turn away.

He could not bear to watch Yolanda's soul escape, so he waited for the screaming to turn to silence. It did not take very long. When that quiet ingulfed the street, he slowly turned around to find the soul of a little seven-year-old girl standing by the car. Her body was still inside, limp and lifeless. Søren looked at her soul, and it looked up at him. As he crouched down to be eye level with her, her gaze followed. He never did this —talking to the souls. But he felt compelled to make an exception with this one.

"...They have jellybeans in Purgatory," the Trainer whispered. "And milkshakes. Pizza, and cheeseburgers too. And candy floss that you can eat forever and never get a tummy ache."

A soft giggle escaped the girl's lips, and it echoed as though she were not really there. Søren knew that she was not —but it was even more heart wrenching to see her in this form; dead and only seven. But she did not have to suffer any more —at least there was that truth.

"...Rest in everlasting peace, Yolanda Russel," he smiled slightly as the words caught in his throat.

She took a step towards him and lifted her ghostly hand up to touch the side of his face. He could not feel it, but it was all right.

Then she melted away, into the early morning air; a sad smile on her full lips and the echo of a laugh disappearing with her.

CHAPTER 14

SØREN

HE HOPED THAT Hermes would not mind a takeaway BLT sub as an offering. He also hoped that the god would not mind the fact that the Reapers were in the Ancient Greece exhibit storage room of the Natural History Museum, attempting to light a fire at one of the fake altars —which was thankfully, made of heat resistant concrete.

Savannah had been baffled at Søren's proposition. She saw no reason for a god to respond to their summoning —especially the Winged Messenger. She thought that Hermes would not care; that he had no time for the petty requests of Grim Reapers. They were barely better than mortals.

However, Søren argued that if any of the gods were to aid them, it would be the ever lawful neutral god of the cunning.

"Have you ever actually done this before?" the trainee whispered, keeping an unnecessary watchful eye on the door.

Although perhaps she was being cautious about the Reapers Organisation Security and not the museum's.

"Can't say that I have," Søren sighed.

"How do you know what you're doing is right?"

The Trainer clicked his tongue. "I looked it up on the internet."

"Right —because that's always reliable."

She was hitting his last nerve. "It's all we have to go on here," Søren snapped,

126

shooting her a glare. "Maybe if you had given me early notice of your intended homicide, I could have better prepared."

She shut up at that, sulking at the wall. The Trainer wondered if she felt anything at all for what she had done; for the life which she had stolen.

The fire then finally lit on the seventh try, illuminating the dark confined space and allowing Søren to free up his hands as he tossed the sandwich into the open flames. Then he began to pray.

He had never prayed to a Greek god before, but it was likely similar to how he had been taught as a young boy: hands together; be respectful; and follow the sequence of worship, then the request and then gratitude. The offering was worship in itself, so he omitted that step.

'*Hermes, lord of travellers, please accept this offering. We are Grim Reapers Søren and Savannah, and we are seeking your presence in order to request your assistance regarding a matter of utmost importance. We desperately need to change an event in the past, but knowing that the gods do not interfere with time, we ask that you point us in the right direction of someone who might be able to help us do it. Thank you in advance for your time. P.S., if we could keep this between ourselves, that would be greatly appreciated. Um…Amen.*'

Søren was not trying to tell him what to do or anything —it was just a friendly suggestion. He also had a shrewd suspicion that Hermes was not one to take kindly to constructive advice.

It was quiet and still for a few moments; the only sound being the crackling fire on wood, which only amplified the Trainer's frustration and impatience. Security could be close behind and they would not know how to deal with them. The two Reapers needed a response and they needed it *now*.

"Isn't something supposed to happen now?" Savannah then hissed into the silence, as anxious as Søren was.

They looked at the altar. The BLT sub was black ashes.

"We have to give him a little bit more time," Søren clipped. "He's a busy guy." He was doing a pretty bad job of convincing himself of that.

There was a beat of silence, before a male voice suddenly quipped from behind them, "I most certainly am."

Søren and Savannah whipped around and comically gasped as a lanky teenager in a blue hooded jersey and early 2000's denim jeans hovered in the doorway —the little wings on his white high top sneakers flapping incessantly before he touched down on the floor. His body radiated a warm golden glow —a godly halo. It then dissipated after a few seconds, rendering him fairly ordinary and mortal if one could look past the silver Caduceus strapped to his back. His arms were folded, his expression amused. "Though I have to be honest; answering a Grim Reaper's call seemed far more interesting than meddling in yet another delivery of a letter to Ares from Aphrodite," he chuckled.

"...*Hermes*?" Savannah blurted in disbelief. The god nodded, evidently used to her reaction. He could not really blame her —he barely passed for Søren's physical age. Understandably, he did not look exactly like his statues and paintings in the exhibit. His mien had altered with time and adjusted to his preference now that he was in the twenty-first century. His short curly hair was still the colour of golden wheat; his skin was evenly tanned; and his eyes were polished star white sapphires.

"You actually responded," the redheaded Reaper spluttered once she accepted that this...*boy*, was in fact, Hermes.

"I heard that entrances are supposed to be more dramatic than that," Søren remarked, narrowing his eyes at the god.

"Well, you see, I just happened to be in the neighbourhood, so..." he drawled sarcastically. "Look kids, I don't know if you've noticed, but stealth is kind of my thing," he smirked. "I can't afford to be bursting forth in a shimmering shower of light to the sound of trumpets every time that someone offers me their leftovers."

"That sandwich was fresh from the store," Savannah snapped in defence.

"Yes, I suppose it was a satisfying change in snack," Hermes huffed.

Søren coughed, feeling the need to remind the two of them why they were even interacting in the first place. "Hermes, we really need your advice. Do you know anyone who would be willing to warp time?"

"What for?"

128

"*Someone* made an irreversible mistake," the Trainer hinted, shooting his trainee a glare. "And she could get reaped for it." Savannah glanced elsewhere again — more stubborn and betrayed than guilty.

"Reaped? That's extreme. Mistakes can be quite catastrophic in your line of work, I see," mused the god. Søren was thankful for his indulgence, something unlike no one had ever given him before in his life.

"Exactly. Which is why we are trying to change the perception of the future; make it seem like the incident never happened."

"I am glad to hear at least that you understand that you cannot actually eradicate the past," Hermes acknowledged. "And you were wise to seek my aid. I take it you know of my adventurous history."

"The god of practical jokes," Savannah scoffed.

Søren elbowed her sharply. "Forgive her," he said through gritted teeth, "this is our first time summoning a deity."

"Well, she is not entirely wrong," Hermes admitted. "I do enjoy a good prank every now and then." The petty Reaper grinned triumphantly at her Trainer. "...But," the Winged Messenger then spoke again, this time his eyes glinting with a sinister shine, "what's in it for me?"

The two Reapers paused. They had not thought of that. They dithered helplessly. Would the god really turn them down now, even though they had come halfway? Their panic must have shown on their faces, because Hermes then slowly nodded in understanding.

"In exchange for information, you must give *me* information," Hermes said, his voice low and eerie. "If the knowledge you seek is to save an existence, then you have to provide me with something that can destroy one. So, tell me why you desperately need to alter this timeline."

The teenage god leaned against steel scaffolding, deadly serious. The Trainer glanced at Savannah. She met his gaze, her eyes shimmering with defeat. She knew as well as he did that they did not really have a choice. Against better judgement and their will, they had to trust Hermes. Even Søren's additional plea to keep the matter private might mean nothing to him.

"I swear upon the River Styx," then said Winged Messenger; his bright, terrifying eyes unblinking. "I will not tell a soul. Not a mortal, not a monster, and not an immortal. Not now, anyway. Perhaps we will see if the information proves useful at another time."

"You can't —" Savannah started, darting forward.

"—I can," Hermes cut her off, "and I will. You summoned me. I don't know you two. I need some sort of collateral."

She glared at him —she really stared the herald of the gods down, her stance irreverent and unapologetic. And he met her challenge, wordlessly and intangibly wrestling with her very soul. Both immortals' irises flickered to life, burning wildly. For a second, it almost seemed as though Savannah might be a match for the god. But Søren's trainee then growled, buckling beneath the pressure and angrily turning away and hissing something impolite under her breath. Hermes retorted with the quietness of a spy; his form almost melted into the shadows, but those luminous eyes anchored him.

"I killed someone," Savannah then huffed, refusing to damper her pride a little by directly addressing the deity. "I reaped a soul ahead of its time, because I let my emotions get the better of me."

Søren drew a breath, impressed and nervous all at once.

Hermes sucked on his teeth. "That *is* quite destructive. Interesting." His expression then brightened, and he abruptly reverted to the laid back, mischievous god of the cunning he had been when he arrived.

"Well, we've held up our end of the bargain," Søren promptly reminded him. "Now what lead do you have for us?"

"Right," he coughed, stretching out his hands. "I actually know a guy."

Silver glowing misted sheets of paper materialised from thin air between his hands, like those from a binder. He then began flicking rapidly through the seemingly endless pages, the spine and covers either invisible or non-existent. After about a minute the god paused, his crystalline eyes gleaming in the light of the dying fire. "...Finnigan Michael Magik," he announced. "I know he sounds like a children's party magician-for-hire but I think you'll find that this guy is surprisingly close to the real deal."

"How so?" asked Savannah, finally glancing over.

"Is he an immortal?" Søren followed up.

"Well…" said Hermes. "He wasn't always. He is only immortal now because of an accident —something with which you might be familiar. And at least, he was born and raised human."

"What changed?" Søren frowned.

"About twenty years ago he was…permanently employed," the god put carefully. "I think you'll understand what I mean when you meet him. But be warned: his boss does not take kindly to those who side with the gods, mind you. She may question your motives."

"I wouldn't say that we particularly side with the gods," Savannah sneered. "We are bound to one against our will."

"Well then, let us simply hope that she understands that," Hermes quipped, shrugging.

"Where can we find this Mr Magik, anyway?" Søren asked, frowning.

"Here is his business card," Hermes said, offering him a small rectangle of shimmering purple card. "Feel free to knock on his front door. He's usually home these days. And he can never resist using a spell."

And with that, the god of the cunning erupted into a puff of storm cloud; the image of his crafty grin lingering. The musty darkness of the storage room was now somehow menacing. Savannah shuddered.

"I feel like we just bought drugs off of a dealer."

"I can understand why," Søren snorted. "But he did potentially give us what we wanted. Which means, I was right. You owe me."

"I told him the reason for my potential death sentence. I'd say that we're even," she said as a matter of fact. "Anyway, we should get going. We don't know how unpredictable Mr Magik might be."

✠

Finding the address was surprisingly easy. Finnigan Michael Magik lived on an obscure street in a back alley behind an old rundown restaurant. Ordinarily, it would be difficult to tell that someone was living in the neglected apartment, but there were flashes of light and bursts of colourful mist which could have been mistaken for a wild rave. If one looked closely, one would notice the things hanging in the windows —hacked legs of small animals, shed reptile skins, an assortment of exotic plants and drying fruit.

Savannah offered Søren a look, not knowing what to expect. "Ten bucks says he's just a madman," she bet.

Søren decided to give Hermes the benefit of the doubt. "You're on."

With the Trainer leading the way, they then cautiously approached the kiwi green front door, before he hesitantly rapped upon it.

At first, the two thought that the owner might not have heard. But the light show suddenly fizzled out, and a loud crash of metal echoed through the detached apartment. Then there was a pause, supressed quickened breathing, and a strange overhanging uncertainty.

"Hello?" the redhead called.

"There's…no one home," a raspy voice responded from behind the door. "The resident is unable to pay his rent at the moment, as he…he's in Hawaii. He left this morning. And if this is Terry, stay away from my fruit."

Søren and his trainee shared a look of pure bewilderment.

"Nice try, Mr Magik," Savannah quipped. "Open up."

"More like *pathetic attempt*. Your first mistake was responding to the knocking," Søren informed the voice.

They were answered with grumbling, and a frustrated kick on the door. "Fine. You got me…Are you the police?" Finnigan asked.

"No."

"Are you positive?"

"The police are not immortal, Mr Magik," Søren smirked.

That seemed to convince him. Several chains were then unhinged, and locks were opened. The door opened just a fraction, to reveal part of a stubbled square jaw and a tired russet eye. He had not gotten much sleep in *weeks*. The eye widened as its gaze travelled the length of Søren and Savannah.

"Grim Reapers?" he breathed.

Savannah raised her brows, impressed. "Hermes didn't lie."

"You owe me again," Søren quipped.

"Nope," she smiled. "He hasn't done anything yet."

"Wait, Hermes sent you?" Mr Magik then blurted, opening the door a little further. The extent of his condition was even more evident: he did not look all that old, but his hair was peppered and he had deep rings of purple around his eyes; not well hidden underneath comically large round glasses. And his skin...it appeared normal from some angles, but at others, it was a burning and angry red. The kind of stark crimson that Demons were. Bits of his form almost seemed to mist and disappear, as if he was not entirely there.

Like a Shadow Man.

"Why would Hermes recommend me to a couple of Reapers?" he asked.

"This *isn't* a regular occurrence for you?" Søren frowned.

"No," he admitted. "I am used to divine beings inquiring about my services, but it has been quite some time. I was told not to —" he began and then did not finish, his gaze falling downwards in guilt.

"This is sort of an emergency," the Trainer urged.

Finnigan's eyes narrowed as he looked back up, studying him. "An emergency? That's why you needed Hermes to back you up. What for?"

"The thing is, we need your help. We need you to warp time."

He hesitated for a moment, before inviting them inside.

CHAPTER 15

SØREN

HE HAD NEVER quite seen anything like it before. The interior of the once modern style apartment was arguably that of a vintage pagan cottage located in the middle of an enchanted forest. A variety of curing ingredients hung from the wooden beams lodged just below the ceiling, and the scent of death and rosemary was thick in the air.

"I'm a wizard," Finnigan offered in explanation as the Reapers took it all in. "As I'm sure Hermes must have mentioned."

"I didn't realise that those actually existed," Savannah bluntly muttered. "Is it like modern aesthetic witchcraft —with cards, charms and chants and that? Not actual physical magic?"

"I am not a wizard by birth," chuckled the eccentric host as he adjusted his glasses. "I have studied magic for a number of years. I believe that we who do not inherit abilities like those of the gods can draw it from within us. From our very souls."

"Then why doesn't everyone have magic now?" the redhead scoffed.

"Savannah," Søren clipped.

"No, no, I encourage questions," Mr Magik sighed. "And that is a very valid one, young lady. I can answer it two ways: first, a majority of humans have evolved to declare such archaic practices to be obsolete in our modern society. They have no interest in the supernatural or even spiritual. Second, I learned under the guidance of my mentor that magic is a thing you must yearn for more than anything. Nothing will take root if you do not make it the centre of your existence."

Søren gave his trainee a wary glance. Would that explain the man's skin? What had he given of himself in exchange for power?

"...I take it that you did just that," Søren breathed, slowly eyeing what he assumed to be a workshop.

Finnigan nodded. "I was mostly toying with charms and chants as a teenager —as you mentioned, girl," he addressed the trainee. "But one day, I meant to summon the goddess Iris. Instead, a handmaid to the Olympians came through, alerting me that Iris was otherwise engaged. She was curious, though, about why I had done it. I spoke to this maiden for quite some time afterwards, and she kept visiting me of her own accord. She is the one who gave me a deeper understanding —gave me a drive."

"Is this the boss that Hermes mentioned?" Savannah asked nervously. The wizard laughed just as uneasily, his expression hiding some sort of lingering pain. "I do not think that '*boss*' is the appropriate title. She was a guide; a friend. She taught me and even gave me, a mere mortal, a scintilla of her magical power. And then she was a lover, but I do prefer to forget that," he muttered more to himself, frowning in thought as he shuffled to the kitchenette. "One should never mix business with pleasure."

Søren was tempted to agree with that notion. After falling for his father's business partner's daughter and facing the consequence of death; and having fallen for a fellow Grim Reaper; he was now sure that he had learned his lesson. Nothing good came from love —not for him.

"If you don't mind me asking," Søren then spoke up to dispel his lingering thoughts, "What exactly *are* you?"

The wizard paused, his stance shifting to that of a person with something to hide. "...I am immortal, in a sense," he murmured. "It...happened about five years ago. I was not meant to die. My soul was cleaved, but because of the Olympian magic within it, I rejected death. I am a dead man walking."

"That's why you're red and wispy sometimes," Savannah realised.

"You two can see that as well?" Mr Magik grimaced. "Is it because you are Grim Reapers?"

"Likely," Søren huffed. Then his eyes narrowed as he realised something. "…You are not supposed to be alive," he said. "Have you been hiding from Death and his minions all of this time?"

"No," Mr Magik answered, almost as confused as the Reapers. "No one seems to know except for Hermes and…her."

"Hermes wouldn't reveal something like this unless he wanted something from our Boss," Søren mused. "That's why he's been quiet."

Savannah drew a sudden breath. "That's why he told us to come here," she hissed. "You were reaped too early."

Finnigan's eyes widened, and the mistiness of him amplified in a short burst, leaking into the air. The Reaper in training was correct.

"Is it just magic that is keeping you tethered?" Søren inquired.

"Yes," the wizard admitted. "You would be the only other beings besides the gods who can see this —the part of me that is still spirit. To mortals, I look human, as I was before. But I have already grown tired of…forever. I am searching for a permanent solution, but so far I've gotten nowhere."

Dying again was clearly not an option.

His expression then darkened, as though he were attempting to be threatening. The wispy ends of him flared out like the tails of snakes; like living shadows. "You…you two are not going to report this, are you?" he asked them in a low, careful voice. "Because I can assure you, I am very prepared to keep this a secret even if it means burning *your* souls."

The Reapers tensed. Savannah's hand curled around the handle of her sword, but she did not dare to draw the blade. Søren shook his head at her subtly, trying to communicate his thoughts.

Clearly, mortals could not contain magic well.

"We swear upon the River Styx," Søren said to the wizard calmly, raising his free hand slightly as reassurance. "We will not report you. We still require your aid, Mr Magik."

"Why should I trust your word?"

Søren glanced at Savannah. She inhaled deeply. "Because our situation is similar. A soul has been reaped ahead of its time. What we do about it now effects our fates," she wisely kept it vague.

Finnigan paused. Perhaps he dealt with betrayal on the regular, and had become accustomed to the need to silence those who turned on him. His defences remained erect, even though he visibly loosened and let out a sigh of relief. "All right. I will do my best to help."

Even with that conformation, Søren suddenly got the terrifying feeling that they were fortunate to still be standing where they were.

Mr Magik began to busy himself at his main table littered with books, herbs and crystal beakers. Some were full of translucent liquid that looked like they had bottled whole galaxies, while others stored preserved plants and weeds. The research of half a lifetime compiled into one space; Søren thought it was impressive that he could sift through it so efficiently.

The Reapers stood stiffly by the door; arms folded and jaws clenched as they had not relaxed completely —just as the immortal was, the two were on cautious alert. Anything could happen to cause a snap.

"...So, um, Mr Magik," Søren went on as casually as he could manage. "About our request...can you really warp time?"

"Well. There are laws in place —" he began dubiously.

"The Titan Lord Kronos is currently imprisoned," the Trainer reminded him. "There is nothing that he can do to you."

The wizard chuckled uncertainly. "That is not what I meant. I was warned that fraternising with time had...unpredictable consequences. It is not a fixed thing that can simply be removed."

"What we need is the perception of an event to be altered," Søren informed him. "We can't erase it —we know that."

"What is the original timeline?" he frowned.

"The soul is reaped, and we will be reaped as punishment," Savannah clipped, keeping it short. It was not as though she would willingly reveal the details of what happened, after all. Yet as Søren thought about it, nothing was preventing Finnigan Michael Magik from concluding whatever he wished with the information given. The wizard might even know that his trainee had been the one to reap the soul.

If he had realised it, he showed no resentment towards her. Given what had happened to him, Søren did not think he would be so cooperative with a Grim Reaper who had unlawfully taken a life.

"If it is your wish and intention to bring this person back to life or prevent their death, I should not do that," the wizard warned darkly.

'*Should not*', Søren noted. Not '*cannot*'.

So, the cursed immortal was very capable of such.

"No," Savannah said firmly. "That is most definitely not the goal."

Mr Magik frowned deeply, as though her words struck a nerve too deep. "…That is disappointing, to an extent," he murmured. "Though I am sure that you have your reasons. I can't judge your motives. But if I may know, what *is* it that you want to do when you get to the past?"

Savannah looked at her Trainer. They had not actually discussed the matter. They knew that they could not stop her from killing the bastard. That would rupture the timeline and make a mess of everything else. Instead what they needed was a way to make it seem as though the mortal *had* been set to die. To make it seem as though it was not an accident. Søren would have to fabricate a fake list for the day with the mortal's name included. It would be more difficult to uniform the hard copy information rather than digital, but he trusted his hacking skills enough to make it believable.

The Trainer explained this to Finnigan —and he certainly was not thrilled about it. He grumbled and muttered to himself in irritation, but agreed that it would indeed be an understandable course of action.

And so he got to work, grinding up all of the necessary ingredients for the spell which he would be using. Søren glanced at his trainee to see how she was handling herself —as it turned out, she was anxious. She tried not to show it, but it was noticeable. What if they did not succeed, and what if they were reaped in the end anyway?

Søren leaned back against the wall and sighed. They were certainly going to long lengths to rectify the incident. He knew how terribly Savannah's mistake would reflect on his reputation —but he wondered if that was the reason for which he was seeking the help of a psychotic immortal wizard with a connection to the divine world.

Savannah had expressed it earlier that she would have preferred to die and pass on. But when Søren looked at her now, stiff and biting on the nail of her thumb, it was obvious that the thought of death frightened her. She did not want to die —not the way it would now come.

"Are you two sure that you know what you are doing?" Mr Magik asked when his preparations were complete. His veins were glowing red softly beneath the surface of his skin, and the range of the wisps had widened.

"Yes," Søren said, despite Savannah's wary glance in response.

"All right," Finnigan sighed. "You will be pulled back when you utter the word '*finite*'. Do not say it until you wish to return. Now, as I send you, concentrate hard on the place and time to which you want to go, and keep your consciousness rooted in that. Do not slip or think of anything else —I have some theories about what would happen if you do, including becoming forever lost in a sea of nothingness."

The two nodded vigorously, and agreed on a time and destination.
The wizard then muttered something beneath his breath that was written in the book beside him, before gathering a little of the potion he had made in his hand and holding it out towards the Reapers. And then he blew.

Blue mist swirled from his palm and into the air, slowly enveloping Søren and Savannah. They marvelled at it for a moment. The amount then seemed to increase dramatically in a matter of seconds, and soon they were surrounded by a blue vortex; whipping and snagging at their clothes with winds that only picked up in speed. Before long, Søren's eyes could not remain open.

His grip tightened on his crossbow, before he suddenly felt a hand fly for his, desperately gripping his fingers. Unfazed, he chose to keep Savannah's hand there —if only to provide encouragement and reassurance.

New York. Home. My apartment. Yesterday evening, he told himself over and over, and he could only believe that his trainee was chanting the same.

✠

Søren opened his eyes to the glare of neon signs on the side of a busy street. Then he heard Savannah gasp beside him, before her hand jerked out of his as she staggered forward, disorientated. The Trainer glanced around and breathed a sigh of relief to know that the spell might have worked —but they could not be sure without checking the date. He did not want to think it, but this could have been a trick; a simple teleportation spell, since it had also been evening when they arrived at Mr Magik's apartment.

"I did not think that would take this much of a toll," Savannah rasped.

"The timeline may be rejecting our presence," Søren suggested.

"Or maybe I'm just not used to all of this magical displacement. You seem to be just fine."

She was wrong. On the outside, he seemed fine. Though inwardly, even he felt a nauseating tug within him —like something was not right.

"It doesn't matter. We don't have time to waste. Let's check where and when we are," he said, walking down the sidewalk towards an intersection.

It turned out that they were a few blocks away from the apartment building. Savannah breathed harshly through her nose as they walked, either deep in thought or attempting to mentally prepare herself for what they were about to do.

Søren was doing something similar; and he was admittedly a lot calmer than he had been before, but he was glad to see that his trainee was finally taking this seriously.

Perhaps Finnigan's dilemma had had a hand in revealing some of the consequences. At least to Søren's knowledge, thank the gods that Savannah's ex-boyfriend had not been tampering with the divine and magic —otherwise the

140

Reapers would have a much larger problem on their hands.

"Hey," his trainee eventually said in a careful and quiet voice, looking across at the opposite side of the road. "When you were out yesterday…I had a run in with the Chainsaw Guy."

Søren frowned, not following. "The —*who*?"

"Oh," she quipped, before shaking her head and laughing. "I mean Melchior. I just call him *the Chainsaw Guy*…in my head…" she added quietly, lowering her voice.

The Trainer could not resist the smirk of amusement which then broke out on his face, before he realised who she was talking about. "…*Melchior*," he said slowly, not hiding the urge to sigh.

Savannah nodded. "He asked me if you were back yet."

"Because he *cares*?" Søren snorted, raising a quizzical eyebrow.

"I don't know," she answered defensively. "All he asked was if you were back yet. That's all. He came up to the door and knocked, which startled Phee-Phee. He set your potted fern on fire," she added flippantly.

"He *what*?" Søren growled, clenching his fists. "*Savannah*. I thought I told you to look after that demon properly."

She shrank away sheepishly. "Let's not focus on that now," she insisted. "The point is, why did Melchior ask for you? He didn't exactly come across as the caring type."

"He's…he's not," sighed the Trainer. "Not really. And I think I knew that even before I asked him out."

Savannah did a double take in utter disbelief. "Wait. *You're* the one who asked him out? And he said yes?"

"Yes," Søren pouted, "Why does that seem so hard to believe?"

She gave him a self-explanatory look.

"*Okay*," he sighed in defeat. "So maybe it took a little persuasion since he would never publicly date a man. But he still agreed, with a few conditions. And we were happy in secret I guess; for quite some time."

She looked at the Trainer, expecting him to continue, but that was where

Søren wanted to end the conversation.

"...*And*?" she prompted.

"And what?"

"What happened to you guys?"

The Reaper shrugged, but inside he was irked. He did not want to have a conversation about his ex-boyfriend any more than Savannah would not want to talk about her own. "...We broke up," Søren said bluntly. Then he stopped walking. "Here we are."

The trainee sighed and looked up with him, before they headed for the side of the building. Søren searched for the security ID button, before pressing it and prompting the face scan screen to pop up.

It quickly approved, before the tiles began to shift.

Søren then beckoned Savannah to the front doors. They ran through the lobby, with no one seeming to notice them, before making their way to the elevator. The Trainer pressed the button to the second floor, and they waited impatiently while tapping their shoes. Savannah glanced up towards the ceiling and sighed loudly as though she wanted to say something.

"What is it," Søren sighed at her indecisiveness.

"Nothing!" she immediately defended herself, shaking her head.

"Oh, really," he smirked as the elevator bell rung, and the doors opened to the second floor. They marched out and headed for number eight, before the two paused at the door and glanced at each other wearily. The same apprehension that Søren felt reflected itself in Savannah's gold eyes, but his hand still moved to open the door.

"...I hope that you didn't lock it," the redhead surprisingly voiced Søren's own concern, but the door opened easily and seemed to beckon them inside. It was empty. Completely silent.

"We must have already left," his trainee murmured, marching inside. "Which means we don't have much time."

"Right," Søren agreed, setting his crossbow down in the living room.

The Reapers then got to work in the computer room.

After activating Angelina, Søren began writing out the codes needed to disable the Reapers Organisation's cyber security defences, allowing him to slip inside undetected.

"How many times have you hacked into HQ?" Savannah frowned, noting how quick and efficient the Trainer had been.

"This…wouldn't be the first time," he confessed nonchalantly. "That being said, the other times were for petty reasons. This is the first time I am using it for criminal purposes."

"You make us sound like convicts —Jesus," she cringed.

Søren completely ignored her statement.

"Okay, I have found the lists for Manhattan, New York. April 21st, 2019," he then announced. "And…it's this one. Bingo."

He pulled them all into Documents to edit them, spreading each official duplicate over every monitor. "So, what was his name again?" he asked.

"…Aaron Finnick Carter," growled the redhead.

Søren typed his name at the end of a pre-existing list.

They both gasped as the name disappeared right off of the screen like a cloud of dust in a light breeze. Søren typed it in again. And again it blew away. He did it over and over, even as dread began to consume his confidence.

"What the…?" he frowned. It was like magic.

"Let me try," Savannah insisted, nudging him aside.

It did not make the slightest difference. She typed the name over and over, her fingers stabbing the keyboard as though pressure might make it stick. It was not working —the timeline was rejecting the change. But Søren's trainee refused to believe that. The Trainer said her name, trying to get her to stop and calm down, but she shook him off.

She kept typing until her hands finally moved from the computer, still jabbing at the air, and several drops of water splashed onto the desk.

"…Savannah," Søren said quietly.

"He tricked us," she whispered, her voice hollow. "I'm going to die."

"You don't know that for certain —"

"He knew that we couldn't change the past like this, but he still let us go," she continued, raising her voice. "Those stupid fucking laws —he wasn't talking about getting into trouble with the gods. Maybe he was referring to the laws of time itself."

"We don't know if he knew that this would happen," Søren said gravely. "What if this was all down to chance? What if this timeline just doesn't want us here, changing it?"

As though time were its own, separate and sentient entity.

"Then Fate says I should die," Savannah hissed, her brows furrowing. "…This was all a waste of time. I'm so sorry, Søren."

"No, it wasn't a waste," he insisted. "We wouldn't have known if we hadn't tried, right? And we still have to deal with Mr Magik. If he knew we wouldn't be able to change anything, why would he send us on a fool's errand? There's got to be something that we're missing."

The redhead frowned. "Mr Magik mentioned that he was searching for a cure to his immortality," she murmured. "What if this is just an experiment to him? If he had known, or if he had left it to chance, what could he possibly gain from our failure?"

Søren drew a breath in realisation. "…Rage."

"What?"

"Rage must be a running theme for untimely reaping —or so he would think. If we failed, no matter the means, he could be counting on bitter and petty rage to attempt to reap his soul once again."

"But it won't work," Savannah pointed out. "Not with the magic binding him. I mean…didn't he already try? Isn't that why he's in this mess now?"

"I think that he's desperate enough not to give a single solitary shit," Søren scoffed. "It must be well worth the risk to him."

"Then…let's go back," the trainee mumbled. "Even if it means accepting death, even if it makes me a killer. And let's agree not to give Mr Magik what he wants." She straightened her jacket, her expression blank and unreadable. "…He deserves to live with his own consequences."

Søren's eyes narrowed as he stood up and grabbed hold of her arm. "Hey," he said firmly. "I have as much responsibility for this whole mess as you do. I'm supposed to be your Trainer —I should have handled it better. I should have stopped you in time."

"You are not the one who killed Aaron," Savannah deadpanned.

"No," he admitted, "But I am not letting you face Death alone."

She looked up at him properly, her eyes pink and her irises a more vibrant gold. "You shouldn't change the past —instead, you should learn from it. Our chance might be gone, but, if you go, then I will go with you."

Savannah blinked in astonishment. Perhaps no one ever said something like that to her before, Søren mused. Had she not known of such loyalty? Judging by the slightly sceptical undertone in her expression, she had not.

But she did not argue. She then mumbled, "…Okay."

As though it was the most casual offer in the world.

She did not need to say anything more, however. Søren knew that there were some forms of apology and gratitude there, that she could not voice aloud.

After he had logged off and deactivated Angelina the two solemnly left the computer room. Søren grabbed his crossbow from the sofa before he solemnly offered his trainee his hand. "Finite?"

She drew a deep, empty breath. "Finite."

CHAPTER 16

SØREN

FINNIGAN MICHAEL MAGIK was very unapologetically surprised to see the Reapers with such neutral façades upon their return.

The wizard seemed to be on edge —quite anxious and more jittery than before. As though he had been fretting over the outcome. Savannah and Søren shared a subtle look. Their suspicions were proving to be right.

"Did you…succeed in your quest?" inquired Mr Magik.

"Not at all," Søren quipped. "The timeline refused to be altered."

"You…do not seem too upset about it," Mr Magik observed.

"Nope," said Savannah. "We've come to terms with it. We are going to deal with the consequences. Thank you for your help, though."

The Reapers moved towards the door.

"Wait!" the wizard suddenly cried. He was met with expectant looks. "I…I don't understand it —if you failed, should you not be enraged? Should you not be cursing me instead of thanking me?"

Søren scoffed. "…You are shameless, Mr Magik."

The man blinked rapidly, appearing confused. "What?"

"You really did mean to manipulate our emotions, didn't you?" Savannah elaborated. "We realised it, after our changes were denied. If you had known from the start that we couldn't do anything, you wouldn't have helped. Yet you were working with the possibility that nothing would change, and that it would anger us. Just what did you hope to accomplish with such a plan? Did you want us to reap you?"

The wizard stood there, dumbstruck for a moment. The wisps of mist flared ever so slightly, before their movement almost slowed to the point where they were barely flickering around him.

Finnigan smiled.

It began as a smirk, then it grew into a grin. Then a low chuckle escaped his lips. "…Oh, I underestimated you," he realised. "I didn't think you would figure it all out. Still. What's so wrong with what I did? Either way, one party was going to win or lose. There was no win-win option. I simply used the possibility of your loss to my advantage."

"You used us," Søren reiterated.

"Yes, but your consequences have nothing to do with me," Mr Magik truthfully mused. "Either way, whether you ended up reaping my soul as you did with the other mortal or not, *that* would not change."

Savannah growled a bit, knowing that he was right.

"We're leaving now," Søren told Mr Magik, tugging his trainee along before she could actually fulfil the wizard's wish. "And you are going to find another way to cleave your soul. Preferably not at the expense of someone else's," he emphasised. Then he paused, glaring at the immortal darkly. "Though maybe this is simply a curse which you deserve."

Mr Magik raised his eyebrows slightly at that. Then he barked a laugh. "That was what that maiden told me as well when she left."

Søren shook his head in pity as he nudged a stubborn Savannah out of the front door, realising that what had happened to Finnigan was precisely why mortals were not gifted with magic.

✠

The Reapers stepped into Søren's apartment physically sound but mentally drained. Savannah selfishly sprawled onto the sofa, sighing deeply. Søren knew that she had wanted to stay longer to give Mr Magik a piece of her mind, but that would have been playing directly into his hand.

"You have got to learn to control your temper," the Trainer advised.

"What's the point in that?" she huffed, staring up at the ceiling. "If I'm going to be put to death, then it won't matter."

"As I keep saying, you don't know that," Søren clipped. "The Boss could have mercy, for whatever the reason." Though even he doubted it.

"And what about Mr Magik? We can't seriously just leave that psycho be, can we?" she asked. "We have to report him. He's a danger to society."

"We swore upon the River Styx not to alert any authorities," he reminded her. "There is nothing that we can do."

She grumbled bitterly.

"...Anyway. I should go and submit a report about the whole Aaron incident. It's better to own up before we're found out instead," Søren then quipped, heading for the computer room.

He opened the door and received the fright of his life as he switched on the lights. A small gathering of people he had never seen before were before him. It consisted of Security officers; bodyguards; all with long gleaming scythes —and in the forefront, was a sharply dressed raven-haired man with a serious, deathly look chiselled into his stony features. A soft golden godly halo emitted from him, like a thin sheet of hazy shimmering light.

"*Security breached,*" Angelina decided it was the best time to announce the security status. Savannah ran in, coming to a standstill beside Søren.

"Did you kids find what you were looking for?" the presumed god in the expensive suit asked, his arms folded coldly.

The Reapers froze. The god glanced at Savannah —at the necklace around her neck, and down at her sword. Søren then narrowed his gaze at the deity's chest. Something was faintly glowing underneath his shirt. The Trainer took a protective step in front of Savannah.

"Aaron," the god said leisurely, and snapped his fingers. He turned slightly to the side, but his bronze eyes stayed glued to the Reapers.

Søren and his trainee tensed at the name, before the Trainer wondered for what exactly the god would be calling that soul.

The red misty form of Savannah's ex-boyfriend materialised next to the deity; the soul's eyes aglow and boring into the Reapers like a predator.

Savannah flinched and inhaled sharply, before clutching onto Søren. The Trainer glared at Aaron, and the soul regarded him wearily.

"That's her," Aaron lifted his finger towards the redheaded Reaper and said; his voice distorted and as ear-damaging as a screeching violin, causing everyone to wince. The god shifted his weight to his right and snapped his fingers again, prompting the soul to disappear again, leaving a vapour of red dust. "*You*, are coming with me."

He was pointing at the trainee.

The Security officers made moves to take her forcefully but hesitated when Søren put his hand up, recognising his authority.

"Who the hell are you?" he asked the god. "And what warrant do you have to search my apartment?"

The Security officers all glanced backwards to their commanding officer, raising their eyebrows. The god flippantly waved his hand in a way of saying that it was fine before smiling at Søren maniacally.

"You know, *Søren*," he started, forcefully fiddling with his shirt cuff links, "Considering how long you've worked for me, I would have thought you would address me with a little more *respect*."

He shoved his hands in his pockets and glared at the Trainer, causing Søren to hesitate. Could it be…this male…was the *Boss*?

Søren dithered. It then hit him that Death himself had felt compelled to visit them personally —or rather, apprehend them.

"Shit," he then blurted out, before Savannah elbowed him in outrage. "I mean — " he coughed as the Boss gave him a look, "…I'm sorry sir. I didn't know that it was you. I didn't mean to speak so disrespectfully to you."

"*Quite*," he spat, eyeing the Trainer spitefully. "It should pain me to say this, but unfortunately for a Trainer with your reputation, I'm going to have to bring you in with your trainee —for harbouring a criminal."

Søren frowned, though it was not news to him. "I…I understand, sir."

Savannah stepped out from behind him and put her arms out. "No. I've changed my mind. Don't bring him into this," she pleaded, "He tried to warn me and stop me but it's my fault I disobeyed his orders. I didn't listen. So, please —don't punish him for my mistake."

There was a beat of silence.

"…Mistake," the Boss snorted, taking a step towards her. His eyes flashed a brighter bronze, the clocks within them more visible; and every vein in his neck straining. "You see, young Reaper, a *mistake* is when you forget to reap a soul on any given day. What you did? That was *murder*."

Savannah shrunk back and hung her head, which made Søren frown.

How dare he lecture her. She had already learned the lesson —she did not need to hear it again. And if anyone was going to speak to her that way, it was going to be her Trainer.

He gently moved her aside and stared the Boss down.

"Look, I understand that what she did was unlawful, but she's still kind of new to this. As her Trainer, I should take more responsibility. I didn't warn her, and that's as much of a fact as her not listening." Søren then paused and glared at the glow coming from under the god's clothes. "And…"

He glanced back at Savannah's necklace, and she looked at him in confusion, before he turned back to the god of death. "…Are you aware that your chest is glowing?"

The Boss glanced downwards, and almost seemed startled. He had not noticed all of this time. Then he looked at Savannah, who quickly clutched at her own chest. The god pressed his lips together thoughtfully; regained his composure and straightened his tie, before clearing his throat. "…Savannah. You need to come with me —immediately."

The redhead glared at him, after having attained some sort of confidence.

"I don't care who you think you are," she started, taking several steps towards him and agitating the bodyguards, "and I don't care what your rank is. What I want to know," she hissed, and stabbed a finger in his chest, from where the glow was emitting, "is what the heck *this* is."

"Hey, that's enough of that," the closest bodyguard then warned, stepping forward and raising his arm.

Savannah's head jerked in his direction and she caught his fist easily, before twisting his large muscular arm away from her until he doubled up in pain and crumpled to the floor. Everyone immediately took a step backwards, but Søren was too surprised to move.

It was almost as though the girl had become a different person.
She then turned back to the Boss and tilted her head to the side, the burning rage in her golden eyes almost rivalling his.

The god did not turn a hair —though he did put on a look of disgust and lean slightly away —and stared back at her blankly. Savannah then dug into the front of her top and pulled out her necklace, holding it in front of his face. He still remained poker faced.

"…You have one too —don't you?" she whispered.

He did not answer, but the way his gaze shifted in discomfort suggested that Savannah, was right.

CHAPTER 17

SØREN

SAVANNAH COULD NOT stop apologising to the bodyguard whose arm she had twisted.

He was over it fairly quickly, but she insisted that she had done it unconsciously —as though she had not even known she had been doing it. It was as if something had taken her over in that moment.

Søren thought about it as they were led to a previously unnoticed black limousine outside of the apartment building; when they were driven to a five star restaurant called *Le Noir*; and when they used one of the Boss' many personal portals to Purgatory —that happened to be in the men's bathroom. Savannah squirmed and was hesitant to go inside, but she eventually got through it after Søren shoved her in with her eyes shut.

After going through, they stepped directly inside of a building. Unlike her Trainer, Savannah did not look as though she minded that they did not get to see the exterior of Purgatory, and walked perkily alongside the Boss as though she had been here before. It seemed that the elimination of a death sentence had cheered her right up.

Søren frowned, narrowing his eyes at her as they walked unaccompanied down the halls of the office building. She did not notice for a while and continued to ask question after question while Death's patience dwindled.

When the god finally told her to give it a rest, she reluctantly turned around and caught Søren staring into space.

She fell back in step with him and punched his arm, snapping the Trainer out of his thoughts. "Quit staring at me," she teased.

"I wasn't really staring *at* you," Søren chuckled half-heartedly, swinging his crossbow back and forth between them. "Rather, *through* you. I was thinking about something, and you just happened to be standing in the spot on which my eyes decided to stay glued."

"Sure," she scoffed, tilting her head to the side. She then undid her falling out ponytail, letting her hair fall around her shoulders.

Søren then glanced at the Boss, wondering what the god and redheaded Reaper had been talking about throughout the journey. "…So what's the deal with him?" the Trainer asked.

She followed his gaze and looked at Death marching along with clenched fists. "He knows my father," she said quietly. "That's why he has the same necklace as me. He says my father gave it to him for safe keeping."

"Why were they glowing though?" Søren whispered, leaning closer towards her so that they could not be so easily heard.

She opened her mouth to say something, but their conversation was cut off by the Boss suddenly clapping his hands to gain their attention.

"All right, this is my office," he said, stepping aside to reveal a door marked '*Head Office*'. "You are not ever to be allowed inside without my permission and or presence."

He gave them both a stern look, and the two Grim Reapers nodded —but as soon as he turned around, Savannah stuck out her tongue and winked at Søren when he elbowed her.

The Trainer drew a deep breath as they entered a dark, musty office decorated with skulls; white and black roses; and accents of dark red.

In one corner, a tall glass case displayed a large, ebony, diamond encrusted scythe —very sharp, and very reflective. Søren shivered when he saw his own reflection in the obsidian, clear and defined. He frowned at it as well as the skulls that decorated the base of the case, before feeling a chill run down his spine. He

153

wondered if the skulls were real and human.

"They're supposed to be ironic," the Boss said as if he could read Søren's mind, before taking a seat in a chair behind a dark Oakwood desk.

Søren shrugged and offered a fake understanding nod. Savannah's eyes roamed every detail, and she too shuddered at the scythe display.

"So…" she started, coming to a stop in front of the desk. Søren stood next to her, holding his crossbow over his shoulder. "Are you going to explain everything now?"

The Boss sighed and waved his hand. A glass of bloodred wine appeared and settled in his open hand. "…I am going to be frank with you. There are things that I cannot tell you. There are things that you are not allowed to know about. But what I can tell you, is that these necklaces were supposed to be a way of communication between you and your father.

"Your mother didn't want anything to do with him after she found out the truth about him, so he gave one to you earlier than he had planned; and the other one was intended for himself. They are meant to glow when anything significant happens. They glowed before because of the close proximity," he ended, nodding at Savannah's chest.

"It didn't glow when I died," the redhead pointed out.

"No," he agreed, "—but it did when you Turned. When you reaped your first soul, as well. And…when you reaped your boyfriend," he added.

"*Ex*-boyfriend," Savannah corrected him, through clenched teeth.

"Whatever," the god clicked his tongue. "The point is, you reaped a soul when it was not yet supposed to. That is why his soul was red. So, congratulations you imbecile —he can never rest in peace now."

"I…didn't know that at the time," she argued truthfully. "Besides. I don't think he *deserves* to rest in peace."

"That is not for you to decide," Death murmured, a shadow passing over his face as he glared at her.

"If you knew what he had done —" Savannah started, before she growled in frustration. "You don't understand. He had been *lying* to me."

Søren understood.

He had been lied to as well; misled and made a fool of. At least Savannah would not have to watch Aaron grow older and be with someone else.

"Okay, look." The Boss sighed as he stood up, bringing his wine with him. "Mortals and immortals alike cheat on each other all of the time. It is not some great, *magical*, inexplicable phenomenon. It's flawed nature —likely on our part. But it is no reason to murder someone."

"Can we please stop using that word?" Søren then spoke up, finding that he was growing uncomfortable with the way it was being thrown around. He knew that he had in fact used it himself, but he had also come to realise the impression it had on Savannah.

It would not help in moulding her into an efficient and notable Grim Reaper.

"Well, why not say it as it is…?" the Boss scoffed, almost mockingly. The Reapers did not respond. "Fine. What do you *suggest* that we use?"

Søren shrugged. "…Homicide?"

Savannah gave him a look, indicating that he was not exactly helping.

"Homicide," Death repeated. "…Is it not still killing?"

Søren wanted to argue that homicide was a milder term, and therefore more sensitive to the deceased as well as being sparing to Savannah's feelings.

"Excuse me, are you going to charge us or not?" the redhead spoke up. "Why did you even bring us here —what's so important?"

"…I'm not going to charge you *very* severely," Death sighed, his brows knitting. "You will both stay here until you have dusted *every single last book* in my library and placed them all in alphabetical order; and also according to size, date, and relevance to my preferences. You will find the list for that at the door." Then he paused, a smirk indicating that it was not as easy as it sounded. "…I own a very extensive library, by the way. Oh! And Savannah," he then went on, snapping his fingers. An old-fashioned maid outfit complete with a frilly apron, appeared on a plastic hanger. "This is for you. You can't take it off until the job is done."

He snapped his fingers again, and in a red smoky burst, Savannah was suddenly kitted out in the maid outfit. Søren stifled a burst of laughter, glancing aside, and Savannah shot him a look of offence.

"Where the hell did my clothes go?" she hissed at Death.

"They will come back when you are done."

"*What*," she spat, "the hell? What *is* this —some sort of kink?"

"*Gods* no," he immediately responded, looking thoroughly repulsed by the suggestion. "It is a punishment."

"What kind of *punishment* —"

"I am not finished," the god cut her off by raising an index finger. She reluctantly let him continue. "Now, I will be keeping a very close eye on you from now on —just to make sure that you do not do any additional stupid things. Oh, I also need to take a look at that sword of yours," he continued, sitting back down in the chair. "It is not enough that you proved that it is yours earlier. I need to run my own tests."

"And when will I have it back?" the Reaper asked, quirking an eyebrow.

Death twisted his mouth in thought. "Eh...tomorrow —or never."

"*What*?" Søren exclaimed, knowing how unfair the proposal was.

"You can't really just take my reaping weapon," Savannah added. "I thought that it belonged to me forever."

"That will not matter if I find even the slightest thing out of place. What I need to do won't take just a few hours. I have to inspect it thoroughly —which means that you should be grateful that I even suggested tomorrow as a possibility," the Boss scoffed, resting his chin in his free hand.

Søren found nothing to say.

The god was truly desensitised; death taken form.

Savannah however, had plenty of words to express her outrage at the injustice. "Yeah —*right* before you suggested *never*."

"*Really* wish I could help more..." Death murmured, rocking the wine glass in his hand. Søren studied the way his muscles were all flexed; how stiff he was in his chair despite his indifferent expression, as if he were not quite as relaxed as he appeared.

The performance was growing obvious.

"*As if*," Savannah spat, throwing her sword onto the floor. A loud metallic clang rang out, and it bounced twice before sliding to a standstill.

"How dare you!" the Boss cried. "You cannot go throwing things down in hissy fits. That is imported marble."

The trainee Reaper glared at him in disbelief, before pushing past Søren and stomping out of the ajar door.

She slammed it behind her, for emphasis. The Trainer glanced back at the god with a grimace, before turning to go after her.

"…She should be beyond grateful, you know," Death said, making the older Reaper pause. "The fact that I did not fire nor reap her on the spot speaks volumes that she refuses to hear."

Søren pressed his lips into a line, unsure of whether or not he should even respond. "I'll…talk to her," he then sighed. He turned to leave again, but the Boss called him back. The Reaper raised an eyebrow expectantly.

"My advice to you, *Søren*," he started, saying his name as though it was a poisonous swear word, "is to keep your distance from Savannah —lest you want to find yourself without a job."

Søren frowned, feeling that something was amiss. "What do you mean? I'm her Trainer —I have to stay close."

The Boss snorted and took a sip of wine. "Oh, it's a good thing that you are so slow witted and naïve," he chuckled. "A Trainer is all you will ever be to her, understand? Nothing more than friends."

Søren's brain then finally caught up, and he scoffed. "No way," he said, "I don't even really like her as a friend, let alone anything more."

Death's expression then hardened. "…What, are you saying that suddenly she is no longer good enough for you?"

"That's not what I meant," Søren assured him. "Look, if you're asking me to back off because *you* like her, then I can totally do that."

The Trainer was not going to judge or call out the god of death —or any deity for that matter —for taking an interest in whomsoever he pleased.

157

Death suddenly choked, spluttering wine everywhere as his bronze eyes widened. He shuddered, disgusted.

"...First of all: she is far too young, especially given her permanent age. Even I have limits. Secondly, there is no way I would ever be attracted to someone like her. And lastly, I don't support incest."

Søren paused and frowned at him in confusion. "...Incest?"

The Boss froze, and then muttered something obscene under his breath in Greek. "...Well, I suppose it will be fine if you know about it. I did not want to tell anyone —not yet anyway," he admitted, avoiding Søren's gaze. "Savannah...she is my *half*-sister," and he shivered as he said it, and looked as though he were about to throw up. "We...have the same father. That is why I also have a duplicate of the necklace. He gave it to me so I could look after it —and not by choice."

The Trainer's brows rose in intrigue rather than surprise.

"Why didn't you tell her?" Søren asked.

Did she not deserve to know she was related to the Boss —to Death himself?

The god sighed and rounded the desk, before sitting on it in an intimidating pose; leaned forward and legs apart. "If I told her the truth, she could work out that her father is a god. She has wild, childish power, Søren," he warned, "—it would be far too dangerous for her to know just how much, when she can barely control it herself."

Søren nodded uncertainly, taking it in. He could not see either of them in each other —he was cold, brooding and dark; she was bright and bubbly and impulsive. Their eyes were similar to an extent —but otherwise the Reaper never would have guessed that the two were in any way related.

"If you tell her," the god's voice said, and was suddenly a lot closer —and so was he; standing right in front of Søren so he could see the miniature clocks in Death's eyes, causing him to jump back in surprise.

"I will not hesitate to feed you to Cerberus," the deity promised. "He has grown rather tired of dinosaur bones."

Søren gulped, and hastily nodded, believing every word.

For his own sake, and for the safety of the world from Savannah's unknown quantity of power.

"Now go and get started on that punishment," Death ordered, waving a hand dismissively and turning back towards the desk.

"Yes, sir," Søren responded as he backed away. He gestured that his lips were sealed, before ducking around the corner and walking quickly towards a hall whose signage appeared to lead to the library.

The Trainer suddenly stumbled into two large gilt doors, face first. He groaned and slowly looked upwards, to see a sign that read '*Library: The Entire Worlds' Information and Creative Centre*'.

He pulled the doors open.

The Boss had been serious when he said that he owned an extensive library. Books lined every available slither of the walls, leaving only the white wooden brackets just below the ceiling. Ladders stood against the shelves every few meters —the fancy sliding ones with wheels on the bottom. Søren could not see an end all the way down to the left of him, nor to the right.

And there appeared to be hundreds of twists and turns ahead and around those bends, similar to a labyrinth.

He drew a breath. Normally, this would have been absolute heaven. But under the circumstances, he might as well have been in Tartarus.

"Took you long enough," Savannah muttered, turning around from facing a shelf and giving him a look. The maid outfit was a little less creepy and more amusing to Søren now that he knew the Boss was her half-brother.

He tried to keep a straight face, but she could tell that he wanted to laugh. She stomped her foot and glared at him, with her hands on her hips. Søren averted his gaze and looked at the numerous books, whistling softly. The redhead huffed and then returned to wielding a black and white feather duster —before coughing and spluttering as dust flew everywhere.

"Does he ever actually come *in* here?" she wheezed, doubling up and clutching at her stomach.

Søren walked up to where she was and ran a finger along the spines of the books. Dust flew out at him too, and more coughing ensued. "…I don't think he's been in here…for *years*."

Savannah huffed and rubbed her nose, trying to get rid of some of the dust. "What held you up? I thought you were right behind —"

"—We weren't talking about anything," Søren blurted out.

"…*me*," she finished, narrowing her eyes and looking at him sideways. He then frowned in an effort to avoid further suspicion. "Oh…kay?"

The Trainer ran a hand through his hair. "…I mean, he didn't say anything of significance. Just…to keep an eye on you," he settled for, folding his arms to assert his false adamance.

Savannah did not look as though she believed him.

"Why is that the new rule for me?" she said through her teeth. "I get it —what I did was wrong, and I should've listened to you. But why the heck am I now being treated like a *child* —"

"Because you *are* one," Søren raised his voice over hers.

She withdrew, as though he had just slapped her, and her face loosened into a frown. She did not understand.

"You're only eighteen years and nearly two weeks old —you're still a *child*," Søren explained. "The mundane world taught you that you'll have all these weird and wonderful entitlements when you turn eighteen, but guess what? Now that you've Turned, you're basically eight. So, grow a pair and suck it up, Savannah —because no matter what you thought you knew when you were alive; you. Know. *Nothing*. Now."

Søren's jaw clenched as he maintained a look of indifference. He did not feel bad for being so harsh.

She was beginning to piss him off —and as much as he hated to admit it, it was because her attitude had been one that he had had when he started out.

This is stupid, he had thought. *Why do I have to take orders from someone I don't even get to see? Death is such a coward.*

Savannah blinked, startled by her Trainer's words, before a layer of tears glistened in the bottom of her eyes. They spilled, one by one, onto her skin and down her cheeks. He watched them fall and he saw the hurt in her eyes.

160

He turned away.

Søren could not handle it when people cried. He had convinced himself that it was a beg for sympathy —and feeling sorry for someone was not a good thing to feel. Especially when trying to correct them.

He walked over to the door and grabbed the other feather duster, and the rolled-up list that hung on the other side.

"…You're right," came a hoarse whisper. He glanced backwards out of the corner of his eyes and waited for her to say more.

"I *am* a child," she said clearly. "And I'm sorry for behaving like one all this time. I know that what happened with Aaron was immature on my part. My temper was out of control. I understand why you'd say all that, but I'm *trying*," she insisted. "…I'm just a Turned Reaper who doesn't know any better. But I'll cooperate and learn. I swear. I'm sorry —I really am."

Søren paused, before turning back around to face her. He brought the list and feather duster over, before leaning against the shelves with his elbow and facing her. She sniffed and wiped her face with the back of her hand.

"When I Turned, I thought that I had turned into a ghost," he told her. She frowned and looked up at him curiously. She seemed to be wondering why he was telling her this. He was not entirely sure either. "No seriously —I jumped right through three walls before crashing into the last one and sticking there like a fly on flypaper."

She then let out a soft laugh, before covering her mouth apologetically.

"…I died in a shooting in 1836," Søren lowered his voice.

"Oh my *God*, Søren, you're so old!" she exclaimed, her eyes widening. "Like…a hundred and eighty-three," she concluded after several seconds, pouting thoughtfully. "Well, if you count from when you died."

"Actually, a hundred and ninety-eight counting the years I was mortal," he corrected her. "I died a month after my sixteenth birthday."

"Oh," she softened. She then bit her lip, thinking for a moment. "…You don't have to go on —I'm sorry."

Søren could not help chuckling, much to her surprise. "I wasn't going to go

161

on." Then he sighed and stood up straight. "Don't be sorry. It's not your fault. It *wasn't* your fault. You weren't even born yet."

"Touché," she said sheepishly, "It kind of slipped out naturally. Whenever someone talks about death, you usually apologise —even if it hasn't got remotely anything to do with you."

Søren shrugged. "I figured," he yawned, raking through his hair. "All right. Now let's get started on this punishment."

Savannah blew a raspberry and slouched but reached for her feather duster all the same. But she was smiling, and occasionally turning to stick her tongue out at him playfully.

CHAPTER 18

SØREN

SØREN WAS VERY tempted to open up and start reading *The Da Vinci Code* by Dan Brown, but Savannah was standing a few feet away from him, dusting vigorously and keeping a watchful eye on him.

She would not approve of him reading on the job.

He dusted the book carefully, before dusting the empty slot of shelf, and the books on either side. Then he slid the book back into its place before he picked up the next one.

"You know, my Mom would *flip* over a library this size," Savannah spoke. "She's only got a tiny one-wall collection of her favourite classics."

"*I'm* flipping," Søren replied. "I really wish that our punishment was to read every one of these books instead."

"God, no," she sneered, turning to glare at him. "There are some seriously boring books here." She then pointed at some examples.

He was severely offended. "They are called classics; and they're art."
"I prefer books with more out of this world fantasy and bloody action to them," she reasoned haughtily. "Keeps you on your toes."

"Mm. I'm sure," Søren deadpanned.
She huffed, before turning her attention back to the shelves. Her hair was almost chestnut in the dark. And in that moment, a thought struck the Trainer. "...Hey. Whatever happened to your fire bird?"

Savannah froze and looked at him with fearful eyes. "Phee-Phee," she gasped, as though it was a recent development. "They…they didn't take him —I didn't see them take him…did you?"

"No…" Søren said slowly, trying to recall what had happened. Then another, *better*, thought stuck him. "You don't think…maybe they scared him so much that he turned to ash?"

His trainee gave him a warning look. "Wouldn't you just *love* that," she snapped. While she did attempt to snarl, he did not peg her as one to tear up easily: a thin film of silver shimmered at her lower eyelid.

Søren sighed and glanced elsewhere. "Maybe it's better this way," he suggested, "—that they never saw him and that he left. Gods *know* what the Boss would have done if he found out we were harbouring a Phoenix. Technically, they're only supposed to work for him."

Savannah rubbed her arm self-consciously. "…Maybe," she mumbled, and Søren frowned as a lone tear slid down the side of her face.

Her behaviour was beginning to get annoying. He had never understood the reasoning behind keeping that thing in the first place, and now that they had a chance of things going back to normal and not worrying about molten lava bird excrement, she was not seeing the bright side —and the *right* side.

Søren had established his distaste for her stubbornness well ahead of time, and he hoped she knew that her tears were in vain. No amount of guilt tripping would soften him up —not even if it had some sort of validity.

"This is how it is supposed to be," the Trainer whispered.
She looked up at him, and suddenly the tears were no more. She wiped them away fiercely with the back of the decorative detached shirt cuffs before glaring up at the older Reaper with hard, intense golden eyes. Unfazed, Søren raised an eyebrow, expecting her to say something.

"You're actually a jerk," she said, throwing down her feather duster. "You're such an insensitive, closed off jerk and a hypocritical *idiot* —and…and I just want to punch you in the face," she said through clenched teeth; her chest rising and falling with effort.

164

Søren folded his arms; mostly out of disappointment. She was really holding back. "Tell me something that I've never heard before."

"*Unbelievable.*"

"The word you're looking for is '*apathetic*'."

"No," she frowned and shook her head thoughtfully. "It's '*liar*'."

Søren paused at this, surprised for only a flicker of a moment. That was definitely not something he had heard before. He never lied —he always tried his best to accomplish what was within his capabilities, and never made empty promises. And when he promised something, he always included the words '*I promise*'. If he did not say them, it was because he knew the outcome was out of his control. So, it hurt when she called him a liar.

He glared right back at Savannah, anger welling up inside of him. The air settled, undisturbed. He was close enough to see the streaks of brown and amber in her irises, melting into the shades of yellow.

Søren did not like them. They sent shivers down his spine.

"I think that you *do* feel things," Savannah whispered, her face softening briefly. "And I'm not sure whether this started before, or after Melchior —but I think you're just afraid of what will happen if you feel again."

The Trainer tensed up, before feeling a wave of heat rising to the surface of his skin. He was uncomfortable at the mention of Melchior's name —as well as her question about feelings. As soon as those words left her mouth, his mind went into shut down mode and a reflex of blushing out of embarrassment activated, very much against his will.

Søren opened his mouth, but absolutely nothing came out. He wondered why he could not deny it; he had always done it in the past.

"...*No*," he eventually managed to articulate. "I —I'm not afraid."

His trainee's golden eyes narrowed and she took a step closer to him, making him back up further and bump into the books behind them.

She frowned, and her eyes moved slightly from side to side as though she were searching for something in his. "Are you...*blushing*?" she whispered, evidently just as surprised as he was about it.

"…Maybe," he murmured.

She withdrew and blinked uncertainly. He knew that she wanted to ask why.

Søren sighed, defeated. "…I got thrown off by what you said. I didn't want to really acknowledge what you were saying. Look, it doesn't mean what you said is true —I am *so* not afraid of feeling things," he insisted firmly. "It's just that…I got upset when you called me a liar."

"Technically, I didn't call you a liar directly," Savannah defended herself. "I used it as an adjective."

"Still," he hissed, balling his hands up into fists. "I am not a liar and I try everything within my power *not* to lie."

Søren then pursed his lips guiltily, remembering that he had done just that when she asked what had taken him so long after she had stormed out of the Boss' office. It had not been his fault —he would very much prefer to stay alive and not turn into three-headed dog food.

"…I see," was all with which she replied, stepping back.

Søren exhaled and moved away from the claustrophobic corner in which he was. He did not know what had just happened, but he did not ever want it to repeat. Hopefully Savannah would not make it a habit to confront him and make him question himself. He did not need that —not from her.

Suddenly the front doors burst open, making the Reapers jump and turn. A young woman with long purple hair stood there, out of breath and quite flustered. We stared at her expectantly, but she took a while to gather her thoughts, simply staring back at the pair.

"…Søren and Savannah, right?" she asked.

"Yes…?" Søren answered.

"There's been a…*situation* —"

An alarm then interrupted her, and the Reapers looked around in confusion. The woman snapped her fingers to regain their attention, before growing serious. She motioned for them to follow her, so Søren grabbed his crossbow before they walked towards the exit uncertainly.

"What's going on?" Savannah asked, putting her hands over her ears and

166

wincing at the piercing sound of the alarm.

"A pair of *Detached* have broken in and at the moment, we are unsure as to whether or not they have taken anything," she explained, picking up the pace, "We need to lock down and do a head count, so you need to come with me to the throne room."

"*Detached*?" Savannah repeated.

"They are Reapers who have run and broken away from the organisation illegally. They've basically dropped off of the grid," Søren filled in for her.

Savannah's eyes widened and a suspicious smile found her lips. "Wait, you can do that?"

Søren frowned and shot the idea down immediately. "Don't get any ideas," he warned. "*Detached* are outlawed, discriminated against —and if caught, will be reaped on the spot."

She gulped, thankfully appearing to be abandoning the possibility.

"That is correct," the purple haired woman continued, nearing the throne room entrance, where the bustle of noise was already at high volume. "*Detached* have no regard for anything and just like us, will not hesitate to reap if confronted."

Savannah shot her Trainer a nervous look as they then entered the crowded throne room and headed for the dais, where the Boss looked just about ready to tear his hair out. "What the bloody hell did you bring these two here for?" he hissed as his eyes landed on the Reapers.

"You asked for everyone, sir," the woman answered in an exasperated tone, before turning on her heel.

Death sighed heavily, before flippantly waving Savannah and Søren off. "Just…go stand in the back or something, and keep your mouths shut."

The two muttered short, sharp comebacks under their breaths as they sauntered off, elbowing past officials and panicked employees. Several snickers were sent their way as they then realised that Savannah was still dressed as a maid. The Reapers paid them no mind, though Savannah did go slightly pink and wrap her arms tighter around herself. "…This is stupid," she hissed as they stood with their backs against a pillar.

"Tell me about it," Søren drawled and folded his arms. He glanced around and then met a gaze of Tiger's Eye; hard and focused on him. He flinched as his gaze lowered, gliding over a large muscled frame and a Security uniform. The Trainer then quickly looked away, but it was too late since they had already made eye contact. The officer began to march over.

Savannah started as she noticed him too, and stood up straighter, sensing the tension. She looked at him in what seemed like disbelief.

"Well, what do we have here?" he smiled, towering over them. His skin was tropically tanned, and his muscles strained against his uniform.

"What's with the getup?" he snorted, nodding at Savannah.

She dithered, until she found her voice. "…Not by choice," she mumbled, glancing downwards and kicking one of her shoes with the other.

"The Boss thought it was funny," Søren explained.

"The Boss punished you personally?" remarked the domineering Reaper. "Harsh. Oh —you wouldn't happen to be the punishment kids, would you?" the officer then grinned, looking between them. Søren frowned at the word '*kids*' and unashamedly displayed his taken offence.

"What's it to you?" Savannah snapped, and her Trainer nudged her subtly, alarmed by her lack of respect.

"Well, I happen to be the Head of Security, so, I wouldn't use that tone if I were you," he warned her with a smile. Savannah shuffled around sheepishly, before murmuring an apology. Søren shifted his weight uneasily, still craning his neck up to look at him.

"Ignore her," the Trainer sighed, "it's been a long day."

"I can imagine," he said while sucking his teeth. "And I can agree, because you two weren't easy to find," he chuckled, pointing at the two comically.

Søren eyed him wearily and was not sure if he was trying to be funny or not, so he remained silent.

The officer was then about to continue, when he turned as though someone was calling him. The portable radio strapped to his side turned on, and filtered in the angry voice of the Boss, demanding that the so-called Head of Security had

168

better move it or else he would be fired.

Savannah and Søren snickered, as the Reaper hissed and muttered under his breath in Māori —before his icy glare shut them up.

"You two just remember old Norman, Head of Security —okay?" he told them as he backed away into the crowd, "He's got his eyes on you."

Once he had disappeared into the sea of people, they burst out laughing.

"...*Norman!*" Savannah spluttered.

"How scary. I thought it would be something more intimidating," Søren snorted, "like Lesley...Or Fred!"

They were in such hysterics, that they almost did not hear a megaphone screech from the front of the room.

"...Is this thing *on*?" the Boss' voice boomed around the marble room. Once he realised that he had nearly burst everyone's eardrums, he lowered the volume slightly and proceeded to inform his employees of the situation. "Everything is now under control. Both of the *Detached* have escaped, but only a few reaping lists were found missing. We have reason to believe they were taken by the vile creatures. But rest assured —we are currently working on investigating the matter further!"

Relieved cheers rang out and Søren and Savannah clapped along uncertainly, not really sure if they could really be included.

The alarm finally faded, and the sweet sound of silence became the background for chatter. Søren then frowned as he replayed the speech in his head, going over every detail. Savannah could tell that he was in deep thought because she let him think without saying anything —until he realised something, and he wagged his finger knowingly.

"What? What is it?" she asked.

"They took reaping lists," the Trainer said in a low voice, pulling her closer so they were further out of earshot. "Lists of souls that needed to be collected. What could they possibly want with that kind of information?"

Savannah narrowed her eyes and pouted, seemingly at a loss. She shrugged, which Søren should have expected, before he looked up in time to see Death making his way over to them.

"Well, you two can go back to the library now," he said with his hands in his pockets. "The situation is under control and you are no longer at risk of being harmed." He smiled, but it was clearly ingenuine.

Savannah returned her own fake smile. "Thanks for the concern."

"Don't mention it."

Søren rolled his eyes and tried to steer the conversation in a more constructive direction. "...Sir?" he started. "You said they might have taken some reaping lists? Well, that deserves some immediate attention. It hasn't occurred to you that maybe they have an agenda behind this attack?"

"This isn't the first time," a woman standing next to the Boss added. "We're missing the lists from yesterday and the day before."

Death sighed and visibly stiffened, unsure of where this discussion was heading. "These are not matters with which to concern yourself, *Trainer*."

"But he's making a point," Savannah backed Søren up. "Can you just bring your ego down a few notches and listen to someone else's ideas?"

Everyone winced and looked between the Reaper and the god, worried about what he would do to her for speaking to him in such a way. He clenched his jaw. His eyes glowed dangerously in a warning, and a snarl made its way up his throat. Yet, he said nothing.

Death gave both of the young Reapers a once-over, and turned sharply on his heel, prompting his posse to follow after him. And that was it.

Savannah and Søren shared a look of surprise, before they were left alone with the remaining stragglers.

"Why didn't he make a snappy comment back?" the redhead whispered.

"Probably because we had an audience," Søren figured, moving to walk to the exit and head back to the library. She followed suit, nodding in agreement. "He's got to keep a level-headed reputation."

A sly smile then spread across her face, and Søren could tell that she was conjuring up something mischievous. "...Maybe I should call him out in front of his employees more often," she voiced the thought.

"You're *awful*," he chortled, reaching out to open the doors to the library as they approached them. They continued laughing as they went inside, before a loud pair of gasps silenced them.

The Reapers paused and stood a little way away from two figures huddled in a corner by a lit candle; their faces smudged with mud and dirt, and their hair tangled with leaves and twigs. A young woman, and a teenage boy. They still wore their Reaper uniform, but their badges were ripped off, leaving the patches of skin that were underneath completely exposed.

All four immortals simply stared at each other, frozen.

Then Søren opened his mouth to speak, but only managed to inhale sharply when the woman pulled out a baseball bat spiked with obsidian coated nails.

The Trainer's crossbow dropped to the floor as he and Savannah raised their hands in surrender.

"Stay back," she warned in a hoarse voice, shakily holding the baseball bat out at them. Her intense pearl eyes glared at them from underneath straggly dark brown hair, but the fear in them was evident.

"I thought that you said no one comes in here," the boy hissed, eyeing the other Reapers wearily. His eyes were a clear shimmering crystal, in a light blue that was almost sea green at different angles.

"Shut it," the woman hissed back.

That was when the answer became apparent to Søren.

"...The *Detached*." he whispered. The woman's eyes widened.

CHAPTER 19

SØREN

WHEN BEING HELD at nailed-baseball-bat point, it is best not to make any sudden movements; so as to not agitate the wielder of said nailed baseball bat. Because if one does, no Fury can possibly conceive the amount of Hell that will break loose.

Thankfully for Søren and Savannah, the woman holding a nailed baseball bat did appear to be posing much of a threat. In fact, she looked miserably weak and her movements were rather disjointed, as though she did not want to be here any more than they wanted her here.

"…Put the bat down," Søren said calmly, lowering one of his hands to be in front of him, and the other to be across Savannah who had wisely taken a step backwards. "And no one gets hurt."

The woman snorted bitterly. "No one gets hurt?" she echoed, shaking her head and furrowing her eyebrows. "Are they still shoving the same lies down Reapers' throats after all this time?"

Søren then frowned as well, and slowly straightened up. "…Lies?" he repeated, concerned that he had heard her correctly.

"How long have you been a Reaper?" the boy then asked, which seemed to irk the woman more than anything.

Søren admittedly hesitated. "…Just under a couple of hundred years," he answered cautiously. "Why?"

The two *Detached* shared a look and appeared to wordlessly reach a consensus of some kind. The woman turned back to look at Søren, before lowering her baseball bat wearily. "…You wouldn't know, but a few decades before you Turned there was an outright war within the organisation." She then paused, making sure they were paying attention. "Kronos, the Titan of Time, threatened Hades and Death and the organisation because he couldn't believe they were recruiting Grim Reapers from eras as far back as Heracles. So, when the gods refused to fire some employees, Kronos took it into his own hands and stormed the Underworld before going for the mundane world. Hades couldn't stop him without the help of the other Olympian gods —but for some reason, they refused to help. They indirectly let half of the organisation get slaughtered —"

"Well, it was more like *disintegrated*," the boy interrupted. "Anyone he touched would break up into ash, and then blow away in the wind."

"Let me *finish*, idiot," the woman snapped, shooting him a glare. Søren smirked, wholly relating to their dynamic.

"The point is, Kronos nearly destroyed the whole organisation. Humans weren't reaped for months afterwards, and the Underworld was bursting at its seams. Eventually Hades and Death were forced to retreat to the Underworld to clean up the mess they had created, but the Reapers Organisation was never the same again. The bosses became hard, tyrannical and cold —vowing that it was the only way to make sure that nothing like that ever happened again."

There was an uncomfortable silence after she wrapped up the history lesson, but while everyone else was feeling either nostalgic or sympathetic, Søren was not so easily won over. He still had questions to ask, and tears were not going to exempt anyone from spilling information.

"Why did you come here?" he asked in a purposefully gentle voice. "And why would you steal reaping lists?"

"Reaping lists?" the woman narrowed her eyes. "What in the gods' names would I do with those?"

"Well, they were reported miss —" Savannah started talking, but Søren quickly clapped a hand over her mouth to shut her up. She glared at him and pulled his hand away, mumbling something under her breath along the lines of, "You could have just told me to be quiet."

Søren ignored it and turned back to the intruders.

"Answer my other question first."

The woman then seemed to flush out of embarrassment, and the boy averted his gaze and scratched the back of his neck. "…If we were to be completely honest, we only came in here for the shelter the library would provide," the woman started. "We've been hiding in an abandoned warehouse for the past year and it's been *hell*, so I thought since no one usually comes in here, we could hide in the many twists and turns."

Søren studied their faces and noticed several cuts and bruises, and their rat's-nest-hair certainly drove in their point. "…What are your names?"

The boy opened his mouth to answer but the woman took on a horrified expression at the request. "I'm Lewis!" he said a little excitedly. "And this is my older sister, Nadine."

"*Great*," Nadine hissed, glaring at him, "So much for secrecy. Now we'll definitely get turned in!"

Søren turned to Savannah and she returned his scheming look. He could tell by the mischievous smile of her face that she was thinking something similar to what he was thinking. He then turned back to Lewis and Nadine, who were engaged in a feeble slap fight.

"Maybe we could reach some kind of agreement," Søren suggested, causing the siblings to pause and show some interest. "You need to stay undetected, and I'd like to know a bit more about your…situation."

"In exchange for shelter, you can help us clean this giant and ancient forsaken dustbin," Savannah added. Søren looked at her sideways and glared, trying to be as stern as possible; silently daring her to say anything more and to see where it would get her.

"We will keep our mouths shut if you cooperate with answering my questions," he reiterated, before they could become confused by Savannah's request. But the redhead then gave a little cough.

174

She was not going to let it go. So, Søren compromised. "...And occasionally lend a hand to this lazy maid, here."

Savannah slapped his arm. "Hey. Who are you calling lazy? You're probably setting up an interrogation just to get out of the punishment."

"*What...?*" he scoffed timorously, as though that were not the case at all.

"Asshole," she clicked her tongue.

"Name call me again, I dare you," he hissed through his teeth.

Savannah opened her mouth to do just that but was interrupted by Nadine's loud coughing. The Reapers both turned to face her, glaring in annoyance.

"I can tell you two aren't really getting along right now, but I still need some kind of reassurance that you'll keep your word and won't turn us in," she said, sticking her nose in the air. Then she paused, causing Savannah and Søren to turn away from each other and grumble out apologies. "...What's in it for you guys anyway?" she asked, regaining the Trainer's attention.

"Why, that's easy," he scoffed, shrugging, "I ask questions and you answer them. I want to know more about what it's like to be a *Detached* and you two are just the ones to help me do it."

Søren smiled, pointing at them knowingly.

Nadine looked at her brother uncertainly. The Trainer then watched and waited as she slowly stood to her feet and walked over to him, coming up to just a few inches short, but being twice his age. She looked up at him sceptically, holding her bat to her side and making him slightly nervous.

From this distance, he could see the light outline of her irises, which made her pearl eyes only marginally less creepy. She lifted up her arm —her free one — and held out a grubby and chipping green fingernail-painted hand. Søren looked at it, before involuntarily leaning away.

"Well," she frowned and shifted her weight. "Do we have a deal or not?"

He was pleasantly surprised, and immediately reached out to return the gesture — before he flinched just before their skin could make contact and very tactfully hesitated, flexing his fingers. Savannah sighed next to him, but she could not understand. She was not the one who had to shake a possibly one-hundred-and-ninety-eight-year-old hand. Nadine decided for him and grabbed his hand, causing him to let out a yelp.

Savannah snickered, while Søren tried not to squirm as Nadine's hand shook his in an amused fashion.

"Cool," she chuckled, mercifully withdrawing.

Søren gave her a grimace as he whimpered softly and mourned the violation of sanitation of his right hand but covered it up with a cough; before turning to his trainee, who abruptly shut up at the sight of his hardened expression.

He then shivered, feeling a tingle run down his spine and a sick feeling settle in his stomach region. "…Back to work," he sighed, tilting his head to the side and smiling slightly to show just a little compassion. "We're not allowed to leave until the whole place is spotless, remember?"

"Really?" Lewis asked, standing up and dusting his trousers off onto the floor —to Søren's absolute irritation. "How come?"

"It's a long, boring story," he said before Savannah had the chance to accidently answer the question and reveal too much.

"Oh, we've got an eternity," Nadine snorted, not buying his excuse for a second. "Because that's how long you'll be in here."

Søren paused before refusing again, and letting her words sink in. It seemed to suddenly dawn on him and his trainee that this punishment was doomed from the start, and…*might* just be an excuse for the Boss keeping his half-sister out of the way. The Trainer frowned at that thought, but honestly it did not surprise him as much as it could have.

"I killed my ex-boyfriend," Savannah suddenly blurted out.

Søren looked at her in disbelief, but she only offered a shrug in response. Maybe now she wanted everyone to know.

"Wow, that's pretty hardcore," Nadine turned to her and smirked in admiration. "…Wait, did you kill him before or after you Turned?" she then asked in a serious tone, her dark eyebrows furrowing.

Savannah dithered, allowing Søren to fold his arms and up the ante on her slip up; now thoroughly enjoying himself.

"…After," the redhead mumbled.

Lewis and Nadine's eyes widened in unison and they gasped. Søren shook his head in disappointment. "You could have kept your mouth shut."

"I couldn't help it," Savannah whined. "They'd find out sooner or later if they're going to be associated with us."

"Nobody said we were going to be associated," Nadine's and Søren's voices overlapped as they snapped the same sentence. They shared a wary look, but left it there. The Trainer noticed the similarities between them, but it was not wise to become friendly with an outlaw —or her brother.

It could spell disaster.

"…But why the maid outfit?" Lewis went on. "You kind of look like our old maid, Paulina."

Nadine face palmed and looked on disapprovingly. "Trust you to focus on the least important detail, *Lew*."

"It wasn't my choice," Savannah grumbled in response to Lewis. "You can thank the Boss' obvious kinks for this."

She gestured downwards at herself.

Nadine snorted before laughing outright, causing everyone to stare. "…What?" she asked, still chortling. "It's funny. He never struck me as a man who had that type of kink, you know. By the way, it doesn't exactly look like you put up much of a fight."

"I *did* protest —but I also value my life, so…" Savannah murmured, turning her head away.

Growing tired of the tomfoolery, Søren clapped his hands and informed everyone of what they would be doing for the rest of the day. Nadine was going to sit down and talk to him, while Lewis and Savannah cracked on with book dusting and organising duty.

"This list is so bloody long and complicated," Savannah complained, unrolling the scroll from which she was referencing. "There's no way we can manage to organise this entire place."

"Not with that attitude, you won't," Søren pointed out. Then he pushed them

177

towards the shelves. "Now let the grown-ups talk."

Both teenagers shot him highly offended glares but did not put up a fight. Nadine chuffed in amusement.

"I'm impressed," she said, nodding at Lewis vigorously dusting three books, "—I can never get him to do as I say."

✠

"So," Søren started, glancing over the notes he had made thus far; because of his prudency, he always carried a pencil with him. "You came from a noble home and died in an ambush during a storm? Do you know specifically what happened to your parents. Were they perhaps targeted?"

Nadine averted her gaze and looked crestfallen, which then worried Søren that maybe he was onto something, and she was not going to feel comfortable enough to share it. "…They were killed," she then mumbled, sighing quietly. "In the ambush. The men who ambushed us told us who they were before they killed us. They…they had worked for my parents' business and trade partner. Apparently, he had wanted out, but my father wouldn't let him. So…" she struggled at the end and hung her head.

"So, he had them killed?" Søren finished, in a tactful and soft voice. She paused, and then nodded slowly. She did not go on, but there was no need for her to, either. "Let's talk about the war instead," he suggested. "You know, what happened before and afterwards?"

She noticeably perked up before looking back at him with those ghostly white eyes. "…Well, it was just a month after Lewis and I had Turned and come off our training. We were both around thirty reaped souls —not too bad for a couple of newbies, right?" she laughed softly, though the strain in her voice was evident. "…Anyway, after a week or so everyone received a warning to stop reaping until further notice. So, we stayed put for a couple of days; just lounging around and doing nothing. It was super boring, and Lewis wouldn't stop playing with a paddle ball —"

"—Paddle ball?" Søren interrupted, quirking an eyebrow.

Nadine smirked, understanding his amusement. "Yeah. You don't know how annoying it is hearing the sound of a rubber ball smacking against a wooden paddle for twenty-four hours straight."

"I can imagine though," he chuckled, glancing at Savannah and hoping she would never discover the sin that are paddle balls.

She then sneezed loudly at that precise moment a few feet away from them, making him chuckle.

"...Hey, Lover Boy," Nadine said, suddenly snapping her fingers in Søren's face, "Eyes over here."

It took him a few seconds to realise what she had called him, after which he stared at her blankly. She raised an eyebrow quizzically, inviting him to respond. He opened his mouth, but nothing came out.

"What, does being in love make you *speechless* too?" she quipped.

This time something did come out of Søren's mouth. Short, sharp words that made Nadine raise both eyebrows in surprise.

"Okay, okay," she murmured, folding her arms. "You could have just said that you weren't a thing —and I was just messing with you, lighten up."

Søren grumbled and got back to his list, wanting nothing more than to resume their previous conversation.

CHAPTER 20

SØREN

HE WAS RATHER surprised that after what seemed like fifteen minutes of interview, Nadine suddenly turned the tables and proceeded to ask Søren a couple of questions. He had had the upper hand all of that time, and now she was catching him off guard. He froze, his pencil poised mid-air, but he knew that he could not show her any signs of instability.

"How did *you* die?" she had inquired, narrowing her eyes. "And how come you've never heard of the war? It didn't happen long before you turned, so I'd think you would have at least picked it up in gossip or something," she continued vaguely, and her gaze shifted away from his.

Søren gripped his pencil tighter and gulped, before flexing his fingers. He was not prepared to answer this kind of question. It was personal, and he had only told Savannah because he thought that telling her would bring some kind of comfort or understanding. It *had* made her stop moping, but it was not supposed to open up further discussion. Sharing that with Nadine —who was a total stranger and whom Søren did not trust in the slightest —would be like posting a super-secret journal on the internet.

Mortifying.

He blinked rapidly, as a series of images then flashed across his mind. He still occasionally had those—not every time someone mentioned his death, but it happened often enough. They reminded him that he could not forget —that he was not *allowed* to forget. Memories of what happened that afternoon whirred like a film reel. They used to unnerve him, but now they were a constant reminder of how he was suddenly plucked from his life and forced to take on a job that would then cause his sensory and emotional systems to shut down.

The images changed faster, but the people in them moved in a slow and blurry motion, and only *her* laugh echoed in the background.

Grass. The garden. A white tulle dress. Tumbling down hills. Long, dark auburn hair, with strands tangled between my pale fingers. A kiss.

It was a puzzle of different scenes inside of his head, and if anyone else could have seen it they would not think that they were very connected. A chill then travelled down Søren's spine and the scenes shifted, growing darker and more ominous. A shadowy figure moved along in every room he saw, omnipresent and quiet. He had learned that this was the Reaper who was supposed to reap his soul that day. It never made the situation any more reassuring. The images then whirred again, more blurred and disjointed.

A garter belt. Tights. Boots. A white tulle dress, strewn across the floor. A red lipstick smile. Dark, and almost black brown eyes. Long, dark auburn hair, with strands tangled between my pale fingers. A kiss.

And another. And another…

Søren closed his eyes, letting out a strangled sound before he felt himself returning to the present, and the images turned fuzzy and distant, leaving his mind to rationalise.

I could have saved them both.

I should have been more alert.

She should not have distracted me.

Maybe I would have lived, and grown up to —

He shook his head, stumbling out of the fog. Everything returned to normal, and he opened his eyes to find Savannah, Lewis and Nadine staring at him.

He coughed and felt a wave of heat rise to the surface of his skin.

How would he explain what had just happened?

Søren opened his mouth, but still nothing would make its way up his throat, which only made him feel even more flustered.

"Are you okay?" Savannah asked gently. "You kind of froze up and…" she did not finish, and looked to Lewis and Nadine for help.

"Was it something that I said?" Nadine asked worriedly.

Yes, he wanted to scream.

But Søren still could not voice it, so he shook his head slowly instead. Everyone then went back uncertainly to what they had been doing, and he could tell that he had rendered the atmosphere stiff. He turned to face Nadine again, who flinched slightly at the movement.

"I suppose I hadn't heard about the war because the Boss wanted to keep things under wraps," the Trainer finally said; completely ignoring the first question. "I wouldn't blame him. Reapers would probably have quit if they were informed of what that Titan…*Kronos*, did."

If she noticed that he ignored half of her inquiry, she did not show it. "I guess…" she murmured, her eyes disappearing into slits.

"Hey guys," Lewis then drew their attention towards the shelves, already slumping over with exhaustion, "Can we swap now?"

"No," Nadine and Søren answered in eerie unison.

"…You're supposed to keep going until nightfall," Søren continued.

"Then we swap?" Savannah grumbled.

"*Then* we swap," Søren confirmed.

After that had been cleared up, he turned back to Nadine and sighed. He felt drained after the flashback, and he was stiff from sitting in the same position with his legs crossed. He then uncrossed them and sat up lengthwise.

He was okay with the fact that no one wanted to bring it up, so he enjoyed the uneasiness to that extent.

"…How long have you been training her?" Nadine asked, nodding in Savannah's direction.

"Almost two weeks now, which is already too long," Søren huffed. "Sometimes I wish she came with a return receipt."

Nadine then laughed at that, and he enjoyed the melodious sound, even if it was a little forced. "...Hey," she then sighed, stretching out her arms. "You want to have a quick lesson on the Greek gods? It'll take our minds off of...things," she suggested tactfully.

Søren thought about it. He only knew basic Greek mythology. Growing up in a strict Catholic estate did not allow for much depth into the study of Greek culture. But he supposed that since his boss was in fact a god himself, he had to start somewhere. "Yeah. Sure, why not."

✠

After two strenuous hours of trying to understand the gods' family tree and their blatant and unapologetic incest and infidelity —namely Zeus, Poseidon and Ares being a few of the guilty parties —it was finally around the time of nightfall. Lewis and Savannah did not really want to interview each other, so they lay sprawled on the floor without exchanging a word.

"Hey Søren," Savannah then said sometime later, before he could finish dusting another book. He turned in surprise before she took his hand and dragged him around a corner so he assumed they could be out of earshot.

"What?" he said, unsure of what she wanted.
She looked down and folded her arms, hesitating. "I just...wanted to check up on you. I don't believe that Nadine had nothing to do with it. I figured that maybe her question about how you died might have thrown you off and kind of...put you into a state of shock," she whispered, looking upwards and meeting his silver gaze, "...or something."

Søren clenched the feather duster tighter in his fist and sighed heavily, cursing himself because he really should have seen this coming considering Savannah's naturally caring nature. He could not tell her the whole truth.

He could not really lie either. So, he settled for halfway, hoping that she would then drop the subject. "I just had some...flashbacks," he said quietly.
"Flashbacks?" she repeated, cocking an eyebrow.

"Mm hm..." he hummed, twirling the feather duster between his fingers.

183

She narrowed her golden eyes at his, and then shifted her weight to the left. "Was it what I think it was about?"

"What do you think it was about?" Søren retorted, raising his own eyebrow. She paused, before looking like she was deliberating over telling him whatever her guess might be. And that made him grow suspicious, because depending on why she was hesitant to tell him, it was not sounding like an idea to which he was going to be open.

"…That *girl*," she finally hissed, being super vague.

"Which *girl*?" he mimicked her tone.

"You know —your computer," she elaborated, "You always seem so protective over that name and I figured it might have something to…do with…" She trailed off as she noticed the angered expression on his face. In that moment, Søren hated her mostly because despite her assumptions based on little evidence, she actually was not wrong.

In fact, she was pretty on the mark. Rage pulsed through his veins and shallow breathing ensued. He hated that she simply had good intentions. He hated that he could not let her in. So, he turned around to walk away before his fist had the chance to prevent her from ever wanting to talk again.

"Hey, wait," she whined, grabbing hold of his arm and stalling him in his tracks. A growl grumbled in his chest as he tried to tug himself free. Somehow, though, she was stronger than him and managed to keep him where he was. "…I didn't mean to hit a nerve. I just figured you wanted me to be more specific," she murmured. She had been *too* specific.

Søren frowned and turned back to face her anxious face, feeling betrayed. "…I never asked for you to be specific," he said through his teeth.

Savannah nodded understandingly, and then she did something completely unexpected. She darted forward, and hugged him fiercely, burying her head in his chest. Søren gasped and stumbled backwards, causing them to crash into the shelves. He was slumped against the hard cover books limply, with Savannah's arms still wrapped around his waist. He tensed, suddenly overwhelmed with the scent of lavender and pine. He felt unsure of how to react —it had been the longest time since someone had hugged him. He then flinched, trying to send a message. The redhead did not move, and he wished that she would, because her hair was scratching his exposed skin and she was way too close; her body radiating warmth where it came in contact with his. "…I'm sorry," she whispered.

He huffed before trying something different and wriggling in her grip. "You're never going to tell me, are you? Though, I would completely understand. But sometimes it's good to talk about the things that are bothering you," she went on, lifting her head.

Her gaze met his and she gave him a pitiful look. His hard glare returned it, and he gently pushed her away from him, creating some space between them. Then Søren thought her question over.

Would he ever tell her? He certainly did not want to any time in the near future. But he looked into her shining eyes and pleading face and felt two things. Guilt, and reluctant yielding.

He softened, knowing that the small detail he would forever avoid could not stop him from telling her one day. He nudged her completely away and her arms finally dropped to her sides, freeing him.

"…I'll tell you some day," Søren whispered. "When I'm ready."
And then she nodded slowly, and a smile found her lips, letting him know that she was just fine with that.

CHAPTER 2I

THANATOS

"THEY WERE NOT the ones who took the reaping lists, were they?" Death sighed, re-watching the security camera footage.

Nina sighed next to him as the technical assistant pressed rewind again. Thanatos glanced at her out of the corner of his eye and watched her frowning at the footage. Nina looked as though she had a pretty good suspicion of who exactly took them, if they simply had not been misplaced. Thanatos looked back at the screens, narrowing his eyes at the two figures onscreen. One was a boy who looked to be in his teens, and the other was a young woman. They were *Detached* —evident in how they walked and looked around as though they were not supposed to be there; as if they were running from something.

"And where are they now?" Death then growled, realising that he never checked up on their whereabouts after the throne room fiasco.

"The footage doesn't show," answered the technical assistant. "It's as if they just...disappeared," she continued ominously, pointing on screen as the two *Detached* rounded a corner that led to a numerous number of rooms and hallways. Thanatos frowned and stroked his stubbled chin. He did not recall not having anywhere in Headquarters where cameras were not operating.

"*Impossible*," he then snapped. "They must still be around. Getting in and out of Purgatory is not that easy."

"They could have used a direct portal," Nina suggested, tapping her clipboard with a pencil.

"Only gods can make those," Death pouted, "How would two low-life *Detached* be able to use one?"

Nina suddenly gasped and her eyes widened with fear. "What if...they were acting on behalf of a god?"

"What god would want *reaping lists*?" Thanatos questioned.

"What about Hades?" Nina suggested.

"He wouldn't have any use for them," he cleared up. "Not his department. Besides," he continued irritably, "He would ask first, before ending up taking the thing anyway."

Nina chuckled softly, stifling her clear amusement with her hand.

The technical assistant then leaned closer to the monitor and rewound the footage again. "...What if it isn't a god?" she whispered.

Nina and Thanatos shared a look.

Death frowned deeply and folded his arms, not liking where this was going. If it was not a god, the next high celestial being was a Titan. But most of the Titans were in Tartarus, banished to spend a torturous eternity there since they could not be killed. The remaining free preferred not to meddle with the affairs of the mundane world.

"...You're not suggesting that a Titan is playing puppeteer, are you?" Nina concluded, raising an eyebrow.

She sounded surprised and perplexed, but Thanatos averted his gaze in embarrassment. It would not exactly be the first time a Titan had targeted the Reapers Organisation. His mind went straight for Kronos, even though he knew the Titan was not going to break out so soon.

'*The time for Reapers will end.*
And I will be the one to end them.
You think that you have won?
You are only postponing the inevitable.
Only I know how this all ends...'

187

Death flinched slightly at the recalling of Kronos' words as he and Hades were finishing him off. It sent shivers down his spine, and the heat of Purgatory suddenly grew ice cold, freezing the golden blood in his veins.

"There is no way…" the god murmured, more to himself than to anyone else. His secretary glanced at him suspiciously, but she did not get a chance to say anything, because he moved away to another computer and signed into the camera system.

"Sir? What are you doing?" Nina asked.

Thanatos accounted for all of the connected camera networks before answering her. "You wouldn't know. None of you would," he addressed the rest of the employees, "—but in 1786 the Titan Kronos confronted the organisation about having employees from the BC era."

Nina raised her eyebrows and blinked.

"He said we were messing too much with the stretch of time, and overly thinning out the Underworld. So…he took all of those souls up to the 1500s," Death added, curling his hands into fists. It still angered him. It was not as though they had been completely changing the space time continuum or some other travesty. "The organisation was struggling to get back onto its feet up until the mid 70s. I had to help out with categorising souls for a whole five years because the Underworld suddenly had this huge influx."

The technical assistants pretended that they were not paying attention and kept typing away and looking through and analysing more camera footage. Nina, however, was glowering at her superior.

"…You mean to tell me, that the Titan of Time told you to let some employees go and you *refused*?"

Death offered a sheepish grin. "Well, what was I *supposed* to do? We needed all the Reapers we could get at the time."

"Did the Olympians help you defy his logical accusation?" she snapped, folding her arms.

"No," he grumbled, remembering the very stern scolding of Zeus and the agreement of Hera.

Nina suddenly slapped his arm, sharp and quick. "Thanatos, how could you do that? You disrespected him and purposely went against his orders. And look what happened! You should take it as a warning and make sure that it doesn't happen again."

"No, obviously," Thanatos scoffed, nursing his arm where she had slapped him. "What do you think I've been doing all this time?"

"…Oh my gods," Nina then breathed. "Are you…are you thinking that he's come back again?"

"Maybe," the god murmured. He did not want to jump to conclusions, but Kronos was the only one who had a vendetta against the organisation —against the gods of the dead. Death could not think of anything wrong they had done recently enough to anger the Titan, but maybe there was something Kronos knew that they did not.

"Sir," a technical assistant said, motioning for Thanatos to come over to his computer. "There are no cameras in the library as well as the corridors leading in that south east direction."

Death frowned. "…We did put cameras there, didn't we?" he murmured, glancing at Nina. She looked away and shrugged, obviously trying to hide what had been her own part in the carelessness.

He sighed and looked back at the technical assistant.

"You think they could be in there?" the employee asked.

"Have a team do a sweep," Thanatos confirmed, nodding his head. Then something clicked, and he remembered something. "Hold on. Aren't those two idiots in there doing their punishment?"

Nina nodded. "Yes, but don't call them idiots, sir."

"Whatever," he grumbled. "…Though, would they not have sang like canaries if the *Detached* were in the library with them?" he thought out loud, stroking his chin. "I doubt a crossbow would prove very defensive."

"You know," Nina started, lowering her clipboard, "It's possible that if they saw the *Detached* that they would keep quiet and keep them hidden. Either just to

189

spite you or they don't want to turn them in just yet."

And for what purpose would they withhold that kind of information?

The god of death turned to face her and give her a look of outrage. He could feel the anger building up and fuelling the glow in his eyes, before he ground his teeth together in an effort to retain some self-control.

"Do you really think they would be that *stupid*?" Death spat.

Nina dithered, unsure of how to respond. "You know you're not the most…approachable person, Thanatos, sir."

He growled, feeling the rumble in his chest. He clicked his tongue and turned away slightly so as to distance himself as he evaluated the situation. Søren would never dare to hide something like this from him, would he? The Trainer held Death in too high esteem and seemed far too afraid of him to pull something like this off. He also refused to believe that Savannah could possibly sway Søren's judgement as well, but then again, with that girl one could never tell. Thanatos tapped his foot in frustration, clenching his fists as the heat of the glow in his eyes intensified.

"…They are as good as dead," he said through his teeth. "If those two are harbouring Detached, I am going to make them wish I had reaped their souls when I was supposed to."

"*Sir —*" Nina started.

"No, Nina," he cut her off and adjusted his cuff links. "What possible excuse could they have?"

✠

The four Grim Reapers froze like deer in headlights as Thanatos pulled apart the doors; his eyes ablaze and the crave for death coursing through his veins.

They could see the fire in his eyes. He saw it in the way they cowered in his presence. Death could feel Nina's hand on his shoulder, restraining him. But it would not stop him. Not in this state.

He could not believe it.

The Reapers really had withheld information. They had really thought that Thanatos would not find out that the *Detached* were still lurking within the walls of his castle, and they thought they would get away with it.

Savannah dropped her feather duster and gasped but shuffled to stand in front of the *Detached* boy with scruffy toffee-brown hair. In each of his hands, were nunchucks with curved black blades on each end.

"How the hell did he find us?" the young woman *Detached* barely whispered, gripping a baseball bat riddled with nails in her hand tightly. "Did you snitch?" she hissed at Søren.

"*No*, we didn't —I…I swear have no idea how he found…" Søren insisted, shaking his head.

The young woman clicked her tongue and moved towards the *Detached* boy, before shoving Savannah out of the way and into Søren's side. "I can't *believe* we trusted you," she hissed.

Søren moved towards her. "Nadine —"

"Don't you dare move any further," Thanatos warned, stepping forward. He looked at each of them, growing closer and closer to losing it. "…I cannot believe that you would do this. I cannot believe that you would endanger every employee who works here by hiding these…these *vermin*!" he spat, violently shaking as he raised his voice.

"They are not vermin!" Søren snapped back. "And they're not a danger to anyone either. You don't know their story. Who the bloody hell do you think you are to accuse them of such motives?"

Death let Søren's words carry on in the silence that followed. This only let the rage fester, and the desire to see him dead only grew. Thanatos had no words left. He could not find anything to say.

Words would not suffice or aid to get his point across. He shook his head, as the noise of reality began to fade into the background.

"…Sir?" Nina's voice said from far away.

He pushed her aside.

She fell, sliding onto her side on the polished floor.

But he did not care.

He looked back at the Reapers and snapped his fingers. In a plume of smoke, his diamond encrusted scythe appeared in his hand, heavy and cold to the touch. His hand burned against it, creating steam. Savannah's eyes narrowed at the sight, before she looked up in horror.

"Stop!" she screamed, darting to stand in front of the others.

Death growled and told her that she could not possibly do anything to stop him. He raised his scythe and its handle end dragged against the floor, causing a screeching sound. Everyone winced, but when Savannah opened her eyes, they were a brighter gold. A glowing gold.

And it unnerved Death.

"...*Shit*," he growled, stumbling backwards. Savannah suddenly took in a sharp breath, before she settled on his gaze.

"Don't do this," she said, holding up her hands.

Thanatos hesitated, and the heat of his anger began to cool. He shook his head, confused and growing frustrated.

"Put the scythe down. Let us explain," his half-sister urged, lowering her hands a little. Thanatos' hand jerked and he raised the scythe higher, making everyone but Savannah flinch.

"*Don't*," she said a little louder, raising her hands again.

"What made you think you could *do* this?" Death said in a low growl, letting the scythe drop so the back end hit the floor. "Tell me why I shouldn't reap all of you *right now*!"

He then mustered more anger induced strength and swung his scythe upwards, slicing through the air.

Savannah screamed, before he was suddenly crushed underneath a force that slammed him backwards into the wall. He hit the back of his head, hard, and his scythe slid across polished marble away from him.

He groaned and reached up to his head.

There was a dull ache, and he could feel a sharp sting in his sinuses. Thanatos gasped and sat up before realising that he had to hold the bridge of his nose.

Savannah jumped and stared at her hands which she was flipping over and back again. Death squinted, wondering why she was doing that, before seeing what appeared to be dying light in her palms.

She looked up, and the glow in her eyes faded.

"Oh my gods," Nina whispered, appearing at Thanatos' side and hooking an arm through his own to help him up. "What was *that*?"

CHAPTER 22

SØREN

SØREN FROWNED AT Savannah, who glanced back at him with a terror that suggested that she was afraid of her own hands.

He too was baffled, but tried to make sense of what had just happened.

Savannah had screamed, raised her hands, and from her palms had shot beams of dazzling light. The light had hit the Boss and knocked him backwards and into the wall, leaving an impression. A wave of heat that had dissipated after the flash of light faded almost as soon as it had burst to life, and had likely left Savannah's hands feeling fried.

Søren, Nadine and Lewis then shared unnerved looks before they hesitantly lowered their weapons.

Søren stepped forward and put a reassuring hand on Savannah's shoulder, but he only succeeded in making her flinch. He raised an eyebrow as she looked mortified, and she slowly shook her head. She then offered him an apologetic look before glancing back at the Boss, who was getting up from the floor with the help of the purple haired woman from before.

"I'm *fine*, Nina," Death hissed in embarrassment, irritably brushing her off. He then turned to glare at Savannah.

"It just…*happened*," the redheaded Reaper squeaked, tensing up and holding her hands to her chest. "I mean…I don't know *what* exactly, happened…but…" she struggled, her face scrunching up in desperation to express herself despite her frustration.

"Did you just…use light projection on *me*?" the Boss tripped over his words, sounding as though he were unable to wrap his head around whatever he had just mentioned.

"Light projection?" Savannah whispered in a trembling voice, her eyebrows knitting into a frown. "What…what's that?"

She glanced back at the other Reapers in hopes of an answer.

They looked at each other and shrugged. None of them knew what that was —not even Søren. Savannah evidently spoke for all of them.

The Boss sighed heavily as he shook his head, before he winced and held the bridge of his nose again. "We…cannot have this conversation here," he hissed. Then he turned to leave. No one moved.

"Hello? Am I talking to myself? Follow me," the god ordered, prompting his assistant to scuttle after him.

Søren looked at Nadine and she shook her head, silently telling him that there was no way Death meant that they should follow him too.

"What about our new friends?" Savannah murmured.

Søren blinked; having been unaware of that title she had now given them.

The Boss skidded to a halt at the doors. "Your. New. *What*," he growled, looking back at them out of the corner of his eye. He did not say it as though he expected an answer. He said it in disbelief, and understandable shock.

"Need I remind you that those are *Detached*, and it is of no consequence to me nor to the system if they are '*reformed*' or not. They are still outlawed." Then he turned to the purple haired woman. "Nina —watch," he barked.

Savannah's jaw set and she huffed but marched begrudgingly towards the doors. She turned and shot Søren a look, indicating that he should follow suit. He scrambled to action and mouthed a quick apology to Nadine, but all she did was sneer and scoff, "*Typical*."

The Trainer fought the feeling of guilt as they wandered down the halls towards the Boss' office.

He was so wrapped up in his own thoughts that it took him a few seconds to notice that Savannah's maid attire had melted away and her reaping clothes had rematerialised onto her as they were walking.

The Reaper herself poked at her arms to check if it was real, before starting with excitement.

"Wait," Søren said, interrupting her relief, "Wasn't this only supposed to happen when we finished the punishment?"

The Boss breathed a deep sigh and exhaled wearily as he opened the doors to the office. "Initially, yes," he drawled, "but since that punishment is going to take you forever, I thought it would be better to address this situation like this," he elaborated, before sitting down right on top of the desk. He rested his arms on his legs and gestured for the two Grim Reapers to take a seat. Søren looked at Savannah and there was the same confusion in her expression that was in his.

"But there aren't any —" Savannah started, but when they turned around again two leather armchairs appeared in front of the desk. "—*seats*," she finished, before shrugging and plopping down in the one closest to her.

Søren sunk down in the other one and sighed, wondering what exactly the Boss was planning to say.

"I did not want to have this conversation until it was absolutely necessary, but now that..." he paused and pointed at Savannah's hands uncertainly, "*that* has happened, I no longer have much of a choice."

Savannah frowned and Søren cast his gaze to the wall, figuring that he partially knew what Death was talking about.

He saw Savannah look at him out of the corner of his eye and he subtly shrank back, before coughing uncomfortably. "...Shit," he then muttered under his breath as her stare turned into a glare. He wanted to kick himself for being so conspicuous, but it was too late.

"Don't tell me," she said, tensing up and hissing in the armchair like a cat, "...You *know* something, don't you?"

Søren scratched the back of his neck and glanced at the Boss, hoping he would save him from having to say anything. Death looked back at him indifferently and shrugged. Savannah started tapping her foot impatiently, gradually getting faster, like she was running on a timer.

"He made me keep quiet," Søren suddenly blurted out, pointing at the Boss without an ounce of fear.

Death did not even turn one hair at the Reaper's betrayal, before he cleared his throat. "He is not actually wrong," he sighed, regaining Savannah's attention, "Yes, I did ask him —"

"—*Threaten*," Søren coughed into his fist.

The god shot the Trainer a look, but he just shrugged innocently.

"Order," Death settled for, "...him not to breathe a word to you until I wanted to tell you. And where do I start? Okay. My name is Thanatos. I am the Greek god of death. The Grim Reaper, if you will. The-Guy-With-The-Scythe —I don't know. Whatever. I do not care," he admitted. "...I am the one who started the Reapers Organisation, and it runs independently of but harmoniously with the system in the Underworld."

"Oh...kay?" Savannah muttered, raising an eyebrow.

Søren was genuinely surprised, because he had not thought that she would be so uncaring. Was she so used to hearing things such as this that the revelation now went over her head?

The Boss seemed as surprised by her reaction as the Trainer was, and he shifted slightly so he could cross one leg over the other. "Well," he said in a more amused tone, "that '*okay*' was rather unexpected."

He waved his hand and summoned another glass of wine, before taking a long, awkward silence inducing sip. "Ah," he breathed, as though it had been refreshing, and set the glass down. "Let's get right to the point then," he beamed. "You are a half-blood god. One of your parents, is not...well, human. They are an immortal Greek deity."

Silence then hung over the room like a thick blanket.

After dropping that bombshell, Søren would expect Savannah to at least gasp in disbelief. But as usual, she managed to pull a hit or miss on his expectations. He glanced to the side at her. She paused, before tapping her fingers rhythmically on the arm of her chair. She ground her teeth together and inhaled sharply, but she did not articulate any form of verbal response.

"I would expect that this is a very sudden and shocking revelation," Søren eventually spoke up, causing Savannah's gaze to flicker momentarily in his direction. "That's why she's so...speechless?" he guessed.

"I am perfectly capable of speaking," Savannah then said in a calm and even voice. "I just...I'm not sure about *what* I should say."

"Anything," the Boss retorted.

"...Anything," she repeated, quirking an eyebrow.

The Trainer looked between her and the Boss, before scoffing in what might have been approval. "Smartass," he smirked.

"That is certainly one word for it," the Boss snarled. "Now. Enough tomfoolery. Savannah, you may be a half-and-halfer, but that also makes you what is called '*game*' or, '*sport*'."

"As in...hunting?" Søren asked.

"Exactly," the Boss clarified. "Some of the more barbaric gods would love nothing more than to hunt you down and collect your blood for display as though it were a trophy."

"Excuse me?" Savannah spluttered, doing a double take. "What's so special about my blood?"

"It *is* silver, is it not?" the Boss frowned, picking his wine glass up again. "All half-bloods have silver blood, as far as I have heard."

Søren looked at Savannah to verify. She avoided his gaze and rubbed up and down her arm nervously. "Have you...*seen* any half-bloods with silver blood?" she whispered, mumbling slightly towards the end.

Søren frowned and looked at her properly, curious as to why she seemed so on edge about this. Did she have silver blood or not?

He silently asked her by giving her an expectant look, but she glanced away all too aware of the intention.

"I will admit that I have never seen silver blood, nor have I seen of any half-bloods with my own eyes. But I have heard stories," the Boss said, taking another long sip of wine. "...From the older gods."

Savannah still twisted her mouth in a shape, reluctant to engage.

"Well, why don't we just slit your finger and see what comes out?" the Boss suddenly suggested.

Søren started, and Savannah jumped in her seat.
She cringed and looked like she wanted to protest, but the Boss started laughing before she could get out one word.

"I'm joking!" he assured between chuckles. The Reapers hesitated, unsure of what to take seriously. "I am not morbid," Death scoffed, and Søren scoffed too. Said the man with decorative skulls in his office —of which their origins are still inconclusive, he thought.

"And, who am I to judge you whether or not you have actually ever seen your own blood before?" the Boss continued.

Savannah shrank in the chair, as though she were trying to make herself smaller. Søren gave her a stern look and she dithered under his gaze, biting her lip. He figured that she had in fact seen her own blood before —at the car crash. But as to why she was keeping quiet, was still a puzzle to him.

"So…I'm a descendant of the gods?" Savannah murmured uncertainly, as if it was now beginning to sink in. "Which one?"

A sudden cloud then came over the Boss' face and he scowled deeply. He did not answer straight away. The muscles in his neck flexed so his veins were visible, before his grip on his wine glass tightened and it suddenly shattered, sending glass shards in every direction. But the glass did not penetrate anything —it melted into a white mist and trickled to the floor where it then disappeared. Savannah and Søren flinched, before shifting uncomfortably in their chairs.

"…*That*, I cannot tell you," the Boss said in a low, hard voice. "The consequences would be…undesirable."

Savannah dared to roll her eyes. "What's that supposed to mean?"

"You cannot know who your godly parent is, that's what!" he then thundered, and the room seemed to tremble along with the echo of his words. Savannah pursed her lips and shrank back, and something in Søren did not like her easy defeat. He looked back at the Boss, and discreetly gestured for him to tell her about their relationship. Death seemed to receive the message, because he then looked very unnerved. He poked a finger into the collar of his shirt and attempted to loosen it, to relieve the strain on his neck. Søren glared at him.

Savannah deserved to know.

"...My father," Savannah spoke up, distracting the two from their silent confrontation. "He's the godly parent. He's the one who left my mother —it was because of his duties, wasn't it? Or that she didn't want me growing up with a god for a father..." she gathered, lowering her gaze.

Søren could hear it in her voice. A shiny layer of tears shone along the bottom of her eyes and he froze in anticipation. "So, I can't have a father because it's constantly half-blood season?" she snorted, looking up again.

"...*Well* —" the Boss started.

"And as for your previous question," she cut him off and reached over to Søren. He flinched away but she managed to grab hold of an arrow from his quiver. He looked on in surprise as she quickly swiped her forearm with the sharp tip. The skin reddened like a burn, before beads of red blood seeped out onto the line of the cut. Søren watched in newfound awe as the red seemed to melt into silver; shiny and solid like liquid mercury. Savannah looked up at him apologetically, while handing him the arrow.

The Trainer paused, not knowing what to do with it.

"It's not contaminated," she hissed. "I only made a cut —I didn't go poking around in the wound."

Realising that she had a point, Søren slotted the arrow back into his quiver before the Boss' cough reminded them of his presence.

"I never imagined it to look quite like that," Death admitted, sitting up. "Also, you didn't actually have to cut yourself to prove that."

Savannah blushed and tried to hide her arm. "...It was a spur in the moment kind of thing."

The Boss nodded, then frowned thoughtfully. "I am sorry that I cannot tell you about your father, Savannah. It really is for the best. And what is worse, is that Titans are more ruthless than gods when it comes to apprehending wrongdoers."

"Titans?" Søren repeated. "Like Kronos?"

He paused. "…Yes."

"Hey," Savannah snapped, leaning forward in her chair. The tears were gone. Instead, her irises lit up and returned to normal in a series of flashes, like a warning sign. "What *really* happened in the war?"

The Boss gulped and looked askance, before waving his hand and replacing the old shattered wine glass with a new, full one. "Where do I begin?" he sighed. "It was an ordinary day, I believe. Everything was going smoothly —and then, the sky darkened. Our systems had crashed. The alarm wouldn't stop blaring, and nothing moved or made a sound. And then…*thud. Thud. Thud.* Huge footsteps echoed in the hallways, but nothing showed. So, we raced to the entrance. And there he was —like, twenty feet tall and made of bright red cobblestone; casting a light in the sky that made it look like it was sunset. He had enormous horns that could slice a skyscraper into ribbons. He had finally shown himself after two millennia…" he then paused, letting the suspense build up.

The Reapers did not really react, but the air felt colder and less dense than before, causing a shiver to run down Søren's spine.

"…Kronos," Death breathed.

CHAPTER 23

SØREN

"I *DID* ASK for help," the Boss frowned, stroking his chin. He made it sound as though he was not entirely sure of it himself. "But the Olympians turned me away and said that it was my problem to deal with. I cannot help but feel that they could have prevented a lot of innocent deaths."

"Well, Kronos did give you a chance," Savannah pointed out, visibly becoming agitated in her seat. "It is your own fault for those deaths —"

"*Savannah*," Søren scolded.

"No. She is right," the Boss surprised them with an agreement. "It *was* my fault. I did not and still cannot see what the whole thing was about —it's not as though it changed the very fabric of reality. But as angry as I am with myself, I am more furious with the gods," he grumbled, moving to rest his chin in one hand. "Perhaps because '*family*' rarely means anything to them."

There was a lengthy pause in acknowledgement of the last sentence, before the Boss realised what he had said. "…Oh, don't feel bad. I should be used to it. They are more like those aunts and uncles who try their hardest to avoid attending family reunions."

Savannah then glanced at Søren and shot him a slightly amused look at that description of the other gods, before turning back to the Boss. "So…you and me. We're like cousins?" she asked.

Søren tensed. The Boss did not look any less unnerved, and shifted again.

"Yes...sort of," he mumbled. The Trainer frowned. Was it really better to lie to her than let her know the real relationship between them?

Søren coughed very obviously, while glancing at Savannah several times once he had gained the Boss' attention.

'*Tell her*', Søren mouthed. Death shook his head slowly. Savannah then cleared her throat and sat upright in her chair.

"Can we talk about light projection," she said, making it sound more like a demand than a request. "*Mine* specifically."

The god of death looked all too relieved and summoned his fourth glass of wine since they had started talking. He sighed deeply, whirling the glass gently in a circular motion. "You can manifest light. Usually through the hands, like in your case. It packs tremendous force and it can be incredibly blinding. It is more of a defence mechanism than weapon. It is also not genetic —so do not get any ideas of thinking that you could be a descendant of someone like the Titan Helios."

"So, it's just random?" Savannah concluded.

"Precisely."

The Reaper pressed her lips into a line. Søren found himself wondering what was going through her head. She was like a kaleidoscope —an exuberant array of different thoughts; and her façade while she did it was as unreadable as a kaleidoscope's outer shell was unassuming.

Her next actions though, reminded him that she was still very much *Savannah*. She glanced downwards, and then slowly raised her hand. The Boss did not stop her, even though her palm was facing him. Søren was about to move forward to divert the direction of her hand, but the Boss was undeterred.

And then the Trainer saw why.

Nothing came from Savannah's hand. She shook her hand vigorously, but no light nor magic sparked. The Reapers both frowned, suddenly uncertain about everything that they had been told.

"Confused?" the Boss drawled in a highly amused tone. They nodded in unison. "...I said that it's defensive. And you are rather new to this, so I would not expect your powers to engage again so soon. And if you're out to seriously hurt someone with light projection, you will find that it's easier to thread a waxed mountain climbing rope through a sewing needle."

Savannah clasped her hands together and looked down guiltily, and Søren saw a rosy hue colour her cheeks. He fought with himself to sympathise because of her clear embarrassment, and instead played uncaring delinquent; folding his arms and pressing his lips into a line.

"Well, that concludes our conversation," the Boss announced, clapping his hands together. "Back to the library?"

"I hope that it's not in that horrid frilly joke again," Savannah grumbled, getting up begrudgingly.

"No," he chuckled, shaking his head. "It was amusing while it lasted."

"And my sword? Is that still going to take a day?"

"Oh." He snapped his fingers. Savannah's sword materialised next to him in a shimmering mist. "Thank you for reminding me," he said, motioning for the sword to float over to the redhead. She grabbed it firmly before examining it. "As it turned out, I had given such a wide window because I was unsure of how long the tests would take. Fortunately, because it is one hundred percent your sword, the results were not anything spectacular," Death sighed, sounding suspiciously disappointed.

Søren stood up and adjusted his quiver before he swung his crossbow over his shoulder and looked at Savannah, expecting her to make the next move. She snorted and sheathed the sword, then shifted her weight to one leg and folded her arms. "By the way," she started, "I think it would be to your benefit to leave those *Detached* alone."

The Boss raised an eyebrow and got off the desk to stand in front of it with one leg crossed over the other. "And just who are you to tell me what to do? I am still your superior —whether there is god blood in your veins or not. So, I think I will do what I see fit with those *Detached*, thank you."

"That's bloody *selfish*," Savannah accused, glaring at the Boss. "We know now that the *Detached* didn't take the reaping lists. They just wanted a safer place to hide. They are not a threat —to the Reapers Organisation nor to your high and mighty ass."

Søren inhaled sharply; and rightly so, because the Boss' bronze eyes then fizzled to life. But Savannah stood her ground, defiant.

"They are not like you say," Søren then quipped, deciding to back Savannah up. "They're just really scared, and really damaged people. They were humans once, too —"

"Don't you dare try and tell me how to run my own damn company!" Death suddenly exploded, making the Reapers take a step backwards. His eyes were wild with molten bronze, and the clock hands sparked like jarring metal. "You're just like father. Don't do this, and don't do that —I am not a *child*, and I can do things by myself!"

The Reapers blinked, surprised by the content of his outburst. Savannah looked away uncertainly, mimicking Søren's unease.

"Get out of my office!" Death commanded; his eyes fully ablaze. A gust of heat that matched his rage blew through the room.

They shuffled towards the door, still shocked, before he barked out the order again. They disappeared around the door and it slammed in their faces, leaving them out in the hallway. Savannah whistled and ran a hand through her hair. "…I wasn't expecting that," she admitted.

"Me neither," Søren sighed.

"But did you hear what he said? He feels as though everyone treats him like a child too," she remarked.

"Don't push that again. You are a Grim Reaper —once human. He's an immortal god. Although…now that I think about it, you two actually sound a lot alike," Søren realised. "It's almost uncanny."

She looked at him sideways.

Maybe he was getting ahead of himself by trying to hint at the fact that they were related to each other a little closer than cousins.

"…Whatever," she huffed. "He makes it sound like all of the gods are the same. Uncaring."

"Surely at least some of them are a little bit caring? I mean, how else do offspring come to be?"

"Just because people have kids it doesn't mean that they care," she snapped, shooting Søren a knowing look.

He paused. "To be honest, his father sounds like he cared *too* much. Treating him like a child —it's as though he wasn't ready to let him grow up and wished he would stay with him forever," Søren sighed. Without even realising it, his voice then dropped to a mumble. "…At least that's better than forcing a child to grow up before they're ready."

"Søren…" Savannah frowned and her expression softened, before he felt her hand land on his arm. The Trainer froze and stared at it, confused. It was such a touching, probing gesture. But he was not in any mood to elaborate.

It was too much too soon, and it left him dithering. So, Søren suddenly turned away and closed himself off.

Savannah withdrew slowly, looking a little hurt.

"So…what a firecracker, right? I told you that Death was unhinged," he then whistled, redirecting the conversation.

Savannah lidded her eyes. "Seriously? You can just say so if you don't want to talk about something. You don't forcibly have to change the topic."

"Well, then excuse me for wanting to keep my private life *private*," Søren snapped, clenching his fists.

"I didn't force you to share anything," she reasoned. "Just be honest with me and tell me if you don't want to talk about something."

"You should be able to tell."

"How?" she pointed out. "I barely know you —and certainly not well enough for deciphering your moods. So, cut me some slack."

Søren could not listen to her voice of reason. He was far too upset. He simply wanted to argue with her and releasing some of the pent-up rage.

"Pfft —you're just using that as an excuse," he snarled. "Soon enough everyone is going to stop treating you like a newbie and you're going to have to take responsibility for your actions. Like, what the hell were you *thinking* in that office, backchatting the Boss like that?"

"It…it wasn't just me," she countered.

"*I* was just paying him back for being an asshole," Søren said defensively. "You wanted to rile him up almost as much as I did —if not more."

"That's not true!" she protested.

"Then what *were* you doing?"

"I don't know —I just…I was trying to do something good —for someone else…I wanted to be a part of saving someone…or something," she struggled, becoming increasingly frustrated. "You know what? I don't know why I'm trying to explain this to you. It's not like you would understand."

She then whipped around and stormed off. Søren's anger then diminished enough for him to realise how much of an asshole he was being. He fought the feeling of guilt and replaced it with resolve. He was not about to apologise, but even he knew that she had not deserved that.

"…Wait, Savannah." The Trainer darted forward after her. He grabbed her arm and stalled her in her tracks, surprising her as she stumbled a little before reluctantly looking up at him. "Why would I not understand about heroism?" he inquired, narrowing his eyes. "Just what do you think I've been doing all this time by tagging along with you in all of this? I could have left a long time ago, Savannah. But I am still here."

That was not entirely true. Søren could not have left her —he was bound by his duties as a Trainer to teach her until she was ready to go it alone. A status of which she was admittedly far from. Savannah made a face and then wrenched her arm free, causing Søren to stumble backwards. She clicked her tongue, but if anything, she looked more hurt than angered.

"…I thought you said that you don't lie," she said in a nonchalant voice, before walking off down the hallway.

Søren opened his mouth and then closed it, unable to come up with a comeback. So, she had caught on. She knew that he could not abandon her. That meant his plan backfired badly. The Reaper growled, disappointed for the way in which he handled it.

✠

Søren was set to give Savannah a proper apology, but unfortunately when the Reapers got back to the library there was something else to demand his attention. "What on Earth happened —"

"—I have no idea," Savannah's answer overlapped his question.

The purple haired woman Søren recalled as Nina was sitting on Nadine's back and filing her nails as the Nadine flailed her arms and legs. Her baseball bat lay a few inches away, just out of her reach.

Lewis was buried underneath a pile of books in a pyramid structure, with his face poking out in the gaps between the spines.

Nina looked up at the Reapers expectantly, but they could not find the words.

"Help us," Lewis' muffled voice groaned from the pyramid.

"What the hell did we miss?" Savannah gasped, rushing over to Lewis' aid. Søren walked over to Nina and gestured for her to get up. She did, but Nadine remained there on the floor like a beached whale. Then Savannah gave Nina the same expectant look as her Trainer did.

The assistant shrugged. "They tried to escape," she put simply.

"So, you sat on her, and put him in a cage?" Søren questioned, pointing.

"What was I supposed to do?" Nina frowned. "The girl was very strong and agile —the boy was scrawny and weak. I had to get creative."

Savannah spluttered incoherently, unable to believe it.

"Well, you can go now," Søren said firmly. "I expect that the Boss will be needing his girlfriend right about now."

"Girlfriend?" Nina repeated, and her cheeks coloured an interesting shade of maroon. She seemed to then gasp in realisation and made an effort to cover her face, before coughing uncomfortably. "I'm the furthest thing from that. I'm his secretary. And…why would he need me right now? What has happened?" she frowned, straightening her skirt.

"He…had a tantrum," Savannah summed up tactfully.

Nina did not react beyond closing her eyes for a moment and then opening them again, in a long blink; before she purposefully headed for the doors. Søren frowned, suddenly struck by the odd colour of her eyes.

"What is it?" Savannah asked when Nina was supposedly out of earshot.

"Nothing really," the Trainer dismissed, reaching out to help Nadine up.

He then flinched as she slapped his hand away and back flipped to her feet, glaring at him. "What was that for?" he murmured, nursing his hand.

"Lewis, duck," Nadine clicked her tongue and picked up her baseball bat, before knocking the top of the book pyramid over with a powerful swing.

"…Did you actually think I'd forgive you and accept your help after what happened?" she growled.

"Oh," Søren mumbled, cowering away guiltily. "Right. But you have to believe us, Nadine. We didn't rat you out. When would we have had the opportunity to do so?"

She snorted and helped her brother up, shoving Savannah aside. The redhead, however, was not about to admit defeat and not prove herself innocent. "Hey! We never gave your location away. We tried to save you when we were talking to Volcano Head," she reasoned. "We were vouching for you when he totally lost it."

"And Savannah did save your souls with that light projection earlier," Søren frowned. "You guys could have been *reaped*."

Nadine glared harder, but Søren could tell that she did not have anything to say to that. "…Whatever," she clipped, turning away and folding her arms. She knew that what they were saying had merit, but she would not admit it.
Søren took this as the closest he and Savannah would get to remorse, as well as a form of gratitude. His trainee then said his name, regaining his attention.

"What was that you said before? The '*nothing really*'?"
The Trainer paused, before recalling what she was talking about. "Oh —no. It was just that. Nothing really," he assured.

She looked at him uncertainly but moved to pick the books from Lewis' prison up off the floor. He may have told her that it was nothing really, but in reality, Søren was a concerned. Nina's eyes were the colour of dravite tourmaline —a crystal bronze gemstone. Saying she was a Reaper would be a stretch —especially in her professional position. Death's other employees were Spirits and willing souls chosen for their roles. Grim Reapers were designed with only one type of job in mind. So that was ruled out.

There was only one other explanation. Nina was a Vampyre —a Demon and human hybrid with blood the colour of dark, almost black, red. It would explain her maroon blush; her surprising strength; and her eyes. Because what Søren was really concerned about, was how her eyes changed from dravite tourmaline to red when had she left. She was thirsty.

The only other question he had was, how could the god of death have tamed such a creature?

✠

Savannah avoided speaking to her Trainer after their argument, and he could not blame her. But whenever their gazes met, she looked at him rather pityingly. And that made him frustrated.

Søren did not want her feeling sorry for him —under any circumstances. However, if she was really feeling sorry for him, what did she think that he was thinking of her? Did she think that he was still angry with her? And even if he was, he would not necessarily give her the silent treatment. There was too much going on around them for him to do that.

Søren just hoped that she did not feel that she could possibly ignore him for however long she had planned.

"Hey, isn't this the 'D' section?" Savannah frowned as she was putting a book back into its slot. She held up a book with a gold embellished spine that resembled something vaguely religious. "This should be under 'T'," she explained. It was called *The Book of Treaties*. "…Or at least 'B'."

Nadine glanced at it before turning her nose up, while Lewis looked on with childlike interest. Søren was about to tell Savannah to just put it where it was supposed to be, but he then realised something. It was a bit too out of place to have just been accidentally misplaced.

He took it from her and opened it up, before both Savannah and Lewis leaned in on either side of his shoulders to read. The Trainer sighed but let them stay there as he skimmed over the page to which he had opened. "The Peace Treaty," he read aloud. "Established 1980 AD."

It went on to elaborate on an agreement between the Olympian gods to basically not wage war on each other as well as the human race.

"Wow," Lewis whispered, causing Søren to grumble and lose his place. Which did not end up mattering, because the *Detached* then flipped the page and went backwards to earlier sections. "It's like a book of contracts."

"Why would someone go to such a length to put it here instead of its proper place though?" Savannah quipped.

"Isn't that the whole point of this punishment?" Nadine sighed. "To put things in order?"

"Yeah, but so far everything has been jumbled up pretty understandably," Savannah retorted.

"Hey look!" Lewis suddenly exclaimed, pointing at a page on which he had stopped. "This one says *The Infidelity Treaty*. Like…adultery?"

Savannah's sharp golden eyes darted straight to the page to assess just how interesting the name was, before they widened and she gasped.

"Søren," she whispered, finally addressing him. "I think that I know why this book was put here."

CHAPTER 24

SØREN

WRITTEN IN ICHOR; the blood of the gods.

The Infidelity Treaty
Est. 1697 AD

This treaty hereby declares that no god nor goddess shall indulge in fraternising with mortals in ways in which a half-blood offspring will result. For the safety of the gods, as well as any existing half-blood offspring living prior to the making of this treaty, no contact is permitted between either party. No exceptions. In the case of death on either part, the half-blood's loved ones may be contacted discretely and given some sort of mortal compensation. Any violations of this will be dealt with by banishment.

Especially in the case of the eldest gods and goddesses, infidelity shall be treated as a criminal offence and the newborn offspring may perish —depending on the level of threat they pose with or without godly powers —under the judgement of the high court. In signing this treaty, one accepts all of the above conditions; indirectly but effectively swears upon the River Styx; and therefore, cannot plead innocent in the high court.

Signed, The Olympian gods.

PART II

THE

JUDGEMENT

CHAPTER 25

SØREN

IT WAS LEWIS who then had the clever idea to read the treaty aloud. It was not the fact that he was reading it out loud —it was that the text seemed a too occult, like one was reading words for a spell. As soon as he said, "*Signed, the Olympian gods*", a cold gust of air suddenly blew through the library and blew out all of the candles. Søren then shivered, praying that they had not just angered any of the gods.

The four of them paused, unsure if anyone should move or not. It could have been a coincidence, but something did not feel right. Even Nadine's eyes widened, and she stiffened like a frightened child.

Then a few seconds passed without anything else happening.

Lewis hummed, unfreezing. "Guess it was nothing."

Everyone else looked at each other and moved disjointedly, still uncertain. What had happened was something out of ancient mythical curses.

"…Lewis, please don't read out loud from cryptic books," Nadine then told him, cringing.

Savannah took the book from Søren's hands and shut the it with a snap. Then she reached out to put it back, but after a pause she appeared to have thought better of it; tucking it inside her leather jacket underneath her arm.

"I think it'll be better to take it with us," she explained.

Nadine scoffed. "And take potential curses with it? I don't think so. It clearly belongs to Mount Olympus, judging by the last line. The most important question is, why was it here?"

"Maybe they wanted to put it in a place someone wouldn't think to look. Whoever it was they were hiding it from," Søren suggested.

Nadine shrugged. "I guess that sounds logical."

"Or maybe it just *ended* up here," Savannah then raised her voice, glaring at them and hugging the book closer. "Don't make assumptions."

"Okay. I was just theorising," Søren said defensively. The redhead mumbled something under her breath and glared at the floor, but then turned away, not wishing to engage in a full conversation. The Trainer narrowed his eyes at her, but he could not decipher what she was thinking.

"Hey, you think it would be okay to take any other books?" Lewis asked, reaching out for one. The floor suddenly shifted beneath their feet and a few books shimmied out from the shelves to smack onto the floor. Everyone froze again, and sure enough another tremor shook the room a few moments after. And again. And again. And then it stopped.

"...*Fine*, I won't take anything," Lewis then murmured, holding his hands above his head and backing away from the shelves.

"Great," Nadine scoffed, throwing her hands up. "You've now not only put a curse on us, but the whole building too!"

"I wasn't trying to," her younger brother protested. "I just wanted a good read for the road."

"But you get travel sickness."

"Only sometimes. Plus, only when I look at your face."

"*Lewis!*"

Søren sighed and rubbed his temples, trying to make sense of the last minute. But he did not get to dwell long on it, because the floor shook again; this time causing everyone to lose their footing —and for him to drop his crossbow.

Savannah met his startled gaze.

She then scrambled to her feet and darted towards him as he got up. He frowned as she huddled against his side, anxiously looking this way and that.

"What…are you doing?" Søren chuckled, reaching up to pat her head. Strands of her soft hair slipped through his fingers and he instantly jerked away, as the action triggered unwanted memories. The action of his hand suddenly withdrawing caused her hair to be pulled slightly and she squeaked, and she shot him a very deserved glare. "Sorry," he murmured.

But she did not move, and her arms wrapped themselves tighter around his left one. Søren sighed softly. It only became worse when Lewis then did it too, and the Trainer cringed; highly uncomfortable with the new position that he was in —the guy everyone thought was a total hero. The quaking then distracted him, and he held onto the shelves for support.

"…Anyone else getting the feeling that maybe this isn't all Lewis' doing?" Nadine spoke for all of them, clutching at the shelves behind her.

They all looked up at the ceiling, before the piercing sound of an alarm blared from all angles. The Reapers winced and moved to cover their ears, but the alarm persisted even through that. Then a thought occurred to Søren. All of the shaking; the alarm —it all sounded rather familiar.

"Hey!" he raised his voice over the sound of the alarm, "Hasn't this happened before? A long time ago, with…"

They all paused and let the idea sink in, even if they did not want it to. But it was a little too sequenced to be a coincidence.

"…*Kronos*!" Nadine finished over the noise, gripping her baseball bat tighter. The rest of the Reapers frowned knowingly.

Savannah then tugged on Søren's arm and pulled them away from the shelves. "We need to get out of here!" she urged, heading for the door.

Lewis finally let go of the Trainer and edged towards his sister instead. She was not exactly keen on that either.

Søren made sure to reach for his crossbow as they then made for the exit. The hallway was as empty as if had been when he and Savannah had gotten there, so they ran without worrying about bumping into someone. A strong wind was now coming from the direction in which they were heading —and Søren realised it was because they were running past a series of open windows made by a row of pillars. A turquoise blue light shone through the gaps and cast their shadows on the far wall. The Trainer did not think much of it until he looked outside.

He came to an abrupt stop, causing Savannah to nearly trip and fall.
Nadine and Lewis then paused too, wondering why Søren had. He pointed to the windows, and they all moved towards them. The light was coming from giant cracks in what looked like a mass of iron ore as large as a skyscraper.

Søren and Savannah decided to look a little higher and stick their heads out of the windows. "Oh. My. *Gods*…" the redhead breathed.

Towering at least fifteen feet above was a giant disjointed and crumbling raw iron being, stomping its way towards the castle. It had two twisted horns like that of a wild buck; gleaming canine teeth; and glowing blue eyes that roamed the area in slow, careful sweeps.

Savannah then suddenly pulled Søren back as its gaze began to move in their direction. "That…that's not Kronos!" she gasped.

"Isn't Kronos *red*?" Lewis added.

"We have to warn Thanatos. This way!" Savannah decided, and before anyone could object, she was already pulling Søren along again. Nadine and Lewis did not have much of a choice but to follow.

They then made their way back to the Boss' office. After rounding a corner, they skidded to a halt by the door, lightly panting. Savannah was about to bang on the door when it suddenly flew open, followed by a frantic god of death. The Boss did a double take when he recognised them, before panicking again. "You need to leave," he told them. "I'm doing an emergency evacuation of all Reapers and employees, so that no one remains in danger. Head to the portal that leads to your district *now*!"

The Reapers all looked at each other nervously and shrugged.

"…You have no idea where the portals are, do you?" Death realised. They shook their heads. He whipped around and called for his secretary.

"Yes sir?" she answered, coming into view. Her eyes were back to their dravite tourmaline colour and she looked noticeably flushed.

"Get them to the New York portal. *I'll* deal with Horkos!"

He then pushed past and left them with Nina.

"All right, follow me," the secretary commanded, taking off down the hallway. They straggled after her, jumping every time the floor rumbled. The alarm still blared, but they were growing used to it.

The newfound problem was trying to keep up with Nina.

She was surprisingly fast in high heels. Or rather not very surprising, Søren thought, since he was sure about her being a Vampyre.

She led them down a different set of turns from where they had come, before thankfully stopping in the window speckled hallway by what looked like a maintenance closet. Nina opened it by holding up a badge of the Reapers Organisation over a sensor, and it promptly swung open.

Søren had imagined the portal that was inside to be more Science Fiction than it turned out to be. It was a swirl of green storm clouds; free standing and not inviting in the slightest, which caused a hesitancy in the Reapers.

"Are you sure this is safe?" Nadine asked Nina.

Nina turned around and raised an eyebrow in what appeared to be amusement. "Nobody ever said that it was," she answered ominously.

The floor then shifted again, and dust fell from cracks in the ceiling. Nina looked up at them worriedly before gesturing for them all to go.

Nadine was the first to put her brave foot forward, and she regarded everyone else wearily before disappearing into the swirl of clouds. Then Lewis went. Søren met his trainee's gaze as she finally glanced at him. Her eyes asked a million questions and rendered him unsure of what to say or do. He then glanced back at the windows across from the open door.

The iron giant was getting closer.

Even with the *Detached* not with them, he knew this was not the time and place for a conversation. So, Søren swung his crossbow over his shoulder and walked up to the portal. "Here goes nothing…!"

Søren leaped into the storm clouds. A jolt of electricity went up his spine, before he marvelled at the portal's interior of jade, emerald and peridot nebula space clouds. It lasted only for a moment as he pushed through the misty green and gasped as though he needed air when he emerged through the other side, stumbling to a halt in front of Nadine and Lewis.

"Took you long enough," Nadine huffed. "Where's Golden-Eyes?"

Søren whipped around to see the portal, which was now inside of a large tree. He glanced around and found that they were in a forest, though it could be any forest in Manhattan. He looked back at the tree and straightened his leather jacket. The clouds continued to swirl undisturbed for a moment —before Savannah tumbled through with a squeal and landed face-first on the leafy forest floor. The treaty book slid across the ground, but she quickly reached for it and tucked it back into her jacket. Søren heard Nadine snicker and fought with himself not to do the same. Lewis was the one to rush over and offer her a hand.

Savannah wiped mud and leaves off of her face while he picked out ones in her hair, before she gave him a grateful smile.

The portal then swirled in on itself and disappeared in a burst of dark turquoise smoke. "…We need to get out of these woods," Søren then cleared his throat and announced, drawing everyone's attention. "We don't know where exactly we might have ended up."

✠

The Reapers walked for about fifteen minutes before finding what resembled a clearing and a tarred road. They stumbled out of the trees and dusted ourselves down, before Søren started searching for signs which could give them an indication as to where they were.

"Queens?" Savannah deadpanned when he broke the news to everyone. Her expression was of vague disappointment. "I think that my Mom took me there one Spring Break when she was fresh out of ideas."

Søren shrugged. "At least it's close enough for us to walk."

"Where do you guys stay?" Lewis asked.

"Lower Manhattan," Savannah sighed, jiggling the handle of her sword back and forth in its sheath on her hip.

"That's about…five hours?" Lewis guessed.

"Four," his sister corrected. "That's still quite the distance. Why can't we just shift the whole way?"

"She doesn't know how to do that on her own yet," Søren pointed out, pointing at Savannah. "It won't work if not all of us have the same destination in mind. Have you guys ever been to Manhattan?"

"…Good point," Nadine pouted. "We wouldn't know where to go."

"Then we're walking," Søren concluded.

After a few grumbles they set off alongside the highway. It was completely silent initially, before Savannah and Lewis and Nadine decided that they could not handle the boredom and began a lively conversation.

Søren preferred the silence.

It was not that he did not like socialising —he simply felt more at ease with his own thoughts, no matter how destructive they were. Or perhaps he was masochistic that way; for choosing the haunting of his past over engaging in the present. He had never attempted to run from the shadows which chased him. If anything, he wallowed in them. Called them home.

The Trainer found himself striding behind the others, his mind beginning to drift. He did not think about 1836 —not about his death.

Søren thought about fire. He thought about how it burned and destroyed — yet it could be contained. He thought about how it robbed and took from people, yet it could make way for new life. He thought about how it killed.

And he thought about the sea.

The sea killed too —statistically more than fire. The sea was more beautiful than fire as well, mesmerising onlookers with the sequence of crashing waves for hours on end. Boats braved those waves and some capsized; some were ripped apart by sheer force; and some just disappeared in its vast expanse. Those boats would never return, just like the lost souls which fell for the ocean. Søren had fallen in love with the ocean. It had not taken anything away from him except the memory of his mother —fire had been the one to take lives.

Lives which he could have saved.

The Reaper shook his head, refusing to let himself get sucked into thinking about people and souls again. Thinking about the sea posed no problems to his memory lapse, so he began whistling a mimic of the howl of the wind in a high tide swell.

Søren saw his mother by the waves, her dress billowing behind her. She had always been there, at the water's edge, in his memories. She probably thought deeply elsewhere too, but from what his father had told him getting her away from the sea had been quite a task. Søren would not have known, because he had not quite gotten to see her alive. And now her existence lingered in the mist of the sea —in his reach and yet somehow still out of it. She was the only one he could think about and not end up freaking out. While everyone else screamed and cried in an inferno consumed chaos, she floated in tranquil silence in a calm ocean; her wild raven hair growing longer and sinking with the weight of water, and her crimson lips chapped and faded from the iciness of the Norwegian sea.

He remembered that he had been dressed up in a little corduroy blue suit with a big pink-purple satin bow at the neck for her funeral. Her ashes had been scattered in the harbour as per her request. For years afterwards, people never stopped telling him how he had only kept pulling at the bow and fussing. It had not been his fault —he had just been an infant.

Søren's father had dumped him on a nursemaid's lap to mourn tearlessly in peace —or experience the effects of cannabis, but Søren would never know. All he knew was that no one cried at his mother's funeral. *He* would have, if he had not been a week old. No one cried because no one cared.

The duke remarried a duchess from France two weeks later. The wedding was not a memory for Søren, but it was where he met Angelina. At least that was what their nursemaids told them.

She had been a year old already and was the youngest daughter of a duke with a vast network of estates across Europe. And for a newborn heir who had just lost his mother and gained a new one who only spoke French; befriending her had

224

been by far not the worst thing that Søren could have done. Unfortunately, his father had not seen it that way.

Søren sighed, then finding himself back on the desolate highway with three people he barely tolerated.

Nadine, Lewis and Savannah all looked back at him curiously.

"…When you're lost in thought, your nose does this cute little thing where you look like a rabbit," the redhead said out of the blue.

"What?" frowned the Trainer.

"Like this." She then demonstrated, scrunching her nose up and sniffing. Nadine snorted in amusement; while Lewis appeared to be lost in thought — blankly staring into the tall forests either side of them.

"Seriously?" Søren hissed, feeling the heat of a blush surface on his skin. His trainee simply laughed.

"What had you been thinking so deeply about?"

He paused. "…My mother and the sea."

"Oh."

All laughter died and Nadine coughed, but Søren did not feel awkward. He did not know why he had told the truth, but it felt relieving to do so. It felt easier to tell them about someone to which he had no emotional attachment. It was like reading a fairytale with an unhappily ever after where one did not actually know the characters.

Characters. Yes, that was what they were. Flat, underdeveloped characters in Søren's own personal fairytale.

CHAPTER 26

THANATOS

fifteen minutes earlier…

✠

HE DID NOT notice Nina standing in the doorway until she rasped. Thanatos' head snapped up at the strangled sound and his eyes widened. She looked at him and grabbed at her throat desperately, gasping for air.

Death jumped and left his rage at his desk, before moving to catch Nina in his arms as she collapsed weakly. He had not been counting the years. A century had already passed. He rolled up one of her shirt sleeves to check the severity of her condition and winced at the sight of her veins pulsing dark red beneath the surface of her skin.

He knew that all Vampyres craved blood in order to soothe the unbearable burning that their half Demon blood caused. Drinking Ichor, the golden blood of the gods, kept the symptoms and thirst at bay for a hundred years at a time. Most importantly, it kept *Nina's* thirst at bay and ensured her usual top performance.

However, when she was like this, she reverted to her initial unholy half Demonic state from when she was born. It was dangerous —and if she did not consume any mortal or godly blood within the next few hours, the existing fiery blood in her could destroy her from the inside out.

She whimpered as Thanatos urged her to keep her volume low and attempted to hold her upright. "Why did you wait this long?" he hissed. "Did you not have earlier symptoms?"

She lifted her head to look at him through strands of purple hair. Despite the pain that she was in, she still managed to give him a dirty look.

"Just let me…suck your blood," she rasped, grabbing at his blazer with iron force. Death tensed but sighed and moved to lock the door.

He then walked her along slowly towards the wall.

She slammed him against it and ripped his shirt open, popping the buttons off. "Nina. That's expensive!" he cried. She snarled and bared her teeth; all of them now morphed into jagged and sharpened canines.

Thanatos sighed in defeat, before flinching as he felt those white teeth graze his neck. Nina stood up on the balls of her feet, and then forcefully pierced through his skin. Death growled and dug his fingers into her arms, but she bit harder, drawing out more ichor.

He struggled not to cry out in pain, and it only worsened as she began to suck. A dull pleasure mingled with the distinct agony but it was not enough to distract him. "…*Nina*," he snarled, throwing his head back. She kept him where he was and did not relent.

The last time she had gotten this aggressive was the first time that she had ever needed his blood. She had been so starved of proper nutrients that she had nearly burst one of his arteries in her fervour.

The Vampyre continued sucking, desperate for that relief; and it was not long before Thanatos could feel the blood which she was consequently missing drip down across his shoulder. But he was equally relieved to see the intensity of the colour of her veins fade, and to feel her grip on him loosen.

He then breathed shallowly and shuddered as she licked up the traces of ichor along his collarbone.

It caused dangerous, wicked thoughts to flash through his mind. Thoughts which he knew that he should not be thinking. Not about her.

He quickly moved to stop her before she dared to begin licking anywhere else

227

and inevitably send him into the depths of no control.

Her breathing was laboured and heavy as she kept her head hung and Death moved her to arm's length. They simply stood there, panting and willing the atmosphere to regress from strained to professional.

This was always the strangest part.

It reminded Thanatos of when he had first found her at the tender age of fifteen on the fringes of Wales; hungry and monstrous. Her eyes had not been tourmaline in almost two years, since animal blood did not satisfy the way human blood did. She would not have found many humans around there though, in the forest she was hiding in.

She had been covered in mud, twigs and forest leaves and nothing else — completely wild and camouflaged like her surroundings. She had bared her predatory teeth at Death, shrieking menacingly. Her nostrils had flared, and she then seemed to recognise him as non-human, because she shrank away and scrambled to climb up a tree.

"I am not going to hurt you..." Thanatos had cooed, reaching out to her carefully as though she were a stray cat. She had flinched and threatened to bite his hand, but he had been undeterred.

After a few more tries she had finally let his hand touch the top of her head, and she frowned as though in wondering about why he had not killed her yet.

He probably should have. Vampyres were not exactly tolerable creatures to anyone —to the gods, to divine creatures, nor to mortals. It certainly would have been easier if he had reaped her on sight all of those years ago.

But Death had looked into her red eyes and seen something in her that he saw in himself —and had therefore shown her mercy.

Vampyres' souls —not their bodies, though those only aged to maturity — were immortal, so it would not have mattered what Thanatos had done.

His behaviour had confused her, causing her to hesitate with her clawed nails held out defensively.

But she had drank his blood ravenously when he had offered, the fire in her system extinguishing before her calm nature had taken over.

Her straggly brown hair had straightened into gentle waves and her newly dravite tourmaline eyes sparkled. Her hands had softened and glistened gold with ichor in the moonlight. Thanatos remembered thinking that she was beautiful — as Vampyres go, devilish beauty was a result of a dazzling demon and attractive human —but he had to restrain himself due to the implications of sparing her life.

She had looked up at him curiously and opened her mouth —but she did not say anything.

She had forgotten how to speak, if she had ever even learned.

She had then screwed up her face and begun to cry. Death had scooped her weak exhausted form up in his arms, while wrapping her in robes.

She had been surprisingly heavy for such a small girl, but he managed to hold her comfortably enough. He had blessed her and brought her to his palace, where their agreement was established: he would satisfy her cravings every hundred years and she would work for him in return.

He named her Nina because as she learned how to speak, they were her favourite syllables to say over and over again.

The experience had changed the way Thanatos saw and treated Vampyres. It showed him that even the most fearsome and wild things could be befriended.

Satisfied Nina was refreshingly quiet and careful; and had stayed away from clothing for a full month before switching her cloak for a simple cotton dress.

She had then started to dye her hair purple when Thanatos told her the truth about what she was.

"No one must ever know what you really are. They do not understand you the way that I do. They would want to hurt you. Never use your powers explicitly around others."

She frowned, not understanding why.

"…There are cruel people out there. If they knew you were a Vampyre, they would take you away from the safety of here."

From the safety of him, he wanted to add.

He believed that she had understood, because she nodded slowly and made an effort to move slower and be less aggressive.

Dying her hair had not been out of self-spite —she *liked* her new look and had sprinted to Death's office to show him afterwards.

And as he had put her through schooling and retaught her English; then taught her Greek, her timid demeanour morphed into something more of mischievous and confident.

She had a knack for being able to organise Thanatos' messes and run around after people to make sure they did what they were supposed to do.

Her skills were fitting of her job. But as brilliant as she was at her work, she was rather forgetful when it came to keeping track of time.

"…I'm sorry, sir," Nina now whispered, reaching up to wipe her mouth with the back of her hand. Her apology brought Thanatos back to the present, and he shook his head slightly to reorientate his thoughts. "I should not…have waited…this long."

He sighed and took off his blazer, before summoning a new shirt. The holes that Nina's teeth had made were beginning to heal and would soon disappear. "You are right. How quickly did it start?"

"Slowly…about a week ago," she murmured. "I suppose it went to full effect after —" She suddenly stopped short and went quiet.

Death frowned and folded his arms. "After what?" he asked. She did not say anything. "Nina," he said more firmly, reaching over to tilt her chin up. She looked up at him begrudgingly with her normal dravite tourmaline eyes.

Gold was smeared on the corner of her mouth, and her all of her teeth were back to their natural variations.

"…Why had you been so upset earlier?" she whispered, frowning.

Thanatos frowned too, not recalling of what she was talking about.

"What do you mean?"

"The Dynamic Duo told me that you had a tantrum," she sighed.

He raised an eyebrow. *Tantrum? Dynamic Duo…?*

It then became obvious to him: Savannah and Søren. That pair of clowns could not get along *less* if one locked them up in the same room.

As for their dismissive term for his outburst, he could not be bothered to retaliate in his state.

"I do not really want to talk about it," Death said in a low voice. "Let us say that things were said and I was just rubbed up the wrong way."

"Oh."

He then stroked his chin, thinking about a sudden point. What did his anger have to do with the severity of Nina's situation?

"…But why did that trigger your symptoms? Why did they fluctuate so suddenly?" he questioned aloud.

Nina's gaze shifted and she bit her lip. Her face flushed a deep maroon. "…I don't know," she whispered.

A thought crossed Thanatos' mind and it made him tense. Perhaps she had been worried about him. Her symptoms had worsened when she had been overly emotional, as he observed.

Which meant it was most likely that she had felt a surge of something —fear or perhaps even rage.

"There is no need to be ashamed, Nina," he smiled weakly. "I cannot help you if you do not talk to me," he said in a gentle tone.

She slowly shook her head. "I really do not know."

She was closing herself off. She evidently did not want to tell him anything. But as much as Thanatos respected her choices, he could not help but feel a little wounded. He did not have time for this.

He shrugged his blazer back on and side stepped her.

"…Clean up and resume work in at least ten minutes," he ordered. "And next time, do not wait until you're on the verge of death to come to me."

"Yes, sir," she murmured.

He walked towards the door, before the room suddenly groaned.

He paused, and slowly turned to face Nina again. She looked as surprised as he did. It shook again. And then a few more times, before it stopped.

"…What was that?" Nina whispered, absentmindedly licking her fingers and walking towards Death. He cringed; yet tried not to imagine her tongue in other places, doing other things. She straightened her shirt and skirt before brushing her hair from her eyes. She then gave him an expectant look when he continued staring. "What?" she asked.

"…Nothing. And, I am not entirely sure what that was," he sighed as he looked upwards at the ceiling. "Purgatory does not have tectonic plates, so it could not have been an earthquake."

Nina frowned thoughtfully. "Maybe it was something outside?"

Thanatos clicked his tongue. "What outside could possibly cause the building to shake?" he snapped but went over to the window and opened the curtains. The ground shook again, more violently than before.

He looked up and gasped.

"What? What is it?" Nina panicked.

Thanatos cursed in Greek and turned away from the window. "Switch on the emergency alarm," he told her. "And the evacuation alarm too."

"Why?" she asked but she moved to his desk obediently with such speed it was as though she had teleported.

"I believe that we have an intruder," Death growled. "Search under '*H*' —for Horkos."

☩

"Who the hell is *Horkos*?" Nina exclaimed, throwing the file down onto Thanatos' desk.

"He is the god of oaths," he said over the sound of the alarm. "If anyone swears upon the River Styx and breaks an oath, he will come to rectify the situation. *Violently*!"

"Well, what is he doing here? What oath have you broken?"

"I…I am unsure, but I think I have an idea of what happened. But first, we

232

need to make sure that everyone gets out of here —now. Including you!"

"But…But what about *you*?" she cried.

"That is not important," he insisted. "I can handle another god, Nina. I do not need you to get caught in the crossfire!"

"But I pledged my loyalty to you. I can't run away like a fool while my boss could be getting harmed," she threw back, stomping her foot. "It is my duty to be by your side!"

Thanatos impulsively grabbed her face and pulled her towards him, allowing him to lower his voice. "…Remember what I told you when you were sixteen? About cruel people who would hurt you?"

She nodded vigorously.

"Well, Horkos is not the kind of opponent you would overcome, Nina. You would lose. Even with your powers. Please *listen* to me and get out of here after everyone else. I…I don't want to see you get hurt. I do not want you to sacrifice yourself for me if I am able to come back. You cannot. Do you understand?"

She blinked, and droplets of tears formed in her eyes.

But she nodded, biting her lip. He reached up and gently wiped the tears that spilled. Then he rested his forehead on hers and whispered that everything would be all right. He had restrained himself from this sort of affection, but if this would be the last time for a long time, he needed it.

He needed to feel some part of her, so that he would not forget the sensations.

He abruptly realised that if he leaned in just a little further, his lips would find hers. He could fulfil that long repressed want —he could kiss her. He was certainly close enough to do so.

Death knew it well, though, that such an action would be difficult to discuss and explain afterwards, should he actually survive.

Nina clung to his blazer in an almost hug and breathed shallowly, trying not to cry. In such an intimate moment, formality had no place.

It was a sad three minutes.

"…Okay," she eventually rasped. "Go and be a hero."

Thanatos then let her go and ran for the door, before swinging it open —only to

233

bump into the party of Grim Reapers. He could not let them get away so easily —
but also realised that all bad blood aside, he needed to get everyone out no matter
who they were. He did not need a repeat of needless deaths.

"You need to leave," he urged them. "I'm doing an emergency evacuation of
all Reapers and employees, so that no one remains in danger. Head to the portal
that leads to your district *now*!"

They dithered for a moment and shrugged.

"…You have no idea where the portals are, do you?" Death growled. They shook
their heads. He whipped around to turn back into his office.

"Nina!" he called.

"Yes sir?" she answered, teetering to the door.

"Get them to the New York portal. *I'll* deal with Horkos!" he declared. Nina
nodded and led the band of convicts away, while Thanatos stormed his way to the
front entrance.

He flung open the doors and a strong wind blew past him into the castle. His
forearms rose up to shield his face as he tried to keep his footing.

The wind then died down and he straightened up to see a fifteen-foot Horkos
in his godly form of iron and blue light, in a toga and with a court hammer in one
hand. Death frowned.

Horkos was usually holding The Book of Treaties in the other hand.
The giant god's blue diamond eyes turned from where he had been looking to
look at Thanatos. And the god of death could feel his anger returning, and he
started marching towards Horkos. As he did, his human form melted away and he
rapidly grew in size.

His body turned to black granite with lava dripping from the cracks in the
surface. Horns protruded from his head and curled into those of a ram's.

He held out his hand, and his scythe materialised in his hold, bigger and
heavier to match his size.

"Horkos. God of oaths!" Thanatos thundered. The sky rumbled and the
ground trembled. "State your purpose for coming here *uninvited*. I have not
violated my oath concerning the Reapers."

234

Horkos glared at him and dropped his hammer to his side. "…I am not here for you, Thanatos, god of death."

Thanatos frowned and his grip on his scythe loosened. "Then what in the gods' names are you here for in such a threatening size?" he demanded. "This is my domain, fool!"

Horkos raised his free hand to tell Death to stop talking. "I am here for the child. Savannah Green; daughter of Hades, god of the Underworld."

CHAPTER 27

SØREN

HIS MIND WAS taking him back to 1836, but this time he knew why. It was an aspect which Søren never wanted to consider. The shadows around his and his father's deaths were the only ones which he did not embrace —the only ones which could maul him.

In the flashbacks, the duke's cries muted as his face contorted in desperation and fear. But mostly anger. He was furious with his son because he had not manage to save him. When Søren acknowledged that fact, he then heard the words he was screaming.

'*You are just like your mother.*
So distracted by infatuation that you forget
about what is going on around you.
This is all your fault. All of it.
If it was not for you and your damned noble-born
whore, I would have lived!'

Angelina's laughter was echoing in the background, but it was piercing his ears. His father kept repeating the words over and over, but they faded as the laughter became overpowering.

Søren knew what was happening. His brain was trying to force him to think of a possibility he could not bear to evaluate.

Not her. She could not have…

…It was not her fault.

Yet a part of him had wondered if Angelina had known all along, even then. Søren squeezed his eyes shut and shook his head, and the images swiftly dissipated. He then started at the feeling of someone suddenly pulling on his sleeve, and he consequently staggered into Nadine. She was holding onto his jacket and tugging him away from the path he had been walking. He whipped around and saw the surprised face of Lewis, and the concerned one of Savannah —though she glanced elsewhere when their gazes met.

She was still pissed off.

"Søren, you seriously need to stop doing that," Nadine snorted, steering the Trainer away from a telephone line pole. "I was really tempted to just let you run into the pole."

Søren breathed out and shrugged, before letting out a chuckle. "Thanks for not letting that happen. And…I was just somewhere else, I guess."

"Yeah, that much is obvious," Nadine grinned, nudging him. "What were you thinking about this time?"

"…Stuff," he murmured.

"*Stuff*, he says," Nadine mocked the Reaper, making quotation marks in the air. "It's probably about some *girl*."

Søren then choked, spluttering and wheezing while she laughed. He coughed sheepishly, not bothering to retaliate. She was simply trying to push his buttons. And if he let her, she would only tease him all the more.

"Leave him alone," Savannah surprised Søren by coming to his rescue. "At least he's actually been in relationships."

Lewis burst out in laughter, insinuating that the taunt held some truth.

"I've just never been interested," Nadine defended herself. "Some people have had other things on their minds in life."

Søren was inclined to side with her. Nadine knew what arranged marriages had been like, and the life of a noble child. As a millennial, Savannah simply did not understand.

"What exactly do you have against my trainee?" the Trainer asked Nadine after witnessing their childish bickering.

"It's nothing personal," she clarified, sticking her nose in the air. "I just know a spoiled brat when I see one."

Søren could not argue with that. He kept to himself though, ignoring the tension. For a while afterwards, he thought about Melchior.

Ideally, the Trainer would like to see the blond get set alight and thrown into a ditch. But unfortunately, his dreams never come true, so he would have to deal with seeing Melchior every day in his existence. Søren wondered whether the he thought about what had happened between them at all. Did he care. Did he miss them. Did he miss…him?

Søren nearly burst out laughing at that thought. Missing him was probably not something of which Melchior was capable. But the Trainer did. Not that he would ever admit it out loud —but he missed him.

…Sometimes.

More not than often. The words miss and hate often blurred for Søren.
He knew that Melchior did not hate him. The blond was not indifferent either. He was a puzzle. And he was always the same, whether the two were together or apart: a narcissistic, emotionally unpredictable asshole. Maybe the Trainer just attracted people with ulterior motives. Perhaps it was his curse.

Søren then glanced at Savannah, gritting his teeth. Would he let his friendship with her crash and burn as well, because of one mistake?

She was smiling —and even he could tell that it hid something deeply buried which she did not want to unearth. But he had to speak to her. They could not continue to pretend that the fight did not exist.

"Savannah," he called.
She actually turned, her feigned amusement wavering. "What is it?"

"I have to talk to you."
Nadine and Lewis immediately and suddenly found something to talk about, giving the two Reapers some much appreciated privacy.

"What do you want to talk about?" Savannah clipped as she fell into step with her Trainer behind the *Detached*.

"The fight."

She pressed her lips into a line. "I…actually want to discuss something else first," she admitted, wrapping her arms around herself.

"Okay."

"So, in the library…when we found The Book of Treaties, you suggested that someone might have wanted to hide the book. I mean, why else would it be in such an obscure location, right?" she asked.

"Yeah, well —you shot that idea down pretty quickly," Søren reasoned, narrowing his eyes. "It could have '*ended up there*', as you put it."

"I know what I said," she huffed. "It's just…I only shot it down because…a sudden thought occurred to me at that time."

Søren paused and studied the hesitancy in her body language. He wondered what exactly the thought had been to cause her to snap unexpectedly. What exactly was she suspecting?

"Which would be?" he whispered.

She glanced downwards at her boots. "What if my *father* had put it there? To hide it from the Olympians."

Søren's eyes widened and he finished the idea. "…Because you were born, and your existence violates the treaty."

"Exactly."

"But are you not already technically dead?" the Trainer frowned. "The Olympians shouldn't be able to do anything if so —at least that's my opinion. You don't pose a threat to the mundane world."

The redhead looked a little hopeful, but then the worry returned. "What about the divine?" she whispered. "I already have light projection. And you've seen what I can do when I get furious. I do the same thing Thanatos does, but to a lesser degree." Then she paused, clenching her fists at her sides. "…Who knows what else I can do?" she barely whispered.

Søren hesitated, unsure of how to respond. He should say something

239

comforting or encouraging. But he did not know where to start. Of course, she was afraid. That much he understood.

He frowned and took in the immensity of the situation. "...You are right. We *don't* know what you're capable of. But...that doesn't have to be a bad thing," Søren pointed out. She looked at him sideways. "They don't know your powers. So, what if you passed it off to the Olympians as how much of a danger you *don't* pose?"

Her face suddenly lit up at that. "You really think that I could get away with hiding my powers?"

"Well...Maybe not with Thanatos and our friends now knowing."

"Oh, so they *are* our friends now?" Savannah smirked.

Søren scoffed childishly. "Whatever. Even though Nadine doesn't seem to like either of us, acquaintances doesn't sound applicable anymore."

Savannah chuckled. Then her smile fell into a frown again. "...If I can't hide, then what am I supposed to do?" she whispered.

"You mean what are we supposed to do," Søren corrected her, softening his expression. "You're not alone, Savannah. We —and I can't specify who, but it's not just me. We will all be here for you. All of us."

She held his gaze, and it was like an understanding was suddenly found between them. Everything she had done now made sense: it had been out of suspicion and fear for her life. Fortunately, it was not clear if anything could be done to her now that was a Grim Reaper.

She was technically no longer alive.

"Don't tell anyone about this, Søren," she then insisted, veering towards him along the sidewalk so that she could lower her voice. "Especially not Thanatos. But I could be...*wrong*," she admitted with some difficulty, "So let's put a pin in this conversation."

The Trainer raised an eyebrow, still frowning. There was something that he did not understand. "So...why exactly did you tell me?"

It was not that he did not want to know —it was just the problem of telling him if she so desperately wanted to keep it on the down low. It would have been better to keep it to herself until she was sure. That was not to imply that Søren could not keep a secret —but he was under moral obligation to speak the truth. If someone were to ask about it, he would tell them everything; no questions asked.

But he did not want to find himself in that situation.

"Because I needed to share the idea with someone I trust," came the unexpected reply. Søren's brows rose.

She trusted him, and he could not understand why. In his opinion, he had not been the most particularly trustworthy person up until then. So, on what basis could she conclude that she trusted him?

Søren scratched the back of his neck as she looked on for his response. He averted his gaze and frowned. He could not seem to formulate any words.

"You aren't sure why I trust you, are you?" Savannah then sighed, as if reading his mind. "Well, let me put it like this. You could have left a long time ago, right? And yet…you're still here."

"But…I don't have a choice," he mumbled. "I'm sorry about earlier —I did not mean to mislead you. It's not that I don't lie; I just do my best to avoid it. As noble as you're making me sound, I'm really not doing this out of free will. I'm not allowed to leave you until you're ready."

She smiled and her eyes twinkled. "Then I hope I'm never ready. And it's okay —if being here is part of your job —"

"It was at first," Søren admitted.

"And…now?"

"Now, I'm choosing to stick around."

She gave him a mocking look of disbelief. "Thanks. It'd be nice to have and keep a good friend around here."

"You want to be friends with me that badly?" Søren teased.

"Well, I don't see many other candidates for the available positions," she teased back, grinning. He smiled back. He did not have a best friend, but Savannah would certainly make for an interesting one.

He thought back to his first so-called friend. *Angelina*.

Savannah was far sweeter than Angelina, and less bossy too. Her hair was redder and wavier, as well as thicker than Angelina's thin but longer auburn hair in ringlets. Savannah's smile reached her eyes, and not much seemed to bother her. Angelina's smile never made her eyes light up —not since her father had died. She gotten more serious after that as well, and found the grounds on which to turn into a manipulative trickster. Yet she still held Søren's heart, even if it meant twisting and squeezing it to her bidding.

The Trainer should say something.

But he did not want to tell Savannah the truth. Not yet. Because he had also fallen in love with Angelina —and he did not want to end up repeating history. The last time that he had felt anything for anyone was Melchior. Before him, Søren had not been willing to fall ever again. But what happened between them had loosened the chains on the cage he kept around his heart —not enough to open it, since he had not been devastated when they split.

But it had been enough to make him cry. Søren frowned and thought inwardly. He was barely over Melchior.

Then suddenly the Boss' words of warning rang in the back of his mind. Training Savannah was a professional obligation. Being her friend, was his own choice. And nothing more.

"You know…you would be the first trainee to even consider becoming friends with me," Søren eventually spoke.

"Why? Did you drive everyone else away?"

He frowned in offence as Savannah laughed lightly —but her amusement faded when she realised that his expression remained sullen. Søren simply shrugged, wishing that it was indifference.

"…No one thought I was worth knowing."

CHAPTER 28

THANATOS

ten minutes earlier…

✠

"…HORKOS. GOD OF oaths!" Thanatos thundered. The sky rumbled and the ground trembled. "State your purpose for coming here *uninvited*. I have not violated my oath concerning the Reapers."

Horkos glared at him and dropped his hammer to his side. "…I am not here for you, Thanatos, god of death."

Thanatos frowned and his grip on his scythe loosened. "Then what in the gods' names are you here for in such a threatening size?" he demanded. "This is my domain, fool!"

Horkos raised his free hand to tell Death to stop talking. "I am here for the child. Savannah Green; daughter of Hades, god of the Underworld."

The god of death hesitated.

He was not sure about what response to give. Instinct was urging him to tell Horkos without a second thought. After all, capturing Savannah would ensure the safety of the organisation. But a strange tug was causing Death to consider not selling her out —and it almost felt like…guilt.

"Let us not waste time and go around in circles," Horkos then continued.

"Reveal the child's location, or *else*."

"Do not *threaten* me," Thanatos said through his teeth, his grip on his scythe strengthened to iron. "I do not think that you are in any position to bargain with me on my grounds."

"I do not think that you are in any position to bargain, either," Horkos countered. "I have every right to uphold the conditions of the treaty by any means necessary. In addition, I am also aware that The Book of Treaties was in fact within your premises all of this time. It was stolen from me and hidden for quite some time. Regardless of how you managed to do it, I need it back. And seeing as it no longer seems to be here, I am under the assumption that it was taken. So, I will not bring harm to your operations if you tell me Savannah Green's location immediately."

The Book of Treaties had been in *Thanatos'* possession? That sounded absurd. Granted, he had not been in the library for a long time.

How on Earth had it been hidden?

Then he realised; the god of death knew exactly who had taken the book —the first time, and the most recent.

"…You dare to accuse *me* of thievery?" Death demanded. "You have no proof. And what would I do with the Book of Treaties, in any case?"

"Do not take me for a fool, Thanatos," Horkos warned him. "You have an extensive library, do not forget. And many gods wish to possess the book —you should be aware of that."

"I think I would know if my library had your book, Horkos," Thanatos said thickly. The god of oaths regarded him wearily before sighing angrily.

"Your defence is unimportant," Horkos snapped. "Give me what I need, or I will not hesitate to destroy what stands in my way."

"Destroy? As in, *my* headquarters? I think it unreasonable that you should punish my entire company because of one stupid employee," Thanatos pointed out.

Horkos smirked, evidently resorting to scheming. "…Indeed. I do agree that it would be most unfortunate and undesirable. So why do you not cooperate and

244

tell me where the child is?"

Admittedly, Thanatos knew precisely where the Reapers were. However, he could not tell Horkos that. Even with the knowledge, the god of oaths would destroy everything just to make a statement.

"…If I reveal her location, will you really leave this place and not harm anyone within the Reapers Organisation?" Thanatos asked, needing confirmation. He was hoping that Savannah and the rest of them in New York would be better equipped to negotiate with Horkos more effectively.

"I am bound by oath," Horkos assured him, raising his free hand and placing it on his chest.

Oh yes! thought the god of death.

One of the best things —but the worst for Horkos —about being the god of oaths was the additional importance of making a promise. Even if he did not swear upon the River Styx, Horkos was essentially unable to break his word.

If he did, he would effective immediately lose all of his power for half of a millennium.

Thanatos smiled deviously. Savannah would simply have to deal with Horkos herself, assuming that he could find her with Thanatos' incorrect directions. Unlikely, but not impossible.

"If you swear it, I will reveal the half god's location," Death told Horkos. "I will not endanger others on her behalf," he added darkly.

"What an interesting sense of leadership," Horkos remarked. "But very well. Be warned Thanatos, that if you do not honour your end of the deal that you will be punished accordingly."

"I…am aware."

"Then I swear upon the River Styx that I will not bring harm to anyone within the Reapers Organisation *if* you tell me where I can find the girl," Horkos declared, eyes as bright as hellfire.

"And so, I swear it too," Thanatos agreed.

He then thought about the perfect lie. Lest he wished for Horkos' confrontation for something as ridiculous as New Zealand, he had to be as vague but as close to accurate as possible.

"The girl used a portal," Death began with the truth. "The portals destinations are not specifically accurate, but I have an excellent idea of where you can find her."

Horkos grumbled and narrowed his eyes suspiciously. But he bought it. "Very well. Now, what is the location?"

The god of death hesitated. "The North American state of Washington."

"Washington?" Horkos repeated. "…Are you serious?"

"Yes," Thanatos said in the firmest tone that he could muster. "Now seeing as you have what you require, please leave my domain. Your size is threatening to my workers."

Horkos paused and seemed to stick his chin up stubbornly. "…I see. My presence reminds them of your previous war, am I right? The one where Kronos sought you out to apprehend some rather *illegal* employees. And the Olympians did not even bother to help —"

"Leave *now*," Thanatos cut him off with a voice that shook mountains, and Horkos actually flinched. Then Thanatos reined in that power and gave him a hard look. "You are not welcome here."

Horkos narrowed his eyes at Death and returned his gaze. Thanatos thought that he would lose his temper, but instead he relented. "…What a pity," he said in a low voice, and reluctantly turned around.

Thanatos watched him storm off to a portal he had made and did not feel safe until he disappeared through it, and before it dissipated after him. Death then exhaled and turned around as well, to walk back to headquarters.

He shrunk in size, regained his human appearance and his suit as he walked back up the steps, dragging his scythe behind him.

Nina met him inside.

"What in the gods' names are you still doing here?" he hissed at her. She gasped, before immediately running over, launching herself at him and then crushing him into an unexpected hug.

Death staggered and dropped his scythe. Nina sobbed as she clung to him, her hair falling out in strands. Thanatos did not know what to do. He felt conflicted between hugging her back and telling her to let go. But he hated seeing her upset. So, he let her maintain the embrace.

But he could not bring himself to return the gesture —physical affection was not something which he often displayed. He was then unsure of what to do with his arms, so he dithered with his fists clenched at his sides.

"I'm sorry, I couldn't help myself," Nina whispered, withdrawing slightly so she could face him. The whites of her eyes were reddish. "I tried to leave after everyone else had, but then I heard thunder. So, I figured you were only having an argument. I take it that it was a...misunderstanding?"

Thanatos grumbled before finally gripping her waist and setting her down onto the floor. "...I hate your intuition," he sighed. "It's a curse to me that you can just...*get* it."

"Not a blessing?" Nina smiled, raising an eyebrow. "*Someone* has got to keep you out of trouble."

He smiled in return. "What am I going to do without you," he sighed, impulsively reaching upwards and tucking her hair behind her ear. She stiffened and then so did he, realising what he was doing. He jerked away and she took a step back, fixing her hair by herself.

Thanatos hesitated.

Had he done that out of habit? He had done it when she had been younger. She would often grow sad at the mention of parents, whether hers or anyone else's, so Thanatos had done a lot of the comforting. She did not tie her hair back then, so it always fell into her face. He looked at Nina now as she wrapped her hair into a secure bun. Things were simply no longer the same. She was no longer a child, and certain things had now changed their meanings.

He needed to be careful.

"We need to get everyone back here," Death finally said, sighing shakily. "Preferably as many Reapers as possible. Horkos plans on going to the mundane world, so everyone would be safer in the divine. He swore not to harm anyone who is here."

247

Nina gave him a look. "You're not planning to leave those other Reapers *defenceless*, are you?"

"It is a factor that I have already taken into consideration," he said firmly.

"Thanatos, sir," she subtly scolded him in a low, careful voice. "That is not very becoming of a leader."

"Excuse me?" Thanatos raised an eyebrow. "I *am* being a leader. It will be better for the greater organisation."

"And not them?" Nina countered. "No matter how you feel about them, they are a still part of this organisation, Thanatos. Maybe not the *Detached*, but the other two certainly are."

"Well, then maybe I will fire them," Death growled.

"What. Why?" she asked. "What is your problem with them? They are not bad souls, so why are you just going to abandon them?"

"Because then I wouldn't have to worry about that stupid part of the family anymore!" Thanatos suddenly yelled, causing the room to shake.

Nina flinched at the power. Then she slowly narrowed her eyes at him. "…Family?" she repeated.

Thanatos took a deep breath and slumped his shoulders, realising that he had exposed himself. He thought about how he would talk his way out of it. But Nina was very observant, and she noticed little details. She would not believe him if he tried to twist the truth. Death did not keep much from Nina.

So, he decided that she could know.

"The girl, Savannah —she is…actually my half-sister," he told her.

"*What?*"

"Eighteen years ago, my father had an affair with a mortal woman. He does not usually do that, so I suspect that she caught his attention because she is a *Profitis* —someone who can see things from the divine world that normal mortals don't. They had a child; a half-blood god, and soon he had to leave them due to a certain treaty. It forbids half-bloods from existing. They are too dangerous and unpredictable. So, Savannah was monitored by me for most of her life through the necklaces our father gave to us. She showed no signs of power or supernatural

248

abilities except for a few incidents that were written off and kept a secret. And then...then she died."

Nina looked confused. "So...does she still technically pose a threat?"

Thanatos sighed and nodded. "Because she is a Grim Reaper, indeed she does. I mean, you saw what she did to get in here. She killed someone, and if she ever had a chance before to be spared, it will be gone now."

Nina glanced down and thought for a moment. "...How many other cases like this have there been? Of a half-blood god who turned into a Reaper?"

Death paused. "Actually, you know...I do not think that I have ever come across another one," he admitted. "I have only heard tales of half-blood gods anyway, but I would not know if we ever employed one. I don't look too deeply into that department..." he mumbled.

"So, she is rare as well as hunted," Nina remarked. Then she smiled softly and shook her head. "...If you fire her, then she really can be dead. Then the treaty will be ineffective, and she can reincarnate or remain in the afterlife. Right?" she suggested hopefully.

"Hm. That does not sound like a bad plan," Thanatos murmured. "Firing her also ensures that we will not be held accountable for any other idiotic things she has done since she died."

"But why did you even hire her in the first place?" Nina questioned. "Surely if you had thought about the implications of her being a half-blood, you would not have done so?"

"Yes, well —I do not actually hold job interviews or anything. She was obviously chosen because she fit the criteria."

"And, is she worth it?" Nina asked, with an edge to her voice.

Death frowned and gave her a look. She just raised an eyebrow. "What is that supposed to mean?" he asked.

"It means," she breathed wearily, "...is she worth keeping in the Reapers Organisation. Is she worth abandoning. Is she worth...losing?"

He blinked rapidly, surprised by her use of reverse psychology. He understood at that which she was getting —was Savannah worth losing in terms of her relation to him. And he thought about it.

Would he really care? It was not as though he had any attachment to her. All she had ever been was a burden, and he despised her almost as much as his mother Persephone did. Not because he did not wish for her to exist, but because his daily life would have been far simpler.

Every time that Thanatos looked upon the redhead, he saw Phoebe Green. The two mortals bore a striking resemblance. And he knew that the unease would be the same for the rest of his family. He knew that Savannah and her mother's existence was something that Persephone especially would rather think of as a bad memory —or even a fabricated bad dream.

It did not hurt as much as Death had figured it would when he reached a conclusion. "…Yes, she is," he finally answered Nina, before turning around and walking away from her.

CHAPTER 29

SØREN

IT LOOKED AS though it would rain soon.

Søren thought about death. It felt appropriate to think of such grim things in the rain. The rain itself seemed to support this, since it nearly always rained at funerals. It had not rained at his funeral.

It had snowed.

And he felt that it had been an appropriate response from the weather to snow. Because his death experience had been *like* the snow: the sensation of being dead was exactly as he had thought.

Cold, numb and sort of hollow.

It had not been any different from living.

Søren had been born a day before it had snowed, and he had died a day before it had snowed. It had been a fitting send-off.

"…Hey, Savannah?" he now quipped. She turned to face him as they walked. The highway had come to an end, blending into the urban cityscape as they wandered the highstreets. Nadine and Lewis were too absorbed in being tourists; jostling about and messing with oblivious passers-by; so Søren had the opportunity to talk to his trainee alone again.

"I had only started watching you on the day that you were due to die. How had your life been before that?"

The redhead drew a shaky breath. "Same old, same old," she murmured.

"How descriptive," Søren deadpanned.

Savannah's heels ground into the concrete in a similar way to her gritting teeth. "It was normal, okay?" she snapped. "Perfectly happy and normal. Nothing was lacking. My life was...perfect," she breathed.

Søren frowned in utter disbelief.

"That's bullshit," he huffed. "No person or life is perfect, Savannah. Why do you think we end up dead? Because we were *flawless*? As if. It's okay to admit things weren't great, you know. It makes for a good story."

"Excuse me?" she huffed, nudging his side. "A good story? What does that mean? I'm not writing an autobiography."

"That is not what I meant," Søren assured his trainee firmly. "I'm just saying, that what someone goes through in their childhood and adolescence shapes them into the interesting person they are today."

"Or a boring person."

He turned around to meet her gaze. "Who said that '*interesting*' always alludes to an exciting thing?"

She opened her mouth and closed it again, at a loss.

So, Søren began to tell her something which he had never told anyone before.

"...It was an ordinary day in early November," he sighed. "It hadn't started snowing yet, but I remember that I couldn't wait for it to do so. I had my studies to occupy my short attention span, but something else was distracting me. A girl was going to pay me a visit."

Savannah blinked before she realised that he was talking about the day he had died. "...Angelina?" she whispered.

"Yes. And don't let her name fool you. She was the furthest thing from angelic," the Trainer answered. "She told me her father was hosting a lady and wished her out of the house. So, she came to mine. My father didn't know, and he was in his study until...until the gunshots."

"Oh, Søren," she breathed.

"She was polite enough when she arrived and suggested that we go outside and enjoy what was left of Autumn. We laughed and joked and chased each other and rolled down hills until mid-afternoon," he murmured. "And pun intended; it was all downhill from there."

"*God*, that's corny," she sighed, smiling slightly. He did not return it.

"She seduced me," Søren stated bluntly.

"What?" Savannah hissed. "Seduced you. Like a stripper?"

"Escort," he corrected, "is the word you're looking for. And no, not like that," he muttered self-consciously. "She wanted to try something with me —to see how far I would let her go. I was so in love with her that I didn't think to say no. I wanted to say no, deep down. But I didn't."

Savannah offered the Reaper a sympathetic look.

"Anyway, we didn't end up having sex, because the sudden sound of gunfire made us pause a few stages prior. Angelina looked frightened enough, but for some reason, she didn't really look like she wanted to stop immediately —she wouldn't willingly allow me to go. But I eventually managed to escape my room, then she slipped from the house…and I got to my father just before he was shot right in front of me. The intruders ran out of bullets after I then fought them, but they injured me with shards of broken glass. Then I was left to bleed to death."

Savannah gasped, but knew not to comment on the deaths. "…What happened when you Turned?" she asked.

"It was strange. I remember thinking, what did I do to deserve this? To not rest in peace. Why had Death chosen *me*…?" Søren then pressed his lips into a tight line and blinked to get rid of the sting of tears.

Savannah remained quiet for a few moments. "…From when I was born until I was almost seven, I thought that my family was the best and happiest in all the world. We always laughed together and played together, and there was so much love that I now wonder if it was too good to be true. And lo and behold, my father left us —me and my Mom."

"Well, at least you have an idea of the reason why now," Søren mumbled, unsure if it would help.

"That's true," she sighed. "…I guess I hated him for a long time just because I didn't know what we had done wrong, if we had even done something. I blamed myself, mostly, because everything seemed to have been going right until *I* was born —"

"Savannah don't say that," Søren then hissed, disbelieving of what he was hearing. "Don't you ever think that. You know your father probably would have stayed if he had not been leading a double life."

She blinked, and then looked downwards. "...Even so," she said shakily, "I can't help but think that their relationship would have turned out better if they hadn't introduced children into their lives."

The Trainer did not respond. He could not relate to what she was saying. In his original timeline, children had only been for affirming an heir; and young girls had been encouraged to marry wealthy for that purpose. Maybe there was some truth in what Savannah was saying, but Søren could not stand hearing her talk about herself like that.

"You are important, you know that?" he said. "No matter what happened after your father left. You didn't stop being loved."

She smirked and shook her head at him.

"I'm serious," he insisted.

"You're Søren," she retorted.

The Trainer said nothing, and shoved his hands into his pockets. He did not know if his pain was then too telling, but he drew a breath, struggling to say the next thing. "...The first soul that I reaped out of training was Angelina's."

"What? Seriously?" Savannah's jaw dropped slightly in surprise.

"It was an assassination job," Søren went on. "Acting on orders, after Angelina had put her oldest son to bed, a man from her father's council came into her and her husband's room. She was better equipped than I thought she might have been. Maybe she understood the perpetual danger of the life she led. She...then fought the assassin until he managed to slit her throat."

Savannah started.

The Trainer chuckled weakly. "...It had been pretty gruesome. The husband had been in on it, because he had purposely ripped his night shirt and carved out a wound to make it seem as though he had also been attacked."

There was a pause, and Savannah's discomfort was overwhelming.

"…Angelina knew it was me when I entered the room. She had seen me around the house before that, as routine, but I wasn't really watching *her*. I was watching her life —catching up with everything I had missed.

I suppose that a part of me hoped that she had actually loved me, and I know it sounds cruel, but I wanted to see her suffer. Not in physical pain, but emotionally —for the fact that I was no longer there. I wanted her to feel as torn as I did. Do you know how much it hurt to see that she was perfectly well? *Happy*, even?" Søren gritted through his teeth. "As though she had completely forgotten me. Like I had been nothing to her."

Savannah's eyes glistened with a film of welling tears.

"…Despite that, believe it or not, I still cared," he admitted. "She might have been wickedly devious, but *I* still loved her. So, when I saw her three children and rich, cocky husband I felt…I felt —"

"—Completely torn apart?" Savannah offered. He nodded slowly. "…I get it," she went on. "It's not the same, but that's kind of what I felt when I reaped Aaron. Like everything had been a lie."

Søren frowned. Not that asshole again. Her relations were valid, but it felt tainted because of that mortal in particular.

Angelina had never gotten the opportunity to tell Søren face to face that she had started pretending after a certain point. That was also a difference between him and Savannah: Angelina had grown to manipulate, while the trainee had been fooled right from the start.

"…I didn't think that you would tell me so soon," Savannah then whispered. "Whatever happened to telling me when you were ready?"

He turned back to her and shrugged. "I guess I just…felt ready."

"*I* didn't really want to tell you about me," she murmured. "I know that's hypocritical, but I guess I was afraid that you would judge me incorrectly and jump to all sorts of conclusions. I…I'm sorry."

Søren paused and thought about those two words. '*I'm sorry*'. He frowned, wondering if he believed that. What was going to stop her from withholding information from him again based on some *emotion*?

"…*Søren*," the younger Reaper said irritably, regaining his attention. "Hello? I said that I'm sorry. Seriously."

He nodded slowly but did not look at her.

"Søren," she breathed, walking closer. "We just swapped traumatic backstories. Now all you can do is sulk?"

The Trainer breathed deeply, gathering his thoughts. He turned to face her, and for a moment, he saw Angelina…and then not. *She is not her.*

He knew that Savannah was her own person, with her own intentions.

His expression softened.

"…Thanks for telling me," he said. "I know it wasn't easy."

"I'm grateful too," she murmured. "I appreciate you telling me. I can only imagine the hurt you had felt. It's…probably not entirely fair for me to compare my pain to yours."

He stiffened. "Probably."

"But I want you to feel like you can talk to me," she quipped. "And even I with you. About the good, and the bad. Sometimes things hurt a little less when you tell someone else."

Søren sulked. He hated how right she was.

They then walked on and Savannah jumped into Lewis and Nadine's antics, while the Trainer remained in peaceful silence a little way behind them.

A small smile tugged at his lips.

The dull ache in his chest that throbbed whenever he spoke or thought about Angelina was beginning to fade.

CHAPTER 30

SØREN

THEY ARRIVED IN Downtown Manhattan sometime at night.

Søren and Savannah led their guests to the apartment in silence while they continued to *ooh* and *ah* at any iconic landmark.

Once they were at the building itself, Nadine and Lewis did a double take when Søren unlocked the facial recognition security system and the normal bricks turned over to turn into white granite slates. They then walked in, past the few stares they received, and headed to the elevator.

The employed Reapers knew that it was risky to bring in a pair of *Detached*, but no one would dare to approach them or a still wanted Grim Reaper while they had a respected Trainer by their side.

"This place is so *fancy*," Nadine whistled, leaning against the mirrored back panel. "Marble everywhere; a grand foyer —"

"It isn't that grand," Savannah deadpanned. "And not everything here is made out of marble. Don't be so culturally insensitive."

"—And an *elevator*!" Nadine went right on, completely ignoring her. "We had stairs back in my day. Only stairs."

"What a tragedy," Savannah mocked.

Thankfully, Melchior was not in the elevator. Søren was not sure if he could have dealt with that right in front of everyone. He pressed the button to the second floor and leaned back against the wall, sighing deeply. His mind was then somewhere else —a couple of years ago. In that very elevator. Melchior had pushed him up against that mirrored wall, and kissed him senseless. He could almost feel the swell of Melchior's lips, the grazing of his teeth.

"…Søren? *Søren*," Nadine's voice snapped Søren out of it as she half-heartedly punched him in the stomach. "We're here. Look alive."

He snorted at the irony of her command before swiftly shuffling out of the elevator after everyone else. They padded along to room eight and then parted like the Red Sea to let Søren through to unlock the door. He took his key out of his pocket and fumbled around —but the door was already unlocked. He started in alarm, before pushing it open.

Then he froze.

The living room was ankle deep in fire extinguisher foam; the walls and furniture also splattered with the stuff; and the dreaded Phoenix was perched on a side table, preening itself. There was a person in Søren's apartment too, holding the fire extinguisher, and covered in some foam in soapy patches.

Then the person turned around.

Melchior's garnet eyes stared back at Søren, caught like a deer in headlights. He had forgotten that he had given the blond a spare key.

"…Chainsaw Guy?" Savannah spoke up, moving out from behind her Trainer. He frowned before remembering that it was in fact a nickname. Melchior frowned at the name too, before glancing at his chainsaw on the sofa and realising from where it had arisen.

He then shook slightly, sending the foam flying in every direction.

"What are you doing here, Melchior?" Søren asked in quiet voice, pressing his lips into a tight line. "You're not supposed to come here anymore. Especially by yourself."

"There was an emergency," he protested, gesturing to the Phoenix. "I smelled smoke, so I came to check up on —"

"You live three floors up," the Trainer cut him off. "How could you smell *anything* from up there?"

He gave the older Reaper a look. "You want me to be honest? Fine. I had come wanting to talk to you, but your door was locked. Then I smelled the smoke. So, I unlocked the door and...there was a Phoenix in the middle of your living room and all of your plants were on fire."

"...You know Phoenixes don't like the colour green, right?" Lewis murmured. "It drives them a little crazy."

Everyone groaned.

Søren smacked his forehead and drew a deep breath in. If Lewis was telling the truth, then why had Phee-Phee not attacked his plants the last time that they had seen him? He dismissed that thought though, because he had another matter that was more pressing.

Søren was not upset at the mere fact that Melchior was in his room. He was more upset that the Reaper had tried to stop his apartment from burning to a crisp. The Trainer did not need him to waltz in and start playing hero.

Now Søren owed him a favour —and he was the last person on Earth to whom the Trainer wanted to be indebted.

The Phoenix suddenly stopped fussing about its appearance and looked directly next to Søren —at Savannah. It hopped off of the table and scurried towards her, before coming to a standstill and cooing softly.

"...Phee-Phee?" she whispered, bending down to be eye level with it. "Look Søren. He survived after all."

"Phoenixes also become aggressive when moulting or after rising from their ashes," Lewis added, believing that everyone was paying attention. "It's when they're at their most vulnerable; so to ward off predators."

"How do you know so much about Phoenixes?" Savannah asked.

Lewis shrugged modestly. "I do a lot of reading."

"And research," Nadine chipped in. "He used to observe them like a scientist. It was a little obsessive."

"*Hey,*" her brother whined in protest, "you promised that you would never tell anyone about that."

"...Oops."

Søren did not care about where Lewis had learned all of that. What he really cared about at that moment was the fact that the demon bird was still inside of his apartment. Was it ever going to leave?

"…Who are they?" Melchior then asked with an edge to his voice, pointing to Nadine and Lewis.

"They are our *invited* and *welcome* guests that we picked up from headquarters," Søren answered in a passive aggressive tone.

"Aw, we're invited *and* welcome?" Nadine cooed; a huge patronising grin plastered to her face.

"I just saved your apartment," Melchior went on, grunting out the sentence through his clenched teeth. "There wouldn't be anything to welcome your precious invited guests *to* if I had not shown up."

Søren growled and folded his arms.

He knew that he was behaving like a child, but he did not care. He was pissed off, and Melchior was going to see that.

"And who are *you*?" Nadine asked curiously, swinging the direction of the conversation back to Melchior's question.

The blond Reaper glanced at Søren briefly for help, but both seemed to share the same look of uncertainty. He then decided for himself.

"…I'm his friend," he answered casually enough.

Søren flinched at the word '*friend*' and found interest in the wall.

Savannah then came to their unwanted rescue.

"Actually, they used to date," she announced.

The Trainer's head whipped around and he glared at her, his face ablaze. Melchior glanced away, stiff and uncomfortable.

Søren hissed at Savannah to shut up, and all she did was giggle sheepishly.

Nadine raised an eyebrow as she put her hands on her hips. "You didn't strike me as a guy who swings the other way," she told the Trainer.

Søren lidded his eyes. What a great euphemism.

"Technically, he swings *all* ways," Melchior corrected her. The Trainer glanced at him; his eyes set. The blond only offered a guilty shrug.

"…He's pan?" Savannah reiterated, raising both eyebrows.

"Wait —he's a frying pan?" Lewis asked, furrowing his eyebrows in confusion. Everyone looked at him strangely. "…What?" he asked with an apparently genuine seriousness. But no one had the chance to explain.

"All right, that's enough," Søren firmly spoke up. "Can we stop talking about me as if I'm not here? Also, sorry to shock you, but my sexuality is *not* a topic to be discussed. And Melchior," he sighed, deciding not to bother to get angry, "—get out of my apartment."

Melchior shuffled around for a moment before he grabbed his chainsaw from the sofa and then made his way to the door.

"…I was really only trying to help."

"I never asked you to," Søren growled, his eyes following the younger Reaper's until he walked out of the door and then closed it.

"He seems like a caring person," Lewis remarked. "He did save all of your stuff after all. So why are you pushing him away?"

Søren ignored his question and shuffled towards his computer room door. He did not need any input from someone who knew nothing about the situation.

Sure, Melchior was somewhat behaving at the moment, but he could snap at any point and prove exactly why he was not wanted around.

"You wouldn't understand, Lewis," Savannah said quietly, finally saying something helpful. "There's some bad blood." Then she looked at her Trainer sympathetically and stopped being helpful. "…But Lewis still has a point. He did help. Think of all those books that could have burned."

"They're still *ruined*," Søren snapped, picking one up and holding it in front of them. It dripped foam onto the already spoiled carpet. Then he saw the title underneath and flinched, realising that it was one of his favourites. "How am I going to fix all of this?" he whispered.

No one answered. The question had not been intended to be rhetorical, but the other Reapers shuffled around and averted their gazes as though a response was still expected. Søren growled.

Maybe Melchior *should* have let it all burn.

It would have been better than dealing with a soggy heap.

"I think someone should lock the two of you in a room," Savannah suggested. "Maybe then you'd learn how to get along."

Søren scoffed. As if that was ever going to happen. He would not be able to let his guard down long enough so that such a scenario could be fabricated.

"I'm going to check on the computer system," he sighed, opening the door. "Maybe there's still something worth saving."

✠

Angelina was okay.

Søren's computer room was left relatively untouched, and no foam had managed to short circuit the boards.

He breathed out a sigh of relief and sat down in front of the main monitor, before he swivelled around in the chair.

"We need to talk," Savannah's voice suddenly said, causing him to jump. She was frowning at him from the doorway, arms folded and foot tapping.

"Don't scare me like that," Søren gasped, sitting upright.
She sighed and came in, before leaning against the desk and looking at him gravely. "…About when you spoke about Angelina —"

"You don't have to say anything," Søren snapped, narrowing his eyes. "I…need to loosen up a bit. It's just hard for me, okay? I'm not used to having someone I can talk to about that kind of stuff."

"I wasn't…actually talking about that," Savannah said dubiously. "I was thinking more about the fate of the world —not of our trust."

He went rigid. "Oh."
"But I'm glad that you see eye to eye with me now," she said more encouragingly. "However, we need to focus on the matter at hand."

Søren nodded. The redhead tucked her hair behind her ears and exhaled deeply. "Look, I'm not sure who that Titan was, but they're probably out to get Thanatos like Kronos did. Which means our lives are once again in the hands of Mr *Oh-So*-Competent," she said sarcastically.

Søren chuckled in amusement.

"I'm kind of worried though," she then confessed. "Will the power I have as a half-blood right now be enough in a battle?"

"What? Light projection isn't enough for you?" he teased.

"*Ha ha*," she mocked. "I just wanted…something else. Death said it was only for defensive purposes."

Søren smirked and stood up. "Well…what if you can talk to the dead but just don't know it, because it sort of comes with the job?"

Savannah titled her head to the side and frowned. "…Doubt it."

"You…could have the power to *raise* the dead," the Trainer suggested. "You could create your own undead army."

"I don't think that's a thing —I'm pretty sure in most mythologies and fantasy lore that you're not allowed to raise the dead. And if you do, it comes with disastrous consequences," Savannah snorted. "…But it makes me feel better to think of possibilities," she admitted, glancing at the floor.

Then she suddenly flinched, as though someone had slapped her.

"Savannah?" Søren said, moving forward. "Are you okay?"

She paused, before shaking her head and breathing out shallowly.

"I'm fine. It's…it's nothing, probably," she mumbled. "I just felt a strange sensation. Like a wave of intense heat pulsing through my veins. It didn't hurt, per se —it was just…strange."

Søren frowned and moved closer to her. She was hesitant to let him touch her, but she did not stop his hand from then resting on her shoulder. She looked up at him blankly, while he looked back with concern.

"Are you sure that you're okay?" he whispered.

She nodded slowly.

Søren then removed his hand. "Okay. But if you want to talk, or —"

"I said I'm *fine*," she then snapped, raising her voice. Søren blinked, surprised. He took a step backwards and put his hands back in his pockets. Savannah bit her lip and averted her gaze. "…By the way, something tells me that you're still thinking about what you told me."

"What do you mean?"

"That you wanted to see Angelina suffer," she elaborated. "Melchior seems to be suffering as well —but you don't look all too pleased. Does it hurt you whenever you see each other as much as it hurts him?"

Søren's jaw clenched. "What?"

"You can't tell me that you don't see the pain in his expression —in his eyes, every time. Do you…still care about him? In a different way?"

He did not. He *should* not. He did not want to think about it. She was right — it did hurt him in a different way. Did it hurt because instead of one of them being left behind and being long dead, Melchior was more physically there, existing in the same timeline as him?

It was as if Søren could not escape him.

The Trainer did recall resolving not to be so petty as to request a district transfer after they had broken up. It did make him wonder though, why Melchior had stayed. Perhaps Søren was not deluded in thinking that the blond Reaper still cared as well —in his own strange and passive way. Søren stiffened at the conclusion.

"…Holy shit," he sighed, raking his hands through his hair.

"I'm going to get him back," Savannah then stated.

"Wait, *what*?" Søren cried, mortified.

"Yeah," she confirmed, sidestepping him and headed for the door again. "I…I think that it would be good for you," she clarified, before walking out. Søren shook his head and flopped back into his chair.

Good for him?

Even back then when they were some kind of happy; since when had anything to do with Melchior been good for him?

264

CHAPTER 3I

SØREN

THE LIFE EXPECTANCY for the average celebrity musician was not very high. It was too bad then that Melchior was already technically dead, because Søren could have sorted it out for him if he had still been alive, with no hesitation. When they had first met, the Trainer had been rather impressed by Melchior's life before he Turned. He had been a rock band lead singer and a model, having died from a drug overdose at one of his tour parties. A tragic story; but he had assured Søren that he regretted none of it.

Maybe that was part of the reason why the older Reaper resented him. He had not died thinking about the people he left behind.

"...I still can't believe that Søren sent for you to bring me back here," Melchior's voice suddenly said from the other side of the door, making Søren jump. "That's not exactly like him."

Damn right it is not.

"Trust me," Savannah said sweetly. "He can't *wait* to talk to you."

Anyone who knew Søren would know that statement was a complete lie. Which meant that Melchior should not be fooled. The Trainer sighed and turned his back to the door, just before he heard it open.

"Søren," Savannah said loudly. "Play nice."

He refrained from saying anything back, and only clicked his tongue. He was above dignifying that statement with a response.

The redhead sighed and turned to leave. "Can you at least try?" she asked, before walking out and closing the door.

Søren glared at Melchior as he just stood there. The blond shrugged, rocking back and forth on his heels. It was as though now that he was there, he had no idea what to say to him. And there was no time for such hesitancy.

"…I'm out of here," the Trainer sighed and got up, heading for the door. He gripped the handle and pulled —but the door did not budge. He pulled on it harder, but it remained shut. It was locked. Savannah had locked them in. Søren then recalled her words from before.

"Someone should lock the two of you in a room.
Maybe then you'd learn to get along."

"Oh, you have got to be shitting me," he murmured, banging his fist feebly against the door. "That scheming little —I can't believe she locked us in."

"What? We're locked in?" Melchior said in surprise, before going over. He struggled with the door as well.

"Perfect," Søren huffed, folding his arms. "Now I can't escape."
"Does this mean…that we have to talk after all?" Melchior asked.

"Like hell it does," Søren grumbled. "I will still refuse to talk to you even though we're locked in the same room."

"Then just listen to me," Melchior suggested. "You don't have to talk back…Just hear me out. Please."

The Trainer glanced at him and raised an eyebrow. The blond might as well go ahead —he obviously loved the sound of his own voice. But he should be prepared for his words to fall on deaf ears.

"I was thinking about you before I came downstairs," he started. Søren tensed in response. "I had been hung up on what you said to me in the elevator last time. I guess I had deserved it. That was kind of why I wanted to talk to you. But seeing you with that girl —"

"Savannah," Søren corrected him. "Her name is Savannah."

266

"Well, she didn't sound very willing to tell me that the last time that we interacted," Melchior justified.

Søren scoffed. *Obviously she had not wanted him to know.*

"...Anyway," he continued. I was curious about your relationship with her."

The Trainer's fingers curled tighter around the wooden edge of the desk as he thought of how to respond, and he was sure that Melchior noticed.

"...You told me that you don't have any interest in your trainees. But then you two just disappear. What am I supposed to think?" the blond sighed, shooting Søren a look.

The dark haired Reaper frowned in offence. "What, do you seriously think we ran away together or something?" he snorted. "Come on. We were arrested and taken to Purgatory to see the Boss."

"No, *you* come on, Søren," Melchior said firmly. "Arrested? That's not like you." He then snarled. "...What did she do?"

Søren looked at him and furrowed his eyebrows. His behaviour —his concern; it made the Trainer jump to one conclusion.

"Are you jealous?" he asked bluntly.

Melchior glanced away for a moment, not wanting to confess to anything. "You seem...close," he said instead. "Are you friends? Or something more?"

"It's none of your business," Søren informed him.

"It's just a simple answer."

"That *you* won't get the satisfaction of hearing."

Melchior growled and then fell into a pace, muttering under his breath. Søren knew that the beast within the blond was awakening and prowling, ready to sink its claws into him. Søren watched him walk back and forth for a moment before he sighed, relenting. It was not worth aggravating him that much.

"...We saw something," Søren murmured. "Something in Purgatory. Something new —and terrifying. It was another Titan; a blue one. We think...the Organisation might be in trouble again."

"Is that really why you're so on edge?" Melchior said with concern.

Søren did not respond.

"…So, this Titan," the younger Reaper said, clearing his throat. "Is the reason you kicked me out and wouldn't thank me?"

"You know bloody well why I kicked you out," Søren grunted. "And when would I ever thank you?"

"Gods, you're so stubborn," Melchior muttered.

Søren pressed his lips into a line and remained cold.

"Look Søren, besides being an asshole, you haven't really been yourself lately. You didn't even shout at me earlier. I know when you are stressed out — you go quiet. It's dangerous. I just want to know how you're…coping."

Søren looked up at him slowly with an expression that was a mixture of anger and disbelief. He did not say anything. He did not think that he *could*. The concern…it felt too foreign to hear that coming from him. So, Søren did something familiar. He raised his middle finger at him.

"Ugh, why won't you just *tell* me?" Melchior groaned.

"I don't have to tell you anything," Søren murmured. "We're not friends."

Melchior raised his eyebrows at that, but then nodded slowly. "You are right. We're not friends. We're just people who used to know each other, deeply. And…I promised you that I would care about you no matter what happened to us, so let me honour that. You look stressed, Søren, and I don't think it's because of this *new Titan*."

The Trainer breathed out harshly through his nose. He did not want to tell him anything. He did not want to do something that showed some level of closeness to another person. Because the two were no longer close.

"Please. Let me help."

Help? Søren thought. *Melchior wanted to* help*?*

"We're just friends!" he suddenly snapped.

Melchior just stared in what appeared to be surprise. For some reason, it made Søren angrier, and he ground his teeth together. "Christ. Nothing happened between us. Because I can't let go of the past; I keep holding onto things and…I don't know what's wrong with me."

Melchior blinked and averted his gaze. "Søren —"

"I'm confused. I was thinking about…someone else from my past. This girl I was in love with a long time ago."

Having told Savannah, Søren was now riding on the coattails of the courage he had had in order to finally tell Melchior about it. His expression turned sceptical. "Who? You've never mentioned anyone before me."

"There were others," Søren exaggerated. "You're not that special."
A sound like a snarl ripped through Melchior's throat.

Søren could not contain his smug pleasure upon hearing it. "Oh, so you definitely are jealous," he smirked.

"Yes," Melchior grumbled, actually admitting it. "I thought…I was your first. That notion was something that was really special to me."

Søren blinked. Given his past behaviour, it had not ever occurred to him that Melchior cared and had held such things in esteem.

"…You were not my first kiss," Søren confessed. "Nor were you the first to arouse me. But you can claim everything else."

That did not completely satisfy Melchior.

There was nothing that he could do to change that fact. It made Søren smile to know that he sparked that jealous side of him. Though Melchior managed to contain his annoyance, and ask the Trainer to give Angelina some background. To explain what she meant to him.

"She was a nobleman's daughter. Her father and mine had been rivals of sorts. He didn't approve of her. But I was naïve, and I fell in love as the years went on. I think that she loved me too, at some point, for a little while. Then she…betrayed my family, after her father's death. His empire crumbled, and she had resolved to restore it by any means necessary. Even if *I* was in the way. She had stopped feeling anything real, I think."

"Do you still love her, in spite of all that?" the blond Reaper asked.

Søren sighed deeply. "It's complicated. My heart is telling me that I still am, but I don't want to be. I want to forget her. And my emotions are completely fucked up right now," he admitted. "I think that part of me…craves emotion that was lost."

Melchior's expression turned into one of hurt, before he took a step towards the Trainer. "*Søren*. It's okay," he said softly. Then he smirked. "...I never expected you of all people to have an emotional outburst."

Søren smiled slightly and feebly swung a punch at Melchior's chest, before glaring at him. "Asshole," he grumbled, which earned a chuckle.

The Trainer wiped his face roughly with the sleeve of his jacket, sniffling. Melchior then suddenly ruffled his black hair. Søren stiffened, remembering all of the times he had done it before. He had not cared much for it back then, but now, it hauled up memories he had worked to bury. He then swatted his arm away. "Don't do that, Melchior," he warned. "We're not *that* cool."

Melchior did not chuckle spitefully. He did not snort in amusement. He withdrew and respected Søren's orders. Maybe it was mostly because he was ranked above him, but the Trainer would like to believe it was a small indication that Melchior was becoming a little more human.

"...Do you like *her* now? Savannah?"

The way he said her name...as if any feelings that Søren might in fact have were her fault. He tried not to react to the question. He clicked his knuckles and stared blankly at the floor. He did not like Savannah —not in that way. But he realised something as he glanced upwards and caught Melchior's eye. That swirl of red and purple made his chest tighten. Maybe he really was feeling something for someone he really should not.

Shit, shit, shit —I cannot let it happen again, he internally hissed.

"No, I don't," Søren clipped aloud.

He sighed and collapsed into his chair, and then swivelled around in it lazily. Melchior folded his arms and leaned against the desk, before they looked up and met each other's gaze again. The intensity rose.

"What happened to us, Sør?" Melchior murmured.

Søren started so violently that he nearly fell off the chair. Melchior had not called him by that name in nearly a year. It had been his genius idea of retaliation after Søren had called him Mel. Then it had become endearing.

He had hissed it in pleasure against Søren's flushed skin; and muttered it in the Trainer's ear when he was in one of his moods.

"You've grown," he then continued. Søren frowned. "No, I mean, you've *matured* since I met you. You've risen the ranks and you…you really seem better off. Seriously —I'm proud of you."

Søren paused, unsure of how to feel or of what to say.

"…*Jesus*, you sound like a teacher," he blurted out irritably; stiffening and averting his gaze as he turned to continue to swivel.

"Learn to take a compliment, Søren."

Søren hung his head. "I don't think that you get it," he clipped. "I'm not ready to be…normal around you, Melchior. And you can go ahead and make fun of me all you want for it, but you…*hurt* me. You would think that after all this time that maybe I would be over it, but I'm not. I'm not any different —any better. So, I guess the time just hasn't been long enough. Not yet."

Melchior did not respond, and all Søren heard was the shuffling of feet. He squeezed his eyes shut, frustrated with himself for letting the blond get all of that out of him. "…I know," Melchior finally said. "And…I'm sorry."

Søren's jaw dropped slightly. The two words that he had waited for so long to hear —had Melchior really just said them? It was a goddamn miracle.

"…Wait. What?"

"I said that I'm sorry," the blond Reaper said more firmly. "I'm sorry for hurting you. It had not been my intention." He then paused, his brows narrowing further. "You were too fragile, okay?" he grumbled in exasperation. "Yeah, you say that you're apathetic, but I could *see*, Sør. You were too innocent and naïve for your own good."

Søren closed his mouth and his jaw set. Of course, there would be a catch. As if Melchior could say sorry and just leave it at that.

The Trainer glared at him and sat upright. "So maybe I was a little unstable and still trying to figure out who I was —but was that your basis to break up with me? Because as you said, it wasn't because you didn't want to '*be gay*' anymore," he spat, making quotation marks in the air.

Melchior glanced elsewhere and frowned, before mumbling, "Not really."

271

Søren let out a hiss. He realised that he had to stop squirming and being afraid of the other Reaper; afraid of telling him how he really felt.

"Bullshit!" Søren cried, jumping up. Melchior hesitated, confused. "It *is*," the Trainer continued. "It is because you couldn't stand being with such a bipolar, depressed prick any longer, right?" he accused. The blond did not say anything. Did that mean that he agreed with the statement, to a degree?

"…I knew it!" Søren declared, shoving his chest —or at least attempting to. Melchior caught his fists and held them, keeping him from moving away. "I knew it," Søren repeated in a low whisper, his voice breaking like large fissures in a desert. "…We couldn't get along from the start."

Melchior said something then. "That's not true," he insisted. "We were great friends. And then I really did fall in love with you. I just…when we…"

"When we what?" Søren scoffed, withdrawing and making him meet his eye. "When we what, Melchior?" he taunted, trying to strike a nerve. He wanted him to say it —to validate what they did. He *needed* him to say it, so he could stop feeling like the entire instance was a fabrication. "…Why don't you just *say* it?" he rasped. "We've been avoiding it ever since you left that night and pretending like it never happened. So? What did we —"

"We slept together!" Melchior suddenly raised his voice, cutting the other Reaper off. "We slept together for the first time…and I left you."

They then stood in silence, staring at each other. Melchior looked into Søren's narrowed eyes guiltily. His admittance did little to satisfy the Trainer —he was thoroughly disappointed. It was not because it came out this way.

Søren was disappointed in himself for clearly being a problem, yet again. He could not figure out in what way he had messed up though, because he recalled numerous pleasured exclaims, from the both of them. Gods; *the touch of his fingers, the sound of his strained breaths, and the* heat —

Melchior had told Søren that he loved him, right before it. Perhaps he had he not meant it, then. Not meant it when he had claimed the smaller male for his own, or taken him in his mouth. He had not meant it when they had lain there side by side, content with the mere touch of skin. He had not meant it when Søren had told him too, sincerity in every syllable.

And he had realised only after we had shared that intimacy that maybe the two of us would not work after all, Søren theorised.

It had been risky to let Melchior take his virginity. It was true, then, what was said —the first time will always stay with you. *Haunting* you.

The memories of it came flooding in a sudden surge for Søren, and he found himself starting to drown in the chaos. His face warmed as he stiffened at the realisation that he was blushing. It intensified as he became self-conscious. He hated looking pathetic in front of Melchior.

"…*Shit*," Søren said, finally breaking eye contact and looking down. A heavy feeling swallowed his chest. Melchior slowly let go of his fists and he held his head in his hands. "I'm sorry," he breathed.

"What are you sorry for, Sør?" Melchior asked. "You are not the one who dumped someone after having sex with them. *I* was the jerk —not you."

"I'm sorry for being such a failure in the first place so that you left," Søren clarified, looking up again. "…I'm sorry for disappointing you."

Melchior paused, before a soft chuckle escaped his lips.

"Oh, Søren. When are you going to learn that it's not always your fault? People are just people —they screw up on their own and the people they care about get affected anyway, no matter what they did or didn't do."

"What do you mean?"

"My disguised selfish choice caused you a pain that I dare not try to comprehend or compare to my own."

Søren narrowed his eyes. "Melchior," he said slowly. "Are you trying to tell me why you broke up with me?"

The blond sucked on his teeth. "You deserve to know. I made a mistake — not in loving you, but with the sex. I didn't realise that being so intimate with you would make me snap. It's not that I didn't enjoy it. I just…things became so real in the moment. More so, actually, when I said that I love you. That's when it really hit. Look, for a long time, I was thinking of letting you go. Everything you did — and gods, your smile, your laugh —it kept reminding me that I didn't deserve you.

273

No matter how much I wanted us, I knew that you deserved better. And I was such an ass that I thought breaking things off would be that '*better*' for us. Better for *you*."

Søren ground his teeth together. "You can't be serious. Melchior, that was not your sole decision to make."

Melchior's answer did not actually surprise him. It did nothing to reconcile the tear in his heart. In fact, he did not feel much of anything. It was an answer which he had been waiting for, but it brought no closure. Was Melchior really suggesting that he had just quit while he was ahead?

"I *am* serious," insisted the blond Reaper. "And I know —trust me, I know that now. But I meant it, Søren. And you meant everything to me. I just…I couldn't wait around for me to fuck it up."

"So, the solution was to fuck it up in advance?" Søren hissed. "Because, honestly, fuck that. You don't know what could have happened if you had stayed, Melchior. So how *dare* you insinuate that you were trying to protect my feelings in the long run, or whatever."

"I'm not giving an excuse for what I did, Søren," Melchior insisted. "I wish that I could take it back now, but I know that it's too late. I know now that I've already ruined everything. All I can do is offer an apology and hope that you won't hate me forever."

"I make no promises," Søren seethed.

"I get that. But I won't stop saying that I'm sorry. And please, don't think it was your fault. None of it was, so stop blaming yourself. You didn't disappoint me." He then paused, before smirking slyly. "In fact, making love to you was kind of better than —"

"—You…don't have to finish the rest of that sentence," Søren cut in. He did not need the fact rubbed in that the sex he was never going to have again had been great. Melchior smiled, before folding his arms. Søren hesitated, unsure of how to continue the conversation. Then he spoke up, "Why do we end up fighting and shouting at each other almost every time we interact?"

Melchior thought about it for a minute, before shrugging. "I guess it's just who we are. Our personalities clash. We are not people who usually get along, so there is bound to be friction."

Søren huffed. "…Sure."

"Plus, it's the only way that we ever resolve anything," he went on.

"Which is kind of sad. Gods, we're a mess."

"Ah," Søren said, "Finally. Something that we can agree on."

He nodded, before frowning again. "Do you ever…miss me?" he asked.

Søren cringed but tried his best not to give himself away so easily. "Wow —I see that ego is still as big as ever," he remarked, laughing lightly.

Melchior sighed and looked at him seriously. "*I* miss you."

Søren blinked in disbelief.

He…missed him? He wondered for a moment if this was what he wanted: for someone to agonise over him. A sharp pain then seared in his chest, and he bit his lip in defeat. He debated telling Melchior the truth.

"I think it's *okay* to miss something that was a part of your past," he started, trying to avoid directly answering the question. "But dwelling there is problematic. Things happen for a reason, and I guess…ours is maybe that we were supposed to learn from each other —from the experience," he went on. As he was saying it all, it finally clicked that he needed to hear the same thing. "I…*I* missed you a whole lot more than you missed me," he then finally caved into the desire to let it out.

Melchior looked genuinely surprised, which made him tense, but personally it did make Søren feel better. Freer.

"But that part of our relationship —the romantic kind —I think we should probably put it behind us," the Trainer murmured. It hurt to tell Melchior all of that; things that he wished were true but were just wishful thoughts. But the truth could wait. Telling him that thinking about him still made Søren melt completely —that would complicate everything.

Right then, things between them needed to be simpler. Easy.

And if that meant that Søren could not tell him how he really felt, and that they might never be a couple again —then so be it.

"Maybe…I do want to be friends with you again," he did offer.

And he meant it.

Melchior was strange —Søren knew that from experience. But what he did next was one of the last things the Trainer had ever expected.

The fearsome blond blushed a deep pink. He tried to cover his face with a hand, but it did not quite work, making Søren laugh. He ended up laughing too; such a genuine laugh that neither had heard in ages.

"Thanks, Sør," he said when they had sighed and exhausted the humour. "I…hope that I can find reason to call you that again."

Søren nodded and bit his lip. "Me too, Mel."

For a moment, there was only a warm silence between them, as though they finally understood. Melchior was not so big and tough —even he had flaws. Søren seemed to have forgotten that when he had held him in such high esteem. Like him, Melchior could grow insecure. He could be vulnerable; he could lose confidence. And perhaps he could fall irrevocably in love.

The door then suddenly unlocked and opened. Savannah's head popped up on the other side. She grinned as soon as her eyes met Søren's —before she glanced at Melchior and the grin fell into a small polite smile.

"I heard laughter," she stated. "Does that mean you no longer want to tear each other's heads off?"

Melchior and Søren shared a look. The burly Reaper gave a curt nod. Søren smiled and went back over to the computer monitors. "Yeah," he answered the trainee, lighting up the main screen. "Something like that."

The soft laughter that ensued was then interrupted by a soldier-like series of knocks on the front door. Savannah and Søren looked at Melchior.

"Don't look at me," he defended himself, "—it's not like I organised a house party and am expecting guests."

Søren looked at Savannah. He certainly was not expecting anyone. She did not look as though she was either.

The knocking then started again; this time more impatient.

"Okay, *okay*. I heard you!" Søren called, getting up and walking through the apartment. Phee-Phee jumped and a few embers flew from his panicked flapping wings. Nadine and Lewis looked up from the books in front of them where they were sitting on the sofa, with vague interest. Søren frowned. Nadine's book was upside down. They had obviously been listening in.

At that thought, he reddened slightly. Although, he should not blame them since there had been shouting.

As he headed for the door he muttered incoherent words under his breath. On the other side of the door stood a man who looked to be in his early thirties.

He wore a severe black suit and tie, and his jasper irises glinted eerily. The man smiled warmly at Søren even when the Reaper rudely raised an expectant eyebrow at him.

"Hello there," he said in a cheerful British accent. He then looked straight at the Phoenix. "What a pretty little bird you've got."

Søren could not tell whether or not he was being sarcastic.

"And you are…?" the Trainer asked sceptically, with one hand on the door handle as though he was ready to slam it shut.

"Why, I am Hades," he answered, chuckling.

Everyone blinked in surprise. Søren suddenly felt bad for wanting to slam a door in the god of the Underworld's face. Hades then tilted his head to the side and looked at the youngest Grim Reaper, still smiling.

"I am here for Savannah, actually."

"Why?" Melchior asked, narrowing his eyes.

Hades looked at them all as though they were beginning to annoy him. "…I am her father," he answered like it was simple.

There was a pause as they all turned to look at the Reaper in question. She looked like she was about to pass out. Then she took a step towards the god, reaching out with her hand shakily —before she let out a sound like a strangled cry and suddenly slammed the door in Hades' face herself.

CHAPTER 32

SAVANNAH

EVERYONE STARED AT me with an array of shocked expressions as I simply stood there with my hand gripping the door handle, speechless. Even Phee-Phee looked at me sideways, cooing as though he was confused.

I did not know what to say.

When Thanatos had explained what I was, I was not as surprised as I thought I would be. It was a fitting explanation for all of the strange happenings. That, or maybe I was simply fighting with myself to really believe it.

"Did you really just do that?" Chainsaw Guy whistled. I squeezed my eyes shut and winced. His voice sounded far off and distorted.

"…Woah, Hades is your father?" Nadine gasped. "*You're* a half-blood Greek god?" She sounded somewhat impressed. Though it did not last long. "Well, no wonder you try so hard with him —Hades is not what I would call the *World's Greatest Dad*," she huffed.

I frowned and clenched my fists. *How dare she.*

If only she knew the power that came from absolute rage. And if anyone was going to be allowed to shame Hades for who he was and for what he had done, it was going to be *me*.

"Shut up Nadine," Lewis surprisingly beat me to it. "Savannah doesn't need any crap from you right now."

Everyone started at Lewis for a moment, rather shocked. I certainly never thought he would have it in him to put his sister in her place.

"...Lewis is right, Nadine," Søren sighed, glaring at her in disappointment as she pouted sheepishly. "This is serious."

"Enough about the rest of our opinions," Chainsaw Guy cut in. He then looked at me with genuine concern, and I flinched in alarm. "Did you mean to slam the door in his face?" he asked.

I swallowed but the lump in my throat would not go down. "I..." I started. But I could not finish.

The walls were closing in on me and I could not breathe —and not in the sense that I had no need to. It truly felt as though I were suffocating.

I abruptly turned around and pushed past Søren and Chainsaw Guy to go into the computer room, before I closed the door and leaned back against it for support. I felt like my knees would buckle at any moment.

I turned my head to the side as I heard them begin to discuss whether or not they should open the door again and let Hades inside.

Hades. The god of the Underworld.

The god of the *Underworld* was my father?

I sank down to the floor and blocked my ears, unwilling to overhear any more. I screwed up my face and felt the tears beginning to pool up, before I blinked them out. I was not going to cry over this.

I was not going to give anyone that satisfaction.

So, what would I do —act cold and uncaring?

No. That was not really me. I sighed and raked a hand though my hair. Why was everything so suddenly crashing down around me?

My existence was threatened; I had a new job I would not have even wanted to apply for let alone be willing to do; and now there was going to be a war because of my blood. Because if that Titan we saw was anything like Kronos, then war would inevitably be the end result.

I hugged my knees against my chest again and frowned, wondering what this meant for me. My father had suddenly just shown up. Was that really real? I pinched my arm to be sure, and unfortunately felt the painful sensation to confirm that it *was* real.

I had not been ready to meet him so soon. After Thanatos's outburst I had begun to wonder if firstly it was a good idea, and secondly if I was actually ever going to meet him at all.

But now that he was actually here...I was unprepared.

What had I honestly expected —a hand written invitation?

Not that I would have accepted it willingly anyway. Perhaps this was the best way —an abrupt meeting. It would force me to make a quick decision, and possibly interact with him.

Half of me wanted to go back out there and see him.

The other half was too proud.

I then jumped at the sound of a knock on the door, before scrambling to my feet and brushing my hair aside. "*What*," I rasped.

"...Savannah. I understand how you feel. Please. Just let me try and talk," *Hades'* voice was the one which filled my ears instead of a familiar one.

I did not respond and folded my arms childishly.

He understood how I felt? Then he should understand that I was not going to come out of the room any time soon.

"Savannah, please," Søren's voice said, which caused me to pause. "At least just hear him out."

"Why are you on his side?" I snapped. "You don't know what happened. How can you say that? You don't *know* him."

"Savannah," Hades called out gently. "No one is on anyone's side. I am here for *you*. And I really need to speak with you. Do you have any idea of the immense trouble that I will be in with Zeus and Hera when they find out that I came to see you?"

"I didn't ask you to break the rules for me," I defended myself. "I didn't ask for you to come here!"

"But I am here now," he said in a softer tone.

I did not say anything to that. Instead, I winced and squeezed my eyes shut to avoid crying again. He was here now —only now?

It was just not good enough.

This was not good enough.

"…*I'm* not good enough," I found myself saying aloud. "To be your daughter. Is that why…is that why you left?" I asked, finding it harder to hold my tears back. They fell down my face indignantly, but at least I was not making the embarrassing sounds that came with them.

"Savannah," Hades said softly. "I did not leave because you were not good enough. I did not leave because your mother was not good enough," he went on. I let out a series of sobs. Then he paused. "You want to know the reason I left? …Because *I* was not good enough."

I gasped, all traces of self-pity vanishing. "What?" I said. "What do you mean by that? You're a *Greek god*."

"No one is perfect, Savannah. Even the gods have flaws," he chuckled. "And if you think they are perfect then it makes you perfect too. Because humans were made in our image. So, you see, it's a cycle."

"…Are you actually using a convenient set of scapegoats as a reason for leaving Savannah and her Mom?" I heard Nadine say.

"Nadine, stay out of this," I asked weakly.

"Then open the damn door," she countered snappily. "This is no way to have a conversation."

I hesitated. I clenched my fists and thought about it. Maybe this was a conversation for both of us to be in the same room, alone.

"…Fine," I said reluctantly, and through my teeth. I opened the door and my eyes were met with jasper irises.

Had they always been that colour?
I had always thought that they were a warm brown. Then I understood. I had only seen what I had wanted to see.

He smiled weakly and looked at me sympathetically —which was not something that I wanted. I did not need sympathy. Not from him. But he looked approachable enough, and I honestly could not blame my mother for being attracted to him once.

"We'll talk in here," I said, glancing back at the computer room. He nodded curtly and marched in past me.

"Excuse me? Who said that you could?" Søren protested. He shut up when I shot him a look behind my father's back.

Then I closed the door behind me. Hades stood there in the middle of the room, stiff and uncomfortable, before straightening his tie and coughing. I did not say a word. So, we stayed like that, awkwardly shuffling from foot to foot. "...There is no excuse," he finally murmured.

"What?" I whispered.

"There is no excuse," he repeated. "Not then, and definitely not now. I...I am really sorry Savannah, believe me —"

"Are you?" I cut him off, glaring spitefully. "Are you really sorry?" I demanded. He just gave me a confused expression.

I growled. "Do you have *any* idea what it was like? Life without you? Do you even —" I started, by then stopped to restrain myself. I breathed deeply and closed my eyes. "...Never mind. You wouldn't care."

"But I was around for as long as my brother would *allow*," Hades insisted. "I did not want to leave. But Zeus had begun to grow suspicious of me. So, I had to manipulate your mother's memory of what happened. Her hating me was not part of that alteration," he admitted, glancing downwards. "That was...that was all on her own."

I paused and frowned, noting how vulnerable and human he looked. I resisted the urge to comfort him.

"I hated you too," I admitted. He looked at me fearfully at that comment. "...Or at least I tried to. I wanted to. I *really* wanted to hate you," I told him, clenching my fists and glaring right into his eyes. "Because if I hated you, then maybe I wouldn't feel this gaping hole inside my chest as much."

Hades looked at me more sympathetically then.

"And I wanted you to hate me too," I went on. He raised his eyebrows this time. "...Because everyone knows that it's easier to hate someone you believe hates you back..."

My voice cracked before it trailed off to a whisper at the end and I dropped my gaze, unable to look at him any longer.

"I most certainly do not hate you," he said, sounding borderline offended. "I never did, and I never will. How could I? You were just a little girl who had done absolutely nothing wrong. Does that sound like a basis on which to hate someone?"

I flinched but kept my lips clamped shut.

"Look, I had no choice when I left. But I should not have left the way that I did. Telling you the truth would have been absolutely out of question though," he said, chuckling softly. This angered me.

"So why are you telling me now?" I asked haughtily.

"Great question," he acknowledged. He frowned deeply. "...Savannah, there is an issue. You see, as a half-blood, you are not allowed to exist. And yes, I understand that you died, but you are a Grim Reaper now —which means that you are not alive but you are not exactly dead either. And therefore, the treaty still stands valid."

I tensed at the word *treaty* and my hand flew to my side.

The feeling of The Book of Treaties still in my possession eased the tension slightly but I could not help but get the feeling that I should not have taken it from the library after all.

"...Now the Olympians know of your existence as well as every other half-blood god child still out there now," Hades continued, snapping me out of my thoughts. "The only question is, how? I thought I was very thorough in finding a good hiding place for that treaty —"

"Wait —so you *are* the one who hid the book?" I gasped without thinking. "I was right..." I murmured to myself.

"Wait," Hades said, narrowing his eyes at me. "What do you mean you were right? What do you know about The Book of Treaties?"

I opened and closed my mouth comically before glancing at the wall. "...Nothing much. I just saw the spine when I was in Thanatos' library cleaning up as punishment."

I could have told him the truth.

I *should* have told him the truth. But I did not need to get reprimanded at a time like this. Unfortunately, the god of the dead saw right through me. His eyes flickered to my waist, right where the book was, before he took a step towards me and held out his hand. I tensed but remained unmoving.

Hades' eyes narrowed and a faint glow began to illuminate them. He sternly glared at me and gestured with his hand again for me to give it up. I let out a sigh, before I dubiously handed it over.

Totally busted.

Hades flipped through it before shutting it with a snap and clicking his fingers, making it disappear in a plume of black smoke. He then turned to the side and refused to look at me for the first time. The slither of fatherliness caught me off guard, and guilt consumed my every thought.

Was he disappointed in me?

"…You lied to me," he whispered. I did not know what to say. I hung my head. "I do not blame you," he sighed. "I would have lied about it too. But unfortunately, because you removed this book from its shelf and the library, Horkos will be able to find it again."

I narrowed my eyes. "Who?"

But Hades did not seem to be that interested in the book or my question anymore. Instead, he focused on something else.

"…Hold on a second, you were doing *what* as punishment for Thanatos?" he growled, making me look back at him. His eyes simmered with irritation. He surprisingly appeared infuriated. "Just what did that boy make you *do* —"

I scoffed and shook my head. "It was just cleaning —calm down. And it was pretty lenient considering what I had done."

"What on *Earth* did you do to receive such a fate?" Hades said with genuine but melodramatic shock, clutching at his chest.

I glanced elsewhere. "I reaped the soul of my ex-boyfriend before he was supposed to die," I whispered.

Hades' shock diminished and he became stony faced. "Oh, I see. In that case you deserved every moment of it."

"Well, that's not very supportive," I complained.

"What were you expecting?" Hades rightly asked. "A slap on the wrist? You took a *life*, Savannah. A pitiful, pathetic and highly-unworthy-of-my-daughter life, but still. That is just as well of an offence in the divine world as it is in the mundane."

I then momentarily smiled at his description of Aaron's life —and how apparently unworthy he was of me —Hades momentarily returned it, before turning still and grave again.

"I do however need you to take this seriously," he said; his icy voice sending chills through my entire body. "Do not think that you will get away without a scolding from your father."

The mood instantly reverted to how it had been before at the mention of the word '*father*', and I frowned at the floor.

Hades sighed and raked a hand through his hair. "…Savvy," he murmured. I tensed, gawking at him. "I suppose that I have not called you that in years," he admitted.

"No one has called me that in years," I murmured.

He pressed his lips into a line and nodded slowly. "I truly am sorry, Savannah. I wish that I could have been there for you all these years and been the support you needed —that you deserved —but I could not. And I am going to regret it for eternity. I will *never* put another mortal family through that ever again. Besides," he then looked sheepishly embarrassed, "…my wife would kill me again."

His wife.

I had been so caught up in the idea of a perfect and whole family that I had forgotten that the illegitimate child, was in fact, me. Hades had his original family, long before my own mother had ever existed.

And Hades' wife, as far as I knew, was as beautiful as she could be lethal. I was then surprised that Hades was actually standing in front of me in one piece. "…Persephone," I breathed, recalling her from myths.

"Yes."

"She is *not* becoming my stepmother," I said through my teeth.

"Oh, that is not something which I meant to imply," Hades said quickly. "Persephone is wonderful and a capable queen —but she has got her hands full with our one son."

I froze. *Son? Hades had a son too?*

Then I glanced at the floor. Of course, he had other children. He had been around for eons —and Persephone too. My mother was not the first. And knowing Hades, she might not actually be the last like he said. But I decided that I did not care. But then my heart ached, and tears pricked my eyes, proving that the flesh did not always cooperate with the mind.

"Savannah —"

"It's fine," I cut him off. "Really. I know I'm not that special. You don't need to feel bad for having children with more than one woman. I mean, Persephone is a goddess. And my Mom…is just my Mom."

"*Savannah*," Hades clipped firmly. "It is not like that. When I met your mother, I was in a very bad spot. Persephone and I were having a break. She does not completely blame me for Phoebe, but she is not okay with what happened either. But the point is, that you can never believe that I would love you less because you are not a god or for whatever reason you have convinced yourself to be true. I love you. You are my daughter. You are *my* beautiful, wonderful daughter."

My eyes grew wide, and my lips parted uncertainly. The tears spilled, but I let them. Those words made something break inside of me. Probably that thick brick wall box of resentment around my heart.

I suddenly darted forward and crashed into him, before wrapping my arms around his torso. He was startled for a moment, but then his arms wrapped around me in turn and he let me cry into his blazer.

"I…we got the letters," I choked out, hugging him tighter. "The ones for Mom…she kept them *all*," I whispered.

Hades gasped but did not say anything. He simply hugged me back tighter, mirroring me. "…I am so glad," he eventually whispered. "That she received them after all."

"I've read some," I sobbed. "Did you…mean all of that?"

"What? Of *course* I did. In fact, I was going to send your eighteenth birthday letter earlier, but then I became so busy and completely forgot. How about I give it to you now?"

"No. Not now," I decided, shaking my head. "How about…when all of this is straightened out? I just…want all focus to be on it when I read it."

He hesitated for a noticeable amount of time before answering me. "All right. But you know, I didn't just come here to reconcile with you."

I slowly withdrew and looked up at him. "No?" I whispered. "What else did you come for?"

"To warn you," he said seriously, frowning. "Thanatos told me. Horkos is coming. And he is not coming alone."

CHAPTER 33

SAVANNAH

HORKOS WAS THE god of oaths —the godly embodiment of a snitching teacher's pet; *not* a noble recorder and keeper of promises.

So, he was really only doing his job.

"Wait, he's only a god?" Søren frowned, sitting down gingerly on the sofa. "We thought that he was a Titan."

"Yes, he is only a god," Hades sighed, "but he is Zeus' right hand man. Which means that he is just as threatening as a Titan, if not more so."

"Zeus?" I echoed. "…Is he the one coming with Horkos?"

The combination of a liar's worst nightmare and the king of the Olympians; the god of the skies…It was not a good mix, and it would spell doom for a master evader of responsibility like Thanatos.

"No," Hades sighed wearily. "Zeus has no interest in the affairs of death. None of the Olympians do."

"But what about the other minor gods?" Søren pointed out. "They always have something to side in a war about."

"You're telling me," Hades sighed, rolling his eyes. His annoyance was momentarily amusing —and got me thinking.

The minor gods must feel every bit as undermined during conflict as when dubbed with the title of '*minor gods*'. Regardless, maybe they were not as much of a threat as perhaps implied.

"So...*are* there minor gods coming with Horkos?" I asked, wanting clarity. "And if so, do we really need to worry about them...?" I trailed off, while tilting my head to the side in an uncertain fashion.

Everyone murmured in agreement, but Hades shot me a very hard look, causing the humorous mood to deflate instantly.

"Horkos is a minor god," Hades deadpanned.

No one was smiling or murmuring now.

"Oh," I swallowed, putting things into perspective. "*Well*. Shit."

"Exactly," Hades agreed, sighing heavily. "So, he might as well bring an entire army of minor gods —mind you, there are a lot more than you think."

"Oh, I don't doubt that," I muttered, folding my arms. "So, what are we going to do?" I frowned deeply. "Do we resist? Give ourselves up?"

"Like *hell* are we going to give ourselves up," Hades suddenly raised his voice, startling us all. "No matter the situation, the gods of death are very proud and stubborn, so do not even dare to *suggest* giving in. It is not a joke."

"...Yeah, proud and stubborn sums it up perfectly," Søren muttered.

"*Hey*," Hades snapped, snapping his fingers and pointing at him. "You watch what you say, young man. You are on very thin ice as it is," he said ominously, tipping his head back with disdain.

Then the god glanced at me. Søren's silver eyes widened slightly as we then made eye contact, frowning in confusion.

Did Hades...think that there was something between Søren and me? Was he spying on my life? Or perhaps I was overthinking things again.

"...Um," I started, biting the edge of my fingernails. "Didn't stubbornness and pride cause all of your problems in the first place?" I murmured.

Søren vigorously sliced his hand in front of his neck —until Hades turned and glanced at him. He stopped immediately and smiled widely, playing innocent. I rolled my eyes and Hades shook his head slightly.

"Savannah," Hades said to me, making me tense. "Regardless of the past...*spats* —we like to maintain a non-helpless reputation in the Afterlife Department. Please understand that I am not stupid, and that I want what is best for those of whom I care. However proud we may be, it does not excuse us from apologising and considering other people."

I held my hands up in surrender and blinked rapidly. "Wait! Okay, okay — I'm sorry; I didn't mean to offend you."

Hades sighed before crossing one leg over the other and smirking at me. "…We do not back down very easily, either."

I lidded my eyes. What exactly did he ever accomplish with those contradictory policies?

"…I think what Savannah is *trying* to say," Nadine surprisingly came to my rescue —even though she did shoot me a disapproving look, "is that maybe you should approach this new threat…differently. Like, different from when you were confronted by Kronos. Perhaps your strategy is…outdated," she put delicately.

I winced.

Chainsaw Guy leaned towards Søren and whispered something with a snarky look on his face; his eyes on Hades. Søren snorted before leaning back against the sofa to say something back. Maybe the conversation they had had helped a little more than they would care to admit.

Hades also raised an eyebrow; in response to Nadine.

"…How old are you?" he asked her.

Nadine blinked, clearly thrown off by the question. "Two and a half centuries —why?"

"Two and a half *centuries*?" Hades repeated, nodding patronisingly. Spite did not look good on my father. "…Just who do you think you are to say such things about how I run my systems? You were probably there during the war but what makes you think that I would give up my ground in this case? Horkos is just a petty toga-wearing asshat —I was not intimidated then and I will not be intimidated now."

I did not think that Nadine had ever been told off like that before. For some reason, I wanted to laugh.

"…Uh, well I wasn't trying —" she started.

"*Exactly* —no, you were not," Hades cut her off, holding a hand up to stop

290

her from talking.

Nadine hung her head and put her hands between her legs, silenced. Not one else here had made her shut up out of shame. I then frowned. I was all for smart mouthing Nadine, but Hades was taking it to a disrespectful level.

"...Dad," I said slowly through my teeth, getting a feel of the word. Hades looked at me and blinked, suddenly unnerved. "That was harsh," I told him, giving a look of disappointment. "Like I said to Thanatos: pride is one thing; a huge ego is another. Putting down other people's input is uncalled for. You should be ashamed —do you think it would kill you to listen to people's ideas and advice? You might actually learn something. Because guess what —we aren't stupid either."

Hades froze. Truly —he looked back at me blankly, his mouth slightly open and his jasper eyes widened. I dithered, wondering if in turn I had been harsh. Then I shook my head. No. It had been necessary to reprimand him. It was inexcusable to talk to anyone the way he had spoken to Nadine. I then nearly choked. I could not believe that I had actually concluded that.

Hades coughed and looked vaguely embarrassed, before he exhaled loudly and nodded. "You are right, Savannah. That was...out of line. I apologise...Miss...What is your name?"

Nadine took a few seconds to register the question, before she quickly responded in a fluster.

"I am sorry...*Nadine*," the god of the dead said through his teeth.

"Anyway," I said nervously, clapping my hands in order to divert Hades' attention and the conversation. "So, what happens now?"
I glanced around the circle for suggestions.

"If we are going to fight back, then we are going to need an army of our own," Søren said.

"Do we have to fight?" I asked.

"Do you want to die?"

"Well, no, but surely there's another —"

"Then we are fighting," Søren concluded. "We have to assemble a defence. I suggest we recruit as many Reapers as we can. Because it's not as though the Olympians will volunteer."

"Exactly." Hades nodded in agreement. "It is unlikely that we will likely get any help from them. And there are many Reapers. I suggest we start now. Like *here*, in this block of apartments."

"Like...give them a campaign speech?" I murmured, narrowing my eyes thoughtfully.

"Convince the Reapers why they should fight on our side," Hades sighed, standing up. "In the meantime, I will see if there are any *Págos* in the Underworld that I can rope in."

"What are...*Págos*?" I asked.

"Ice giants," Hades grinned.

We might stand a chance with those on our side. The god then straightened his blazer, before walking towards the front door. I got up and walked him out. We then stood there in the hallway in silence, unsure of what to say.

"...I am fighting because I do not want to hand you over," Hades eventually murmured. I glanced up at him and blinked. "I do not want to lose you. Now that I can be here for you," he went on. "It is like losing something that you just found after years of searching —frustrating and enraging. I do not want to give you up."

I smiled softly. "Aw, *Dad*..." I sang, before we both chuckled. Hades then enveloped me in a hug and patted the top of my head.

"You do not understand how much you mean to me, Savannah. Always remember that," he whispered.

I nodded, before withdrawing. I waved him off, before breathing out and leaning against the wall. I smiled and clutched at the necklace around my neck. At least I could still see my father in this new life. Assuming that I would survive the war. That then got me thinking. The whole situation was about family, in a way. So, I decided that I wanted to see my mother again. Just once more, in case I would never get the chance again.

I went back inside the apartment to the others and paused as they all looked ready to leave.

"Where are you all going?" I scoffed.

"Nadine and Lewis are heading downstairs to the lobby and Melchior and I were going to go across town to see a friend," Søren answered. I smirked, to which he responded with a dirty look.

"Later," Nadine said as she held up her hand in a way to saying goodbye, before she and Lewis left. Søren then offered me a smile before I glanced away and folded my arms. "Do you...want to come with us?" he offered.

I did not respond.

Søren, Savannah and Chainsaw Guy. *Not* a good combination.

"...Are you okay?" Søren asked, walking over to me and then putting a hand on my shoulder. I was so startled that it took me another second to realise he was asking me something.

"Hm? Yeah," I breathed, nodding for emphasis. "I just...I was just thinking about my Mom."

"Oh," he murmured. "Is it to do with the possibility that you might never see her again?" he guessed. I nodded slowly.

He hesitated, but then he suddenly pulled me into a firm hug. I froze and stood there stiffly, before uncertainly wrapping my arms around him in turn. He towered over me and he was not as soft and warm as Hades, but I liked the way I fitted in his arms. This was new. I liked it.

Chainsaw Guy did not.

"...Hello? I'm still here," he announced loudly.

Søren playfully shushed him as he let go and comfortingly patted my shoulder. He went to grab his crossbow, as I put my hands on my hips and tapped my fingers on the handle of my sword.

Phee-Phee looked up at me curiously before I realised that there was no one staying with him. "Guys...who's going to stay and watch Phee-Phee?"

"Not a goddamn chance," Chainsaw Guy immediately declined, cringing. "Never again."

"Well, we can't leave him here alone," I argued. "Because look how *brilliantly* that turned out the last time," I huffed, rolling my eyes.

"And whose fault was that, *Princess*?" he scoffed.

"Don't call me Princess," I snapped.

He raised a weary eyebrow. "…I'm still not pet-sitting," he grumbled. "How about you just let nature take its course and let the damn thing turn into ash? Besides —you're going to get way too busy to take care of it pretty soon," he snorted, straightening his jacket.

I scoffed. "Well…Maybe he could be an asset. He has been pretty loyal so far. And Phoenixes can breathe fire. He could *help* us."

"Well, then I guess that you will just have to see how loyal it can be when we get back," he spat.

"About that," Søren interjected, swinging the crossbow back and forth. "You know, Melchior. I was thinking maybe…I take Savannah to see her Mom, and then you can go get Abby?"

"What? Wait Søren, you don't have to come with me," I started.

"You shouldn't be alone," he countered.

"What about Chainsaw Guy?" I jerked my thumb in his direction.

"I have a name," the blond Reaper scoffed. "…And *I* do not need a babysitter," he smirked, making me gasp in offence at what he implied. "But she's right, Søren. You don't have to go with her."

"*Melchior*," Søren said in a sudden firm tone, unnerving us. "Don't push it. Go and get Abby. We'll meet you back here in about…an hour and a half."

His jaw clenched tightly. "…*Fine*," he snapped back, picking up his chainsaw. He shot me a glare, before making for the door. "Later," he murmured, before leaving the apartment.

I almost felt bad, as though I had stolen Søren away.

"Don't worry about him," Søren told me. "He won't mind. He knows what boundaries he's pushing."

I huffed. "It must be nice having the upper hand like that. Especially with someone like him."

Søren shrugged. "Yeah, kind of."

✠

Walking to my house after shifting to Fulton with Søren was not as weird as I thought it would have been. We were actually managing to hold conversation. I inhaled sharply as I finished laughing at a joke he had cracked and shoved my hands into my pockets.

"It's been quite the three weeks, hasn't it?" I said to the sky.

"Has it really been that long?" Søren frowned, chuckling. "Time really shortens when you live forever."

He kicked a pebble across the path as we fell into silence.

I frowned and thought hard about Hades' battle strategy —or lack thereof. I could not see the point of endangering more innocent lives of Reapers and other semi-mortal souls alike because my father wanted to play '*house*'.

It was just not the kind of thing that I would do.

"Søren —" I started, turning towards him.

"Savannah —" he said at the same time.

We then paused and stared at each other, wondering who should speak first.

"Okay, you go first," Søren decided.

I chuckled. "So…it's about the war. I…I really don't want to fight. It's not me. I mean, I am capable of fighting, but I don't feel okay with acting as though Reapers are expendable. It feels like we're using them. You know —this could all be solved over a cup of tea or something."

Søren snorted. "Yeah okay, Savannah. The gods do not solve conflict over a '*cup of tea*'."

"Well, they should try," I laughed lightly. "Green tea can do wonders for the restless spirit."

"Indeed," he agreed. Then he sighed and looked up at the sky. "…Look Sav, I understand that you would want to explore alternative ways to ensure that no one dies —but the gods are very serious about their fights. They're not the kind of beings to be rational. And that's just the way it is. There is nothing that we can do about it."

I frowned and looked at my shoes. I did not want to believe that. There had to be another way —a way to make them see reason, or even just to bargain. Any solution that did not result in a repeat of the last war.

I sighed and looked up at the sky again, suddenly reminded of how insignificant our existence felt. I then paused as something registered in my mind. "…Did you just call me *Sav*?" I asked, grinning.

Søren glanced elsewhere, but nodded. "But it's no big deal. I thought it was just a nickname. It just…it kind of just came out naturally."

I laughed softly and playfully bumped into him. "No —it's not really a big deal," I confirmed, straightening up. "My friends called me Sav. It's just…that's the first time that *you* did."

"Oh," Søren said a little nervously.

"No, it's okay —I said," I insisted. "We *are* friends."

"Okay," he chuckled, glancing at the houses we were passing.

"Oh, what did you want to say?" I asked.

"Hm?" he murmured, looking back at me. "…Oh!" he started, scratching the back of his neck uncertainly. "Well…look we're here!" he then said quickly, abruptly stopping by the front gate. It was in fact my house.

He had managed to stop right in front of my house —without getting too distracted or understandably lost. "…Should I be concerned that you know exactly where I lived?" I smirked. He simply sighed.

I looked up at the house, before feeling flooded with a sense of loss and longing. Here I was again. *Home*.

CHAPTER 34

SAVANNAH

I WAS NOT entirely sure what I had expected when I looked into the house from the windows, but Ron Weasley II's curious face definitely had not been it. I yelped and jumped backwards, tripped over a bush, before consequently crashing into Søren and knocking us onto the freshly cut lawn.

"…Gods," Søren rasped as I groaned. He was really bony and did not make the best landing mattress. "Are you okay?"

"I think so," I murmured, staring upwards at the sky and closing my eyes in utter unwillingness.

"Good. Now get off me."

I gasped and scrambled to my feet, before sheepishly offering him a helping hand. He raised an eyebrow at me, to which I responded with a huff. I rolled my eyes when he just stared at my hand begrudgingly.

So, I started withdrawing, pouting tauntingly. He finally took it, shaking his head, and I pulled him up. "Sorry about that," I apologised. "I just kind of freaked out when I saw my cat."

"What —you mean that one?" he asked, pointing to the windows.

I turned around and saw Ron scratching at the glass, mewling loudly. "Oh, Ron…" I whispered, moving to put my hand on the other side where his paw was. "How can he can see me?" I asked Søren.

"Wha…'cause he's a cat," he said obviously.

"What, cats can see souls and the undead?" I snorted.

"Yes, they *can* see souls," he actually confirmed. "The undead? Well, who wouldn't be able to see those? But I hope you weren't referring to *us* as the undead. Because we're not zombies, Savannah. We're Grim Reapers."

"Right," I mumbled, turning back to the windows.

At this point in time, I could not see a difference between zombie, ghost and Reaper. Reapers followed blindly and were Turned in order to kill —like zombies. But they could walk through walls, disappear and go undetected —albeit rather uncontrollably, but who could really complain —like ghosts.

So, what was so special about being a Grim Reaper?

"Ron? You silly cat, what are you doing?" a voice then said from inside the house. I flinched back. That was Phoebe's voice.

"Who's that?" Søren whispered.

"It's my...my Mom..." I stammered.

I then inhaled sharply as her figure moved into my field of view. Then her gaze landed right on me. Her dark grey eyes widened too, before a loud crash suddenly rang out as she dropped the dish in her hands. My mother took a step back, before blinking rapidly. I was frozen, unsure of my movements. And she stared back with the same uncertainty.

"Savannah," Søren then murmured. "Your Mom can see you. And since she doesn't recognise you, she's going to think that you're trespassing."

I was speechless —and still staring at my mother.

She then suddenly sprang to life and made for the front door with a speed I had never seen before. I turned, just in time to see her burst out and stumble on the pathway. I tensed, not knowing what to expect. All I had wanted to do was see her. But I knew she would not recognise me. She would think I was some crazy teenager trying to steal her cat.

She slowly walked towards me. I took a step backwards when she was close enough to reach out and touch me.

Why was she not shouting at me to get off of her lawn? Her gaze simply bore into my eyes, unable to be torn away.

"…How?" Phoebe finally rasped. "How are you here? How are you…"

I blinked rapidly. "What do you mean?" I asked nervously.

My mother then gasped. I flinched, unsure of what to do.

She leaned in, her eyes darting back and forth slightly, before raising up a hand towards my face. I paused and frowned, but I let her advance.

I then breathed out shakily as her skin came in contact with mine. I looked into her eyes, before I felt the prick of tears in my own.

I blinked again, hoping I was not imagining this. It felt good to feel her warm hand against my cold cheek.

"…Savannah?" she whispered so softly as though it was only for me to hear. I drew a sharp breath, and I heard Søren do the same.

"Savannah how are you…*alive*?" she went on.

My jaw dropped and I suddenly flinched away from her, holding out my hands in front of me. She started in surprise as I somewhat glared at her. I was confused.

"How do you even…know that it's me?" I frowned in response, raising an eyebrow.

"Savannah," she breathed, clapping a hand over her mouth.

Then she started sobbing, letting the tears free fall. "Oh my God…Savannah —you're alive!" she cried.

I opened my mouth to start explaining myself, but I was speechless. How in the world could my mother recognise me? She was only meant to be able to see me —but now it really was as though I was the *Walking Dead*. We stared at each other for a few more seconds, before my mother walked forward, stopping right in front of me.

"…I lost you so suddenly," she started. "For a while, I couldn't…function. I didn't eat, I didn't sleep —it all felt so surreal. It was like being in a dream, but wondering if you'll ever wake up. Don was so patient with me, bless him. But all of this time I blamed myself. I should not have kept you so sheltered that you felt that you had to keep things from me. I didn't realise how I had raised you would result in such a —"

"Mom, no," I cut her off, shaking my head gently. "It's not your fault. The

299

car accident was just that —an accident. I had been drinking. Aaron had been distracted by me. I wasn't myself. If it's anyone's fault, it's mine."

"But I could have…" my mother struggled.

"Mom, you did your *best*," I insisted. "I really couldn't have asked for a better mother," I whispered.

She glanced downwards and did not respond for a moment. "…I love you, Savannah," she murmured. "I really wish that I deserved you."

"What do you mean?"

She looked up and smiled at me while a few tears streamed down her cheeks. "You are the best thing that ever happened to me," she told me.

A small smile then spread across my face as my own tears fell. I suddenly darted forward and hugged her tightly. She gasped, then hesitantly wrapped her arms around me in turn. We both cried. Tears of joy, and tears of sorrow.

Then a thought occurred to me. "…Mom, if you can see me now, how come you didn't see me at the funeral?" I asked.

She suddenly withdrew from the hug and stared at me with widened eyes. "Wait —you were at your funeral?" she said with genuine surprise.

"Yeah —I was thinking of posing as my own long-lost twin sister," I said before I could stop myself.

My mother was confused. "…What?"

"What?" I immediately echoed, averting my gaze self-consciously and trying to seem equally surprised.

"Uh, does anyone want to explain what is happening right now?" Søren then said from behind me.

Phoebe then withdrew further and turned to face Søren. She looked between me and him, and then raised an eyebrow at me suggestively. "And who is this? Your new boyfriend?"

Søren snorted a laugh.

"*Mom*," I clipped, shaking my head. "No." Then I paused and frowned. "…Wait, how can you see him?"

She frowned as though I was the one who was making no sense. "Like I can see you," she scoffed. "I can see the divine, unlike most mortals. It's a special and rare thing your father once told me about. It's something in Greek —I can't quite remember the name."

I frowned curiously. I had not been aware of such an exception. Then I decided to answer her question. "This is my…Trainer. Like a guide and mentor. Just…I will explain," I chuckled softly.

"Right," my mother murmured, moving to tuck her hair behind her ears. "Okay. Well, why don't you come inside, then? It's cold out here."

"Sure," I agreed, before turning and beckoning Søren.

He had safely put his crossbow away but did not look all too thrilled to be invited inside. "This is not what I was expecting, Savannah," he whispered in my ear as he walked beside me.

"Me neither," I whispered back. Then I climbed the steps and stepped into something familiar.

✠

Nothing had changed.
Of course, I would not have expected anything to have changed in the short amount of time I had been gone; but it brought a dull comfort to see an environment so recognisable.

I chuckled softly as Søren and I sat on the sofa opposite Phoebe. "…It's like I never left," I breathed.

"Yeah," my mother said, pressing her lips into a thin line.
I glanced at Søren for some help but all he did was raise an eyebrow and shrug. I hissed at him in warning before turning back to my mother.

"Mom. I…I know about Dad," I started confidently. After studying her expression, I realised that it might not have been the best topic to start with. As anticipated, my mother tensed up and breathed out heavily. She then looked away and tried to clear her thoughts.

"Sorry," I apologised. "That wasn't the best thing to start with. But it was the way to start with what I am, and why I'm…here."

"Did he set you up to this?" she asked. "Did he send you here to torture me or something? Did he…do something so that you would still be alive?" she whispered fearfully.

"No," I assured her. "He didn't do anything. But…you should know that I'm not technically alive."

She frowned at me. "And just what is that supposed to mean? You're sitting right in front of me. I *hugged* you two minutes ago."

"Yes," I agreed. "But…even Søren and I can't understand why you were able to know it's me. You see, I'm a Grim Reaper now. I work for Death. And when I Turned, I *had* died, but my soul didn't go to the Underworld —in these semi human bodies we're in a sort of in-between stage. We knew that you would be able to see me —but you were not supposed to be able to recognise me," I said firmly. "But now…you knew that it was me and were able to touch me. And I don't understand why."

Phoebe Green suddenly looked very guilty. I frowned, wondering what had resonated with her.

"Look, I knew what your father was when…when we created you," she admitted. Then she paused, narrowing her eyes at nothing in particular. "…I knew what I was getting myself into," she whispered. Then her face hardened, and she clenched her fists. "I knew…I knew, and I still did it, *damnit*," she hissed, banging her arm on the armrest.

We jumped in surprise.

I then drummed my fingers on the sofa uncertainly. "Is there something that you want to tell me?"

Phoebe looked back at me with a face of regret. She brought her hand to her mouth and choked out a sob, before looking away.

"Savannah," she croaked. "I am so sorry. It's all my fault. I…I shouldn't have…You're going to hate me for the rest of your life. It's just…"

She was struggling to say whatever it was. "Look, I know that you're a half-blood god. I always have. I just thought that maybe, if I pretended nothing had ever happened, that it would be so."

I stared at her blankly as she then continued sobbing. Søren shifted next to me and put a hand on my shoulder.

I shook him off and blinked as my vision blurred from tears.

Phoebe had known.

Well, I had not thought she was completely clueless. Of course, she had known Hades was who he was. But she had repressed my nature knowing full well that doing it could hurt me and the people I cared about.

That did not sit well.

"I think that I'm going to be sick," I stated, before standing up and storming to the bathroom.

I flushed the toilet when I was done.

I was surprised that something had actually come up —considering that Grim Reapers did not eat. It must have been excess bile left over from before I had died. I stumbled to my feet and looked at myself in the mirror. I was paler, and pinkish-red bags hung underneath my eyes.

I scraped my hair back against my scalp, panting hard.

How could she have done this?

I closed my eyes and breathed out deeply, before I flinched at a series of knocks on the door. "Who is it?" I whispered.

"Søren."

I sighed and moved to open the door.

"Hey," I murmured, avoiding his gaze.

"Hey," he returned. "Are you okay?"

I snorted. "Do I look okay?"

He paused. Then, "No," he sighed. I breathed unnecessarily.

"Your Mom —" he then started.

"No," I immediately cut him off. "I don't want to talk about it. Let's…let's just get out of here," I told him, sidestepping his tall frame and making for the door. "…I need some time to think."

"Okay."

303

I walked into the living room and stopped short as my mother looked up at me. "Savannah," she whispered hopefully.

I gave her a look of indifference and shrugged with my hands stuffed into my jacket pockets. I strode for the door, and momentarily paused only to spit, "This was a mistake."

"*Savannah*," Søren said after me, but I did not stop.

I threw the door open and stomped outside. I walked down the steps and onto the pathway. I gasped at the sight of Hades, decked in a black suit, standing in the driveway but I still did not stop. In fact, I sped up.

"Savannah!" Søren called.

Hades' slight smile fell at the notice of my hostility. "…What happened?" he asked. I stormed down the path, making a beeline for him.

"You knew *too*," I growled as I roughly pushed past him, before turning to walk down the street. I could not handle any of it.

CHAPTER 35

SAVANNAH

I ANGRILY WIPED my sleeve across my face as I continued stalking down the street. But the tears would not stop.

I was fuming —but it felt like there was a gaping wound in my chest. My heart had been ripped out, and I could not bear to think, speak —or have the will to remain conscious. I wanted it all to end. To *stop*.

Maybe I really was a Grim Reaper now. Even my thoughts were more morbid. Or maybe I was simply angry. I could not grasp the fact that my parents had tried to treat what was fundamentally half of my existence like a bad memory that they could ignore and pretend had never happened.

And what was worse was that it had actually *worked*.

I then shivered and hugged my jacket closer against me.

It was not necessarily because it was cold —it just gave me a weak sense of comfort. I did not know what I was feeling more; rage or utter *betrayal*.

Then abruptly more than anything, I began to feel that strange tingling heat in my veins I had felt in Søren's computer room again. I frowned, and uncoiled from my self-hug, before coming to a halt altogether. It started small, but then the temperature slowly rose. I winced. It was getting hot —uncomfortably hot. I hastily took off my jacket and looked down at my arms.

I then started in alarm and dropped my jacket as I saw a faint white glowing illuminating and pulsing through my veins; as though I were a freaky Science

Fiction alien entity.

"...*Savannah*!"

I jumped at the sound of Søren's far away holler. I glanced back, meeting his gaze. We gave each other the same look of regret. I saw him sigh heavily and shake his head. Then he broke into a run. I panicked, dithering as I thought about what to do. I knew that I could not outrun him.

But I bent down and took my jacket, then started walking away, and faster this time. I was not giving myself time to think. I was feeling frustrated, and now I was beginning to panic about my luminescent arms.

"Savannah. *Stop* —you need to stop!"

I winced and shook my head, picking up the pace again. I stomped around the corner before a searing pain shot up both of my arms and I consequently stopped walking and screamed. Søren's footsteps instantly quickened —and I started when I turned around as he finally caught up with me.

He gasped at my teary face and then at my arms.

"Oh my gods," he hissed. "Savannah...what *happened*?"

"I...I don't know," I cried. I bared my arms to him and trembled. "It just started. *Help* me, Søren —I don't know how to make it stop. It hurts!"

"Okay, okay," he said, reaching out to grab hold of my shoulders. "Ow!" he suddenly shrieked, holding his hands to his chest defensively. "Holy shit, it's like you're made of fire."

"*Do* something," I whined.

"Okay, calm down for a second," he suggested. "Maybe Hades will be able to do something."

"*Screw* Hades," I went on, screwing up my face to match. "I don't want to talk to him!"

"So, you want to find out what your arms are going to do?" Søren deadpanned. "What if you combust?"

My eyes widened as I stared at him with my mouth hanging open in shock.

"...Okay, I shouldn't have said that," Søren realised. "I'm sorry. You probably won't combust —it's just...well I don't know why you're heating up.

What else could happen?"

"Do you *want* me to explode?" I whimpered.

"No!"

I flinched. He then looked downwards and sighed, rubbing the back of his neck. "…I don't want you to explode. You…you mean too much for me to just leave you here," he explained disjointedly. "…Please, just come back with me. It's *because* I don't want you to explode that I'm asking you to come back with me."

I softened at his speech and glanced downwards as well, feeling guilty. I was tempted to smile too, at the fact that I meant too much for him to just leave me. He really was just trying to save me. I should stop being so stubborn.

"Oh. Søren, I —!"

I was cut off by my own scream.

The pain in my arms cranked up tenfold and my knees turned weak for a moment, causing me to stumble into a wall.

"Savannah!"

I stiffened and clenched my fists to see if it would lessen the pain. But it did nothing. I then gasped repeatedly, beginning to hyperventilate.

"What's happening to me? Help —!"

I screamed again, and this time my knees buckled entirely. I dropped onto the ground, folding my legs underneath me as I tried to keep my arms from touching anything. Søren crouched down in front of me and dithered for a second, unsure of what to do. Then he frowned.

"…What?" I rasped.

"I am not leaving you," he murmured, reaching for my jacket.

He then suddenly hooked his arms underneath my knees and around my shoulders before lifting me up off of the pavement.

He inhaled sharply at the contact of my arms, but he did not let go.

"Søren!" I cried, noticing the steam starting to rise from his skin. "Put me down. Look —you'll burn!"

He managed a soft chuckle and looked down at me. "I'll live."

He then turned and started running back, hissing every time my skin touched his

307

as I tried to hang on. I wanted him to drop me. I could already see the reddening on his skin, and I did not want to see what third degree burns looked like. Contrary to what Søren had told me, this was not worth it.

I was not worth it.

But I could not think about that any longer, because I then screamed again. I had never been inside of a burning oven, but I imagined that it felt like this.

"We are…almost there," Søren panted. I nodded, unable to bring myself to give a verbal response.

The least I could do for him was to do as little as possible.

I heard Phoebe's voice first as we approached the house; hysterical and demanding to know what had happened to me.

"Don't touch her," Søren warned as he gently lowered me down onto the lawn. "Her skin is searing hot!"

I laid back and spread my limbs, palms facing up. I screwed my eyes shut, trying to contain the agony.

"What is going on?" I heard Hades demand.

"She said that her veins just started glowing like this," Søren answered. "Can you do something about it?"

"…Yes I can. On the other hand, you should really get those burns looked at," Hades answered.

Someone then knelt down next to me.

I opened my eyes to see the god of the Underworld looming above. He reached down and hovered his hand over my forehead. I stiffened —then he made contact and let out a hiss. But his touch was somehow cooling. The cold began to spread slowly, allowing me to relax slightly. It felt *heavenly*. I slowly sat up, and breathed out deeply, bringing Hades' hand up with me to rest on my shoulder.

"How…are you doing that?" I rasped, confused. I glanced down at my arm and blinked at the sight of something thin and light blue coating my skin.

"Frost," Hades said. "It should cool you down."

"You can…make frost…from your hands?"

"Yes."

"I didn't know…that you could do that."

He winked. "There is a lot you do not know that I can do."

"Excuse me, can you tell me what the *hell* is happening to my daughter?" my mother then cried.

Hades looked up at her. "Right," he murmured. "Do not be alarmed. She's going to be perfectly fine —as long as her veins can withstand the intensity of the fire —"

"Withstand the *what*?" I spluttered.

"The reason why it is burning is because your threshold of pain is being tested," Hades said a little more firmly. "If you are going to be able to manipulate fire, then you are going to need durable vitals. But judging by how quickly you seemed to be deteriorating, I do not think you will gain much power from it."

There was a pause.

"…Manipulate fire?" I repeated.

"Yes," Hades confirmed. "It appears that your first godly ability is ready to be harnessed."

"It's…not really the first."

"What do you mean by that?" Phoebe asked suspiciously, looking from me to Hades and back again. "What does she mean by that, Solomon?" she then demanded from Søren.

He gave her a look of offence as I snorted in amusement. "…*Søren*," he corrected her bitterly, nursing his arms.

"I already have another ability," I answered my mother.

"Really?" Hades was pleasantly surprised. "What is it?"

"Light projection."

Hades' expression then wilted. "Oh. Light projection is all right, but I would not go bragging about it."

Interesting. Thanatos had reiterated the same thing.

"But that doesn't seem too dangerous," Phoebe said. "This fire thing though, I don't think that's a good idea."

"It is never something you choose, Phoebe," Hades sneered. "Abilities reflect the god as well as the half-blood. They choose you."

"So, what is the fire trying to say about Savannah?" my mother snapped. "That she is dangerous. That she's a hazard. That she is…dare I say, *destructive*?" she suggested. "It doesn't make any sense. Because I do not understand why she couldn't have ended up with something cold, like you. I don't think I like all of this mythological business."

"Well, she is not *like* me, now is she?" Hades pointed out. "There is a reason why I can manipulate ice. It reflects my nature —my essence. It has got nothing to do with irony. If you ask me, Savannah reflects the Underworld better than I do."

"Are you implying that it's somehow my fault our daughter is going to be a fire manipulator?" my mother clipped in a low voice, taken aback.

"No," Hades sighed in exasperation. "I am saying, that she obviously has more…passion, than perhaps I do."

"And what exactly does *that* imply?"

"It is a good thing, Phoebe," Hades assured her. "Passion means she feels things intensely —with vigour and purpose. She is driven."

My mother sucked on her teeth and shook her head. "…Then it is no wonder that you got ice."

I raised my eyebrows at the insult and then glanced at Hades. I expected him to look vulnerably wounded —but he was glaring back at her as his jasper eyes shimmered like a thousand suns. I inhaled sharply as his grip on my shoulder suddenly hardened and the cold intensified, so steam billowed from where our skin touched. "Ow," I winced as a short burst of burning cold then emitted from Hades' hand.

"Oh my gosh, Savannah!" Phoebe gasped.

"Dear gods…" Søren added.

Hades instantly let go of my shoulder. I looked down at it and started at the sight of an arrangement of sharp pointed ice spindles protruding from the surface of my skin around a handprint.

"Savannah, I am so sorry," Hades murmured, standing up and moving away from me. "I did not mean to —"

"Look what you've done now," my mother accused as she rushed over to me. "Do you really have that little self-control that you would unintentionally freeze your own daughter?"

"I wasn't trying to freeze her," Hades protested. "I just got very upset. It happens when you insult someone —did that ever occur to you?" he retorted in a snarky tone.

"Whatever," Phoebe growled at him. Then she turned to me. "Savannah, are you okay?"

I clicked my tongue and held my hand in front of her when she tried to touch me. "Don't," I quipped, moving to get up. Søren stumbled to my side to help me. He gripped my arms with covered hands, but from the way he hissed I knew it still burned.

"...Right —you're still burning," Phoebe murmured sadly, withdrawing.

"Well, yes," I confirmed, straightening up. "But I also don't want your help. Or for you to be near me right now."

"What?"

I sighed and looked at her seriously. "Goddamn it, Mom, I am not a kid anymore. And I'm not alive either. I...I don't belong here. I belong in the divine world now, and you have to realise that you won't be around to '*mom*' me anymore. I am tougher than you think I am."

I concentrated the heat towards there, and the ice began to drip away.

"And please stop being so childish with Dad," I went on, looking back at Hades. "I understand that you don't want to get along. I know you didn't expect to see him, and I know that you don't *want* to see him either —but for my sake, at least don't be so harsh about it."

She blinked up at me. Turning sheepish, she glanced downwards at her lap and stiffened. I felt no remorse. I was still rather pissed off at her for her earlier confession about my childhood.

"Be civil," I then clarified. "Accept the fact he's here and work it out without getting me caught in the middle. Especially not this literally."

I pointed at my shoulder.

My mother pressed her lips into a line and stood up. "You're right, Savannah. I suppose memories bring out the worst in me. I'm…sorry."

"Good," I said.

I was surprised by her swift surrender. My mind then started ticking with a follow up idea. "…So now, why don't you two to talk it out here? You seem to have a lot to say. And I don't think you should come inside until you are both okay with being in the same room together."

"Wait, what?" blurted Hades.

"Exactly —what?" Phoebe added.

"I don't think you realise just how hostile you can be," I put carefully. "Whether you like it or not, you two are my parents. I need you both. And I would prefer it if you are *not* constantly at each other's throats."

Somewhat of a truce formed between them, even though they both scowled. It was a moment later when they started mumbling and grumbling subtle apologies. Deciding to give them privacy, I then gestured for my Trainer to follow me and we made our way back to the house.

"Are you sure that it's wise to leave those two out there?" Søren asked nervously, glancing at the window. "It feels like a bad idea."

"It'll be fine. They're not children —contrary to popular observation," I quipped. "I think that they really need this closure."

He simply shrugged. "All right."

I sighed as I then sat down gingerly on the sofa, careful to step over the smashed dish on the floor, before Ron Weasley II came running.

"Oh no, Weasley don't!" I gasped, moving to get up.

But he rubbed against my legs without a problem, purring longingly. I smiled and kneeled down, reaching out to pet him. Then I remembered the fire in my veins. Only…it was no longer burning with that same intensity.

"That's weird," I said, narrowing my eyes.

"What's weird?" Søren asked, flopping down on the sofa beside me.

"My veins are still white, but the pain has lessened," I explained. I touched my skin experimentally. It was a bearable heat.

"But you're still hot, right?" Søren chuckled lazily. "It would be a shame for that to go away."

"Shut up," I scoffed as I ran my hand down Ron's back.

I then turned to face him completely, which caused Ron to jump down from my lap. "How badly are you burnt?" I demanded.

"Hm?" he murmured. He then took off his jacket and rolled up his sleeves. I winced at the patches of dark red.

He had *really* been burned.

"Søren," I breathed, looking at him. "Why didn't you say anything?"

"They don't hurt," he said. "They're just pulsing, and warm."

"You idiot," I whispered, glancing downwards. "You shouldn't have carried me. Besides, it turns out it was nothing anyway."

"That's not true," he retorted. "And you were in pain. *Serious* pain. I would never let anyone experience that, especially not alone."

I blinked. "…Really?"

"Of course. Look, I don't regret doing what I did. I would do it again if I had to. You are that important."

I softened and smiled weakly. "You are too sweet, Søren. I really didn't deserve all of that."

He did not respond. He glanced away and pressed his lips into a line. Perhaps my compliment had been too much for him.

"…How hot is your skin? Can I touch it now?" he then asked. "I think that you could use a hug."

I paused. "I think that it's fine now," I whispered.

He then turned back to face me and hesitantly reached out with one hand. I shivered as his hand then made contact with my arm, causing him to flinch. But he then put his other hand on my other arm. I stiffened, suddenly very self-conscious about the tank top I was wearing. Then he hugged me, like letting go might cause me to disappear.

"Savannah," Søren whispered, making me look up into his eyes as he

313

withdrew. "I was…scared. I thought that something truly awful would happen to you. You know I don't have that many friends. I didn't want to experience what it would be like to lose one."

I had been that lost friend to someone already. I could not bear to think of putting someone else through that again.

I nodded slowly in understanding. "You don't have to be afraid," I told him. "Like I said. I am tougher than you think."

"I…I know," he sighed, glancing down.

I smiled softly and put a hand on his spindly arm. He looked back up in surprise. "Thanks for caring about me though."

He smiled at that.

"…Hey, I hate to be a cockblock, but we have got a situation."

"Dad?" I frowned, turning and craning my neck to see to the entrance.

"Yes," Hades sighed, walking in. "Your mother is kind of…frozen?"

"Frozen?"

"Solid."

I growled and got up, before pushing past him to stomp out the front door. "Jesus Christ, Hades, it hasn't even been five minutes!"

CHAPTER 36

SAVANNAH

I NEVER THOUGHT that there would come a time when I would need to thaw my mother out of a statuesque cast of ice.

I never thought that it would be because of my father, either. But I figured that now was the time to get used to the strangeness and idiocy —myself partially included —that ran through my family.

"I can't believe you've done this," I breathed circling the frozen Phoebe.

"Really?" Søren piped up. "You *didn't* see this coming?"

Of course I had anticipated this. I was not so naïve to believe that a single conversation could smoothen years of wear and tear.

But I was not going to admit it. "Not now, Søren," I hissed.

"It was an accident," Hades informed me. "She said something insulting and I flew off the handle," he confessed, glaring at nothing.

"You need to learn how to control your temper," I sighed. "If you keep flying off the handle, you might end up doing a lot more damage than just freezing someone," I said earnestly.

Hades shuffled from foot to foot.

"So, about unfreezing her," I reluctantly changed the subject, "am I just supposed to put my hand on her and hope for the best?"

"I usually wait for time to run its course, and allow it to thaw. Melting someone free has never been tried before," Hades admitted.

My expression did not change. "…Hoping for the best it is."

I looked down at my palm and willed heat to form there. To my relief my hands then warmed; a dim glow emitting from them.

I stood in front of my mother in her shocked frozen state and thought of the best place to concentrate the heat.

I reached past her outstretched arms and placed my hand on her chest, figuring that going with the heart was the best bet. Steam then quickly rose at the contact, assuring me that it was likely working.

"Hey," Søren frowned, unwittingly reviving the conversation, "What exactly did Savannah's Mom say anyway?"

"Yeah," I added, turning to face Hades, "I want to know too."

Hades lidded his eyes and sighed deeply. Then a rose blush coloured his cheeks and my eyes widened in surprise. He coughed and turned away slightly, but it was too late —we had already seen.

Hades was blushing.

"Woah, I didn't think that someone who gravely embodies cold and disillusionment could do that," Søren whispered, mesmerised.

"What? Blush?" I murmured. "What a development."

I smirked as Hades started and looked directly at me, alarmingly mortified.

"I was not *blushing*," he shakily assured us, straightening his waistcoat. "I just…I was just recalling what your mother had said and my face suddenly warmed up for some reason."

He then frowned as though he was aware that he was simply trying to convince himself as well.

I snorted. "Regardless, what did my Mom say to make the almighty stony-faced Lord of darkness *embarrassed*?"

"Mind you, I am not embarrassed either," Hades snarled. "What Phoebe said was…hurtful, that is all."

"Which *is*…?" I prompted, turning back to face my mother to check on the progress. Her chest was almost completely thawed, so I moved my hand a little lower to focus on her lower half. I turned back to look at Hades when he did not

316

respond to me. "What did she say?" I reiterated.

He hesitated, and the blush came back. He hung his head and did not say anything for a few seconds.

Søren and I shared an uncertain look.

I did not want to laugh and tease him this time. This time I noticed a thin film of silver in his eyes. I shook my head as I then softened. "…Dad, if you don't want to, you don't have to —"

"She asked me why I came back," he cut me off, before looking up with a hard, passive aggressive expression. I immediately shut up and stared at him semi attentively. "I stupidly told her truth. I had learned that The Book of Treaties had been taken and that Horkos was coming for us, so I came to check on you. I tried to apologise for not giving her notice, but she would not hear it. She kept saying that I should have considered other people's feelings and wants, like I was unaware of the implications of my visits. And so, I called her a hypocrite."

"But what was the shocking insult?"

Hades hesitated again. "…She called me a cold, malevolent, unfeeling and selfish bastard," he finally answered. "And she said that none of this would be happening if we had never met. She said that directly to my face —that she regretted it…all."

My blood halted. I flinched away from my mother, before cradling my hand to my chest. I blinked rapidly, running Hades' words through my head. One sentence stood out. *She regretted it all.*

So…she regretted me?

"Savannah?" Søren murmured, reaching to put a hand on my shoulder.

"No," I whispered, turning away. I had not mean to be harsh, but I did not want pity or sympathetic affection. I looked at Hades, who was looking back at me expectantly. "…She regrets everything?" I deadpanned. Then I bit my trembling lip. "Good…good to know."

Hades frowned in confusion before his eyes widened in realisation. "I am sure that she does not mean that she regrets you, Savannah. You *know* her. She wouldn't —" he said quickly.

"I don't care. It doesn't matter," I rasped, making him stop short. "…It's not

317

as if you can vouch for her right now," I pointed out, reminding him that she was still frozen. "It does not matter what you think or hope that she meant. Only she knows."

I turned to go back into the house.

"Savannah, wait," Hades tried again. "We should talk about this."

I looked at my mother and then back at him. "…Seeing how this recent discussion worked out, I don't think that I want to do that right now," I told him. "I just…I need to think. Alone."

I purposefully marched towards the front door.

"Hold on," Søren spoke up, making me pause again.

I turned to him and gave him a weary smile. "You were right, about before. It was a terrible idea."

✠

I cried for ten minutes.

I was not sure if that was adequate or too long for what it was worth. I probably should not have cried at all, but I could not help it. I was being dramatic, but it felt like everything had just shattered in front of me.

I was hoping that seeing Phoebe would heal something.

It had worked at first.

"You are the best thing that ever happened to me…"
"…I regretted it all."

Then it ended up stabbing me in the back. Which one did she truly mean? I screamed into my hands and aggressively ran my fingers through my hair, becoming increasingly frustrated.

But despite not knowing what my mother felt, I reached the conclusion that maybe if I had been in her shoes, I possibly would have regretted the situation too. It was just that without that, no matter what she would try to tell me, one thing could not be ignored.

I would not exist.

"…Savannah," a quiet voice said from the doorway. I looked up after wiping my face. Søren offered me a sympathetic smile.

I turned away and hugged my knees to my chest.

"Please don't push us away," he continued, coming to sit next to me on the floor. "We're trying to help and be there for you and it doesn't help if you're being stubborn."

I slowly looked up at him. I did not have anything to say. So, he took it as invitation to carry on.

"Parents do stupid things all the time. They will say things they don't mean and flare up —but more often than not their care and love don't just go away. Unplanned things will always hold some form of guilt and regret. But…your mother stayed, didn't she? She had you, and raised you, through thick and thin. She never abandoned you."

"Are you trying to tell me that actions speak louder than words?"

"Yes," he admitted. "Think about it this way. Would you really believe the words '*I love you*' coming from a psychopathic abuser?"

"Well, no."

"Then you can't believe that someone hates you when they clearly show that they love you," he concluded. "Actions say a lot more. And when they don't quite match up with words, they speak louder."

I sniffed and stared at him in intrigue. That sounded so profound and wise. "Don't be *too* hard on your Mom," the Reaper then murmured. "I mean, she did give birth to and raise a half Greek god."

I chuckled along weakly and nodded a little, feeling a little less burdened. "Thanks, Søren," I whispered. "I needed that."

"You're welcome."

"How are you so good at this?" I smirked. "Knowing what to say?"

"It comes with age," he boasted, sighing as though it were a tragedy. "I have a lot of wisdom," he quipped, tapping the side of his head. I immediately regretted thinking he had sounded wise and consequently cringed.

I laughed and shoved him playfully. "As if!"

"No, I'm serious," he insisted, shoving me back.

"Whatever," I chuckled, shaking my head. Then I paused, glancing at him out of the corner of my eye. I leaned over and suddenly enveloped him in a hug. "…Thank you," I mumbled.

He stiffened, before he surprised me by putting his arms around me in return. "You already said that."

"I am saying it again," I defended myself.

"I didn't say I minded."

I did not have Luca anymore, but Søren was coming close to becoming a best friend. It could have been the influence of having him as a Trainer, but he knew how handle difficult situations. He knew how to handle *me*. There were few people in existence who knew how to do that.

What he had done since we had arrived —it was borderline romantic, but I saw it in another light. That we could be friends, and that would be what we both needed. I withdrew from the hug and got up before stretching my arms above my head. "I should get back to Hades."

"Yeah. He's worried."

I tilted my head to the side. "Interesting."

Then I marched to the door and took several deep breaths. I hurriedly wiped my face as I came into Hades' view and made for Phoebe.

"…Are you okay?" the god murmured.

I pressed my lips into a line and concentrated on thawing out the ice. "I don't know how to answer that. And I still don't want to talk about it."

"Are you sure?"

"*Yes*," I snapped, turning to shoot him a glare.

"All right, all right," he surrendered, holding his hands up.

I paused, not wanting to come across as spoiled. "…I will be fine with a little time. And no offence, but I don't think you would get it," I added, managing to crack a slight smile.

320

"I…I *do* get it actually," he murmured, raising an eyebrow. "You might not think so, but I do. You just looked so upset, so naturally I thought that I would ask how you were."

I smiled genuinely at that. "Nice fatherly instincts," I told him. "It's also nice to see that you still have those."

"Very funny," Hades huffed.

I shook my head and went back to melting Phoebe. Out of the corner of my eye I saw Søren looking out at the front yard from the window.

"Savannah, what is up with you and that boy?" Hades asked, suddenly standing next to me. I looked up at him.

"What do you mean?" I asked. "He's my Trainer. And a friend. A *good* friend. And that is all that I need right now."

Hades nodded encouragingly. "That is quite mature of you," he noted. "I am glad that the Aaron disaster brought something useful to the table."

"We are not going to talk about him either," I said firmly.

"I know, I know —it is still a touchy subject," Hades said quickly. "But…you *should* talk to your Mom when she is thawed."

I stiffened involuntarily.

I knew that he was right. And even though Søren had comforted me, it did not make the feelings disappear. The anger was still bubbling up, and I found myself grinding my teeth together in frustration.

"Savannah, you are a little distracted," Hades sighed. "You might end up accidentally setting your mother on fire if you are this unfocused," he warned. Then he paused. "I was…wrong, by the way. Your fire manipulation skills are going to be very powerful —the flames are white. I hope at least that makes you feel better."

It did not.

I looked down at my hands. I gasped. White flames were flickering at my fingertips, and they grew larger before I made the effort to stop snarling. Hades was right. I nodded and walked to the side of the driveway to the low laying brick wall. I jumped up and sat there, inhaling and exhaling deeply but shakily. I looked down at my arms. My veins were still glowing, and I felt hotter than before. I sighed and hung my head in shame. There I was lecturing my father about controlling his emotions, while I could have inflicted worse damage due to the lack of controlling my own. I clenched my fists and squeezed my eyes shut.

"I hope that you're not still crying," Søren's voice suddenly quipped.

I started and nearly fell off the wall. Then I opened my eyes and blinked stupidly. He sat down next to me as I shifted and sat more securely.

I did not say anything.

"I don't think that your mother meant to make you cry. I don't even think that she meant what she said."

"I know," I responded. "I *know* that she didn't mean it that way. But I can't help feeling the way I've felt for a long time without realising it," I admitted. It hurt to say those words out loud. "...I was thinking about what you said, and I realised something."

"What?"

I turned to face him. "What if we don't survive?" I whispered. "What if...what if we don't get a chance to live after all of this, because..."

I could not complete the sentence.

"Because we'll die," he finished for me.

I stared at him. "How can you say that so casually?" I asked.

"It's an occupational hazard."

I lidded my eyes.

"What, can't I make that joke?"

I shook my head.

Søren sighed and glanced at Hades, who was sitting cross legged on the grass next to the frozen statue of my mother. He was talking, seemingly outwardly to himself, but I saw in the quiet sadness in his smile and darkened eyes that it was as if he was talking with her.

"I'm afraid of being alone," I suddenly whispered.

Søren turned back to me with a look of surprise. His lips parted like he was going to respond, but then he hesitated. I drew a sharp breath as he remained silent;

leaving me feeling a little stupid.

"It's…okay," he murmured. "I don't think that anyone *truly* wants to be all alone. At least not forever. And it's okay to feel that way. It's okay to talk about it. And you know sometimes…I grow fearful too. After what happened with Angelina and Melchior, I got paranoid that I would be doomed to remain alone."

He tried to laugh it off at the end, but I could hear the pain in his voice, in his tone. It made me feel awful.

"Søren, you don't have to downplay it," I said gently. "As you said —it's okay to feel that way. It doesn't make you pathetic or needy. It makes you…human. You know what I mean?"

Søren paused before he frowned thoughtfully. "You know what? I do know what you mean," he murmured. "I understand. Maybe in the future things will be different —*better*. But I suppose that we will just have to wait until we get there."

I smiled, glancing up at the sky. "I guess so."

CHAPTER 37

SAVANNAH

HADES WISELY KEPT his mouth shut as I headed back to continue thawing out my mother.

I did not *want* him to say anything.

I did not want him to ask what anything meant, or about what Søren and I had been talking. I did not feel ready to have that kind of existential conversation with my father.

I reached up and tied my hair up into a ponytail with strands of my own hair in order to keep it out of the way. I did not have a hair tie, and I was too lazy to go inside to search for one. It was however, more secure than the previous one; I made sure of that by mercilessly tugging at the strands.

I had a far more levelled head, which meant that I could *concentrate*.

But I knew that Hades wanted to say something anyway, because he could not keep an aloof façade for too long.

"So —what happened?" he finally asked.

I started and tactfully took my hands off of Phoebe, instantly extinguishing the flames.

I narrowed my eyes at Hades as he met my gaze.

"I mean, *did* anything happen," he amended the question.

I scoffed and raised an eyebrow. "What, are you trying to be more invested in my life now?" I deadpanned.

"Well…yes," he frowned. "But I am also just…checking up on you."

I blinked, surprised by his answer. It was not what I had expected. It really seemed like he was trying to make the effort to reach out to me at a pace that suited me.

"We had an existential crisis," I sighed. "We're both pretty unlucky in love, and we both realised that we do not want to repeat mistakes."

Hades was looking at me with a stupid grin.

"Dad," I said firmly. "He is *not* my type."

His smile fell and he nodded importantly.

It seemed to satisfy his curiosity at last.

I then refocused my concentration again. I was actually quite chuffed with myself at how quickly I had managed to master manipulating my newfound ability. It was surprisingly simple —it was like switching a light on and off. Except if I did not pay attention, I could very well render something to ashes.

Hades and I sat in silence afterwards, which I was not opposed to, but it only resulted in him unintentionally glowering at me or at my mother while he was deep in thought.

"…Do you really think that you're a cold, malevolent, unfeeling and selfish bastard?" I eventually murmured, glancing up at him.

"What?" he snapped, starting in surprise.

"Do you think what Mom said about you is true?" I deadpanned. "Because if you don't think that about yourself, it wouldn't bother you —and she wouldn't be frozen."

Hades opened his mouth to respond, but something then made him hesitate. He glanced down at the ground and sighed. "A part of me would like to believe that she is wrong. That those words are just words. But…another part, deep down, knows that she is quite right."

I raised my eyebrows.

He offered a sad smile. "Do you want to hear about how we met?"

I nodded, suddenly eager.

"Eighteen years ago, Persephone and I had a really big argument about our son and where the future of the Underworld was going. He had moved out, and Persephone was worried about how he would do on his own. He is not that old, by god standards, so think of it as though a fifteen-year-old was leaving home," he started nostalgically.

I raised an eyebrow at his interesting analogy but did not say anything. "...In the end, we could not really stop him. So, Persephone and I argued for what felt like days, before she kicked me out and I came to the mundane world."

I did laugh at that.

"I bumped into your mother while she was grocery shopping one afternoon. She was young —barely twenty, and she had just started living in her own place close to where she worked. We quite literally bumped into each other —she was coming around the corner and I had not been looking."

"Is this real life or a romantic comedy?"

"Shush —it really did happen that way," Hades insisted, flippantly waving a hand at me. "And I remember looking at her and thinking...I had never seen a more beautiful mortal," he went on. Then his gaze flickered over me. "...You definitely take after her."

"Don't joke..." I scoffed.

"Again, I am serious," Hades deadpanned. "You were spared my dull aesthetic genes. Your mother is beautiful. And I did not hesitate to tell that to her face either, after picking up a head of lettuce that had fallen out of her basket when we knocked each other down."

I smiled softly and moved my hands as I noticed how the ice had almost completely melted where I had been concentrating on before. "I bet she called you a creep," I murmured.

"Oh, of course," Hades chuckled. "But only after she had stared at me in surprise for a few seconds. She would not admit it, but I do not think she had heard that compliment before then. After she called me a creep, I immediately lost all of my confidence and stopped making sense. So, I just turned around and walked away, wanting to kick myself."

I laughed, beginning to picture it.

"Yes, yes," he murmured reluctantly and wearily. "Your old man is not actually very smooth; surprise."

"There's no surprise —I never thought that he was," I chuckled. He pouted slightly in mock offence, which only made me laugh more.

"All right, can I continue now?" he snapped.

"Fine, fine," I sighed, genuinely smiling.

"Thank you. As misfortune would have it, I did not see her for a week; in which I was trying to sort myself out with accommodation and whatnot. But when I realised that I actually needed food, I went back to the grocery store. And Fate decided that I had not quite embarrassed myself enough, and so we bumped into each other again. This time though, your mother's orange juice spilled all down the front of my suit."

"*Ha!*" I blurted, pointing at him comically.

"Yes, it was hilarious —for everyone but me. Luckily for me, Phoebe is as beautiful on the inside as she is on the outside, and insisted that she get my suit dry cleaned. Because I could not possibly say no to her, I agreed. We kept seeing each other more often after that," he sighed and leaned back to look upwards, before developing a far-off dreamy look. "…And although I should not say this, your mother was the first mortal to make me momentarily forget about Persephone."

I blinked, dumbstruck. "I don't think that Persephone would be too pleased to hear you say that."

"Of course, she would not," he agreed, looking back down at me. "But I cannot deny the truth. I really did fall in love with your mother. As deeply as a seabed dweller. And maybe in an alternate reality, where I was not a god and Persephone and I were not together…perhaps Phoebe and I could have lasted," he said quietly, growing pitiful.

I frowned and bit my lip, unsure of what to say.

What exactly *was* I supposed to say?

Did he expect me to agree with him?

I had always known that he had loved my mother, but it had not occurred to me that he might still be thinking about her and alternate happy endings for their tragic love affair all of these years later.

He sounded as though he truly cared.

"How did you react to Mom becoming pregnant with me?" I then dared to ask. I had wondered for while what he had thought. My mother had told me all sorts of stories, but I really wanted to hear it from Hades.

The god of the Underworld blinked at me and did not say anything for a moment. "I mean…the fact that she become pregnant was not ideal," he started, "I was apprehensive about having a child; knowing you would be a half-blood. Phoebe was stubborn and insistent, only caring for the moment and not the consequences.

"But I do not regret bringing you into the world. Phoebe assured me that she knew what she was doing. That she knew what she wanted. Contrary to popular speculation, your mother knew I was Hades as early as our fifth date. And she did not care after the initial shock," he chuckled. "I really loved that about her. I was momentarily overjoyed when she told me. Then I remembered the last millennium," he deadpanned.

It made me snicker just a bit.

"I tried my best to be a father again when you were born," he admitted, before pausing and looking crestfallen. "I really did try to stick around —you know that, right?" He asked me earnestly.

I pressed my lips into a line and simply nodded.

"I do not regret it all," he then unwisely quipped.

My own limbs seemed to turn to ice. Up until that point, I had almost forgotten about what my mother had said and about why I had been crying. Hades had just reminded me, and the mood instantly dampened.

"I…should not have said that," he murmured, finally realising. "Savannah, I did not mean —"

"It's fine," I spoke up, shaking my head. I smiled weakly and willed my words to turn to truth.

"…Okay."

I went back to thawing out Phoebe. She was almost free. So, I increased the intensity of my flames —and accidentally over accelerated the process. The ice turned to steam under my touch and evaporated even when I let go.

Phoebe let out a strangled cry as she regained mobility and suddenly fell forward...into Hades' arms.

"That was close," he quipped.

"How did you get to her so fast?" I frowned. "You were standing just there."

"You forget who I am, don't you?" he smirked, helping my mother to straighten up. I shook my head in amusement as I helped her too. She was shivering, and understandably freezing. She then staggered, disoriented, before she shook her head and sneezed.

"Bless you," Hades said.

She suddenly stopped trembling, and the blue tint to her skin dissolved. She gasped, flipping her arms over. She shot the god of the dead a glare.

"*Hades*," she growled.

"What?" he quipped, arching an eyebrow. "I can't help it. You sneezed. And so, I said, '*bless you*', therefore so it was."

"I don't need your help," she snapped. "You are the one who froze me in the first place." She then paused and glanced at the ground. "...By the way, I heard what you said. Both of you." She looked at us gravely as my father and I stiffened. "...And I'm sorry."

Hades and I gasped in unison.

Phoebe Green was not a woman who put her pride aside often. When she did, it was not for just anybody. She was apologising —and that was an enormous deal.

"I'm mostly sorry to Savannah," she added spitefully, turning to me. "I didn't mean what I said like the way that it sounded. I don't regret you, sweetheart. I love you. I just...just regret *how* it happened," she admitted.

"But what's done is done. I can't rewind time and I can't live in regret anymore. I am sorry for making you cry."

I blinked, bewildered. Then I darted forward and firmly hugged her, squeezing my eyes shut as the familiar prick of tears started coming back. "I'm

329

sorry for thinking that you regretted me."

"Don't you even dare blame yourself," Phoebe warned me, withdrawing to hold me at arm's length. "I should have known better. Plus, your father is a pathetic blabbermouth," she accused, glaring at him.

"Aw, come on Phoebe," Hades chuckled uneasily. "I had to explain why you were frozen."

"You could have left that part out."

"And what good would it have done?"

"Showing how self-assured you *should* be," my mother deadpanned.

Hades gasped and glared back at her.

"Okay!" I said, moving to get in between them. "That's enough; both of you. Mom, what you said to Hades was not called for. I would have gotten upset too. But Hades, it wasn't worth freezing someone over."

I glanced between my parents earnestly and it was almost a relief when they both sighed and appeared to relent.

"Now," I quipped, turning back to my mother. "The reason I came here in the first place…" I trailed off and took a deep breath, preparing myself to say it. "I came to say goodbye."

Hades looked justifiably nervous as Phoebe gawked at me. "Goodbye?" she repeated, her green eyes widening. "What do you mean by goodbye —I just got you back!"

"I know, I know," I sighed. "But there is a god out there who is ready to wage war on the Reapers Organisation, and technically it's because of me, so I'm kind of obligated to participate —"

"Are you serious?" Phoebe cut me off. "War? Hades," she then hissed darkly at him. "we're going to talk."

"*Mom*," I raised my voice. "This is not all of his fault. And I'm actually looking for an alternative, by the way. I don't want to die again," I mumbled, folding my arms.

"Well, I don't want you to die again either," my mother scoffed. "And going headfirst into a war is exactly how to ensure that you die again."

"But what if we didn't have to fight at all? What if, I found a way to reason with Hor —"

I did not even manage to finish my sentence when Hades suddenly started laughing hysterically. I looked at him in confusion.

"I'm sorry," he chuckled, "it is just that…you think that you can *reason* with Horkos!"

I lidded my eyes as he continued laughing. Phoebe gave me a sympathetic look before sharply elbowing Hades in the ribs. He doubled up and spluttered appropriately, but he still could not stop laughing.

"It is a valiant effort, sweetheart," my mother sighed. "But your father's twisted sense of humour actually holds some truth. The gods are not the negotiating type."

Unfortunately, Phoebe Green was well versed in dealing with the divine.

"Well, I will have to *make* him listen," I still insisted, frowning. "He doesn't know what I'm capable of."

"Well, I don't see how that would help your case if you're trying to convince him that you're harmless," Søren suddenly said from directly behind me.

I started as he then came around and stood beside me. I stuck out my tongue at him childishly.

"He's right," Hades sighed, over his amusement. "It is contradictory."

"I refuse to give up though," I remained adamant.

"Well, you can come up with a new idea," my mother suggested. "And while you do, I'm going to talk to Hades."

"Mom…" I said in warning, giving her a look.

"Relax," she dismissed. "It's about the story he told you. And…things he said before, when I was still frozen and you were busy with…uh, Stormin'."

"It's *Søren*," the Reaper sighed in exasperation.

"…*Gesundheit.*"

He grumbled in disbelief; whirling away in frustration to tug at his hair.

"Fine, Mom," I said through my teeth, diverting the conversation back to something important. "…But if I see any funny business —"

"Yes, yes, you will have my permission to interrupt," she cut me off and gently pushed me towards the house. "Now run along."

I trudged to the front door, unable to rid myself of worry.

"So," Søren started when we sat down on the sofa. "Let's brainstorm."

I sighed in defeat. "All right."

CHAPTER 38

SAVANNAH

"WHAT IF WE took advantage of the element of surprise?" Søren mumbled, absentmindedly biting the end of the pencil in his hand. We had migrated to my bedroom in search for stationery, so that we could list ideas. He was sitting at my desk, and I was sitting on top of it, overseeing our progress. Which was not much.

"Don't put that in your mouth," I told him, leaning forward and snatching the pencil. "You don't know where it's been."

"Sorry," he chuckled. "It's a bad habit."

I huffed and leaned back against the wall. "I find it hard to believe we actually can surprise the gods," I murmured. "I mean, they're all powerful. But yet they can't see us coming?"

"I'm sure there's a god for specifically that," Søren smirked.

"Of course," I snorted. "If there's a god of wine, there's probably a god of superstitions and fortune telling."

"Anyway," he then said firmly, tapping my thigh, "Focus."

I frowned, now impatient and irritated.

"Ugh, what's the point?" I groaned, holding my chin in my hands. "We have no chance no matter what we come up with. Horkos will have the advantage of being a know-it-all and getting more people on his side. Like seriously, who the hell is going to listen to us?"

It had finally sunk in that our situation was pretty hopeless. Every option we had looked at ended up with either me, Hades and Thanatos, or the Organisation being executed. I was beginning to think of accepting my inevitable demise.

Søren did not respond straight away.

He gave me this look of complete disbelief, before shaking his head in rather offensive disappointment.

"That's not the Savannah I know," he eventually said, narrowing his eyes at me. I shrugged indifferently. He continued, "The Savannah I know always does things her own way. She doesn't listen and she doesn't easily get deterred. She keeps going —even when it seems pointless."

I raised an eyebrow.

"We're in this together," he reminded me. "I know you don't want to fight, but if you don't defy the policy, then who will?"

I let his words sink in before I sat up straight. He was right. Who would, indeed? "If I fight," I quipped, "I fight for others like me."

"Exactly."

I gasped and jumped off my desk. "I have to fight not just for my existence —but for other half-blood gods alike. I have to completely abolish that treaty," I realised, and I turned around to smack my fist down on the desk. "And I think I might have an idea of how to do it."

✠

HADES

"DID YOU REALLY mean all of that?" Phoebe asked the god of the Underworld once the Grim Reapers were out of earshot. "When you said those things about an alternate reality?" she elaborated.

Hades paused and stared at her. She was looking at him with a face that showed that she did not want to believe him, but she had already concluded that he was right. "Yes, I did," he murmured.

"And the other things you said before…" she trailed off and glanced at the ground. Hades did a double take as he saw her blush slightly.

"Yes."

"*How*?" she asked, looking up again. "How can you mean it? Don't you have Persephone? Why do you still care about me?"

He frowned at her accusing expression. "Of course, I still care. I fell in love with you, Phoebe. We may no longer be together, but it does not mean that I will suddenly stop feeling something for you."

She pouted and glanced away. "It would certainly make things easier if you did," she mumbled.

"Yes, it would," he agreed.

There was then a solemn pause as neither of them knew what to say. Hades understood what she was talking about. He knew what he was doing was a completely foolish idea —but he could not deal with her hatred towards him any longer. Persephone was ecstatic to be rid of her, but Hades could not bring himself to let go as of yet.

The memories he had created with Phoebe were some of the happiest ones which he cherished. He could not just forget about them.

He could not just forget about *her*.

"…Don't you even feel slightly guilty?" Phoebe finally said softly.

"Guilty?" he echoed. "For what?"

"For cheating," she snapped. Then she huffed and folded her arms. "And I know I sound like an awful hypocrite, but if I was Persephone, I would have skewered you. I knew that you were married —we just pretended that you weren't. I feel sort of stupid now when I think about it. I want to say I regret it…but I think we both know that those years were some of the best part of our existences," she breathed.

Hades' eyes grew in intrigue. "Do you really feel that way?"

She stiffened. "Do not make me repeat myself. Yes, I loved you. Once upon a time. Because I am human, Hades. I have my flaws. Just how disloyal are the gods anyway? Do any of you have morals?"

"Persephone and I were on a break," Hades deadpanned. "She knows that these…occurrences do not really count when we do that."

"So, she's *okay* with this?" Phoebe gestured between them.

"Of course, she isn't," he sighed. "But when you have been married for as long as we have, you would understand that even through unconditional love, *feelings* come and go," he explained. "…Truth be told she would not cheat on me — whether we were on a break or not. But if she ever did, I would not blame her. I would eventually grow sick of me too."

She snorted at that, before laughing softly.

"So, when I said that I loved you, I wasn't patronising you," Hades continued. "And when I say it now, I still mean it —just probably not in a romantic way anymore."

There was a big, raw wound that they were both plastering up with pretty words. Neither of them were willing to rip it away; to let it air and heal. It was as though they had become accustomed to that agony, and found an odd sense of comfort in it. If it never closed and healed, they would never have to part ways and say goodbye.

Despite the bickering and petty insults, Hades would be lying to himself if he said that he did not treasure every moment he spent in Phoebe's presence —in the way that a madman loved pain. Unlike what Persephone did to bring blooms after his wintry rage, Phoebe Green ignited undeniable fire in place of his ice.

She melted him.

The fiery woman standing before him now shook her head and sighed. "I must be insane for falling in love with the god of the Underworld," she murmured. "But…I think that he was crazier for falling in love with me."

He smiled sympathetically.

"I want you to stick around," she then surprised him by saying. "Not for me, but for Savannah. I do not know if she's forgiven you or ever will forgive you, but I want you to take responsibility for what happened and to be a parent in my absence."

Hades kept smiling but then it wavered. "What do you mean, '*in your absence*'? She can still see you. You are a *Profítis*, remember?"

"She said it herself, Hades. She doesn't belong here anymore," Phoebe said, her voice cracking. "She belongs in your world now. I can't be there for her." She pressed her lips into a line as tears slipped down her cheeks. Hades stiffened and clenched his fists. He could not stand seeing her cry.

"I swear upon the River Styx," the god of the dead said through his teeth, "that I will do my best to make up for being a pathetic father and be the parent Savannah deserves."

She held his gaze as more tears spilled, those grey eyes thunderous.

"Thank you," she choked out.

He nodded, really wanting to embrace her, but he knew that she would just end up punching him if he got any closer to her than he already was. So, he just stood there awkwardly as she silently cried. Hades meant his promise to Phoebe. He was determined to make it up to this family.

SAVANNAH

"YOU CAN'T TELL anybody about this yet," I whispered, guiltily looking into Søren's silver eyes. "I don't want anyone to stop me. And I am trusting you. This is…something that I have to do."

He frowned, possessing little faith.

"If I have a chance to save other lives then I have to do this," I continued.

"I…I understand," he forced out. "but I don't want this to end up going wrong. If you don't make it —"

"I will make it," I cut him off. "You know why?"

"…Confidence?"

"Not really," I admitted sheepishly. "It's because…I have reason to come back," I said. "For all of us."

His expression did not change, but his eyes gleamed with a feeling which I could not place. "Okay. Good luck then," he whispered.

I gave him a determined smile, partly for my own motivation. "I don't need luck. Now, go and guard the door."

He nodded and marched off. I sighed as I heard the door click closed. I wiped my face indignantly and willed myself to focus on why I was doing this rather than why I should not be. I knelt down beside my bed and brushed strands of my hair behind my ears. I closed my eyes and clasped my hands together, like I was about to pray.

That was because I was.

That was the plan: to pray and try to bargain out of full out war. I knew it was likely to reveal my location —which would spell disaster if my negotiation did not go well —but it was a risk I was willing to take, for everyone else's sake.

I sighed deeply and bowed my head, deciding to get it over with.

'*Horkos, god of oaths,*' I began. '*Hear my prayer. I know that you have been*

tasked with retrieving me because of the treaty against my kind. With all due
respect, I think that you are overreacting. Half-blood gods do not have to be as
dangerous as you believe them to be. With the right to see their godly parent, they
could blossom and turn into a versatile asset. You do not have to fear us. Please,
give us a chance —give me a chance. Amen.'

I opened my eyes, staying still and silent.

I knew that he could not really answer me, but I felt that if I made one wrong move, I could blow my chance.

When nothing happened for ten seconds, I breathed a sigh of relief and stood up, before dusting myself down. I had put the plan into motion, but I was still nervous. If it did not go accordingly, step by step, I could end up dying completely.

I then jumped at a sudden knock on the door.

"Are you done?" Søren asked.

I breathed out and shook my head. "Yes —but don't scare me like that."

"I'm sorry," he apologised sheepishly, before slowly opening the door. "So, what now?"

I pressed my lips into a tight line. "Now all we can do is wait. It can't be too long before we get a response of some kind."

"Right," he murmured, looking away.

"Thank you for not trying to shoot down the idea," I then quipped. "That means a lot to me."

"That's because I think it's brave," he responded. "If you feel that you have to do this, then I'm here for you. That's the best that I can do. You're fiercely independent anyway —I don't think that I would be able to really change your mind." he chuckled softly.

"That's true…" I agreed, smiling momentarily. He was really beginning to understand the way I worked —Aaron had only been able to chip away at understanding that attribute after three years. It then made me frown and wonder about something. "I'm not being too selfish, am I?" I whispered.

"Elaborate," he huffed.

I wondered if my reasoning made any sense. "I mean…I'm thinking of others

339

as I do this, but what if that is actually coming across as selfish? For putting myself at risk and…willing to leave everyone behind?"

Søren inhaled sharply, looking offended. "You are a hero," he said simply.

I blinked. "What's that got to do with —"

"What do heroes do?"

I frowned. "Save people? Keep the peace?"

"Exactly. They sacrifice their own desires and safety for the greater good. They know that justice comes first. No matter what happens to them —they always put others first."

I pressed my lips into a line and gave him a pained expression. "You really think that I'm a hero?" I mumbled, glancing downwards.

"Yes."

I scoffed softly and smirked. Then I looked back at him. "I hope that justice wins in the end," I quipped. "No matter who is left standing."

Søren's expression softened. "So do I."

It certainly felt good to have support.

'*Savannah Green…*' a voice then wafted into my ears.

I suddenly flinched, unsure of what I had just heard. "Did you…just say my name?" I asked Søren uncertainly.

"No," he frowned. "Why?"

"I just heard someone saying it," I grumbled. "My full name, as if they were calling me."

'*Savannah, daughter of Hades*,' the voice spoke again. '*Do you not recognise my voice speaking to you? You are the one who sought out my council after all.*'

I whipped around, trying to decipher from where it was coming. I then paused as I went over the words. Shit.

"Savannah, what's going on?" Søren grumbled, frowning.

I gasped. "Horkos?" I whispered uncertainly. Søren's eyes widened and he immediately readied his crossbow, even though it was unlikely there was actually something at which to aim.

'*I received your prayer, young Reaper,*' Horkos went on. '*I am surprised by your efforts, actually. This was not the best move which you could have made. You knew that I would be able to find you, did you not?'*

"Yes, I had my suspicions," I confirmed aloud.

Søren lowered his crossbow and looked at me sideways. "...Is he talking to you in your head?" he gasped.

"Yes, so shush for a minute," I hissed. "...Yes, Horkos?" I asked nervously, glancing up at the ceiling.

'I have reviewed your plea and I have decided based on your distinct and blatant stupidity or bravery, to agree to your terms. I will give you my council and will be open to hearing what you may have to say. Be warned however, that I am not easily swayed. The choice is yours though.'

I clenched my fists and growled softly. "I am not stupid but thank you for your...cooperation."

'Indeed?' Horkos chuckled softly in amusement. *'We will see. Now, in regard to our meeting —'*

"It will be on Mount Olympus, with all of the other Olympians," I cut him off and filled in. Søren raised his eyebrows.

I had not told him about that part.

'That will not be necessary,' Horkos immediately countered. *'Only Zeus, Hera and the gods' of death presences are required.'*

I ground my teeth together in frustration, knowing he could not be bargained with —especially since he had already agreed. "Fine," I spat.

'Excellent. Please be prompt within two hours if you still wish to hold council. I swear not to do anything before then. Oh, and there is one more thing,' he added.

"What...?" I asked suspiciously.

'You cannot bring anyone else with you —not even that Trainer. If you do, the consequences will be...undesirable. You must come alone.'

"What? Horkos," I said. "What do you mean by *'undesirable'*? What would me bringing..." I trailed off, rethinking what I was about to say, "I mean, what would defying that instruction, *do* exactly?" I asked instead.

But there was no answer.

341

He did not need to say it, however. I knew that it was death.

"Savannah...?" Søren said uncertainly.

I gritted my teeth.

I was supposed to go to confront Horkos with Søren as somewhat of a form of backup team. Now I was being told I had to go completely alone. Reality began to seep in, and I tensed up. This was really happening —my plan had worked at first, but then it had backfired.

"Savannah," Søren said more firmly, marching up to me and putting a hand on my shoulder. "What did he...*say*?"

I could not find the words to answer him. In fact, I could not say any words at all —I was in shock. A million thoughts whirred around in my mind, making me feel sickeningly lightheaded. But one thought kept screaming out at me.

What was I going to do now?

CHAPTER 39

SAVANNAH

THIS TIME, SØREN was very much against my idea. He did not want to let me go to meet Horkos alone.

"I wouldn't be completely alone," I told him. "Horkos said that the gods of death were also required to be there. That means both Hades and Thanatos will be there with me."

"As if Thanatos would willingly be on your side," Søren scoffed. "And I don't think that Hades is good in a crisis."

"And *you* are?" I smirked.

He shamelessly averted his gaze. "I'm arguably better," he mumbled, folding his arms like an infant.

I put a hand on his shoulder. "Søren, honestly, I'm touched that you're only thinking about keeping me safe —but that is not the priority. Remember what you told me? Heroes make sacrifices. They sacrifice themselves for others. So, let me do that."

He looked at me with a pained expression but did not answer me right away. He then took hold of me and hugged me against him, in a grip that felt like iron. "At least try to be safe," he whispered.

I smiled softly and wrapped my arms around his neck. "Okay."

I understood why he did not want me to go. Even though Horkos was bound by his word, gods were particularly known for finding loopholes in any situation. It was hard to hold them accountable whenever there was a grievance. And for that reason, this '*meeting*' was not going to go favourably in any way, shape or form —regardless of the outcome.

But I did not have time for having second thoughts. Horkos had only given me two hours. And I did not even know where Mount Olympus was.

"Søren?" I said, withdrawing. "I need to reach a conclusion immediately," I urged. He withdrew reluctantly but nodded in understanding. I softened. "…I'm scared too."

The Trainer looked like he would rather die than admit his fear.

"I'm not going to stop you," he then sighed. "I will support you in the choice you make. I promise."

"Thank you," I smiled. Then it fell. "…Oh. I need to talk to my parents."

"Indeed you do," Søren breathed, turning me around and then walking me towards the door.

"Prepare for worse arguing."

"Right," I winced.

We made our way downstairs and out the front door, before uncertainly walking over to my parents. I had no way of gauging what kind of reaction they would have, so I was honestly not that prepared to argue. They abruptly turned around as we approached. I paused.

They were standing quite close —which was odd, because Phoebe Green would never condone such a lack of distance.

My mind then began to wander and I skimmed through multiple scenarios of what could have happened during their talk. Some were admittedly a little too hopeful. Others were more realistic.

But judging from the tears my mother was wiping from her face and the stoic expression on my father's face, I figured that I was getting ahead of myself. Phoebe then looked at me with what seemed like disappointment afterwards. It unnerved me, and I then hesitated, wondering where to start.

"Is this about the invitation to a council on Mount Olympus?" she sighed.

"Yes," I frowned. "How did you know?"

"Because Hades just got one," she said. "About you."

"Oh. Right," I said guiltily.

"Would you care to explain?" she went on.

"Of course. Let's go inside so you can...sit down."

My mother simply marched past us to the front door. My already little confidence then disappeared, and I concluded the worst. "She knows everything, doesn't she?" I murmured.

"Oh, you think?" Hades quipped sarcastically.

"I didn't mean to make her angry," I protested. "I'm trying to save her."

"Well, let us see if you can convince her of that," Hades sighed, moving to go after my mother.

I looked at Søren. "...You're not going to comment?" I asked. He shook his head solemnly. For that, I was grateful. I took a deep calming breath, before determinedly marching back inside after my parents.

We all sat down in the living room stiffly, unsure of what to say. I had no idea how to reason with Phoebe.

At least Hades understood what I was trying to do. But my mother would not even look at me, as though I had disgraced her.

"...I think that it's a little selfish, by the way," she eventually murmured.

I narrowed my eyes.

How could she even think that, let alone say it?

I understood that she did not want to lose me but her calling what I was trying to do *selfish* felt like a betrayal.

"I'm sorry that you feel that way," I clipped.

Søren and Hades looked at me with wide eyes.

"What did you say?" Phoebe breathed, finally meeting my gaze. She did not look particularly angry or offended. She looked wounded.

I hesitated, but this seemed like the only way to get my point across. "I said that I'm sorry you feel that what I'm doing is selfish," I repeated. "Look, I'm trying to save countless innocent souls here and you're just shooting the idea down. I can make my own decisions and face the consequences. I'm old enough

345

to know right from wrong, and I think that *this* the right thing to do. I am going to try and negotiate with Horkos, and that's that. Whether you support me or not."

She stared at me in disbelief. Then she looked at Søren. "Why aren't you trying to stop her?"

"Don't bring him into this, Mom," I snapped before he could answer. "He is a trusted friend. And you're my mother. How much more do you think that your faith in me would matter?"

"I'm not sentencing you to death!" she finally cracked, standing up. "I will not do that to my daughter."

I pressed my lips into a line. "You are not sentencing me —to anything or otherwise. *I* am," I said firmly.

"So, this is suicide?" my mother scoffed.

"No, Mom," I scoffed in return. "It's *sacrifice*. I am trying to be the hero who is needed. I want to save people. I want to fight for other half-bloods. I have to fight for myself."

"Alone?" she questioned.

"Hades will be there," I quipped. "I won't be completely defenceless."
She glanced at my father. "That's very reassuring," she sneered.

"All right, you know what?" I raised my voice and stood up to face her. "We don't have the time to be arguing. I cannot satisfy everyone's concerns, but I *can* save everyone's lives," I said firmly, putting on my leather jacket and adjusting my sheath. "I'm doing something to prevent needless war. I'm trying to *save* you. How can you accuse me of being selfish?"

"Savannah..." Phoebe gasped, tears beginning to collect in her eyes. Something in me felt bad but I pushed it away, determined not to give up room for compromise.

"Don't give me that," I suddenly snapped. She gaped at me in shock. I had not meant to be so rude —she was simply not listening. "...I've had enough Mom," I told her, my voice cracking. I then grabbed Hades' and Søren's hands before dragging them both towards the front door. I quickly ushered them both outside. As I then hesitated, the feeling of guilt welled up inside me. I paused, but

346

only to tell my mother one last thing. "…If you really care about me, you'll realise how much this is about you."

And then I slammed the door behind me. I was too upset to feel remorse. I glared at Hades and Søren when I got outside, expecting them to say something to deter me. But they just stood there, speechless.

I took this as a sign to carry on.

"Hades, Søren and I have come up with a plan," I started, feigning confidence. "And I'm going to need you to trust me."

He nodded uncertainly.

"I had planned on going to Mount Olympus with backup, but that's no longer an option," I admitted. "So, Søren," I turned to address him, "just in case something…goes wrong, I'm going to need you to gather whoever you can while Hades and I go to Mount Olympus."

He blinked, and then nodded convincingly.

"And Dad," I turned back to Hades. "You'll be the transportation."

"…Sure," he finally verbally responded, thankfully becoming serious.

I then gave Søren a sad smile. "We will try our best not to make you worry too much," I said. "But if we don't come back after…let's say, two more hours, you have my permission to come rescue me."

"Right," he breathed. "Got it."

I gave him a thumbs up. "See you on the other side," I whispered.

"Which other side?" he said a little worriedly.

I smiled weakly. "The right side."

He snorted. Then his face grew grave. "Don't die."

"Only if you promise me the same," I whispered. He nodded, and then turned to walk down the street. He stopped to wave before he disappeared around the corner. I detachedly watched him go.

I nervously looked at Hades after Søren had left. He looked back at me and whistled. "So, you actually told your mother off…like a child."

Of course, he would not let that go.

"The truth hurts," I deadpanned.

347

He chuckled nervously but nodded. I then frowned at the idea that Hades was now a little derailed by me. Had I somehow scared him with my short temper? No way. Senseless rage was hereditary for me, after all.

"So," I whistled, "how do we get to Mount Olympus?" I asked in an effort to change the subject. I put my hands on my hips and chewed my bottom lip uncertainly.

"Via portal," Hades answered wearily, noticing the shift in mood. "I'll just make one for us," he said, before waving his hand.

I looked on as a swirling golden portal then appeared in front of us. "I didn't know that you could make those!" I gasped. "I thought they were built into a wall or pre-made. That's how Thanatos' portals work, at least."

Hades chuckled and shook his head. "Yes. That is because he cannot actually *create* portals. It's rather strange. He is one of the only gods who is unable to use a portal at will."

"Seriously?" I spluttered, growing amused.
"Unfortunately," Hades confirmed.

I was about to ask who the other gods were when I suddenly heard my mother's voice calling my name.

I turned around and was then crushed into a tight hug.

"Savannah," she whispered endearingly. "You didn't think that I was going to let you leave without saying goodbye, did you?"

I struggled to answer '*yes*'.

"I'm sorry for calling you selfish," she apologised as she let go of me slightly. "You're right. *I* was the one being selfish. But can you really blame me? I'm your mother. I guess…I'm not ready to see you go and act like the strong, independent young woman I've always wanted you to be. You're still my little girl in my eyes," she sniffed.

I softened and smiled a little. "I get it, Mom," I said. "But I've set my sights on doing what I can for those I love. So, I'm doing this."

"Then…I will support you," she told me. I blinked. "I have to understand that you are grown up now, and are free to do whatever it is you wish. I should be so

348

grateful for such a compassionate, selfless daughter. So, go save the world, Savannah. I love you. Never forget that."

I smiled wide. "I love you too, Mom," I told her, hugging her back.

She paused to give Hades a glare when our embrace ended, but it did not seem as though it would start a fight.

"Try and bring her back somewhat *alive*, Hades," she snapped at him. "Or *you* won't go back to the Underworld —alive, at all," she threatened.

"Of course," he agreed.

I snorted. The god of the dead then stepped through the portal, and then vanished to the other side. I paused before I moved to follow after him, turning to give my mother a wave goodbye.

She waved back. And then I stepped through.

✠

I would have loved to walk through and see Mount Olympus in all its glory, but unfortunately Hades' portal was rather direct.

We emerged in a gigantic grand foyer made of white marble and gold. Everything was fifty times normal things my size. I gasped as I looked up and around. There was not a ceiling —just the dazzling blue sky. The marble columns around us were laid out concentrically. In the centre, a cherub marble fountain was gushing out crystal clear water.

"Oh my gods," I breathed, figuring that I could not get away with saying '*oh my God*' here. "This is absolutely gorgeous. Everything looks like its own little sun; shining and demanding my attention."

"Too bright," Hades immediately dismissed.

I pouted. "Well damn, I know that it's not your style, but you have to admit its magnificence."

"No, I do not," Hades chuckled bitterly. Then his mocking amusement faded; a shadow darkening his features. "…I hate this place."

I folded my arms but left it at that. I looked around the foyer again. "Where are we supposed to go for the council?" I asked.

"Throne room," he clipped. I turned to look at him and my jaw dropped as I noticed he had grown three times as big and was still growing. His human form was replaced with a body of reflective black rock that worryingly and suspiciously looked like obsidian; wrapped in a black and gold toga; with blue fire flickering in between the cracks of the stone. Two large twisted horns curled their way out of his forehead, and his jasper eyes shone like stars. He then stopped growing at twenty feet. "I will carry you," he offered, lowering his hand to the floor.

I stared at it, wide eyed, with my jaw hanging open. I had just watched my father grow into a blue volcanic giant.

I did not have any words with which to react appropriately.

"I know," he drawled. "It is so unnecessary, isn't it?"

I still did not say anything.

"Savannah, we need to go inside. Get on my hand. Any day now…"

I suppose I then realised that my father would not ever offer to have me come into contact with obsidian, knowing full well what it would do. I then narrowed my eyes at his hand, and finally identified the rock as basalt.

My body moved for me, and I gingerly climbed onto his hand. I avoided the blue fire around the plate of rock on which I was standing and stared into the distance as Hades stood up and started walking.

My mind had been totally overloaded and fried by the demonstration that I did not pay attention to the interior of the palace. We walked down a fancy hallway and turned right, but that was all that I remembered.

"We are here," Hades then announced when he had stopped.

The doors to the throne room were gilt and white painted wood. Even the door handles were elaborate. They were beautiful —but the throne room itself made them seem like falling-apart doors to a little makeshift shed.

I had to shield my eyes momentarily as Hades opened the doors. A bright light shone through, before I squinted at two giant figures seated on thrones of brilliant gold. One of the two others I recognised as Horkos in his godly form, standing to the right of the biggest throne to the right.

350

The other one was standing off to the left of the other throne. I guessed that it was Thanatos.

I figured that the two figures on the thrones were Zeus and Hera. Hera's godly form was made of white marble, with liquid gold within her cracks. She did not have any horns. Perhaps only the male gods did. She did have hair though — braided chocolate brown waves that cascaded down to her shoulders. Her rose quartz eyes studied me carefully through large eyelashes.

She was beautiful, even as a terrifying giant.

Zeus was made of silver, and blue lightning sparked in between his cracks. His horns were big and thick; curving beautifully.

His intense sapphire eyes sparkled curiously as he crossed his giant legs and leaned on one of his golden throne armrests.

Thanatos' bronze eyes regarded me lazily, and his expression remained neutral —or bored. It was only Horkos who looked at me as though I were already condemned.

Hades stopped in the middle of the room. "Presenting Savannah Green; Grim Reaper and daughter of Hades, god of the Underworld," he announced.

I awkwardly did a half curtsey and bow.

"Greetings, brother," Zeus said to Hades. "I see you are keeping well —and warm. Is Hell still frozen over?"

"Please do not patronise me," my father drawled.

The younger god chuckled softly.

"...So, you came after all," Horkos' voice then boomed too loudly, and I immediately cringed and covered my ears, whimpering.

"Careful, Horkos," Hera warned him in a soft and considerate whisper. "The girl has tiny eardrums."

"Is it necessary to be in these forms right now anyway?" Zeus muttered. "It seems like too much of an effort."

"It *is* necessary," Horkos grumbled. "This is a formal council, so may we please treat it as such?"

"Very well, very well," Hera sighed as her husband grumbled irritably. "Let

351

the council begin," she declared, "The half-blood god Savannah pleads to overthrow the Infidelity Treaty that says she must be executed."

I did not like the way that her eyes then twinkled as she said that.

"What have you to say, half-blood," Zeus asked in a bored murmur. "Make it quick and concise."

"Uh...yes sir," I finally spoke up. Apparently not quite loudly enough. I then shouted it, and they all nodded. "I am here to fight for my soul!" I declared. "And the souls of half-blood gods alike!"

Horkos grinned manically. "...This should be good."

CHAPTER 40

SØREN

WHEN SØREN WALKED back into the apartment building lobby, he was rather taken aback at how packed it was.

He had to push and shove his way through to get to the front, where he spotted Nadine and Lewis standing at the announcement podium.

"…We need to band together!" Nadine was saying. "Not really for the sake of Savannah —but for all of our lives," she elaborated. "She may be trying to convince the gods to leave us alone, but we should know better. The gods don't just change their minds. We must prepare for war!"

A surprisingly large amount of cheers rang out in agreement. Søren started, and then finally stumbled into Melchior, who also happened to be at the front. Abigail turned at the same instance and squealed excitedly.

"Oh, you're back," Melchior quipped, catching hold of Søren's arm and preventing him from falling over. "…Where's the gremlin?"

"Gremlin?" Abigail echoed, furrowing her eyebrows. "It's been like, a week if anything since I saw you. Who in the world are you talking about?"

The Trainer scoffed and straightened his jacket as he shook off Melchior's hand. "Don't call Savannah a gremlin," he clipped. Then he quickly answered the question. "She's gone to Mount Olympus with Hades. She's going to try and change Horkos' mind."

The lobby suddenly fell silent around them.

They glanced around at everyone's blank stares. Søren supposed that was startling news. Nadine coughed loudly and redirected the attention.

"Søren," she said slowly, looking at him with a panicked expression on her face. "What the hell are you talking about?"

The Trainer sighed and walked up to the podium, before shoving her out of the way. He cleared his throat and proceeded to fill everyone in. "Savannah has gone to Mount Olympus to reason with Horkos. She believes that this is the right thing to do. She doesn't want to render the Organisation expendable. She wants to try avoiding physical conflict like…last time."

There were some hushed murmurs.

"She's trying to change the rules so that others like her can exist," Søren elaborated. "Right now, there's a treaty created by the Olympian gods to eradicate all half-blood god offspring. Savannah doesn't see the point of that, as well as living in fear of what half-bloods can do."

Someone then raised their hand. It was a cocky trainee in a red leather jacket with a jagged dagger twirling in between his fingers. Søren could not actually tell that he was recently Turned simply by looking —but rather by how the Reaper was attempting to question his word.

No fellow Trainer or fully-fledged Reaper would dare to do that.

"Have you seen any other half-blood god besides this Savannah chick?" he asked. "Because her powers may be pathetic enough for *her* not to pose a threat, but it doesn't mean that all half-bloods and any in the future aren't dangerous. Why do you think the treaty was made in the first place?"

Søren clenched his fists and frowned as the murmuring grew louder. "What is your name?" he asked, raising an eyebrow.

"Kyle," the Reaper sighed, rolling his smoky quartz eyes. "Why won't you answer my question?"

Søren stuck his nose in the air and glowered at him. "Well, *Kyle*," he drawled. "No, I have not. You know why? Because they're all dead. And do you actually think the gods waited long enough to assess how *dangerous* a half-blood god was? They probably didn't let them live past thirteen."

Kyle scoffed as the Trainer's rebuttal seemed to gain back some favour.

"…Why do you care, anyway?" Søren then asked. "It's of no consequence to you if Savannah isn't exactly successful." He was not saying that in any way hopefully —he was only trying to get a reaction from the trainee.

Kyle did not turn a single hair. Then he glanced down and shuffled from foot to foot. "…I knew a half-blood god," he surprisingly admitted, frowning and looking back at Søren. "And she did not deserve to die. I just think…what can this *Savannah* do?" he deadpanned.

Søren paused, feeling a little guilty. He had not expected that loaded answer. "I understand. No, she did not deserve to die. But think about it —do any of them?" he pressed on. "And…you would be surprised by what Savannah can do," the Trainer smiled knowingly.

Kyle did not return the smile, but he did not ask any more questions.

"So, what do we do now?" someone else in the front then asked.

"I've been given instructions to assemble backup for Savannah in case things don't go according to plan," Søren answered. "So, I'll need a team who is willing to go to Mount Olympus for an emergency."

He waited.

No one volunteered.

Everyone lowered their gazes and avoided making eye contact with him, while shuffling around awkwardly. Søren sighed, waiting for the excuses to start. Then he realised that he did not have time for that.

It disappointed him to a degree that no one was willing to help. He understood that no one really knew her anyway, so they did not need to feel obligated to do her or him, a favour. After all, Reapers were not known for their selflessness — or lack thereof. More than that, though —who would willingly walk into the palace of the gods?

"Fine," Søren said flatly. "No one has to come with me. I'll be the only backup. Because it seems that I'm the only one who cares that Savannah might be trying to save all of your *ungrateful* sorry asses right now."

He then stepped down and stormed off towards the door that led to the stairs, unwilling to awkwardly stand in the elevator that faced the lobby.

He did not regret giving the Reapers a piece of his mind. They were all a bunch of pretty sad excuses for human beings —figuratively speaking —so even expecting at least one or two volunteers was expecting too much.

As Søren got to his floor, he asked himself an important question. If he had not known Savannah and gone through an emotionally changing journey because of her, would *he* have stepped up for her?

It hurt that he hesitated to answer.

And it hurt more to know that he would not have.

So maybe he had been a bit of a hypocrite. It was not as if he was going to march all the way back down and apologise.

No one else would in his position. And that made him feel worse.

Søren was tempted to just crumple and fall down against the wall, contemplating what made him any better than the Reapers downstairs.

But he did not have time for self-pity.

He got over it and stomped to his door. After unlocking it he barged inside, momentarily cursed at the sight of fire extinguisher foam that was still very much there, before making his way to the computer room.

Phee-Phee was surprisingly —or maybe not so surprisingly at this point — still there, but now asleep and not on fire, curled up on the side table and glowing in time with his breathing pattern.

Perhaps Søren could bring him along.

The Reaper then realised that he actually did need him for something else, given the unpredictability of the foam damage, so he cautiously made his way to its side and gently poked the bird with his crossbow. It took a few more tries but it finally stirred and uncurled, spreading and igniting its fiery wings. One of its red eyes honed in on the Reaper and its pupil contracted rapidly before Phee-Phee stood up and turned away from him.

"Yeah, I know you don't like me," Søren grumbled. The Phoenix made a sound that resembled scoffing. "Okay, I'm sorry for trying to shoot you and chase you out. You're not so bad. I should have listened to Savannah."

Phee-Phee perked up at the sound of Savannah's name and then hopped around as though he were trying to spot her in some obscure corner.

"She's not here," Søren said quietly. "She's gone to do something very important. But…I'm going to need your help."

Phee-Phee looked at the Trainer with clear disdain.

"Please? It's important. For Savannah; not for me."

He almost seemed to relent at that notion, and hopped down from the side table to follow Søren; who then sighed in relief and led them into the computer room.

The plan was to send a message to Purgatory for a portal to be opened to the Trainer's location on Earth. Then he could find a connecting portal which lead to Mount Olympus, and slip in without detection.

All Søren had to do was write the letter for Phee-Phee to send.

If he had been confident in his own Phoenix fire tubes, he still could not risk electrical safety —nor could he risk the letter going to the wrong place. If Phee-Phee sent it, it could hopefully go directly to Nina.

URGENT

Please open a portal to this message's traceable location. Once I have arrived in Purgatory, please have a portal to Mount Olympus ready. This is of utmost importance.

Signed, Trainer Søren of the New York District.

After hastily scribbling down the message Søren waved it in front of Phee-Phee. The Phoenix tilted his head back and breathed fire into the air, prompting the Reaper to toss the paper into the flames. The letter disappeared, before Phee-Phee breathed out the last flame and coughed, screeching loudly in a way Søren knew was just to annoy him.

"Søren!" a sudden shout then came from the living room. The Trainer and

Phee-Phee shared a look before he went to the door.

It flew open before he had the chance to put his hand on the handle. Abigail and Melchior stood before him, vaguely pissed off.

"Søren," Abigail started sympathetically. "What are you doing?"

The Trainer frowned. "What does it look like?" he deadpanned. "I'm trying to create some sort of backup. No thanks to anyone else."

"But in *Mount Olympus*?" Melchior interjected. "Where the gods are? It sounds like a trap. No wonder no one volunteered. You really think anyone is stupid enough to go with you?"

Søren gave him a look. "Wow, thanks."

"That's not what he meant," Abigail cut in. "It's just...no one else wants to risk themselves for an already doomed mission. You've got to understand and think about how the other Reapers feel and think. I mean, be honest, would you risk your life for someone you didn't know?"

Søren clenched his fists, and suddenly found fault with the floor. "I do *get* it, okay?" he growled. "But I didn't ask you guys to come back and make me feel like more of a jerk. If you're just here to make me feel shitty, then please leave. I need to concentrate. Phee-Phee and I are going to help."

Phee-Phee squawked in agreement.

Abigail eyed the Phoenix wearily and did not seem all that convinced. "We didn't come here to make you feel bad," she sighed, glancing at Melchior. "We came here to volunteer."

There was a beat of silence as Abigail glanced between the two males with a hopeful smile on her face.

"Wait, seriously?" Søren questioned.

"Yeah," Melchior grumbled. "Turns out *we're* stupid enough."

Søren had just about had enough. "Call me stupid one more time and I'll ask Phee-Phee to set your hair on fire," he threatened.

Melchior then raised his hands in surrender but rolled his eyes all the same, mocking him.

"So, you want to help me in case things turn sour?" Søren reiterated Abigail's offer. "Why the sudden change of heart?"

"It's not a sudden change," Abigail corrected him. "When you stormed off, I realised that maybe this is really important to you. And as my friend, I felt that I should support you in your most stubborn times. I brought Melchior along because he's big, grizzled and strong," she added, giggling softly.

Melchior gave her a sideways look, and then glanced at Søren; his vibrant garnet eyes dark and emotionally strained.

The Trainer ignored the feeling that they erupted within him.

"*Oh*...kay," he said slowly, narrowing his eyes at Abigail, "I'm going to pretend that you *didn't* just say that about Melchior, and I'm going to focus on the fact that we're friends and you're doing this for me."

"Fair enough," Abigail sighed, clasping her hands together. "So...What exactly is happening now?"

"I'm waiting for my message to Purgatory to be received," he explained. "I requested that we use Thanatos' portal to get to Mount Olympus."

Melchior raised an eyebrow. "All right. And how long will it take for that to be confirmed?"

Søren shrugged. "Any time now."

"Great, we're working with estimates..." he muttered, leaning against a table and folding his arms. "Might as well get comfortable."

"Hey, it's not my fault that the mailing system isn't better organised," Søren defended himself. "Besides. We've got an hour to kill anyway."

"What do you mean?" Abigail frowned.

"Savannah told me to bring backup if she wasn't back after two hours," the Trainer informed them. "It's already been one. So, we might not even need to do anything if she comes back before another hour."

"Seriously?" Abigail scoffed. "You could have told us that sooner."

"What would it have changed?" Søren deadpanned.

"I don't know," she scoffed. "We wouldn't have rushed —that's one thing. Now we have time to prepare."

Søren sighed and sat up on the table next to the main computer monitor. He hoped that Savannah was doing okay. He hoped that she was still alive.

Well…Hades would have come and told them if for whatever reason, she was…gone, would he not? Unless the Olympians had already punished him too. Søren frowned and resisted the urge to panic.

He needed to have some faith.

Maybe Savannah was actually winning an argument right at that moment. Or…maybe not.

But he still trusted her abilities. After all, she changed every person in which she came into contact. There was a slither of a chance she could actually succeed in getting the treaty abolished civilly.

Perhaps she could bring out the humanity in Horkos.

Søren then suddenly started and nearly fell off the table as Phee-Phee shrieked to gain his attention. He frowned, but grew anxious as the Phoenix tilted his head back and breathed fire again. An envelope then landed beside him. Søren hastily opened it and took out the piece of paper.

```
                            REPLY


        Your request has been received and acknowledged by
        the CEO's secretary, Nina. She will comply shortly.
               This may take between fifteen minutes
                 and half an hour. Please be patient.


                    Reply to: 40.7831°N, 73.9712°W
                        From: Purgatory HQ
```

"…It'll take fifteen minutes to half an *hour*?" Søren raised his voice, jumping down from the table. "Are they serious?"

"Damn," Abigail drawled sarcastically. "Whatever happened to that entire hour we had to kill?"

"I put *urgent* on it, I swear," the Trainer protested, clearly flustered. "They're just fucking with me. Surely Nina knows about the situation and can put two and two together?"

"Who's Nina?" Abigail frowned, along with Melchior.

Right —the two Reapers had yet to encounter the tamed Vampyre.

"Death's secretary," Søren filled in. "And she's pretty quick from what I've seen. Whoever replied to my message is an unfeeling little asshole."

"Calm down, Sør," Melchior sighed. "There is no point in getting all worked up. It won't make things faster. All we can do is wait, I guess."

The dark haired Reaper hesitated and breathed out deeply. "Fine. We'll wait. But if Savannah ever asks, tell her it wasn't my fault."

Melchior flashed a fake smile. "Sure."

Søren chose to ignore him and sat up on the table again. He really hoped that Savannah would end up not needing a backup team.

Because at rate that things were going, they might get to Mount Olympus when there would be nothing *to* back up.

CHAPTER 4I

SAVANNAH

one hour earlier…

✠

I KNEW THAT Horkos would be entirely against me, but Zeus and Hera were going to be left significantly impressionable —which would be my biggest advantage.

"For centuries, many gods have fallen for human mortals and created offspring that resembled man but harnessed their own godly abilities," I began. "When the Olympians signed a treaty to get rid of these children, I wonder if any of them had a basis for executing the half-bloods. What physical evidence was laid before you and held against countless children? And if one or two of them were actually held accountable for their misdeeds, then why were *all* of them punished —?"

"Little girl," Hera's voice instantaneously drowned out mine. She gave me a look that was not a glare, but was nowhere near friendly. "…Know this: we eradicated half-blood gods because of *many* generational misdemeanours. There was no account for one or two children —but rather one or two hundred. The number of half-bloods that posed no threat was little to none compared to those who did," her voice then grew softer and more sympathetic and she lidded her eyes. "It would have been strange and unbefitting for us to leave those handful and explain why. It was easier to group them together and punish the whole race."

"So, you committed genocide just to escape speaking for a few good half-blood gods?"

"That is not what my wife meant," Zeus then said firmly, overcoming his boredom. The simple and slight raising of his voice amplified and sounded like thunder to my ears, causing me to flinch. The god of the skies narrowed his eyes at me. "…Know your place, Reaper."

I pressed my lips into a line and clenched my fists.

"If you had the means to erase an entire species in one fell swoop, then why couldn't you have at least let the good ones go off and live peacefully?" I asked. "What bad would have come of that?"

"And what if they would then turn against us with time?" Horkos interjected. "We could not risk having pending loyalties."

"And what if they were *terrified* of you?" I countered. My voice cracked at the end and I found my emotions welling up inside of me, threatening to overflow. "What if…their loyalty would have swayed because they had had enough of living in fear that the gods too would change their minds and suddenly rain fire over them?"

Hera looked between her husband and me before narrowing her eyes. Her grip on the arms of her throne tightened and she stiffened considerably. She appeared to be confused. Perfect.

"Whatever do you mean?" she asked. "Are they…our creation…are they *afraid* of us?"

She seemed terrified herself, at the idea.

"Because I assure you," Zeus began before I could answer, "that it is very much the other way around."

"And I can assure *you*, brother," Hades spoke for the first time since the discussion started, "that there is little to no greater fear in the hearts of mortals than death, and what comes afterward. Mortals fear judgement —both for what they have and have not done. And with the thought in the back of their minds, mortals can be drawn to act…heinously…towards themselves and others. It

363

destroys them every day; and it is a wonder it has not completely destroyed them yet."

"That is quite enough," Zeus said quickly, holding up a hand. I felt Hades stiffen underneath me and I felt bad that I could not outrightly thank him for helping me. Zeus cleared his throat and slowly turned to Thanatos, someone who I had almost forgotten. "…What is your opinion, Thanatos? You have been awfully quiet."

To me, Thanatos was no more intimidating in his godly form than his human one. I glared at him without fear and silently challenged him to *dare* to say something stupid. Thanatos met my gaze and a sparkle that never meant anything good momentarily shone in his bronze eyes. He showed me no other sign, so I prepared for betrayal.

"…As the god of death, I spend quite a bit of time with souls," he started vaguely. I frowned. Where was he going with that? He almost smiled as he went on, "Souls are the purist and realist part of both mortal and immortal beings. They reflect their character and intentions and provide a basis on which to be judged. But just as you would still prosecute a murderer with no intent nor knowledge of wrong and right even though less severely than one with vicious intent; it does not remove the fact that *both* committed murder," he concluded with a self-satisfied grin on his face, nodding knowingly.

We all paused and tried to make sense of what he had just spewed.
"Are you trying to say that instead of killing all half-blood gods, we simply lightly punish the relatively innocent few?" Zeus mused, stroking his chin.

"Excuse me?" I gasped, outraged. "You would punish someone simply because of their ancestry?"

"Well, how else do we make an example of them?" Hera quipped.
"You *don't*," I raised my voice. "Instead, why don't we all face the music and suggest punishing the real culprits: the gods who created the half-bloods in the first place —!"

"Insolence!" Horkos suddenly cried, pointing an accusing finger at me. "How dare you suggest a punishment of the *gods*. Who do you think you are. You are *beneath* us!"

I screamed and covered my ears, before falling to my knees. The pain was comparable to the tolerance test that my fire ability had conducted. The ringing in my head was numbed by a sound that had no measure, but rather pierced through me, high pitched and hollow.

My vision whitened and an ache formed in both of my temples.
I then began hyperventilating at the feel of something wet in the palms of my hands and dripping down my neck.

Blood.

My ears were bleeding.

"By the stars —it seems that you have burst her eardrums, Horkos," Zeus remarked, though his tired sounding voice was an echo that barely reached me. "I told you that this form was unnecessary…"

I winced and bent forward, though that only caused all of the blood to rush to my head.

"It is not my fault that she is a half-blood. This is just a complication that comes with that defect…" Horkos said defensively.
I groaned and found that the room was beginning to feel a little less solid and real; swimming up and down in my limited field of view in giant sickening waves.

"How *dare* you imply that my daughter is like a defective supermarket product," Hades defended me, and I felt him draw the hand which I was on closer towards him, like a nurturing mother. "I cannot believe that you would put your pride ahead of life. You are supposed to stand for justice. Although —I actually should not be surprised. You are a Greek god. And the gods are always *so good* at distorting things…"

That was all that I remember hearing.
I could not hear anything anymore. It was getting harder to keep my eyes open. And so, they fluttered closed, heavy and burdensome. My hands fell away from my ears, and my body collapsed underneath me, causing me to fall sideways on my father's palm.

I breathed out, no longer possessing the energy to voice my pain. I went completely still.

Is this it?

Was I really going to lose because of Horkos' clear insecurities? My insides turned to lead. I was losing blood. I fought not to let go, but I was soon unaware of the chaos which ensued as my consciousness slipped.

✠

I woke up like I had been having a nightmare. I gasped, instinctively clutched at my chest, and waited for the pounding of my accelerated heartbeat to start echoing in my head. But it did not.

You are dead, idiot. Remember?

…Right.

I sighed and drew a head-clearing deep breath, before glancing around me. There was nothing but a blur of cream wall, and then a mass of black rock. Recollection then hit me as I winced at the sharp pain that then stabbed the inside of my right ear. That asshole Horkos had burst my eardrums with his childish outburst while I was supposed to be having a civil meeting about *not* killing me. I growled and glared upwards, narrowing my eyes in hopes of recognising something around me. My gaze landed on big fiery jasper eyes with interestingly terrifying void-like dilated pupils. I cringed at the sight of my reflection in them.

"Can. You. *Hear.* Me?" Hades asked hopefully, mouthing the words individually in an irksome exaggerated manner.

"Yes," I frowned. He sighed with relief while I continued to readjust.

I was still sitting upright in Hades' palm. The room that we were in had no windows or doors —just four corners of wall between a marble floor and a cream ceiling, with a simple light fixture. I frowned at the realisation that we were trapped in some way.

"Where are we?"

"We are still on Mount Olympus," Hades sighed. "I gave Horkos a piece of my mind and accidentally —very on purpose —destroyed my brother's throne when I threw Horkos at it," he said in a rather cheerful tone. "…Anyway, the meeting is now in recess," he informed me, "and they have put us in a holding cell until further notice. I managed to get you some *ambrosia* before though — which is why you can now hear me."

I paused and reached up to touch my ears. The pain was quickly fading, though my ears felt a little tender. The blood was still there, but now drying; and I assumed it was because Hades' fingers had been too big to do anything about it. But I was grateful. I recalled what I had learned from reading stories on Greek mythology. *Ambrosia* was the nectar of the gods —a super medicine of magical sorts that could heal just about anything except reverse death; and keep Immortals young and healthy forever. It was only found in one, super inconvenient unreachable place. Mount Olympus.

Although, I did not entirely blame the gods for withholding.
Chaos was avoided by a lack of immortality in the mundane world.

"So, you mean, I lost my hearing?"

"Yes," Hades murmured. "Horkos wailed like a spoilt brat and ruptured the inside of your ears. I think he might have even done some damage to your brain too. That would have been enough to kill a mortal. But do not worry —Reapers cannot die that way. I did not let him get away with it though."

I smiled properly then. "Thanks, Dad."

"Well, who else is going to defend your honour?" he chuckled softly. I nodded in agreement, before a thought struck me.

"How long have we been here?" I asked.

"Time is not the same as it is on Earth," Hades explained. "Time runs slower here. We have been here for approximately an hour now. Two hours and a bit in Earth time."

Two hours…Where is Søren?

"…What's the matter?" Hades asked.

"Remember how I had asked Søren to rescue me if I wasn't back in two hours from the time we left?" I said hurriedly. "Well, that time is up. So…is he coming?"

Hades frowned and averted his gaze. "Hopefully he has the sense to wait a few minutes in case you are scarily punctual?"

"That is not making me feel better," I hissed. "He *knows* that I'm not punctual."

"So, you think he is on his way?" Hades said with a little more concern. I gasped and looked at him fearfully. I did not want to think it, but there was another possibility. "What if he's already here?"

Hades looked back at me uncertainly and did not respond. Perhaps he did not want to think about it either.

"He won't stand a chance if he's by himself," I hissed, getting to my feet. I made sure I had everything with me, before I straightened my jacket and adjusted my ponytail. "We have to find him."

"Savannah, we cannot just get out of here," Hades pointed out. "It is not sealed by a lock and key."

I paused, deterred. "How *is* it sealed?" I grumbled in exasperation.

"Horkos alone has the ability to open and close the cells," Hades sighed. "It is in his veins…and job description," he added begrudgingly.

I cursed in frustration.

"We need to get out of here," I said firmly, falling into a pace. "I don't know how, but we can't let Søren and whoever might be with him to fall into what Horkos will clearly orchestrate into a trap."

"I understand what you are saying but we cannot get out of here. *Only* Horkos can let us out," he reminded me again.

I let out an indecisive cry. I was getting increasingly frustrated and the walls around us were beginning to feel closer and closer; pushing in on us.

"Savannah —" Hades started, but our attention was then suddenly diverted.

An outline of a door seemed to draw itself in the north wall. The line was made of light, and it shone so bright that it felt as though we had been in the dark all this time.

"Is she now awake?" a deep and familiar voice then called out. I instinctively stiffened.

"…*Yes*," Hades answered reluctantly.

I clenched my fists and frowned up at Hades. "Is that Horkos?"

"Yes. Remember," he sighed. "This is the only way. But Horkos is resuming the council now. Hopefully no one will be caught," he added subtly. I scoffed. But he was right. This *was* how we would get out.

What mattered was what we did afterwards.

The light door opened inward towards us to reveal Horkos on the other side. He looked at us almost pityingly, before gesturing for us to come out. I glared up at him determinedly. Hades walked out of the cell and the door sealed shut behind him, leaving a lone silver *XVI* on the wall. I looked on ahead as I noticed a series of them, marking the multitude of cells. Horkos then led us up a set of stairs before I recognised our fancy gold embellished surroundings. Walking with giants obviously takes longer than desired, so we took what felt like an entire minute to get around a corner. My gaze drifted as I sighed and gave up my frustration, before I started at the sight of a line of ants coming from an adjacent hallway. I squinted. No. Not ants. *People* —in my size.

I inhaled sharply and widened my eyes, searching for a black haired, silver eyed boy with a crossbow. And I found him, leading three other people — Chainsaw Guy, a blonde woman who I assumed was Abigail, and a cocoa-skinned male —and…Phee-Phee!

I bit my lip to keep from gasping. Then I started as I made eye contact with Søren. I panicked. He jumped and hastily aimed his crossbow, before I frantically waved my hands around in an effort to make him stop. He hesitated and frowned, allowing me to slice a hand in front of my throat and shake my head. '*Not. Now*', I mouthed. '*No. Rescue. Too dangerous.*'

He looked at me in confusion, but then he suddenly panicked and led his team back around the corner as Horkos then paused and turned around to us.

"…What are you doing?" Horkos asked.

I stiffened and slowly turned to look at him. I then realised that I had still been shaking my head.

"Stretching?" I said, but it came out like a question. "Actually, it doesn't matter. You almost killed me, so why should I answer to you?" I retorted.

Horkos glanced behind me suspiciously before he rolled his eyes and sighed. I was relieved to see that he found nothing. "You certainly are your father's daughter…" he muttered.

"Excuse me —what exactly is that supposed to mean?" Hades demanded, stiffening. "Did you not learn your lesson when I smashed you into Zeus' throne? Shall I do it again?" he threatened, almost growling. "I will be far less *civil* this time."

"Exactly!" I cried, raising a fist. "What he said."

"Oh, do shut up," Horkos snapped. "Save your theatrics for the council. Zeus, Hera and Thanatos are ready to see you again. I would advise accepting defeat now so we can get this over with," he sighed.

"And you should take your own advice," I retorted as we walked back into the throne room. "By the way, we're not the dramatic ones. *You're* the one who screamed like an infant."

I blew a raspberry and felt pretty satisfied —until I looked at the mess in the throne room; from Hera's deadly glare, and Zeus' lightning bolt clenched within his grasp.

CHAPTER 42

SAVANNAH

"IT IS CLEAR now that the entire branch of the gods of death are extremely temperamental," Zeus started, his eyebrows furrowing together in anger. "In theory, I should prevent further implications by eradicating all of you —but getting rid of Hades and Thanatos will backfire on me eventually, so they stay. Your removal however," he spat, pointing his lightning bolt at me, "has no consequence. So, your execution shall be held later this evening, after dinner," he declared.

"…He hates doing business on an empty stomach," Hera chipped in, placing a hand on Zeus' shoulder like a devoted housewife.

I stared at them with wide eyes.

"Wait —wait, what?" I spluttered. "…*Execution*?"

"This is great," Horkos chuckled in amusement. "How clean, quick and painless," he sighed. Then he glanced at me as an afterthought. "…Well, for the rest of us anyway."

"Zeus, I demand that you reconsider," Hades then urged, and I felt the rumble of his voice as his hand quaked beneath my feet. "My outburst was completely justified. Horkos hurt my daughter. Whether she is allowed to live or not, I do not tolerate nor condone such vile intent. He deliberately messed up the council and pinned Savannah in a position that made her seem disloyal and rebellious. She is not here to threaten you, do you not see that? She is just a girl who wants to live.

371

And she wants you to *understand*."

I turned around and looked up at my father in slight awe. He surprisingly had a wonderful way with words.

"Understand *what*, Hades?" Zeus grumbled begrudgingly. "That despite her half-blood powers we should let her roam free?"

"Then *teach* me," I then spoke up, narrowing my eyes in all seriousness. "Teach all of us —in the way of what is good and just. If half-bloods could be trained, you would not have all of this uncertainty."

"You say that with confidence, Reaper, but you cannot speak for everyone," Hera snapped sharply. "How would we even go about it?" she questioned.

I frowned and thought off the top of my head. "I could teach them," I suggested. "They are more likely to listen to their own than someone they fear. You can't raise kind people without kindness," I pointed out.

Thanatos, who had been silent, then whistled lowly as though he were impressed by my words.

"Why would we even consider that?" Horkos then said, glaring at me. "The half-bloods have been nothing but troublesome. Zeus, tell me that you still see reason?" he asked the eldest god hopefully.

The king of the gods was not impressed.

"Actually, that is not a bad idea," he countered Horkos' childish attack. "Having a half-blood pave the way for future half-bloods —it is quite innovative, do you not think so, dear?" he asked his wife.

Hera glanced at me with a slight smile on her face. It was not a high and mighty smile. It was a smile that gave away that she, to my surprise, believed that there was potential.

"I think that it *is* interesting," she murmured. "A half-blood god teaching other half-blood gods —it seems like an excellent way of assessing the durability of a permanent operation, at least to begin with."

Wait, what? Was she doubting my ability to keep an operation running? Or maybe she was planning to test it in some way, before proving how much of a disaster it could really be.

That was not what I had been implying.

"If she could succeed in training half-blood gods and satisfy the wrath of the Olympians, then *I* am all for it," Thanatos stated smugly.

I looked up at him suspiciously, narrowing my eyes at his ominous smirk.

"Why are you on her side?" Horkos frowned as he recoiled in disgust. For once, I was actually with Horkos.

Why exactly *was* Thanatos on my side?

The god of death chuckled softly and smiled at me, which made my skin crawl. "...Because she is my half-sister," he smirked. "I don't know —maybe this family thing is growing on me."

The room then went silent. But only my jaw dropped. Had I heard him correctly? Was I Thanatos —*Death*'s half-sister? I then recalled the first real conversation Hades and I had —how I was not exactly his only child. He had another son. Hades...and Persephone...

He was the son. Thanatos was Hades' godly son.

I blinked rapidly, trying to process and rationalise the concept of me being related to Death —who was my boss and a standard pain in the neck.

"Oh my gods," I stated in disbelief; bewildered as well as a little out of it.

Everyone was probably expecting me to say something more, but I just continued to have a mental short circuit.

"I apologise for not telling you before," Thanatos addressed me. "But you have to understand that telling you would have been dangerous."

My eyes flickered upwards to Thanatos' face and I stared at him blankly. "Dangerous for what —your job?" I deadpanned. "I just...I can't...What the hell were you thinking when you decided to keep this from me?" I demanded. I turned around to my father without giving Thanatos a chance to answer.

"And why didn't *you* tell me either?" I asked, glaring up at him. "You acted like you were just...business partners or something."

"To be fair, we *are* business partners," Thanatos murmured.

"Shut up," I told him. "I'm talking to my —our father."

I frowned thoughtfully.

That does not sound right…

Thanatos huffed and grumbled reluctantly as though in agreement that calling us siblings made both us nauseous, but he said nothing more.

I turned back to Hades. "Why?" I asked.

Hades tensed. His gaze moved away from mine, and a breathy sigh escaped his slightly parted lips. "…If you had known that Thanatos was your brother, it would have implicated both of you further. You finding out now was the second best possible outcome. I am sorry that we could not tell you, but you have to understand that the more you know, the more your life is at risk."

"But he's family," I insisted, growling the statement through clenched teeth. "And you know what? I don't care if we don't tolerate each other —but…you don't get to pick your family."

"But you can protect them," Hades said gravely, meeting my gaze again.

I considered it. Perhaps knowing that Thanatos was my half-brother would have changed how things turned out —especially for the worst. Regardless, I still did not feel okay with the fact that the announcement had just been bomb-shelled somewhat randomly. I then coughed self-consciously, too embarrassed to try to continue arguing.

"So," Hera said softly, inhaling sharply at the tension. "That was…unexpected. But Savannah's relations with the gods of death is not what is on trial here," she pointed out.

"Precisely," Zeus agreed gruffly. "Now, about this mentorship proposition —"

"It is preposterous," Horkos cut in. "I do not know who this girl thinks she is, but she cannot just waltz in here and change rules that have been in place longer than she has been *alive*," he said firmly. "This is ridiculous. Can we just end this and execute her?"

"*Horkos…*" my father said in warning.

"Unfortunately, Horkos has a point, brother," Zeus murmured gravely. "The treaty was made a long time ago. It is not something that can just be…*abolished*. Overturning such a law would require time and the signatures of those liable —"

"Lots of signatures," Hera insisted, widening her eyes.

374

"Many, many signatures…" Zeus mused, furrowing his eyebrows.

"Twelve signatures," I deadpanned.

Zeus and Hera paused, eyeing me wearily.

"I know how many Olympians there are," I quipped. "And I know how good all of you are at making excuses. But I think that a gesture this grand would really restore some faith in the gods." I smiled craftily. "You wouldn't want the mere mortals to continue to fear you, would you?"

Hera's expression then hardened. "Fear is the best tool in controlling a world," she said darkly. "If the humans feel no respect for us…then maybe this mentorship idea is not the best thing after all," she frowned doubtfully.

"Hark, someone who sees sense," Horkos remarked.

"Silence, Horkos," Zeus snapped. The minor god dithered accordingly. Then the king of the gods turned back to me. "Hera is correct. The mortals are our creation. And they need to fear us. Otherwise we would live in a world without consequence."

"But if you kill me you won't get respect," I tried, beginning to panic slightly. "Mortals will see you as merciless and ruthless tyrants —they won't see fair rulers who do what's best for everyone. This treaty…it will continue to create distrust and terror."

"Well, the wayward gods should have thought of that before they defiled the mortals," Hera sneered. She stuck her nose in the air and folded her arms. "…What is done cannot be undone," she whispered, glancing at Hades.

Then she turned around sharply and headed for her throne.

"This isn't fair —!" I started.

"Get this girl out of my sight," Zeus cut me off, raising his hand up in a gesture of silencing me. "The execution *will* be held after dinner. Tell the chef to make something…rich and saucy."

"Of course, dear," Hera agreed.

"*What?*" I cried. "No —you can't. Is anyone actually *thinking* —?"

"Well, that settles it," Horkos spoke up, smiling. "Thus, concludes the council. I will personally see to it that our prisoner gets plenty of rest before her rather…*final*, appearance."

I gulped as Horkos marched over and stuck out his hand in front of me. Hades was having none of it. He withdrew and brought his hand closer to him, refusing to give me up so easily.

"You are not touching her. Ever," Hades said thickly. "If she has to go somewhere, I will be the one to take her."

I pouted, feeling conflicted. On one hand, my father was defending and protecting me. On the other, he was indirectly volunteering to be my personal prison warden.

"Not a chance," Horkos stated. "As her father, I do not believe that you should be trusted with that task."

"Then ward me too," Hades taunted.

"Why are you being so difficult about this?" Horkos questioned, furrowing his eyebrows together.

"Why are you all still here?" Zeus snarled. His question went ignored.

"I don't trust you," Hades answered Horkos, making it plain and simple. "I do not trust you with the law; I do not trust you as a warden; and I certainly do not trust you with my daughter. I am determined to keep her alive as long as possible. And that means keeping an eye of those dirty hands of yours," he then hissed, leaning further away.

Horkos gave him a look and then glanced down at me. "…Fine. I will accompany the both of you back to your cell."

Hades grunted and gave a slight nod, before turning towards the doors.

But one of the doors then creaked open, and a series of small shouts caught everyone's attention. We looked down to the floor to see a small group of leather clad Grim Reapers.

A sudden arrow whistled past my ear and struck Horkos in the side of his arm. I studied its sleek glossiness, and recognised it immediately.

It was Søren's arrow.

Horkos visibly winced, before picking out the arrow as though it were a small thorn. He frowned, before letting out a hiss at the burn of the obsidian.

"What is the meaning of this?" Zeus demanded, darting forward.

"We cannot let you execute Savannah, Lord Zeus," Søren said firmly, lowering his crossbow.

"And just who *are* you?" the god of the skies snapped.

"And where did you get that Phoenix?" Thanatos asked suspiciously, narrowing his bronze eyes at Phee-Phee. The fiery creature began flapping excitedly at the sight of me.

"We're Savannah's friends," Søren answered.

"Uh, do not put me in that category," Chainsaw Guy was quick to interject — which earned him an elbow jab to the stomach from Abigail.

"I'm not really her friend either," the male whom I did not recognise added. "I'm just here for vengeance."

Søren rolled his eyes at his dysfunctional rescue team before looking back at Zeus. "Regardless of what we individually think of Savannah, we are all here for the same reason. To prevent another death."

I looked on hopefully, as Zeus hesitated.

"You are trespassing on the land of the gods," Horkos said, narrowing his eyes in disdain. "That is an offence punishable by death."

"Wait, Horkos," Zeus ordered, raising his hand to silence him. "I want to hear what the Reapers have to say. Start by stating your name and why you are here — give your own personal reasons."

Søren and the others shared confused looks, before Chainsaw Guy stepped forward confidently.

"I am Melchior. And I'm here, honestly for him," he started, pointing back at Søren. The Trainer stiffened and blushed softly. "As a favour," Chainsaw Guy continued. "It doesn't matter, and I don't care who we're saving. I'm just here to do the right thing."

He shot me a begrudging look, before stalking back to stand next to Abigail. I shivered, rendered uneasy.

Søren walked forward next, sighing deeply.

"My name is Søren. I am here to do the right thing too —but I'm also here for

Savannah, because she's important to too many people," he stated with all seriousness. "I will not let her die."

"I am Abigail," the blonde then announced, forcibly pulling Søren behind her as she then stepped forward. "I am not friends with Savannah either, but I'll do what I can to save her. This was a favour…until I heard how unfairly this trial was going," she hissed darkly, glaring at the gods.

Zeus raised an eyebrow, clearly unimpressed.

We then all looked at the last Reaper, who had not spoken up yet. He paused, before stepping forward and folding his arms.

"The name's Kyle," he quipped. "I'm here for one thing only. Answers. My question?" he got straight to the point, "Why did you kill my mother?"

Silence followed as everyone just seemed to be hearing that information for the first time. Kyle himself was glaring at Zeus; an intense expression laced with pain and indignation.

Everyone turned to the god. He dithered, as though he were unsure. "Ah, well. Who was your mother?" he asked somewhat gently, almost as though he possessed some kind of concern.

Kyle tightly clenched his jaw in furious disbelief, but he let Zeus have the benefit of the doubt.

"…Elizabeth Roland," he said. "A daughter of Ares."

CHAPTER 43

SAVANNAH

WE STARED AT Kyle in awe and disbelief in the silence that followed his unexpected revelation.

I looked at Søren for some sort of explanation, but he appeared equally surprised; obviously having heard of this part only now as well.

"Your mother was a half-blood god?" Hera was the first to start. "*How*…is that even…What are you, child?"

She was raising all sorts of valid points —because half-blood gods did not normally live long enough to have descendants. But Kyle's mother had lived — or more appropriately, survived —long enough to meet someone and settle down. That made him intriguing.

It also raised the question of what exactly made up the half of his DNA. In other words…what had his father been?

Kyle clicked his tongue. "I do not know exactly what I am, but I can assure you that I do not have any godly powers," he assured. "My mother, though, was a very skilled pyrokinetic."

I immediately stiffened.

If she had had fire manipulation abilities but still got hunted down, what chance did I have? My powers were not exactly helping my case in the context of that fact. Luckily for the time being, only Hades and Søren knew about it.

"She might have been executed with some of the others in 2001," Hera murmured, more to Zeus than anyone else. "But unfortunately, Elizabeth Roland does not ring a bell."

"It certainly should not," Horkos remarked.

Kyle glared at the reigning god and goddess as his grip on his dagger tightened considerably. "Oh, I'll ring a damn *bell* —because what I'm hearing is that not only did you not hold fair trials, but you also can't be bothered to remember those from whom you rob lives."

"Do not use that accusing tone with us, Reaper," Zeus snapped. "It is not necessary nor practical to remember the name of every half-blood god if they are just going to die anyway."

Most of us were understandably offended.

"How can you say that?" Kyle demanded, stomping his foot. "How can you trivialise murder? Do mortals mean nothing to you? In fact — that makes it all the worse. How *dare* you!"

"Kyle, cool it," Søren said firmly, putting a hand on his shoulder. Kyle glared at him but hesitated, and then reluctantly held his tongue. "…Think about what you're saying," Søren advised him.

Then he turned to Zeus.

"He's really…emotional right now," the Trainer assured. "He's just lashing out at you —and you know what? He has got the right to. You took his mother away from him. He doesn't have anything else. And he will never forgive you for it."

"You're damn right I won't," Kyle spat. "You gods have no idea of the suffering you have inflicted over the years. It will never be okay." His voice broke at the end, and he turned around sharply to hide his face from everyone's view.

There was a beat of silence.

I bit my lip with worry. Assuming that his father was human, Kyle was the child of a half-blood god —so that made him…a *quarter*-blood god?

I then frowned. That did not sound right. There had to be a word for what he was. Or at the very least, another recorded or known example of his kind.

I titled my head to the side as I studied him. He seemed on edge. I did not blame him for lashing out and screaming at the gods —that was very appropriate. My concern was if the treaty extended to half-blood god offspring too. I glanced at Zeus and Hera, who were sharing grave looks between themselves. They seemed to be having a kind of telepathic conversation —the slight change in their expressions suggested consideration and even a little surprise.

"Was your father a mortal?" finally Hera was the one to ask the burning question. I would have asked but speaking out of turn at this stage felt like an instant death penalty.

"Or…something else perhaps?" Zeus added, narrowing his eyes.

"He was a human mortal," Kyle assured them with a mocking smirk. "So, as you can see, I'm not a threat to you."

"The fact that *you* do not possess any godly powers is irrelevant in this discussion," Hera quipped, sticking up her nose in a desirably superior gesture. "The issue at hand is if the possibility is still…well, possible."

"You think as a little mixed blood immortal that I could still get powers?" Kyle questioned, narrowing his eyes right back at them.

"Mixed blood?" Zeus scoffed. "Do not flatter yourself. I doubt there is enough ichor within you for you to even call yourself *mixed*."

Kyle growled, but this time it was Chainsaw Guy who stopped him from doing anything.

"All the guy wants is some answers," Chainsaw Guy started. "You already took away his mother. The least you can do is give him an explanation."

I raised an eyebrow. So maybe Chainsaw Guy was not as much of a selfish prick as I had previously thought.

I might even consider calling him by his real name.

My attention then turned to Hera, who had stood up and cleared her throat. Her rose quartz eyes swept over everyone, before settling on Kyle.

Her expression did not show any remorse, nor pity. She was as still and neutral as a statue; passing silent judgement. Her husband stood by her side with a similar look —but there was a hint of regret glinting in his sapphire eyes; as though he understood what had been done.

381

"The half-bloods were killed off because of the danger they posed to both the divine and mundane worlds," Zeus explained. "Their inherited powers are unpredictable and clearly threaten mortal lives. Revealing the truth about offspring of the divine would be catastrophic for the mundane plane."

I gawked at him. If that were the case, then how much of a threat did I really pose as a Grim Reaper. Or potentially, even Kyle?

"...Reapers are no exception," Zeus then added, glancing directly at me.

Hera then stepped forward. "I am not going to stand here and lie to you that I regret or feel sorry for the death of your mother," she started. "And I am not saying that I wanted her dead, either. My feeling towards the half-bloods is pure indifference. It does not affect me, and I certainly never wish to be involved in the actual executions. *But*," she sighed, "I understand the human condition and the love of family. After all, I am the goddess of it," she said rather smugly, placing a hand on her chest self-righteously. "So, I am prepared to offer you a deal. In exchange for taking your soul, you will have immunity in the Underworld to be reborn into a favoured upbringing which I will oversee myself."

"Excuse me?" Hades quipped, with an edge to his voice. "You have the audacity to attempt to override my ability to assign judgement on the dead? What gives you the *right* —"

"This is not an offer that will be repeated," Hera warned, completely ignoring the younger god. "Nor will it be offered to anyone else. Think very carefully about your answer."

I gasped as everyone's jaws dropped. What she had just said seemed unreal. I looked at Kyle, who had not immediately reacted, but whose facial expression was of one musing. I frowned in disbelief.

No way.

It looked as though he were actually thinking about it.

"What kind of a deal is that?" Abigail then demanded in outrage, glaring at the goddess. "How is it fair?"

"Silence," Hera snapped. "I was not speaking to you, Reaper. This concerns *Kyle* only."

382

Everyone looked at the Reaper.

His head was bowed, and he still did not say anything. But then I frowned as I realised something. Maybe it truly *was* a feasible option. He had no family and he was somewhat immortal. Doomed. This was a kind of existence out of which he could not get.

Maybe it was a good deal after all.

"Kyle, please don't do this," Abigail then pleaded. "You *know* that you can't fully trust the gods."

"I take offence to that," Hera hissed.

"I don't," Zeus shrugged.

"Well, I too am offended," Horkos spoke up again, much to everyone's annoyance —not just the deities. "I am the god of oaths. If any god deserves to be trusted, it is me."

"What a load of *bullshit*," Hades immediately scoffed. "I cannot believe my ears. If any god *shouldn't* be trusted, it is you. You are supposed to be the god of oaths, but you always manage to go out of your way to be a two-faced *conniving* little —"

"I beg your pardon, but I am in fact the god of oaths, and not the god of justice," Horkos cut him off.

"The only thing that you are the god of, is the god of screwing people over," Hades raised his voice slightly, and I felt his hand quake beneath me.

Horkos' eyes pulsed a warning as he growled. "How *dare* you —"

"Enough," Hera sighed, reaching up to rub her right temple. "You two are going to give me a headache."

"And you fight like little children," Zeus remarked, rolling his eyes.
Hades snorted. "*You* would know, brother."

"What was that?" Zeus sneered.
The gods could have carried on insulting each other and bickering forever if you let them, but we did not have the luxury of such time.

I supposed that if you were a god and had spent millennia with the same beings and pretended like you were all one big happy family; you too would have snapped at every chance that you got.

"Would everyone just *shut up!*" Kyle finally shouted, silencing the throne room. His shoulders heaved up and down in anger, before he stomped his foot and growled. "...I am trying to make a really hard decision right now. I don't know if it's right, but it doesn't feel...wrong."

I blinked.

Abigail was about to kill someone.

No one was happy to hear the words that had just come out of his mouth —except for Hera. She stood there with a rather smug smile on her marble face.

"So, you would really throw all of this away for another life?" Abigail asked him. He turned to face her. He did not look guilty.

He looked like this was something that he *had* to do.

"...How can you be so sure that she'll keep her end of the deal?" Abigail then spat, glaring at Hera in disgust.

"I swear upon the River Styx," Hera answered, her eyes widening in earnest. "He has no reason not to trust me," she assured.

No one looked too sure about that.

"...I lost my mother," Kyle then said quietly. "I can't see my father —he won't recognise me for me. I have...no reason to stick around. Not even as a Grim Reaper," he murmured, glancing downwards. He dropped his dagger, and it hit the marble floor with a melodious clang. "So, I'll take your offer, Lady Hera. I will give up my soul."

The goddess smiled triumphantly and clasped her hands together in what appeared to be excitement.

"No!" Abigail cried, lurching forward.

Chainsaw Guy immediately grabbed her at the waist and stopped her from moving too far. "...Kyle, please," she pleaded, struggling to escape Chainsaw Guy's strong grip. "*Please* don't do this. Remember what we talked about. You are not alone."

"I have made up my mind," Kyle announced gravely. Then he softened as Abigail stopped struggling, looking at him with indignant eyes. "I'm sorry.

There's nothing you can offer me that will make me stay. Thanks for trying, though," he smiled weakly.

Abigail shook her head, as tears started streaming down her face. I looked between her and Kyle; confused if anything. She was trying extremely hard to stop him. That was not what I was confused about —of course wanting to save Kyle from a scheming goddess was a valid cause. But what I did not understand was why she was so...angry.

What was their relationship?

"I am so glad you have agreed to my offer," Hera gushed as she picked up her skirts and scurried over to him.

Søren and Chainsaw Guy took several steps backwards in disdain; taking Abigail with them. Even Phee-Phee cowered away from the vast goddess; ducking behind Søren and dimming his flames.

Kyle, however, did not move an inch and bravely stood his ground; looking Hera right in the eyes.

It was a moment to be described as, '*staring down certain death*'.

"Let this be a milestone and example for all mortals with divine blood in them," Hera smiled. "Perhaps we just might offer this to half-bloods instead of executing them, after all."

"So, you won't execute Savannah, then?" Kyle concluded rather hopefully. I bit my nails nervously and hoped along with him.

But Hera laughed dejectedly like it was intended to be an offensive joke — with the marble around her eyes unable to crease like skin, so she looked manically creepy. Her smile wavered as she did not manage to get a reaction out of the Reaper.

"...I said that I *might*," she murmured, turning up her nose. "Besides. You no longer have to concern yourself with her —or any of these rebellious creations, ever again," she smiled wider, before raising her hand.

Everyone froze, uncertain of what she was going to do. Abigail and Chainsaw Guy seemed to have an idea though, because their eyes grew to the size of saucers.

"Have a pleasant next life," Hera smiled. Then she slowly waved her hand from side to side.

A white mist wafted out from the centre of her palm, curling through the air down towards Kyle. The mist enveloped him; circling around his body like a masochistic shiver of sharks.

Kyle became nervous then.

I drew a sharp breath as I noticed how the mist began fading away and taking his form with it, starting from his feet.

He looked up at me guiltily when his bottom half had completely disappeared. He mouthed the words, '*I'm sorry*', before closing his eyes and succumbing to the mist —leaving a shower of dust where he had been.

I blinked, and a tear slid down my cheek.

"No…" Abigail gasped. "…No, no, *no!*"

Chainsaw Guy still had his grip on her, to keep her from charging at the goddess and only to be consequently flicked at the wall like a small irritant bug.

So, she turned to me instead.

"This is all your fault," she accused. "You made him do it. He would still *be* here if it wasn't for you. It's all your fault!" she screamed, fighting against Chainsaw Guy.

"No, I didn't mean to cause anyone harm…I didn't ask him to sacrifice himself —" I panicked, desperate to be understood as genuine.

"It's all your fault!" she cut me off, crying again. "It's all…your *fault*," she sobbed. I dithered as Chainsaw Guy pulled her away into a hug and shot me a look. I had never felt worse; so torn up.

"It's not Savannah's fault," Søren defended me. "It's not *anyone's* fault. You did what you could. There is nothing more that you could have done."

Abigail continued crying and did not seem like she wanted to hear any of it.

I looked up at Hades for some sort of reassurance, but all that he could offer me was an unconvincing shrug. I indignantly rubbed my no doubt reddening face, before folding my arms and turning my back to what was left of my rescue team. I could not face them after that.

Abigail was right.

I should have done something, not just stood and watched. I clenched my fists and dug my fingernails into my palms.

"You are right. Kyle made his choice," Hera then sighed, dusting her hands and turning to walk back to her throne. She paused, before glancing over her shoulder nonchalantly.

"…Now it is time for you to make yours."

CHAPTER 44

SAVANNAH

"WOULD YOU REALLY offer the same deal you gave Kyle to other half-bloods?" I asked Hera, admittedly with a bit of bite.

I was not completely asking for others anymore. I wanted to ask for myself too. Because perhaps it really was a viable option.

I glanced over my shoulder and met Søren's gaze. I hesitated, and my frown wavered. I would have to leave everything and everyone behind. After everything we had done thus far; would I really throw it away for reincarnation?

I stiffened, glancing aside. I wanted to believe that I could actually be selfish enough to consider it. But I looked back at him; the hurt evident in his expression —and realised…that maybe I was not that selfish, after all. I could never bring myself to choose willingly to leave.

"Certainly not if they ask as begrudgingly as you are asking me," Hera remarked, clearly offended. "And it would depend on the threat level the half-blood posed," she continued. "The higher the threat, the more likely I *would not* —because power like that does not simply leave a soul. Certain powers stay with a soul even through death and cling to its essence. It is possible for some powers to be taken through reincarnation. In short," the goddess concluded, "the lower the threat level, perhaps the more inclined I would be to offer that deal. Oh, and in case you were wondering," she quipped, "*your* threat level is very high," she said firmly, narrowing her rose quartz eyes down to slits.

Perfect. That ruled out that idea.

There would be no such luck in getting out of this.

"You're horrible," Abigail then spat. I could not tell for whom she had intended that, because I still had my back to her.

"Excuse me?" Hera snarled.

"Not you," Abigail hissed, confirmed my suspicions. "I meant *her*," she said. I tensed, knowing that she was glaring holes into the back of me. "I can't believe that you would think you could get out of this so easily. Do you even care about the countless others? Do you even know how many Reapers are willing to back you up on this?"

"Don't say that like it's a lot," I scoffed, turning around. "And don't tell me there's no way I would know. Because I can clearly see three people and a Phoenix. Only two of those would actually choose to be here. The *other* two couldn't care less about me —especially *Chainsaw Guy*," I then raised my voice. I was not exactly singling him out on purpose.

I was simply furious.

Confusion flickered over Abigail's face before she realised who I was talking about. She glared back at me, before opening her mouth to retaliate.

"You're pretty ungrateful, you know that?" Chainsaw Guy interjected. "We're here risking our souls for you and the only thing you can talk about is our lack in numbers."

"That's not true," I gasped. "And *she* started it. And last time I checked, my soul was the only one in definite danger," I growled.

"That is *enough*," Zeus said, loud enough for the room to shake. "I cannot believe the amount of disrespect being displayed here. I would have thought you would show a little less…hostility towards your friends."

"She is not my friend," Abigail snapped, folding her arms and leaning on one hip. "And surprise, surprise —mortals taking after their creators? Who would have seen that coming," she added sarcastically. "We are made in your image, right?"

I actually wanted to laugh.

"I see your point," Zeus grumbled. "But I have grown tired of this, regardless. Horkos, please escort them away to the cells."

Horkos smiled. "It would be my pleasure."

"Yeah, I'd bet it would," I remarked flatly.

Søren snapped back into action as Horkos walked forward —and he raised his crossbow. A series of arrows shot through the air and struck Horkos' shins. The giant god hissed and paused, feeling the stinging.

And then Phee-Phee decided to join in the action and breathe fire at Horkos' feet. Horkos winced, before doing a heavy little dance on the spot. The throne room seemed to rumble with the movement.

"Why you little —" he seethed when the heat lessened, his eyes burning and turning molten with anger.

Søren's eyes widened and he started, not having thought his plan through. Horkos lunged forward towards them all, but they scattered, yelping in alarm. The room shook with every heavy thud of the god's feet. It became a game of cat and mouse as Horkos tried to scoop up my failed rescue party.

I dithered helplessly, unable to do anything. I was too high off the ground to survive jumping to the floor. It would not kill me, but I would not be of much help to the situation with broken legs.

"Horkos, remember your promise," Thanatos clipped, suddenly launching to his feet. I shot him a look.

What promise? What bargain had he struck with him?

The hardened expression he gave me in return did not give much away.

"Leave them alone!" I finally commanded, having had enough. "Let them go. They haven't done anything. You…can keep me."

"No!" Søren protested. "We're not leaving without you!"

"It is too late for that," Horkos huffed. "They are going to be imprisoned for an indefinite amount of time for assaulting a god."

"But *we* didn't do anything!" Abigail cried, ducking and rolling.

"…You are guilty by association," Horkos stated.

I clenched my fists and growled, feeling the rage boiling inside of me. And mixed with the heat in my veins, I did not realise that I had summoned fire until the gods gasped. I gasped too —immediately extinguishing the white flames. I clasped my hands to my chest and backed up worriedly.

"She has…pyrokinesis?" Hera breathed.

Her discovery rendered the whole room still and silent. Even Thanatos gawked at me like I had finally managed to impress him.

I shook my head hurriedly, putting my hands behind my back. I could not find any words with which to defend myself. I stumbled into my father's wrist as his hand curled inward in a protective manner.

"It is not as bad as it seems," Hades tried.

"The flames are white," Hera continued, "—so it is not as bad as it seems…It is *worse*."

"At least they're not…blue?" Thanatos offered hopefully.

I gave him a pained expression.

"Zeus, this girl is absolutely dangerous. She should not be existing. What should we do? Move up the execution?" Hera panicked.

"No!" I suddenly found my voice. They looked at me curiously. I paused, shivering in fear. "I'm…I'm not a danger. Not to you —not to anyone. Please don't kill me…I don't want to die again."

Horkos scoffed. "How sickening."

He was right.

"Please," I begged shamelessly. "There has to be another solution. I'll…I'll serve in Mount Olympus or something —I'll even serve out a prison sentence, anything. Just please…don't execute me."

I somehow always thought that I would be brave when faced with death. But it turned out that I was a complete coward. I did not want to die —now faced with the consequence, I realised that it was some fundamental human trait to tremble at the prospect of predicted death.

A part of me was still mortal —still pathetically mortal.

A rumble then came from behind me. I turned to look up at Hades. He looked down at me; his jasper eyes twinkling. Then he raised his other hand and waved it in a circular motion. A green portal appeared in front of me, the wind coming from it blowing my hair and tears back. He waved his hand again and another portal appeared next to Søren on ground level.

"*Hades* —" the god of the skies started, but that did not stop my father from doing what he was doing.

My eyes widened as I figured out exactly what that was. I shook my head and backed up. There was no way I was going to just allow him to let me abandon him. And I was not about to anger the gods even further.

"Run," he said. "I will buy you time."

"Wait, Dad —"

He then jerked his hand forward and suddenly launched me into the swirling green circle.

✠

"No —!" I cried as I landed on wet grass, face first.

I gasped and scrambled to my feet, before blowing the hair that had fallen out of my ponytail out of my face. I could not believe that Hades had let me escape just like that. But it did get me thinking —why had he not done it sooner? Now he had to face Zeus, Hera and Horkos alone and deal with their wrath.

I started as the sound of far off thunder then tumbled in the sky —as if Zeus was the one behind it.

I gasped as I remembered that I was back on Earth. I glanced around me, worried that I had ended up somewhere I did not know.

It was a huge relief to see Søren's apartment building behind me. Hades was obviously better at portals than Thanatos.

I paused and rubbed my arm.

It was still pretty weird to learn that Thanatos was Hades' son —which made him my half-brother. I shivered, thoroughly put off as I recalled every encounter between us that had happened. Especially that stupid maid punishment. It was even more disgusting now.

"Savannah!"

I then turned around at the sound of Søren's voice. Phee-Phee was flying alongside him, completely ablaze. My eyes widened but I did not have time to react though, as the Trainer suddenly crushed me in a fierce hug. I blinked, before tightly hugging him back.

"I'm glad that you are still alive, first of all," he admitted, withdrawing. I smiled back weakly. "Second of all, you won't believe what just happened back in the throne room."

"Oh?" I frowned curiously, reached out to stroke Phee-Phee's back. Phee-Phee jerked away alarmingly and tried not to let me touch him. I laughed lightly and finally succeeded in stroking his feathers, which evidently confused him.

So, I held out my hand and summoned a small flame in the palm of my hand. "...See, Phee-Phee?" I said softly. "I can touch fire now." The Phoenix cooed and flapped around excitedly, before nuzzling against me.

"Well, you know who can't touch fire?" Søren then redirected my attention. "Horkos," he said smugly.

"How come?"

"Oh, you should have seen it," Søren then gasped. "After your Dad sent you off, Horkos flipped out and went ballistic. Zeus then snapped and threw a thunderbolt —and it hit Horkos *right* in the —"

"Hey!"

We were suddenly interrupted by Abigail, who then forcefully pulled me backwards and away from Søren. I nearly fell backwards at her strength.

"*Hey*," I protested. "What was that for?"

Phee-Phee squawked in agreement and raised his wings at her somewhat threateningly.

"Oh no you don't," Abigail growled. I flinched. "You don't get to have a damn touching reunion moment. You don't *deserve* it."

I pressed my lips into a line and did not try to deny her.

Phee-Phee rubbed against my leg affectionately, but it did not do much in the way of comforting me.

"Abby, are you still going off at her because of Kyle?" Søren sighed.

"*Yes!*" she cried, baring her sharpened nails at me. "It's all her fault."

"No, it isn't," he insisted.

"I'm on Abby's side," Chainsaw Guy then declared, running up to us with his weapon sickeningly gleaming in the early morning sunlight. "Because Kyle would still be alive if —"

"If *what*, Melchior?" Søren challenged, taking a protective step in front of me. "If you hadn't volunteered to come with me? That's bullshit. Did I beg either of you *or* Kyle?"

"Don't you dare try to blame Abby," Chainsaw Guy snarled, putting a hand on her shoulder.

"I'm not blaming her," Søren huffed. "I'm not blaming you either. I'm blaming Kyle himself —no one asked him to come along."

Abigail gasped as we all went silent.

She looked at each of us. I turned away awkwardly. Chainsaw Guy was stunned. Søren daringly did not turn a single hair. The blonde paused, appearing to come down from her rage high, before she angrily wiped her face. She looked back up with an unreadable expression.

"How dare you," she said nonchalantly, her face a cold blank wall. As though she could not believe what she was hearing. No one responded. "Fuck you," she breathed. "Just...*fuck* you, Søren." Her words lacked anger or any sort of emotion at all. They were tired. Void of conviction.

Abigail then turned away and stomped off down the street.

I looked at Søren, but he had not wavered.

"I'll talk to her," Chainsaw Guy sighed reluctantly, before he wandered in the same direction after Abigail.

"Yeah, good luck with that," Søren snarled, and then walked off the opposite way. I dithered, before following the Trainer and letting Phee-Phee follow after me.

"Søren, wait," I called, reaching for his sleeve. He stalled, before looking down at me. "That was really harsh," I said.

"What was harsh, exactly? What I said, or what Abigail said?" he seethed, turning away from me.

"No one was justified," I said quickly. "But…that was awful. I understand why she was mad at me, but I can't believe that you would treat your friend with such insensitivity."

"Well, I'm apathetic remember?" he snapped. "I don't feel anything, for anyone." His tone was forced, as though he were trying to convince himself that it was a matter of fact.

I paused and blinked rapidly, taken aback. I knew that he was upset, but that hit me hard, and hurt me in a place I had not known that it could. He paused too, re-evaluating his words.

"…Do you really mean that?" I asked, glaring at him. The heat Phee-Phee's was emitting then intensified as though he was on my side.

"Savannah, of course I don't," he said gently. "It just came out. I'm sorry. Of course, it's not like that."

"How?" I demanded.

"What do you mean?" he scoffed. "I do care and feel things —you *know* that. And I'm becoming nicer. I'm not *completely* apathetic."

I glanced down and bit my lip. "Do you ever wish that you were?"
"No," he insisted. "Because then I would miss out on everything that makes me human. Love; pain; sadness; happiness —I wouldn't get to experience any of that. And I don't know if I'd be able to live that way."

I softened, much to my slight disappointment; I would have liked to see how much further I could push the fight. Phee-Phee seemed to be thinking similar things, because he was still arching menacingly.

I sighed and put my hands on my hips. "Even though I'll end up forgiving you," I breathed, "I don't think that Abigail will be so easily swayed."

"I…know. You were right. I wasn't being tactful. Maybe I shouldn't have said anything at all," he sighed, glancing downwards.

"No, I think voicing the idea that it was Kyle's own fault was something that she needed to hear," I whispered. "It was difficult, but it had to be put down on the table."

Søren nodded solemnly. "But now Abigail wants to use my head to break that table in half."

I chuckled softly at that, before offering him a hug.

But Phee-Phee was having none it; he kept nudging my leg in the way which dogs do to signal a problem.

I sighed in amusement as Søren and I withdrew.

"What happened to us becoming friends?" the Reaper frowned at the Phoenix. Phee-Phee disapprovingly stuck his beak in the air. "Oh, I see," Søren grunted. "This really was only for Savannah."

"He's just jealous," I whispered to Phee-Phee, tossing my head in the Trainer's direction —which earned me an unamused scoff.

"Look, I'm sorry that I made you doubt me," Søren then apologised. "I was just really pissed off. It's just unfair for Abby to keep picking on you."

"No," I whispered. "I think that I deserve it. I could have done something, Søren," I said earnestly.

"No Savannah, don't start," he said firmly. "He chose to get reincarnated. I'm not sure there is much that you could've said to him that would have changed his mind. You should've heard the talk Abigail gave him. She went on and on about family and accepting him into the group —all good things, but they slid right off of him. He had always been alone when he was alive, and after the death of him and his mother, I don't think that there were any words that could dull that pain."

"That's so awful," I murmured, frowning in concern.

"Exactly. So, what could you have said? Now all we can do, is hope that he'll do better in his next life."

"I suppose so," I mumbled. "But I don't think that I will ever stop feeling like this —almost guilty."

"The wound will scar eventually."

"But there it will always remain," I said softly.

Søren then looked at me in disappointment.

"Christ, Savannah —you took something that was supposed to cheer you up a little and turned it into a depressing quote."

"Half of my existence is depressing quotes," I deadpanned.

"But the other half is motivational," he quipped. "I don't think that you can dispute that one."

I paused, mulling it over. "…Yeah, you're right. I can't," I admitted. "I've been cursed with my mother's persistence."

Søren chuckled softly. Then his eyes widened as he remembered something. "What are we going to do now? I mean, we have no way of getting back to Mount Olympus. Are we just supposed to hide and wait for the gods to seek?" he suggested rather pessimistically.

"No," I frowned empathetically. I turned away and started pacing on the sidewalk. Phee-Phee hopped around back and forth, cutely mimicking me. "…I'll think of something. Probably."

"Well, it had better be fast," Søren breathed, looking up at the sky.

I looked up too and gulped. That far off thunderstorm was now fast approaching. "…Zeus looks impatient."

CHAPTER 45

SAVANNAH

I HAD NEVER been comfortable with people staring at me —especially if it was because I was suddenly the sole subject of attention.

Or if the room was completely silent. And the worst option: if me walking in had to result in any and all of those.

I froze as I came to a halt after running into the apartment block lobby, and everyone around me seemed to do the same as they turned around in my direction. I did not know why. It was not as if I was that noticeable —I had hoped to blend into the crowd for a while longer. After a few awkwardly silent seconds I cleared my throat and straightened up, trying to be a little more casual. The stares were not exactly condescending —in fact, the Reapers standing around me looked concerned and a little anxious.

"…What?" I finally asked.

"Savannah!" a familiar voice then called from the front. I craned my neck before spotting Nadine as she ran towards me. She stopped in front of me, and for a scary moment I thought that she might hug me.

She seemed to be considering the same, before she thought better of it and gave me a slap on the shoulder instead, making me flinch.

"Ow —what was that for?" I questioned.

"You're…really here," she went on, posing it as more of question than an exclamation. "And you're still…alive?"

"Yes…?" I frowned, nodding slowly.

Hushed whispers wafted around me, and I heard my name and several curses.

I turned to look at Søren, who was dithering guiltily behind me and scratching the back of his neck. Phee-Phee flew in and landed beside me, gaining several more gasps.

The Phoenix paid no mind to the uneasy Grim Reapers and ruffled his alight feathers in an ostentatious way. I understood the prejudice that hung thick in the air, but it needed to be abolished immediately. I was not going to let Phee-Phee be raised in an ignorant and toxic environment.

"The bird is with me," I announced as a general rule. "Hurt him and I will hurt you," I promised.

The Grim Reapers seemed to shut up and be less restless at the threat.

I was surprised that they believed me —I had not exactly done anything to earn their respect.

I then turned back to Nadine, who was still staring at me in disbelief. "Would you mind telling me what's going on?" I asked earnestly. She blinked rapidly as she came back to the present, but then she looked unsure of what to say.

"Everyone thought that you'd be completely dead by now," someone then said from behind me.

I turned around to see a neutral-faced Abigail and frowning Chainsaw Guy. And even though neither of them looked like they wanted to kill me, I paused before awkwardly glancing at the floor.

I still felt bad for earlier, and for what Søren had said.

"Søren had tried to assemble a rescue team but everyone thought it was suicide," Abigail sighed. "*We* joined because we can't just let him die. He's our friend, and whatever is important to him, is important to us. Even if it has to do with you," she added sourly.

I looked back up at her in surprise. So, the talk had been effective after all? I wondered what exactly Chainsaw Guy had said to Abigail. She had shown us that she was not the type to easily change her mind.

"Oh, don't think we've now *forgiven* you," Chainsaw Guy scoffed. I hung my head in acceptance. "...But we *are* willing to set aside the events of Mount Olympus for now and help," he went on. I perked up considerably at that. "Generally, obviously —not help you personally," he then added.

"Okay, I get it," I grumbled, lidding my eyes. "You hate me but you're willing to work with me. I'll take it," I sighed, figuring it was far better than getting strangled, kicked —or worse, *shot* at —by Abigail.

"Um," Nadine then leaned to the side in front of me, eyeing Chainsaw Guy suspiciously. "What happened in Mount Olympus?"

Abigail and I both inhaled sharply. We shared a glance and somewhat understood that neither one of us could be the one to say it. We glanced at Chainsaw Guy —but he did not look like he even knew where to start.

"...Does anyone remember Kyle?" Søren then stepped in. Abigail turned away uneasily and folded her arms. She was not going to let him live that fight down. Though I really hoped that they could make up before Zeus had the chance to start smiting anyone.

"Wasn't he the guy who left with you?" one Reaper who was standing next to us asked.

"The one with the red leather jacket and dagger," another went on. "He had some balls, having the nerve to question a superior like that."

"*Shut* up," Abigail then snapped, startling them. "You didn't know him. He might have not been polite about it but he had valid reasons to question Søren. So don't you dare say things like that."

"Abby," Chainsaw Guy said softly, nudging her.

He shook his head and put a hand on her shoulder. With some notable effort she clamped her mouth shut and said nothing more. I wanted to feel less guilty but seeing her like that only made me feel worse.

"All right, that's enough," I spoke up, my voice as cutting as ice.

Everyone turned to me. I clenched my fists and turned to march up to the announcement podium. I faced the crowd, all attention on me. I then gulped at the magnitude of Reapers. Every one of them was somewhat depending on me. I was responsible for preserving every soul in the lobby; not to mention the whole

Organisation. That was a daunting truth.

Then I realised something else.

Another one of my weak suits was public speaking. I dithered, suddenly becoming nervous. My empathetic passion had seemed to fizzle out just as quickly as it had sparked, leaving behind a confused puddle of growing paranoia.

What do I say?

My eyes then found Søren's in the crowd, who was steadily making his way to the front. He held my gaze until he was just in front of the raised platform, and then smiled at me encouragingly.

I gulped, before taking a deep breath. I felt myself calm down as the air whistled out of my lungs. Then I cleared my throat to address the crowd.

"What happened at Mount Olympus was not the fault of anyone here; though I would like to take the responsibility," I decided, solemnly glancing downwards. "A deal was made…and a soul which was too far gone was lost. And…we can't afford that," I said earnestly, then finding the courage to lift my gaze back up at the sea of people.

"We cannot afford for any more souls like that to do the same. Abigail tried to prevent it, but Kyle…he *chose* to go on his own. Even though none of us wanted to believe that he was that alone, maybe our efforts weren't enough at the end. Maybe a fresh start really is what he needed. And although I did not know him personally, he still thought of me when he had made his choice. He still valued my life as he gave up his."

I then paused, letting that sink in. I truly hoped that Kyle had a good next life ahead of him. He deserved it, wholeheartedly.

"Did the gods kill him?" someone asked from the back.

"No," I answered quickly. "No one '*died*'. I mean…Kyle wasn't exactly killed," I clarified. "He gave up his spirit willingly to be reincarnated."

"He did *what*?" the Reaper cried.

The reaction rippled through the crowd, and soon the lobby was abuzz with arguing. I dithered, unsure of what to do. I became hopeful as Søren then stepped up onto the raised platform and came to stand next to me. I gave him a sheepishly guilty look. He sighed, before turning to the crowd.

"Hey!" he yelled. "Shut up for a second!"

The lobby fell silent at the mere sound of Søren's voice. Even I cowered away slightly. I knew that he could be intense, but I had never witnessed him command a room like the night devoured the sky.

"It was Kyle's own choice. No one killed him," Søren firmly clarified. "…And if you must know, he was the son of a half-blood."

Several gasps of surprise were heard. So it had been news to all of us.

"Lady Hera said that she thought that Savannah's proposition sounded like a good idea," the Trainer continued.

He then turned to me and gestured for me to elaborate.

"Oh," I said as I turned to face the crowd, "I offered to be a mentor and train half-bloods to control their abilities. The gods said they executed them because of their unpredictability, which would make them a danger to both worlds. But no one has to live in fear. If they could simply be *trained*, then there would be no need to kill them."

"And did the gods agree?" Nadine asked.

I sucked on my teeth. "At first…"

"What exactly does that mean?" someone else questioned anxiously.

"It means it's *indefinite*," I snapped. I was then met with understandable uncertainty. "…Look, I know I was supposed to come back with answers, but sometimes things don't go according to plan. The gods themselves are unpredictable —so of course the outcome of my venture could not have been for sure. Even now, as the god Zeus hunts me down, I am trying to prepare a contingency plan. Ideally, I'm hoping for some Grim Reaper reinforcement," I admitted. "But only those who choose to be. No one is being forced."

The Reapers shared various looks at that. Then noise levels rose as they all started talking over each other again.

I turned to Søren desperately. This was already a disaster. At this rate, the Organisation might actually end up destroying itself entirely without the gods' aid. Søren put a hand on my shoulder and offered me a sad smile. I dithered, unsure of what he meant by it.

"You can't win them all," he then said over the other voices.

I frowned. I knew that he was right. But I wanted to walk away from this knowing that I had done all that I could.

I did not want to go into battle with lukewarm effort.

"Hey everyone!" I yelled at the crowd. No one stopped. I clenched my fists. "*Hey…*!" I shouted, longer and louder than before. The noise finally dwindled, and the attention returned to me. I nodded in approval and sighed. "This is unfair. I know that," I started. "And it's unfair to ask you of this but *please* can some of you contribute to numbers? I'm not going to lie to you and say that no one is going to die. The risk is there. And you know what? The second-best case scenario would be that only I don't make it back. So how about that —?"

"—That is not a hypothetical scenario. That is precisely what will happen," a familiar and gruff voice then said from behind me.

Søren and I turned around to see a grave Thanatos in a burnt suit and with singed hair. I jumped and blinked rapidly, wondering how, why and what on Earth —*where* he had come from, and what he was doing here. Hushed whispers then appropriately dispersed from the crowd.

"Thanatos!" I exclaimed. "What the *hell*? Where…where is Dad —is he here too. And the other gods. Shit —are they already here?"

"Calm down, fool," he sighed, shoving me aside from the podium. "I followed your friends out of Hades' portal. I was offering the other Reapers across the city temporary asylum in Purgatory. I would have recruited them too, but unfortunately, they do not know you nor about your cause. And the gods are not here…yet. But they will be here soon," he added darkly.

"Hey," I whined, stumbling upright. "That's great and all, but just because I'm your little sister it doesn't mean that you can push me around," I grumbled. "Or call me a fool."

"On the contrary, dear *half*-sister," he quipped, "that is exactly what siblings do. Now, do you want my help or not? I've been back here long enough to see that you have been struggling."

403

I pouted but reluctantly relented. I was not in a position to argue, even I could see that. I still was not going to let it go, though.

"Why *are* you helping?" Søren then frowned.

"For this…family thing, I suppose," Thanatos sighed. He looked at me. "I guess I don't actually want you to die?" he said like he was not all that sure.

I raised my eyebrows in surprise. Thanatos was *feeling* something for me?

This needed to be documented.

"Who are you and what have you done with the real Death?" I then mocked, though in all seriousness I was quite suspicious.

"The guilt —and Nina —would weigh on me too much," he added, looking down at me blankly.

I lidded my eyes. There he was.

"Wait. Death is your brother?" someone in the crowd then spoke up. The whispers grew louder.

"Yes, surprise," Thanatos confirmed emotionlessly. "But that is not the thing on which to focus. Listen up. Regarding Savannah's proposal: I can assure you all that as Grim Reapers you are safe from harm —from Horkos at least. However, be aware that if you are pro Savannah not getting killed, Zeus will not hesitate to squash you like a fly."

I gawked at my half-brother, wholly taken aback.

"Do not get me wrong," he went on, "it is completely up to you. Just be prepared. I myself will be fighting, unfortunately, but even I do not compare to the king of the gods and the *sky* —"

"*Thanatos*," I interrupted, giving him a desperate look. "That. Is. *Not*. Helping," I emphasised ever word.

"Let me finish," he demanded, raising a finger at me, before addressing the crowd. "Honestly if I wanted to, I could order every last one of you to fight. But I will not —that would be a waste. Besides, if you do not want to fight, Nina will be opening a portal to Purgatory where you may hide out.

"But what I *will* ask, is that you show a little empathy just this once, as a favour to me as your Boss," he suggested; not surprising me at all with the attempt at emotional blackmail. "I am fighting for someone I never thought I would care about. You will be fighting for justice. It is an honourable cause. And I hope for all of your sakes that there are less cowards here than I think," he then added rather harshly.

Silence followed his speech.

I was unsure if people had yet gotten over the fact that Death was actually here, in front of them. Thanatos then turned away from the podium and gave me a brief nod. I gave an uncertain nod back, still at a loss. It sounded as though he gone for a reverse psychological approach at the end.

"...Okay," Søren was then the one to take charge. "In addition to all of that, we are running out of time. Those going to Purgatory, stay in here. Those who will fight, regroup outside."

The lobby then became a disorderly scramble as everyone tried to get to the place they wanted to go. Thanatos instructed Søren to go upstairs first and gather up all of his back-up weapons, because we would find that we might need them. I offered to help but I was needed outside.

"I'll get Abby and Melchior to help," Søren decided. "But mostly Melchior. I mean, he's probably strong enough to carry all of them."

I nodded and gave him a thumbs up, before heading for the front doors. I could not tell how many Reapers we had managed to convince to help, but it did not look to be too few from the amount of people that I saw leaving.

Thanatos and I burst out into the street to find a fairly sized cluster of Grim Reapers. I inhaled sharply at the numbers, but it was better than no one standing in front me. And I had to be grateful for these lives being risked.

"Søren will be back soon," Thanatos told me. "Why don't you take a breather for like, five seconds?"

"Sure," I agreed, sitting down on the curb.

I glanced up at the sky. I gasped at its glowing blue colour. Lightning cracked brilliantly, and the wind picked up. Tension rose, and I could sense everyone's nervousness. They had never dealt with something like this.

They had all once been ordinary people, now tasked with being divine hitmen.

I was dragging them into a new type of conflict entirely.

I took a deep breath and exhaled, before hanging my head.

Was *I* ready?

I had not even bothered to think about how this was going to affect me. I had been too busy avoiding death.

Now that I was alone with my thoughts, I knew how I felt. My heartbeat would have accelerated so much that I might have had a heart attack.

I was terrified.

I looked down at the sword by my side. I unsheathed it, before holding it up in front of me. The obsidian and gold glinted, and I caught sight of my reflection.

Who is that girl, I wondered as I sheathed the sword again. *And why does she matter so much?*

"Savannah," Thanatos suddenly said, putting a hand on my shoulder. I started, before hugging my knees to my chest. "You're not alone."

I sniffed. I knew that. Theoretically.

"I will not let Horkos get anywhere near you," he went on. I looked up at him curiously. "You're a Grim Reaper, so he should not be able to kill you. But please, can you do me a favour and kick his ass?" he chuckled. "I have been wanting to do it for a while now."

I gave him a half-hearted smile and nodded slightly.

I could not actually promise that, but it made me feel better to hear Thanatos try to lift my spirits a little bit.

"You probably do not want to hear about this again, but you went into an interesting fit of rage when you killed Aaron," he then sighed. I stiffened a bit at the name. "Your eyes glowed and your strength increased —and you looked like you were on fire. If you could do that again, that would be really helpful," Death hinted, tilting his head.

I scoffed. "I was beyond enraged in that moment," I explained. "I had never been so angry."

"Then try to bring that feeling back," Thanatos suggested. "Oh, I know. Think of it like…the gods never loved you, and Horkos is the one who stole them

406

from you."

"Okay, stop," I quipped, holding my hands up in surrender. "Thanks for trying to be helpful but that analogy has many things wrong with it."

"Hm. Fine, so maybe I should move away from the relationship parallel," he scoffed. "But what I'm trying to do is get you to be furious. Nothing fuels a fighting spirit like rage," he sighed contently.

I looked at him sideways and raised an eyebrow. It made me wonder how often Death got into fights.

"Hey," Nadine huffed, coming to a stop in front of us. Lewis gave a small wave and apologetic smile for the failure to rein in his sister. "Why didn't you tell us that you two were related?"

I sighed and rolled my eyes. "It's not something that I knew until like, a couple of hours ago."

"And I don't particularly like talking about the bastard child of my family," Thanatos murmured.

"*Hey*," I snapped, offended. I hit his arm sharply.
He surprisingly flinched. "*Ow.*"

Nadine and Lewis shared a knowing look. "They are definitely siblings," they smirked in unison.

"We're back," Søren then announced from behind us. I immediately stood up. Søren, Abigail and Chainsaw Guy held up a duffle bag each, before lowering them onto the sidewalk.

"Great," Thanatos said. "Distribute them amongst yourselves —no one can go into this battle with only one weapon."

Everyone then gathered around and started taking various other deadly tools to pair up with their chosen reaping weapons. I took another sword —one that looked like the one Søren had used when we were training.

It strangely gave me a little comfort.

"Why do you have so many other weapons?" Abigail grumbled when everyone had taken most of them. "You don't even use them."

"I blame him," Søren pointed at Thanatos, as though being a Trainer had

407

nothing to do with it. Petty hatred sizzled between them like electricity.

"Let us focus please," Death breathed in irritation, clapping his hands together. He called everyone to gather around. "Savannah?" He turned to me. "Would you like to say anything?"

I glanced at the Grim Reapers around me. Some gave me encouraging looks. Some looked as fearful as I felt.

And I understood.

"We need to be a team —to stand together and have each other's backs," I said firmly. "The gods will not show mercy. Not to me, anyway. And I'm grateful that I have people on my side who won't let me die," I smiled at Nadine, Lewis and the others.

They smiled back.

"…But many half-bloods are not as lucky as I am. Most were disowned. If there are still any more out there, which I believe there might be, they are in need of people who won't let them die. People who care. I want to be that for them. I want to show them that somewhere out there, they are being thought of, and they are known. And they deserve to live.

"What I'm saying is…just look out for someone other than yourself. Because at the end of the day, whenever each of our times come and we stand before Hades, we are all part human," I reminded them. They needed to remember. "We just have to retrieve the courage…to act like it."

The Reapers cheered and whistled, making me blush. I could not believe that they had liked my pep talk.

"You heard her," Thanatos then said, looking upwards at the clouds. "We need to fight for each other."

We all nodded but looked up fearfully. The thunder was rolling louder and for longer. The sky was going to open up. Which meant that the gods were close. Everyone drew their weapons. I dithered, the weight of the swords in my hands making me uncertain.

"Hey," Søren then murmured, nudging me. He had also doubled up with a sword. "Are you ready?"

"I sure hope so," I breathed, holding the swords more securely. "This is the fight of my life, after all."

"And I'll give anything to help you keep it."

I looked up at him and smiled softly.

Did he really mean that?

The smile that he gave me in return told me that he did.

"Thank you," I told him. "For everything."

CHAPTER 46

SAVANNAH

I WONDERED WHAT the mortals saw; when the clouds were pierced apart by a sudden burst of light and the Olympians rode down from the New York sky in their blazing chariots.

Because to the rest of us, it looked exactly as it sounded —completely awing and mind numbing.

We all stood stunned for a moment. Seeing the divine and being a part of it proved to be quite different from each other —it was almost like a spell was cast as our eyes took in what simply put, was the splendour of the gods.

Even in their human forms.

But then we snapped out of it, as Zeus' thunder and lightning reminded us that this was far from a friendly visit. A wall of rain followed suit; heavy and sudden, soaking us instantly.

I blinked through the torrent, focusing on the number of opponents heading our way.

I counted eight chariots. I glanced at each rider and I knew who each of them were, as though instinctively, even though I had never seen them before — especially as humans. Two carried Zeus and Hera; another with the goddess Artemis; one with her brother Apollo; Ares, the god of war himself in another; one with Poseidon and another with Hermes. Either he truly was neutral, or he had been forced to participate. But I received my answer as he looked directly at me, and tapped the side of his nose. He could prove to be an ally of some kind.

The last chariot, led by Horkos had my father in it with him; his hands tied to one of the winged wheels.

"Hades!" I cried, lurching forward.

Thanatos put an understanding hand on my shoulder. "I will get him," he promised. I gave him a frustrated expression in return, but I was grateful. He looked back up, and then narrowed his eyes suspiciously.

"…Wha —why is *Apollo* here?" he remarked distastefully. "What, is he going to be the backing track or something? Document the event in rhyme? Dazzle us with his *smile*?"

If I was not facing death for the second time, I might have laughed.

"This battle may yet prove to be entertaining, though," he went on. "All of the eldest sons of Kronos are here."

I gulped. That was definitely a bad thing. But at least, two of the gods were on our side. I looked up again and I met the fire in Horkos' eyes; a slow simmering burn of pure unrelenting prideful judgement. He looked like he could not wait to skewer me with the two sickles he held.

"Oh my gods," I gasped, gripping my swords tighter. "This is it. We're all going to die."

Søren turned to look at me a little condescendingly. "We volunteered our lives for this. So now, I am offended."

"Why?" I questioned. "There are eight angry celestial beings about to land and pummel us. What could possibly be a more appropriate response?"

"How about some positivity?" Thanatos suggested.

"…We're all going to die *quickly*."

"*Savannah*," they scolded simultaneously.

"Sorry," I deadpanned, shrugging. Lightning then fizzled in the sky and I swear I heard my name in the thunder that followed. "…Shit, get ready!" I cried.

Zeus and Hera's chariots landed first, before coming to a standstill at the end of the street. The others landed in a migrating V formation behind them. Then everything was suddenly still. The rain trickled to a drizzle and the wind died down. Lightning flashed without thunder; only possible because of Zeus. But the lightning highlighted the gods' faces —fierce, angry and deadly. I glanced at the Reapers beside me and saw the growing fear in their expressions.

But no one ran off.

They all stayed with me.

Zeus admittedly appeared only slightly less intimidating in his golden toga and cleanly shaven beard —but his sapphire eyes gleamed with the strength of a fluorescent light. He paused as he assessed our small defence. He did not chuckle or seem amused. He did not look hesitant or unnerved either. He actually had the audacity to look at us as though this was all a minor inconvenience that he really could not spare the time to deal with. I clenched my jaw.

He was clearly not going to take this seriously.

Hera then stepped out of her chariot and somewhat floated in her white floor-length toga over to the midway of both sides. Her golden laurel wreath shone and shimmered in the streetlights, along with the flecks of gold in her hair and around her eyes.

"Didn't she get the memo?" Thanatos hissed. "This is a very important battle; not a *Red Carpet* event."

"Oh my gods —shut up," I hissed back, shooting him a look.
Hera glanced at us and raised an eyebrow. Being the goddess of family, she could easily see how much Thanatos and I rubbed each other the wrong way. But then again, so could anyone who had functioning eyes.

I held my ground and looked Hera dead in the eye, but inside I was trembling, ready to get on my knees and beg like my life depended on it, if need be. She had this air about her like an empress scorned.

"Grim Reapers," she began. "And gods," she shot Thanatos a look. "This is an effort in a warning. Surrender now, and we can avoid the catastrophe that a battle would bring."

There was a pause as we all shared looks. Was she serious? If anyone was anticipating a catastrophe it was the gods for making a grand entrance which screamed, *prepare to be murdered, mortals!*

412

"How about *you* all go back to where you came from so we can avoid catastrophe, instead?" I dared.

Hera frowned. "I don't think you are in any position to speak out of turn, Savannah Green. I shouldn't have to remind you that we are all here because of *you*."

I clenched my jaw and glared at her.

"Well, we are here because we know that what you are trying to do is wrong," Thanatos defended me. "Savannah hasn't done anything wrong and you all know it. So why don't you drop the fake concern and just do what you really came to do —to sound the bloody starting horn."

I stared at him in amused disbelief, before looking back at Hera. She did not exactly react. Maybe she had to admit to herself that Thanatos was right.

"…Very well," she said, abruptly turning on her heel. She walked back to her chariot and got on, before taking off and hovering above us. "But remember this. We gave you a chance." Then she turned to her husband. "Let us get this over with."

I looked over at Zeus. He raised his hand upward and clenched his fist. Stray bolts of lightning crackled down from the sky and around us and collected in his hand, before forming one large unstable bolt. Then he looked directly at me, making me tense. The electric look in his vibrant blue eyes sent shivers through my body.

"You made me skip dinner," he grumbled. "So, I am in a worse mood than usual. Expect us to clash swords. Or, I suppose —cause a *spark*."

The lightning in his hand crackled.

Athena simply turned her nose up at me. Artemis looked grave and almost a little reluctant —but Apollo was just sitting on the side of his chariot filing his nails. Maybe he really was here as a joke.

"Your soul is mine, Savannah Green," Horkos then said ominously. He looked down at me with eyes as bright as the moon as he twirled one of his sickles. "You and your entire family will meet their end on this day."

I gulped and unconsciously took a step backwards. Thanatos took a step out in front of me. I looked up at him in confusion. "I won't let you get close enough," he said firmly. I blinked rapidly.

Then I frowned. What he was doing was sweet, but he was painting a different picture of me from the impression I had made in Mount Olympus.

I could fight for myself.

I moved in front of him in turn and raised my swords. "And *I* won't let any of you get close enough to any one of these Grim Reapers, either," I declared.

Zeus smirked. "While I admire your unnecessary and ultimately useless courage, I feel like I need to remind you," he started, walking forward. Then he suddenly appeared right in front of me, in the blink of an eye. "—that actions speak louder than *words*!" he thundered, bringing his lightning bolt down to strike me.

For a split second I was completely frozen. Out of the corner of my vision I saw Søren and Thanatos attempt to shield me. But then my body moved automatically, and I pushed both males out of way and moved to block Zeus' attack with both of my swords. Lightning struck the tar beneath my feet and knocked back everyone within five feet.

"Savannah…!" Søren's voice cried.

"I…I've…*got* this," I growled determinedly, clenching my jaw. I met Zeus' eyes and did not waver. I pushed back against him, and he faltered slightly, seemingly surprised that I had actually managed to block his move.

"Charge!" someone then screamed.

More cries then rang out and everything blurred around me as Reapers and gods ran at each other and collided in a resonating clang of iron, obsidian and steel. I huffed out a breath, beginning to feel the strain in my muscles. Zeus was starting to increase his force, which then involuntarily pushed me backwards, with my feet still grounded. I struggled under his weight, and I was about to pull back —when he suddenly cried out in pain.

He fell down onto one knee before me and I stepped back into a defensive stance, pointing out my swords at him cautiously.

"*Thanatos*," growled the god. I glanced a little way past him and noticed my half-brother standing behind him with his scythe drawn. "You have wounded me."

"Good," Thanatos spat, coming around to stand beside me. "Just be grateful that I didn't aim a little higher."

I then realised that there was smoke coming from the back of Zeus' right leg. Thanatos had slashed his calf and golden ichor was now dripping onto the ground. I smiled up at Thanatos and he returned it.

"Thought you could use a hand," he quipped.

I nodded, and then brought my sword down to Zeus' neck. He looked up at me with honourable surrender, but I was not going to go that easy on him.

"You have done nothing but confirm my notion that half-blood gods are nothing but trouble," Zeus grumbled.

I frowned. "And so, what if we are?" I challenged. "It's not as though *you're* perfect. The apple does not fall far from the tree."

"There will always be those who will fight," Thanatos added. "Most of what that treaty states is profoundly unfair. It is outdated and needs to be revised. If you're still so afraid of half-blood gods, then maybe you're not fit to reign as king."

Zeus then started.

He glared at us, with all traces of humility gone. He struggled, but slowly managed to stand up, with one of my swords still at his throat. "How dare you," he said. "Do you know who I am? You dare to question my authority? I think that position of yours as the Reapers Organisation CEO is getting to your head —"

"He *deserves* that position," I cut the god off.

Thanatos blinked stupidly. "...I do?"

I sighed, focusing my attention on Zeus. "You on the other hand, aren't even the oldest child of Kronos. What makes you think that you're so qualified to be king of the gods?"

"I maintain order," Zeus raised his voice. "I ensure that the future of this world as well as others is sustainable. Hybrids like you do not aid in reaching that goal!"

"You're just afraid of change!" I shouted back. "You would rather brush everything under a rug than think about a future where there are endless possibilities. Change is inevitable, Zeus. And we must all either change with it or get left behind."

"I would rather eradicate change all together!" Zeus declared.

"Without change you would not *be* here," Thanatos pointed out. "None of us would. What do you think evolution is? Growing up and taking responsibility? The wars you have waged and the lives you have taken —everything that you do influences everything you become. And frankly, you have become something of a monster, Lord Zeus."

The godly king paused, and his anger wavered.

He then looked rather grief-stricken. He clearly knew it —or at least he could now see it. He knew that we were right, and that he was just too proud and too safe up in Olympus to realise just how much had changed.

I slowly began to let my guard down. Maybe we could even draw a conclusion to this sooner than expected.

"Daughter of Hades," Zeus then gravely addressed me. "Perhaps…some change is indeed due."

I stuck my chin up in the air, showing my definitely condescending, but genuine approval. It felt…good, to have finally convinced him.

Then I tensed, remembering the other gods around us.

I turned and saw Chainsaw Guy as he brought his chainsaw down against Ares' sword, causing sparks to fly.

I saw Søren deflecting arrows from Artemis' bow with his sword.

Abigail roared to my right, jumping to avoid Athena's spear before firing her gun. Hermes weaved in as silent as shadows, expertly slashing the ankles of Reaper and god alike; like a chaotic assassin.

All around us immortals fought; blood splattered, bodies thudded the tar, and red bursts erupted in their wake.

It really hit me then —that souls were being taken.

"I'm going after Hera," I told Thanatos, sheathing both of my swords. "Keep an eye on Zeus, and make sure he doesn't try anything."

"Please," Zeus rasped, giving me a pained expression. "Do not hurt Hera. She means well, deep down. She does care. And she is still my queen."

"Oh, I won't hurt her," I scoffed. "*Physically*."

Zeus swallowed uneasily.

"And don't worry," Thanatos smirked at me, bouncing his scythe up and down in his hand smugly. "One well-placed hit, and this can send him straight to Tartarus."

"Good." I gave him a curt nod.

I turned away and faced the raging battles.

My eyes narrowed as wisps of humanoid entities wafted in and out of existence amongst the gods and Reapers. They were clad in armour and wielded blades of crystal clear ice —at least, it seemed that way whenever their icicle-spiked, giant lanky bodies were given physical form. The warriors moved with such precision and swiftness that it resembled a dance. Like flurries of snow and blizzard, they gyrated and slammed into anyone in their way. Though their sole targets only appeared to be the Olympians.

I then knew what they were. Servants of Hades.

The *Págos*.

Their strikes did not kill —they were designed to weaken and freeze. Shuddering and thankful that I was not an enemy to them, I ran for Hera's chariot. It was quite a distance off the ground.

I took a running jump, aiming for the wheels.

Hera watched as I launched myself upwards and gripped a slippery wheel, ducking underneath the flapping wing.

She did not react.

"Child," she said gently, offering a hand over the side. "What do you hope to accomplish from all of this?"

I growled and tried to hold on more securely. "You said that you liked my idea of training other half-blood gods. Why did you change your mind? Using fear to subdue your subjects isn't a good leadership trait. I've already convinced your husband. I can convince you too."

Hera then motioned for the chariot to lower to the ground. I stepped back as it landed, before she got off and stood in front of me.

She was more dazzling up close.

"My husband is stubborn. I know that," she sighed. "But I am not. I recognise a need to admit defeat when I see one. Why do you think I am not taking part in this?" she asked, gesturing to the battles raging around us.

More red clouds burst, and shrieks filled our ears.

"It was never my intention for this to go on as far as it has. But my siblings ever rarely see eye to eye with me."

"Oh, I know that," I quipped, unsheathing one of my swords to have it at the ready. "Your ways are dated, Hera. Things need to change. And that can't happen without you."

She chuckled softly. "You do not have to tell me twice," she smiled. "I would like to prevent war, if and when I can help it. I *understand*, Savannah. And…I do like your idea, by the way. I just…sometimes I think that I live in Zeus' shadow," she confessed, glancing downwards.

I raised an eyebrow. Well, I supposed that being somewhat second in command would result in some feelings of inferiority.

"You are one of the eldest gods," I said. Hera looked up at me again. "You were born with power and influence. It would seem that Zeus has forgotten that as much as you have. Remind him."

Hera's rose quartz eyes sparkled. And she smiled.

I still wished that I could have hurt her though. A sudden shiver then ran up my spine and I frowned. Hera then frowned too, in confusion.

Then suddenly, "Savannah, watch out —!"

I heard the sharp gasp and swing of metal before I whipped around. Red blood splattered out in my direction.

Time came to a halt and my eyes locked with pearl ones; wide and terrified.

Nadine fell forward onto her knees, with half of a sickle blade sticking out from her stomach.

I stared, completely stunned.

I could not say anything.

I could not even draw a breath.

It felt like everything had just *stopped* —so abruptly that it did not seem real.

I did not want it to be real.

But Nadine was looking up at me, tears streaming down her face as her baseball bat rolled out of her hands and onto the tar road.

"Nadine…" I whispered, reaching out shakily.

What could I do? Pull the blade from her midsection?

Horkos looked on, with what appeared to be slight surprise as he assessed the situation, before he flippantly remarked, "I missed."

CHAPTER 47

SAVANNAH

DEATH FAVOURS NO man. I would know —he was my brother. And he would likely do me no a favour by singling Nadine out and possibly saving her soul. Why hers, and not the countless others?

It was not as though I had expected everyone to make it out alive. But why had Nadine done this? I had done nothing to earn her blood and loyalty.

Honestly, in that moment there were only four people for whom I would willingly jump into the path of danger.

Nadine...had not been one of them.

"Oh my," Hera breathed, backing up rapidly.

"I...I'm *sorry*," Nadine choked out. Smoke curled out from the wound, indicating that Horkos' sickles were at the least, plated in obsidian.

"Nadine...no," I rasped, shaking my head. I kept a careful eye on Horkos, who was still frowning at the fact that he had stabbed the wrong person. "You shouldn't have...Why would you...?"

She tried to respond —but coughed up blood instead.

I gave Horkos a murderous look. He sheepishly met my gaze and then gestured down to Nadine. "Give me a moment," he said, tugging and making Nadine jerk backwards. "...It's stuck."

I growled and gripped my sword tighter. Nadine looked at me desperately. I hesitated. Then she gasped again, as Horkos finally yanked the sickle out of her.

A shriek pierced through the air as Nadine's body fell forward, and her soul remained. My eyes widened.

Her soul was as red as the others.

And then it burst.

I blinked. She was...gone. Nadine was gone —truly. I screwed up my face as I though I would start to cry. Then I froze.

Lewis.

I quickly looked around me, but I could not see him. I looked back at Horkos and I realised something. This could all be blamed on one being. Anger overlapped devastation and I started shaking.

"The sickle was supposed to impale *you*," he sighed, shaking his head with pure disappointment.

"You...damn son of a *bitch*," I accused.

He then kicked Nadine's body aside as if it was absolutely nothing.

I could not think straight, and all my mind was telling me to do was get revenge. We might not have known each other so intimately to be called true friends, but Nadine had not deserved this.

And Horkos deserved to *die*.

I unsheathed my other sword. No words could describe how desperately I wanted to slice him into ribbons at that moment. I felt absolute rage coursing through my veins as I channelled the anger like Thanatos had suggested. And the power manifested tenfold. My insides burned as though they were engulfed by fire; and then my swords were set ablaze —the white flame raging and flickering over the gleaming obsidian.

I inhaled sharply, before lunging at him.

The flamed obsidian blades clashed with Horkos' sickles as he blocked my attack. I pushed him back, absolutely seething.

"You'll pay for this, Horkos. I'm going to *kill* you!" I swore. I screamed so hard that I thought my vocal cords would break, and Horkos had the nerve to just stare back at me expressionlessly.

"Well, well. The rage of the gods of death," he quipped, pushing against me.

"I was not sure that you had it in you, but it will certainly make for an interesting fight —"

"You *monster*!" I cut him off, before overpowering him and making him fall to his knees as I knocked one of his sickles out of his hand with one of my swords. I blocked his path with a sword as he tried to reach for it, causing him to flinch back. The flames had burned him —though they had actually barely touched him.

"Your fire is hotter than I anticipated," he said carefully, nursing his fast reddening hand. "Which honestly, just further supports my case."

"You have *no* right to talk about my abilities!" I raised my voice, leaning down to him. "You just...*killed* one of my friends. There is nothing other than your spilled blood that will avenge that crime!"

"So is the way of war, half-blood," Horkos sneered, frowning in disappointment.

I roared; a sound so wild and raw, before swinging at him. He parried it with his other sickle effortlessly, holding my gaze. Challenging me. *Daring* me. I wavered for a moment. He pushed against me, and with my guard down, he managed to stand up again. My anger returned and took a step forward, insistent on regaining the upper hand.

"You know something," he said nonchalantly, with his cold and dead blue diamond eyes boring into mine, "Maybe it is your own fault your friend is dead. Perhaps it will teach you a lesson. That you should never drag the people you care about into situations like this. Her brother will definitely blame you for this —"

"She was *protecting* me!" I cried, pushing him back. My voice broke at the end as more tears streamed down my face. He skidded a few feet away, raising his eyebrows in surprise. "And it's all your fault that she's gone!"

I lunged forward, but he dodged. I continued to slice at him, but he kept blocking every strike, every attempt.

I growled in frustration —before glancing downwards.

His legs were completely exposed.

I swung one sword at his side, and he took the bait, allowing me to swing the other sword lower. He unwittingly stepped right into the path of the blade, and he let out a satisfying cry as it sliced his leg from the shin down clean *off*.

"…That is for stabbing my friend," I told him.

Smoke billowed from the burning wound, along with a fountain of golden ichor. My nostrils flared at the sight, and I felt a surge of accomplishment. Horkos dropped his sickle, fell and writhed in pain as I stepped closer.

The battle raged on around us, but all I could see was him, and his eyes suddenly desperate for mercy.

I kicked his sickle further out of his reach, before I bent down and grabbed him by his toga and yanked him up closer to me.

"I was thinking of giving you a quick death," I murmured, "but now I realise that would be too good for you."

"I…underestimated you, Savannah Green," he winced.

I scoffed. "That is not my name anymore. It's Savannah the Grim Reaper; the half-blood who's going to kill you," I said, before drawing back my fist and hooking his jaw.

He gasped, before turning to look at me again with a big and growing grin on his face. Luminescent golden blood dribbled down out of his nose and from his lips, which only made his smile look even more psychopathic. I snarled and punched him again, this time breaking his nose.

He fell over onto his side, and then started *laughing*. I frowned. I kicked him square in the ribs and heard a crack. He doubled up and even coughed up more blood, but he still kept laughing.

It was disturbing.

"What the hell is wrong with you?" I demanded, kicking him again, but at his spine. He rolled onto his back, clutching his stomach. I drew my sword and pointed it an inch away at his throat. The fire immediately started to burn his skin, making him whimper sharply.

"Savannah, wait!" Hera suddenly cried desperately, running up beside me. I momentarily turned my head to face her. She had her hands over her mouth and was shaking her head. "You shouldn't kill him."

"Why not?" I growled, glaring back down at Horkos. "He had no regard for

Nadine when he killed her. So, a life for a life, right?"

"But —"

"Do you know...the punishment...for killing a god?" Horkos then struggled. I hesitated. I had not really thought about it.

However, I then realised something. I would not be killing a deity if he was in fact unworthy of such a title. Everything which he had done up until that moment, had tarnished the names of his kind.

"...You are no god," I retorted flatly.

He actually paused and looked me dead in the eye, surprised. It was as though he were almost...human. Mortal. As if those words made him so.

"Go to Hell, where you belong," I ground out. Then I plunged and dragged my sword through his throat down to his stomach.

Having not realised that gods and mortals differed in souls, what I then witnessed startled me. The slash that my sword had made began to glow. I took a cautious step backwards, an ominous feeling setting in.

And I had been right to move, because a bright golden light then emitted from Horkos' body —before it suddenly exploded with the sound of a firecracker, into golden dust. A few Reapers and the gods seemed to pause in the middle of their battles to look over.

The force knocked me and Hera backwards and off of our feet. I grunted, before looking back to where Horkos had been. There was no trace of him besides a torn and bloody toga, and a pair of sandals. I glanced down at my sword and watched as a golden *III* glowed at the hilt.

I blinked rapidly, processing it for a moment. I scrambled to my feet and stumbled over, inspecting my handiwork. I had done it. I felt a little giddy with satisfaction and growing blood lust, but ultimately, I felt that part justice had been served for Nadine.

"What have you done?" Hera gasped as she shakily rose to her feet.

I gave her a blank look.

We had no opportunity to argue though, as a sudden *whoosh* went by my ear. I whipped around, before meeting the gaze of Artemis, who had her bow poised in my direction. I cursed and winced in realisation, reaching up to my ear and drawing back blood.

"…I missed," she clicked her tongue.

That was the exact same thing Horkos had said before.

"What the hell?" I snapped.

"You have killed Horkos, the god of oaths," she declared, her moonstone eyes cold and deadly and luminous, "so now I must kill you."

"No —what you need to do is to stop this senseless violence," Hera interjected. "Taking her life would mean nothing. And Horkos is not lost forever. You especially should know that."

Artemis hesitated, before slowly lowering her bow. "Maybe not taking her *life*," she began, glancing away suspiciously. "But a warning is definitely in order." She then shot an arrow before anyone could react.

A sharp, blazing pain suddenly erupted in my thigh. I cried out and dropped my swords, before falling to my knees. I screamed —mostly out of shock, but I had also never experienced such a level of pain. It was as though my leg was being burned, frostbitten and electrocuted all at once.

It was *excruciating*.

How much worse had it felt for Nadine?

"*Artemis*," Hera scolded.

"What? It won't kill her," Artemis scoffed. "I did not bring my lethal obsidian arrows to this. It was not worth it."

"Artemis," her brother Apollo then said in a low voice from where he was perched above us. "Do not let your emotions cloud your judgement. You would be no better than she is."

Both the hunting goddess and I growled at that, before the wound screamed again, searing with heat and pain.

"Besides," Apollo sighed, then jumped down and strode over to me. The agony flashed away for just a moment as my eyes travelled the length of the god. He was taller than I realised; his broad frame corded with muscles of iron. If any god represented the Greek marble statue standard, it was him. "She is more useful

425

in good health."

I struggled to look up into his sunstone eyes, but I only hissed as I had finally managed to control my voice. Then I paused and stared. He was unnaturally good looking. I was not into beards but his was neatly trimmed and somewhat smouldering, almost shimmering against his golden bronzed skin. He frowned down at me, so I spitefully glared back, shrinking away. He then looked down at my thigh. He carefully grabbed hold of the arrow. My eyes widened at the realisation of what he might do. He suddenly yanked the arrow out, making me cry out again. Red and silver blood flowed down my leg. He then tossed the arrow aside and waved his hand over the wound. Light shone from his palm and a sudden warmth overwhelmed the pain.

I inhaled sharply and gasped as the wound closed itself up and healed, without a trace of blood on my skin. Deep crimson lingered on my jeans though, as did the ripped tear.

Apollo raised a smug eyebrow as I averted my gaze, feeling the temperature on my face rising. "…Thanks," I murmured begrudgingly.

"You're welcome," he quipped, then held out his hand. I stared at it distastefully, before turning further away from him. "…I understand why you would be hesitant, but I can assure you that I have no intention of harming you, Savannah Green."

I sneered, before getting up on my own. I then picked my swords back up and sheathed them, before folding my arms and shifting my weight onto one leg. I was not about to indulge this male's deluded charms.

"She's adorable," Apollo then smirked, turning to his sister. "I like her." He nodded thoughtfully in approval.

"Ew," said Artemis.

"Hey!" Thanatos' voice then called from behind us. We turned to see him and Hades running towards us. The god of death stopped beside me and pulled on my arm, much like a scolding guardian. "Get away from her," he told the Olympians.

He drew out his scythe in front of us in a protective arc. My father glared at the other gods, while unconsciously rubbing his wrists.

"What have you done to my daughter?" Hades seethed.

"Nothing," Hera said innocently.

"Nothing indeed. You are rather late," Artemis scoffed. "We are no longer trying to kill her."

"Don't you mean that *you* are no longer trying to kill her?" Apollo corrected, giving his sister a look.

"Well, at least *I'm* not flirting with her," she shot back.

Apollo gave a sheepish grin in his defence.

Hades' eyes shone a brighter, sinister shade of jasper as he clenched his fists.

"Excuse me?" Death growled, glaring at the god of light. "You had better back off, Pretty Boy."

The golden Olympian raised both hands in surrender.

"*Thanatos*," I grumbled, feebly slapping his arm.

Of all the brotherly things which he could start doing, I had hoped this would not be one of them.

"There is no time for this," Hera swiftly pointed out. "We need to put a stop to all of *that*. I think we can —"

"Actually, I believe that Poseidon just beat us to it," Artemis breathed, looking skywards. We followed her gaze and stilled.

A giant wall of frigid water was slowly moving over the skyscrapers towards us. Screams rang out as most of the fighting came to an abrupt stop.

"…Always so *dramatic*," Apollo muttered.

"Everyone, to the chariots —quickly," Hera ordered, picking up her skirts and running. We scattered as everyone else took cover. Artemis took off in hers with Hera and Hades, as Thanatos and I got into Apollo's. We took off and flew up over the wave to a safe distance, but I then realised how I had just left a multitude of people on the ground.

"Thanatos," I quipped worriedly, "can Grim Reapers drown?"

"No," he answered. "But that, unfortunately, is not the only way to die in this situation. They could be crushed beyond healing."

"What?" I cried. "Are you telling me I'm up here while everyone who risked

427

their life for me is down there?"

I then put my leg up over the edge of the chariot. "I have to go back and protect as many of them as I can!"

"Savannah, no." Thanatos pulled me back in. "If you jump from this height, you will be of no help to *anyone*. This is all about you. Their sacrifice will be for nothing if you too were to perish."

I hesitated and looked up at him. He was right. And I hated it.

I glanced at Apollo and met his gaze. His eyes smouldered, a fire simmering in them; and a curious unnerving shiver ran down my spine. For a fleeting moment, the wave disappeared and the cityscape blurred. No battle had raged. Nothing but those golden slithers of sun anchored me to the Earth.

Then Apollo suddenly turned, his face solemn, and the spell dissipated.

I started, glancing back down at the ground. The impending doom grounded itself once more. *Focus*, I urged. Was there truly nothing that I could do?

I then looked down at my hands. *Wait a moment.*

I moved to push my way to the front of the chariot. "I'm going to get as close as I can to the wave," I declared.

Death did a double take.

"I know what I'm doing," I insisted. "…I think."

I then steered downwards sharply, causing us to crash into the chariot's one side.

"*Savannah*," Hades cried, noticing our chariot falling away.

"Trust me," I called back.

I came to a halt in front of the wave, feeling far more intimidated. Raging waters surged before me as solid as a concrete wall.

But I had to swallow my apprehension. I raised both of my hands out in front of me and took a deep breath. I summoned fire, and the flames flickered to life on my palms. I concentrated harder and willed the flames to lengthen.

The white fire began to grow.

"…Are you trying to do what I think you are trying to do?" Thanatos asked suspiciously.

"Fire cancels out water. I'm going to turn as much of that as I can into steam,"

I confirmed.

"That is a great effort theoretically," Apollo then spoke up, "but I fear that your power alone is not enough."

I faltered.

I looked down to where the fire was hitting the water —and barely doing anything. I cursed but did not stop shooting fire. "…What else am I supposed to do?" I said through my teeth, willing the fire to increase.

"Savannah, if you go on any longer, you are going to burn your skin off," my half-brother then warned me. Genuine concern filled that brilliant bronze.

I frowned, before realising that my powers were in fact causing my skin to blister and redden. I hissed but I did not let up.

I have to endure the pain.

"Oi. You there!" a gruff voice then thundered. We looked up to see the god Poseidon himself, clad in a sea-green toga that only covered him from the waist down; yielding a golden and emerald trident.

"What'd ya think yer doin'?" He then frowned thoughtfully. "…Or at least, tryin' to do?"

He had the twang of an old-timey pirate.

"I'm trying to stop your doomsday device," I growled at him. "Everyone will be crushed to death if you don't do something to stop this."

"Oh, it ain't my intention to kill anyone, girl," Poseidon drawled. "I just be tryin' to stop the fightin'."

"You don't have to do that with a thousand-foot wave!" I reasoned.

"Well, shoutin' didn't help."

"Just call it off, you stubborn old seahorse," Thanatos then snapped.

"Fine, *fine*," Poseidon grumbled. "There ain't no need for name callin'." He then paused. "…But ya better stop the fightin' afterwards."

"We will," I swore. Or I would die trying.

The god of the sea turned back to the looming wave. He raised his trident, and with the motion, he split the liquid wall into three smaller spheres. He then waved the ornate trident from side to side, and the bodies of water swirled high into the

429

sky, before bursting and falling like heavy rain. We were once again drenched, but it helped to finally extinguish my flames —just as I stumbled backwards into Thanatos out of exhaustion.

He had been right about burning my hands. The water stung but ultimately soothed my hardened palms, creating steam.

It was a long, breathless pause before the survivors below began emerging from where they had hidden. For a moment since the battle had begun, everything was still. Blood was washed away by the water, but the bodies remained. I wondered for how long they would lay there.

Apollo then took the reins and flew us back down to the ground. I jumped out immediately, running towards a tall dark-haired Reaper and a squawking Phoenix.

"*Søren*," I gasped, launching myself at him in a hug. Phee-Phee shone brightly in surprise as Søren staggered beneath my weight. Then his arms wrapped around me in turn and he chuckled weakly. "You're alive!" I breathed.

"Yeah. But be careful," he begged, gesturing to his wounded arm. "Artemis got me with one of her arrows."

I grumbled. "Me too."

"But you look fine," he frowned, before his gaze landed on my hands. "...Except for your crispy palms."

Phee-Phee then nuzzled against my leg affectionately. I bent down and gently stroked him, though my skin stung horribly; the burns screaming at the touch of fire. "Apollo healed me," I answered Søren.

He raised an eyebrow at that.

"Oh, you survived," Chainsaw Guy then remarked as he came up to us, before Søren could say anything in response to me. "Great."

He hooked an arm around the older Reaper, who was evidently too tired to remove it, because he did not squirm away. The former had a few cuts on his face and a slight limp but otherwise he looked fine.

"Right back at you," I deadpanned, straightening up. Phee-Phee squawked at him with equal dislike.

"What's your damage, Melchior?" Søren scoffed, turning his head to eye

Chainsaw Guy's injuries.

"Oh, I got into a fight with Ares because of what happened with Kyle," he explained rather proudly. "He blamed me for not doing anything to stop him, and I guess I understood why. I now know how Savannah felt."

I nodded solemnly.

He then paused, as a maniac grin spread across his face. "…He did admit that my chainsaw was cool though."

"Oh wow," I mocked. "Achievement unlocked."

Chainsaw Guy glared at me. "Well, sorry that *some* of us aren't that special to have all of the gods wanting our heads."

"Oh, stop it you two," Søren sighed heavily. "The battle is over. Can we just celebrate that?"

I was about to say something more when I spotted Lewis running around to the other Grim Reapers; helping them up and telling them that everything was all right. A sharp stab of pain punctured my chest as I bit my lip, fighting back tears. How could we dare to celebrate anything?

"Hey guys," I whispered. "I…I'll be right back."

CHAPTER 48

SAVANNAH

I THINK THAT it would be easier to jump into a vat of acid than to tell someone that their sister had jumped into the path of a psychopath's sickle for you. Of course, that alternative could not really do much in terms of killing a Grim Reaper. But it would still hurt less than the pain I was feeling.

As I was walking over to Lewis, I was trying hard not to cry. The heavy lump that formed in one's throat when they were on the verge of tears was not something that I should have been feeling.

Yet there it was, suffocating and restricting my empty lungs. With every step I took, the more unsteady I became. Phee-Phee walked beside me but even he could not comfort me.

Nadine had given her life for me; for my cause.

Her death had not been in vain. But telling the people whom she had left behind...they might not see it that way.

Lewis was smiling, innocently oblivious to the impending development; with his adorable dimples and curly brown hair. I could not help but picture how I was about to shatter that into pieces with one sentence.

How can I dare to do that to him—

—Oh my gods, I cannot do this.

I was about to stop and turn back around like a complete coward when he spotted me and called out my name. I froze.

"…*Shit*," I hissed, and then tried to look a little more presentable, but I still could not shake the guilt.

"Hey…" I breathed, giving a small wave.

"Hey. Hello to you too, Mr. Phoenix," he said to Phee-Phee. Then he frowned and glanced around uncertainly. "Oh, have any of you seen Nadine anywhere? I've been asking around and no one seems to know," he chuckled softly, scratching the back of his neck. He had a deep bleeding cut along his bottom lip, which made me start in alarm.

"Oh —I did that, actually," he admitted sheepishly, holding up one of his nunchucks. Blood glistened at the end of the curved blade. "I ran into Hermes. He didn't do much though —only a quick stab," he then gestured to his side, where there was a dark red patch.

"Wait, it wasn't an obsidian weapon?" I checked, looking closer at the wound. It seemed to be healing fairly normally. Thank goodness —Hermes really had been trying to be as least deadly as he could.

"No, I think that it was regular iron," he confirmed, sighing. Then he shook his head, refocusing and looking at me intently. "…So, about Nadine. Do you know where she is?"

I flinched, and then glanced away. He had done an effective job at distracting me until just then. Now I could not stall any longer. I wondered where to start — and more tears consequently spilled. I looked up at Lewis and watched his smile fall. It made me feel worse, and my shoulders jerked up as I then let out sob.

"Savannah…what's wrong?" he asked nervously.

I shook my head, my vision blurring.

"Why are you crying?"

My crying then suddenly became audible, and I rushed forward and hugged him fiercely. He staggered backwards in surprise, but then he wrapped his arms around me uncertainly. I continued crying, letting out all of the emotion which I had been suppressing. It was such a sudden release that I wondered if I had ever let the fact sink in before.

Lewis patted my back comfortingly, but I knew that I could not leave him guessing —though he probably now had an idea.

"Lewis," I sniffed, withdrawing. "I'm *so* sorry."

"For...what?" he asked, frowning softly.

"It...it was an accident," I assured. "It should've been me, I know that, but she just jumped in front of it —Lewis, I need you to know..."

I then trailed off as he did not interrupt me in any way. Was he simply processing? "...Lewis?" I asked again.

He was completely still.

He stared at me blankly, and his eyes looked completely empty. It was as though someone had taken his soul. I shook him gently, but he still did not respond. It began to frighten me.

"Lewis...please, there wasn't anything that I could do," I went on. "It happened so fast, and I was busy with Hera. Horkos came up from behind me and he had obsidian plated sickles —"

"No," he finally said; in the quietest and emptiest whisper. I felt all and no emotion in its singular syllable. "...No way," Lewis said a little louder, clenching his fists. I stiffened. He was becoming angry. "She's not...she can't have...She *wouldn't*. She wouldn't *do* this to me."

I could see a layer of tears glistening in his eyes, but none of them fell. It made me wince, as a sudden sharp pain sliced through my chest.

"I'm *sorry*," I whispered.

He did not respond. His expression slowly became distant and unreadable. As though the Lewis I had gotten to know was disappearing.

"She gave her life for you," he eventually stated flatly, unblinking. I pressed my lips into a line and averted my gaze. Then I nodded slowly. "...She had promised to do that for me," he murmured.

I blinked. "Lewis, I would be *more* than willing —"

"Don't," he suddenly snapped in a much firmer tone, grabbing my arms and forcefully shoving me away from him. "Just...*don't*, Savannah."

He looked at me with such wretched anguish that it almost felt as though *I* had been the one who had killed Nadine.

434

"I don't need nor want whatever it is that you're trying to do," he deadpanned. "So, don't even."

"...Okay," I said shakily. I could not force it upon him. "But...at least hear my apology," I asked earnestly.

He then scoffed. "You know —it's actually kind of funny," he said bitterly. "I always knew this day would come —a day when she would be gone. When it happened the first time, it wasn't that bad because we were together. I guess I was naïve. Because now...it's as if I'm being forced to live on without her, as mortality intended."

"Aw, Lewis —"

"Make this count," he cut me off, narrowing his eyes. I beheld the roaring requiem within that blue. "At least promise me that. Do not let her death —her *sacrifice*," he amended quickly, "...be for nothing."

I nodded slowly, before glancing aside. I could not bear to face him. He had such a cold and hollow look; an expression that did not suit him. I had not anticipated this kind of reaction. I knew that I was fairly terrible at delivering bad news. I was not any better at dealing with it either. I could not compare my pain to the pain he was experiencing.

"Hey," Abigail made me jump as she suddenly came up to us.

Her jacket and jeans were frayed and tattered, her hair loose and wild; and she had torn off the hem of her t-shirt to wrap around her wounded arm in a crude bandage, that was now stained red.

"Zeus wants to talk to everyone..."

She paused as she then read the situation. Solemnity replaced her hardened displeasure when she saw our faces.

"Give us a minute," I whispered.

She nodded curtly, before walking off.

Lewis' clear aquamarine eyes turned to slits as I looked back at him. "What do we need a minute for?" he commented nonchalantly. "I have nothing more to say to you."

Then he turned to walk after Abigail.

I could not move. I was utterly shaken. Phee-Phee cooed and brushed against my leg but it made me want to crumble to dust.

Perhaps I had expected Lewis to be in denial. Or I had wanted him to confide in me and cry on my shoulder.

But whatever reaction I had selfishly thought he would have had, did not compare to the sudden cold change in character. Or perhaps, it shook me more to think that that part of him might have always been there.

✠

Zeus was on his feet again —the wound on his leg having ceased to bleed, though he had a slight limp. The colour had understandably drained from his face, and he was looking grave as he tried to be his usual *Lord Zeus*.

He regarded us wearily along with all of the damage we had caused. So few —there were far too few Reapers standing with me now. The bodies of those who had lost their souls had been blessed by Thanatos and were burning away into mist by his magic. Ice blue frost and snow were the only signs that the *Págos* had even been there and fought.

And I tried not to stare, tried not to remember that I knew none of their names —but I knew that I would never forget a single one of them.

"Poseidon," the god of lightning started, "We are going to have a few words when we get back to Olympus."

Poseidon grumbled.

Hera marched to her husband's side and took his arm. "Are you all right, Zeus?" she asked. "Your injuries do not seem too severe, though. I can go and get some *ambrosia* if it is urgent."

"I will live," he answered gruffly. "Right now, we need to worry about what we are going do about this *mess*."

"And what about Savannah?" Hades asked.

The Lord of the skies did not look all too willing to address me.

He sighed and tilted his head from side to side. "…Your courage did not turn out to be completely useless," he admitted. "You even helped me see that change is in order. However, you did kill a god. By law, you should be killed as well," he pointed out. I rubbed my arm self-consciously as everyone who had not known gasped and gaped at me. "But technically, you also killed the law. And you did it in retaliation. And I can understand that rage."

I raised my eyebrows.

"Can we please stop talking about it like that?" Artemis grumbled, glaring at me in particular. "As though he is completely gone forever. Because he is not," she said darkly.

"Well, he is not here right now," Hades said dryly. "In fact, I can tell you *exactly* where he is —"

"If you dare to say it, I will not hesitate to shoot you in the eye," she threatened, waving her bow for emphasis.

"*Shut* it, you two," Zeus snapped, glaring at them.

The rest of us looked on in amusement as soft thunder rolled across the sky. Both of the gods wavered, before reluctantly backing down.

"Savannah," Hera then addressed me. "You must understand that we are not letting you get away with anything —rather, there is no point in punishing you properly for a crime that momentarily does not classify as one," she clarified. "Given the help that you offered me, I found it fitting that you should be given a less severe penalty."

I blinked, before nodding in understanding. I supposed that the queen of the gods and I could now be considered even.

"So," Zeus went on, "I have given some thought to a different form of a way to reprimand you."

I paused. But I should not be complaining —the gods were not going to kill me after all. But if so, then what exactly did the almighty Zeus have in mind as an alternative punishment?

"…To make you a god."

There was deathly silence.

My eyes widened and I nearly choked.

He did not repeat himself. He did not need to.

"Zeus," Hades clipped his brother's name. "What do you think you are doing? If this is some form of a practical joke —"

"Why would I joke about this?" the god asked, taken aback. "It is not exactly a gift, mind you. As a Grim Reaper you can still have a degree of mortality. But if I make you a goddess, you will be cursed with *im*mortality."

"Cursed," Hades echoed, clenching his jaw.

I swallowed nervously.

"Zeus, you have to tell her the rest." Hera then nudged him. "Your reasoning doesn't sound too enticing right now."

"Oh," he quipped, nodding importantly. "Right. I was thinking —there is no god of half-bloods. What we propose is that you can put your idea into practice and look out for the half-bloods of the world. You will train them, teach them to abide by divine and mundane law, and how to master their abilities. You should know that if a case fails, it will be your responsibility to do what has to be done."

"You're actually willing to take my offer seriously?"

"Well, yes," he said as though it were obvious.

Though I knew what his last point meant. *I* would have to be the one to execute them. *No*, I decided. *It would never come to that.*

I closed my agape mouth and glanced at those who had fought by my side. They did not look too sure. I looked up at Hades. He was frowning at the ground now, deep in thought. Thanatos was looking disinterested, as usual —which was strange, because I would have thought that he would be very much against the idea of having me around forever. My gaze slid to Abigail and Chainsaw Guy.

The blonde raised an eyebrow, which probably meant that she did not have an opinion; or that I should not be asking for one from her. Chainsaw Guy simply shrugged, which was not a surprise.

I then glanced at Lewis.

He was twirling one of his nunchucks thoughtfully, glaring at his feet. He looked up and met my gaze. He did not look away in a huff. He stared right back at me; completely deadpan. I could not blame him for the way he was feeling. I bit my lip as I felt the sting of tears.

The news had not had time yet to sink in.

I swallowed hard and then turned to look at Søren. His expression made me waver. I could see the apprehension in his eyes. He did not need to say a word to tell me not to trust the gods. I knew that well —it was not as though they had given us a reason to trust them in the past.

"It is not an easy course to take," Hera then said.

"There will be things to leave behind," Zeus sighed.

"But not your friends. Grim Reapers are essentially immortal," Artemis then murmured. "So, where is the issue?"

I paused and realised what she was saying. I would not outlive any of the people I knew —except for my mother. Oh *gods* —what would Phoebe think about this? But it was not as though she could prevent it. At least eternity would not be lonely with most of my family already being gods.

"…Nothing is undying," I finally said, stepping forward. "Everything fades eventually. But this isn't it. It's just the beginning. I have an opportunity to make a big difference in the world. I…I want to shoulder that responsibility. I want to be there when no one else is."

"Forever is a long time," Thanatos then sighed. "And half-blood gods will keep popping up everywhere."

And whose fault would that be?

"I know," I quipped, sticking my nose up. "But I really want to offer the support that so many others didn't receive. I want to stand for something. That's all this was about," I said earnestly. "Fighting for lives like mine."

Grim Reapers and gods alike murmured uncertainly, but no one offered any further arguments.

"*I* certainly have no objections," Apollo smirked, which was followed by a swift jab in his side from Artemis.

"All right. Fine," I said quickly in an effort not to let my voice break. I straightened my spine, before walking forward and facing the god of the skies. "…I accept my punishment," I declared.

439

I glanced back at Søren out of the corner of my eye. He was frowning at his boots. I looked away, unable to deal with the feeling of guilt. I knew what turning into a god would mean. I would have to say goodbye to him one day. But I could not think about that right then.

"Let the ceremony preparations commence," Hera declared, raising her arms and waving them in a beckoning manner. "We shall host it on Mount Olympus."

"Before any of that," Zeus then cut in, "We need to clean up down here. We caused much of the destruction —it is only right that we must help with major repairs."

"But if we fix anythin', the mortals may get suspicious," Poseidon rightly pointed out, much to everyone's relief. "As far as they know, it be a tsunami that tore through New York."

Zeus looked on wearily. "…Right."

Everyone then dispersed, gathering their weapons and things.

I walked around amongst them, earnestly thanking all of the Grim Reapers who were left and accepting half-hearted congratulations. Most of them would be going to rest in their apartments —I was allowed to invite only my friends to the Rebirth ceremony. I decided that would mean Søren and Lewis.

But then I felt as though I owed Chainsaw Guy and Abigail a form of gratitude for risking their lives, so I extended the invitation. They were genuinely surprised —though even more surprisingly, they accepted.

As for the family I had around; Hades' frown did not disappear, and Thanatos had developed a scowl.

"Savannah," Hades sighed. I held my breath in trepidation. But there was no resentment in his eyes. "I know that it's a punishment, but…I am actually elated that you're alive. This has never happened before —a half-blood being granted the title of a god. But we need it. We need you." He then put his hands on my shoulders, a smile tugging at his lips.

I smiled up at him weakly.

"I can't believe I have to put up with you forever," was the start of Thanatos welcoming speech. "…Is that one of my Phoenixes?"

He eyed Phee-Phee suspiciously.

"He's mine now," I told him proudly, stroking Phee-Phee's back as he perched on a branch beside me. "And what do you mean by '*put up with me*'?"

"Uh, just that?" Thanatos scoffed. "You are insufferable. Yes, we may be siblings, but siblings fight all the time, don't they?"

"Exactly —just look at mine," Hades quipped.

"But I thought we bonded back there," I scoffed, lightly punching Thanatos' shoulder. "You even saved my life."

"Savannah," he then said seriously, grabbing me by the shoulders. "Now that I know you, I would *die* for you."

I blinked, slightly taken aback.

"But, I would also want kill you. It's a contradictory notion," he smirked.

I snorted. "Feeling's mutual," I returned, removing his hands.

Phee-Phee and I then went off to offer our aid, because I wanted to keep myself occupied. I *needed* a distraction. I had the feeling that if I just stood around and took it all in, everything would hit me at once and I would go into shock and I would never be able to move again.

I knew that it was not good for me —but there was too much that had happened in the last few hours.

Søren then caught up with me as I was helping someone carry a giant sledgehammer inside the apartment building.

"Hey," he said. "Are you...okay?"

"Peachy," I deadpanned, then waving the other Reaper off.

Søren frowned, unamused by my sarcasm.

"How are you really?" he asked gently.

I sighed and ran a hand through my hair. "Honestly, I'm a little out of it. I feel like everything is moving so fast. And I know it's not exactly a choice, and that my immortality is going to be a good thing in the long run; but I can't help feeling like I'm standing under another one of Poseidon's waves."

"That's understandable," he quipped. "But look, I'll be around as long as I can. I'm practically immortal too."

"True," I admitted, smiling.

Then my gaze drifted and caught sight of Lewis across the street. He held my gaze for a moment, before turning away and waking off.

I sighed in defeat and rubbed my arms.

"Hey, where is Lewis going?" Søren asked. "Isn't he going to stay for the ceremony?"

I stiffened, realising that I had gotten my hopes far too high when I expected him to stay for such a thing.

Søren softened, looking concerned. "And...where's —"

"*Don't*," I cut him off quickly. "Don't...say it."

He frowned, a little offended.

"It's just..." I struggled. "Nadine...she's gone."

He stiffened, then knowing why Lewis was leaving. "*Oh.*"

"She...died for me," I rasped.

He flinched as I kicked at the ground, pressing my lips into a line.

"I think...I think it's best to leave Lewis alone and let him grieve," I murmured, watching his retreating figure.

I hoped that he would be all right, wherever he would be going.

CHAPTER 49

SAVANNAH

I DID NOT recognise the girl staring back at me in the floor-to-ceiling gilt mirrors. She had gold flecks around her eyes and long, sooty eyelashes. Her golden irises sparkled, and her curled hair flowed down to below her shoulders. She wore a deep crimson floor-length gown; designed to be a modern twist on the ancient Greek toga. The slightly revealing two-piece empire waist was fitted with golden ribbons, matching the gold cuffs above her elbows which secured a pale red gossamer cape that flowed into a train behind her. Digging into her head, was a shining golden laurel wreath; like those of the Olympians. On her feet, were intricate black sandals.

She looked devastating —a princess of death indeed. Like she was ready to be a goddess; capable of shouldering that honour.

I knew that the girl was me, but I could not figure out why I was not feeling comfortable in my own skin.

The lace scratched my skin and hugged like a leotard that was a size too big; and the netted skirts felt stiff.

This is simply a formality, I assured my nerves.

I placed my hand over my chest, where a necklace would usually be. It was the first time that I had taken it off for an occasion such as this. I would wear it again, but no longer for the reason I had before.

"…I hope this isn't like a wedding, where it's bad luck to see the bride before the ceremony. In which case, sorry —I asked Hades where you were and I was directed here," a voice said from the doorway.

I turned around to face Søren.

He was all cleaned up —but he was still sporting his usual black jeans, leather jacket and navy blue sweater.

"What, you're not even going to dress up a little for this?" I chuckled, stepping off of the platform and walking over to him. "I expect you to step your game if and when I get married. I can't have my best man looking like he just stepped out of a slasher movie."

"I can't be the bride's best man," Søren pointed out. "And don't even think about making me your maid of honour. Besides —I *am* dressed up," he scoffed. "I'm wearing my best jacket," he bragged, popping the collar, "*and* my jeans without holes."

"Wow," I deadpanned. "Now I totally see it."

He chuckled in amusement, before sighing and reaching behind his back and handing me a beautiful yellow chrysanthemum.

My brows rose.

"This is for you," he said. "Don't think too much about it —it's more of a thank you gift than a present."

I had not spared a single thought to it.

"…Aw," I cooed teasingly, twirling the flower between my fingers. "That's so sweet. You remembered my favourite flower."

"Yeah," he murmured, averting his eyes and going slightly pink. "Anyway, like I said —*thank you gift*."

"Sure," I smiled.

"By the way. You look really…well, you look like a goddess," he then said as a matter of fact. I blushed slightly and lifted the skirts.

"I know. But I'm not sure how I feel about it."

"Too much?" he guessed.

"No…" I frowned. "Okay, maybe a little," I then admitted, slumping my shoulders. "I don't know, Søren —I'm just feeling so anxious."

"That's completely understandable," he assured me, putting a hand on my shoulder. "Look, this *is* a big deal. You shouldn't downplay it. But you're not going into it alone."

He offered me a smile. I huffed, but then smiled back.

"Thanks," I told him.

"No problem. Now, let me get to the throne room before I'm told that I really shouldn't be here," he said quickly, turning back towards the door. "And don't stress about it…you'll be fine."

I nodded and waved him off, but I wavered when he disappeared around the corner. '*Don't stress about it*'?

That was easy for him to say. I was not even sure about the details of the ceremony. What exactly would they do? Would the process hurt?

I had all these questions which I had conveniently not bothered to ask beforehand that were now overflowing. I took a deep breath and exhaled.

One small step at a time, I internally encouraged.

"Miss Savannah?" a more feminine voice then said from the door. "The ceremony is set to start soon. Please allow me to escort you to the throne room."

I turned to see a Dryad floating towards me. The first thing that I noticed was that her eyes were just a solid mass of green void of irises, that were outlined with long yellow lashes and small pointed spines. There were more spines all over her —on her arms and legs, making her look like more of a sea urchin than a nymph. A shower of mist and leaves swirled around her as she gently touched down onto the marble floor, making her knee length dress flare upwards. Her feet were dainty and wrapped in vines, tinging some of her pale yellow-ish skin a shade of green. Her hair was a bouquet of sticks growing out of her head from a thick vine flower crown blossoming with wildflowers. I had never seen a nymph before, so I stared in awe as she approached and stood three heads taller than me.

"I am Sych," she smiled.

"Oh. I did not realise that Dryads could get sick," I frowned. Then I started to wonder why she was working in the first place if she was sick.

She laughed softly; the sound like cool Spring. "No, my *name* is Sych," she said. "I am a sycamore tree spirit."

I flushed, feeling silly. I apologised very self-consciously, but she told me to think nothing of it.

"You seem ready now," she then said, glancing down. Her eyes then narrowed in on my chrysanthemum. "…Was that a gift?"

"Yes," I murmured. "I thought about putting it somewhere on my outfit, but I have no idea where," I sighed, wishing that I had pockets.

"Oh, I can help if you would like," Sych offered. She held out her hand. I hesitantly pressed the flower into her palm. She took a step back as it then disintegrated in her hand, before she waved her hands at my gown. I looked on nervously as a green mist enveloped me. I could not tell what she had done until the magic had dispersed. I gasped as I looked down at beautiful charcoal impressions of chrysanthemums and leaves now painting the entire ensemble. I twirled around in admiration.

"Does it please you, Miss?" Sych asked.

"Are you kidding?" I breathed, suddenly darting forward and grabbing her in a hug. "It's nothing like I imagined. It's absolutely perfect!"

"Oh," Sych said unenthusiastically as I then let her go. She moved backwards rapidly and flushed a dark shade of green, attempting to hide it with her hand. "…It was no trouble, Miss."

"What is the matter?" I asked, immediately picking up on her body language. "I love what you did."

"Well," she mumbled. "I should never be embraced," she confessed. "The goddess in charge of the gardens, Lady Aphrodite, instructs that personal space is imperative, and that we refrain from touching or being too friendly with our superiors."

"Seriously?" I deadpanned. "That is the reason?"

"Yes, Miss."

"You don't have to call me that."

"Yes, I do, Miss —it is the one rule that I cannot break."

I frowned. I was finding that all very unfair. Her expression gave little away —

her features were so soft and rounded and her eyes were so vacant that it was difficult to decipher what she was thinking.

"...Do you enjoy your work?" I asked carefully.

Sych paused. "No one has ever asked me that," she murmured. "...I cannot say that I find grievances in any task that I perform. I have grown used to everything. This is all I know. What else is there?"

"Oh Sych," I softened. "There's so *much* more out there. And I'm not saying work shouldn't be done. I know that you are a tree spirit, but you should not have to be confined like a tree."

"But I cannot leave," she informed me like it was as a matter of fact. "I am a palace garden Dryad. And my place is here."

I frowned. "Are you even allowed to stay for the ceremony?"

She shook her head slowly. I looked at her sympathetically. I knew there were rules attached to Mount Olympus and how things ran, but I still could not help feeling horribly undeserving. Simply because of what ran through my veins I was automatically entitled to a high status; completely leaving those without godly anointing below. It did not feel right to me.

I wanted to do something for Sych.

She continued to stare at me, that dark green tinting her cheeks again.

I tilted my head to the side curiously. "What is it?" I asked.

She glanced elsewhere. "Nothing. You are very beautiful."

I blinked. It then made sense to me —her actions. My own cheeks heated. No female had ever called me beautiful. I was unsure of how to react, and of what to say. Sych was beautiful, there was no question about it.

However, I was not quite that way inclined.

"...Well, let's head to the throne room," I suggested stiffly. "I can't keep everybody waiting."

"Yes, Miss," she said curtly, turning towards the door. She rose up from the floor and then floated ahead of me. I felt slightly guilty for my unease, but she thankfully paid it no mind. I followed her out of the room, the sound of my heels clacking on marble echoing in the halls. I had my first chance to properly take it all in. But the further the walked the more I realised why Hades hated it. He was right; it was rather blinding and ornate.

When we finally reached the throne room I hesitated, the feeling of dread seeping through me. I gulped, trying to maintain my composure.

The doors were opened, and the throne room was revealed. A set of pews had been set up with an aisle in the middle like a chapel. In front of them, all twelve of the gold thrones were filled, and were regular human size. A makeshift iron throne sat at the foot of Zeus' —and Hades was the one sitting in it.

I almost snorted.

I had not known that the thrones could be adjusted to accommodate the gods' varying forms and sizes.

The Olympians were dressed in long cream togas and silver sandals, with golden laurel wreathes atop their heads. They all looked deathly serious, and I nearly bolted out back to the hallway as I reminded myself that this was in fact a punishment and not a reward.

My invited guests turned back to look at me as I walked forward. They were also stony faced, but not in an intimidating way like the gods. Søren and Thanatos offered me smiles, which settled my nerves. I then stood before the semicircle of thrones, just as Hera rose to her feet.

"Presenting the half-blood Savannah, daughter of Hades," Sych introduced me, standing to the side.

Hera nodded, prompting the nymph to turn around and head for the doors to leave. I paused, before calling out to her. Sych stopped and turned back to face me. She looked confused. I walked back to her, ignoring the whispers, and stopped as she touched down onto the floor.

"You are hereby invited to stay, as a guest," I told her. Everyone gasped, not only the Dryad.

"Is such a thing…allowed?" Dionysus hissed.

"This girl really *is* something else…" Apollo smirked.

"Shut it, Apollo," Artemis growled.

"This is not a normal ceremony," Lady Aphrodite herself whispered. "The rules cannot be bent just for her."

"She is allowed if she's a friend," I spoke up. Eyebrows were raised at my audacity. "So, I'm inviting her."

Uncertainty ensued, and Sych started to look fearful of her very life. I frowned in worry. I knew full well that Aphrodite would not hesitate to cut her tree down for something like this.

"The Dryad may attend, if the half-blood wishes," Hera eventually raised her voice above the hushed discussion, silencing the room. "So long as we may finally *proceed*."

Sych looked down at me curiously. "Are you sure that you wish for me to be here, Miss?" she asked.

"Yes."

She looked surprised, but then walked over to the congregation of invited guests and sat there shyly as she endured the stares.

I then made my way back to Hera and mirrored her raised eyebrows. She sighed, but held out her hands. A thick leather bound golden book materialised between them. She opened it to the middle as she cleared her throat.

"Gathered Olympians and guests," she began. "Welcome to a Rebirth Ceremony. This ceremony will be for half-blood Savannah, daughter of Hades. She will be transformed into a goddess —the goddess of half-bloods. Athena, please come forward to write her human name on her page."

The goddess of wisdom rose from her throne and summoned a fountain pen. Though instead of writing in the book, she turned and beckoned me over. I glanced at Hera, and she nodded in agreement. I walked forward uncertainly and stood before them. Athena took my hand, before she suddenly slashed the sharp pen's tip across my palm. I winced, staring at the line of silver and red blood that appeared in my skin.

Athena dipped the pen in my blood, and then wrote my name on the page that Hera was holding out to her. The letters glowed on the shimmering silk-like paper, before turning into completely silver ink.

"And now, Apollo —the cordial please," Hera called, turning to the other side of the semicircle.

The god stood and a small crystal bottle appeared in his hand.

"This is a sacred potion used only at these ceremonies; made by mixing ambrosia and ichor in a certain ratio. It is not possible to be made by anyone who attempts to imitate it," Hera said firmly.

Apollo popped off the cork and presented it to me. Our eyes met, and that shiver tingled my spine again. The gazing lasted too long to be casual; the glint in his bright irises too hypnotic.

I barely heard her voice as Hera then said, "Drink."

I managed to tear my gaze from Apollo's in order to gawk at the queen of the gods. Did she really mean for me to drink god blood?

I narrowed my eyes at the caramel coloured liquid sceptically, but took it from Apollo's hand. The skin of our fingers brushed, and I could have sworn that the god of light also tensed at the touch.

I then took a cautious sip. It tasted like mud. I retched, sticking out my tongue. Hera raised an unamused eyebrow, making me cower self-consciously. I promptly stomached half of what was in the cordial, before handing it back to Apollo.

There was an anxious stretch of silence from the onlookers.

A tingling sensation then began to spread through my limbs. Stray tendrils of golden mist circled my feet and fluttered along the hem of my gown, as well as beneath my hair as it curled higher; enveloping me. When it dissipated, my veins popped, before being flooded by a soothing warmth —reflecting the returning mortal state my body temperature. I then gasped, starved of air, before my stomach grumbled. I flushed, feeling a stab of hunger.

And then…the drum of a heartbeat.

"Athena," Hera then addressed her again.

The younger goddess took my other hand and cut into my palm with her pen again. And this time, golden ichor dripped from the wound. I gasped in awe.

Athena then wrote a new name with the ichor on the other side of the same page as before. *Kóri*.

"It means '*daughter*'," she explained. Those letters glowed as well, marking it as mine forever.

"This is your page in the Book of Olympus, young one," Hera then informed me. "In it your story will be written for generations in the future; like gods before you and however many to come," she smiled, closing the book and letting it disappear. "Create a legacy for the ages."

I curtsied. "Yes, Lady Hera."

She then motioned for me to turn around to face our audience.

I held my head up confidently but my heartbeat was blaring in my ears. This was it. I could feel my newfound power coursing through my veins.

"All rise, for Kóri: goddess of half-bloods."

CHAPTER 50

SAVANNAH

'**KINDNESS IS MEASURED** not by what we do, but by how we live. It is not found in deeds; but rather in the smile you wear and the love you spread. Without the right attitude, helping someone can turn out to be all for naught.' At least that was what my mother always told me.

I wished that she could have come to the ceremony —but Mount Olympus was not voluntarily revealed to just anyone. Especially mere mortals.

Persephone had told me that in an understandably indifferent tone.

She was just as I had imagined: beautiful, reserved and regal. But when it came to the tolerance of the result of her husband's infidelity for eternity, her darker and more hostile side made itself known.

I did not like her as much as she did not like me.

Persephone's mother tolerated me even *less* —she did not like my red hair or my attitude because they were too similar to my mother's. I decided that it was absolutely fine because even Hades could not stand her. Thanatos was ironically the most accepting of the blending of families.

Even so, the feeling that I was intruding still lingered.

I began to wish that I could go back and live with Phoebe again, just the two of us. I knew that things were not so simple anymore.

"…How am I going to tell her?" I huffed aloud. I was putting off even simply calling her to tell her that I had survived, because one thing would lead to another and my transformation would have to come to light.

"She will definitely have a heart attack," Hades' voice then chuckled from behind me as he patted my shoulder half-heartedly.

"For just how long have you been standing there?" I asked without turning to face him.

"A while."

I stared off at the horizon of clouds and watched the temples and palaces glow in a golden sunset. I had been on the balcony alone until my father decided to offer his company. "I don't want to kill her with this," I said. "I mean, next to '*I'm pregnant*' this shouldn't be so catastrophic."

"I do not think that Phoebe would even care about your bedroom related conquests when you tell her that you are now a celestial being that can transcend space and time."

"*Dad.*"

"Sorry," he apologised sheepishly, tossing his head back. "It's going to take a while to get used to boundaries again."

"I am sure that Thanatos didn't appreciate your strange attempts to relate to him either," I retorted dryly.

"No," he sighed. "And I know, there are many times where I messed up raising Thanatos. Maybe he wouldn't be so isolated if I had not been so focused on a family that I couldn't have. But he is still my son for eternity, whether he likes it or not. And I still want to try."

I frowned in thought. "You know, if you really want to relate to your children, you should try and imagine things from their perspective. You won't build relationships by trying to put on an act or trying to make everything about yourself."

"I know how I can come across," he admitted. "And honestly Persephone nags me about it all the time. I get it."

I turned to face him and offered him a smile. "I have faith in you," I assured him.

He smiled back and then let out a yawn. "When are coming back inside? You should be very hungry."

453

"In a bit," I said flippantly. "I want to watch the sunset."

Hades dithered. Then he reached into the inside pocket of his jacket and pulled out a black envelope. He stared at it for a moment, before handing it to me.

"…This is your eighteenth birthday letter. You can read it now, or with your mother when you tell her about all of this later. Either way, happy belated birthday, Kóri."

I took the letter, recognising the same stamp and shimmering paper. It felt warmer in my hand than the last time I held one of the letters. I realised that it was because of the increase of ichor in my system.

I watched Hades walk back inside before thinking about when to open the envelope. I wanted to read it now —my curiosity was outweighing the notion of being considerate and reading it with my mother. Then I realised how worried — or rather, eaten away at by sheer terror —my mother must be after watching the news. The mortals described the battle as a freak weather system, accounting for the lightning, streaking chariots and Poseidon's wave. She might as well believe that I had not survived. I needed to tell her in person.

"Goddess Kóri," a voice then snagged my attention. I turned around before smiling at Sych. "There is someone here to see you."

I frowned. I was not expecting any more guests. "Who?"

"Follow me."

She led me back inside and to the banquet. She then stopped by the salad bar. I glanced around —and then froze as I met a familiar grey-eyed gaze. They froze in the same instant.

We then walked towards each other hesitantly, as though neither of us could believe that we were here, and my heartbeat started beating faster.

"…Mom," I breathed. "What are you doing here?"

What a stupid question, I realised. *Why not start with something like: 'Hey Mom, look at how I'm not dead!'*

She actually smiled. "Your father invited me. You didn't actually think that I'd miss this, did you?"

I shook my head in disbelief. "No, of course not. But I meant how did you even get in? You're mortal."

"Yes," she acknowledged. "But since I was personally invited by a god, I have the right to be here." She then looked around at the room. "It's absolutely beautiful here. And you," she said, gesturing to my ensemble. "Your hair is redder than it used to be. It suits you."

"Thanks," I whispered, accepting the compliment since it came from her. She was the one who knew me the best. Then I frowned, realising that she knew half of what I wanted to tell her already. "Uh...listen Mom —"

"It's okay," she cut me off, waving her hands. "I...know. Hades told me. I...didn't take it as well as I would've thought I would."

"You...anticipated this?"

"Well, not exactly," she admitted. "But I had prepared myself for a scenario where I would lose you. And now...you're going to outlive me like your father? It's kind of crazy," she laughed lightly.

"So, what *do* you think?" I asked.

She looked at me intently, which was slightly unnerving. "Goddess of half-bloods, huh," she said. "Way to come up in the world, honey."

I paused. *Wait what? She is...fine. She is not in shock.* My eyes widened before I grinned and wrapped my arms around her in a hug. She embraced me just as tightly and gently stroked my hair. "I love you, no matter what you are."

I withdrew and told her the same.

"...Is that for me?" she then asked.

"Hm?"

"That letter."

I then remembered the envelope in my hand. "Oh. This is for the both of us. It's a letter for my birthday."

"You think it's as generic as the others?"

I narrowed my eyes. "What do you mean?" I asked.

"Don't try to evade the truth, Savannah. I know that you took them. I figured it out after I had planned to get rid of that box after you had died," she smirked, holding me firmly by the shoulders.

"Well…why didn't you tell me about them? Why didn't you tell me that my Dad was writing to you the whole time?" I countered, deflecting from the issue of my snooping.

My mother sighed in defeat. "If I had told you, it would have done more harm. If you knew that your father was sending letters you would've asked where he was —or worse, run off to find him. I couldn't have you asking questions about who he really was. Not then."

I pouted. "It was still selfish."

"I know. And…I'm sorry," she said in a small voice. "I shouldn't have hidden them out of spite. But what I did then, it wasn't just because I wanted to forget him. I also did it because I wanted to protect you."

"Well, turns out my life isn't normal like you wanted," I murmured.

"It was never entirely in my control," she admitted. "I did try my best to keep you unaware of this world," she sighed, glancing around us, "but looking at you now and what you've accomplished…I couldn't be prouder."

I smiled bashfully. "Thank you, Mom." She was taking all of this quite well. Better than I had imagined.

A thought then struck me, though —if I had been able to open that box with my necklace, how had Phoebe done it for all of those years? I wondered if she received one from Hades as well.

"Do you have a black winged necklace?" I asked outright.

"What?"

"That necklace that I never used to take off —the one that Dad gave me. I used it to open that obsidian box. But I've never seen you wearing or holding one. How did you unlock it?"

Phoebe hesitated, and shuffled on her feet. My brows rose. I had caught her off guard —and whatever she was about to tell me might have been something which she had never planned to disclose.

"…I wanted to tell you about the box when you were going to move out and live your own life," she began. "As I said, telling you too soon would have ruined all of those defences I had worked hard to erect. I'm sorry, Savannah. But I can

456

tell you now," she breathed, as though a weight were being lifted from her shoulders. "That box had been a gift from Hades. It was a jewellery box — designed to lock that way for obvious security measures. When he had to…when we parted ways," she corrected herself, "I refused to have anything to do with it. I tried to destroy it —to destroy that memory of him —yet it lingered. The box was indestructible, and I thought of him every time that I looked at it. I couldn't escape even that.

"I did have a necklace. But Hades took it with him. It wasn't to spite me or get one up on me. He took it so that he could watch over *you*; be with *you*. When I told him that I hated him, he realised that you were the only thing he had left of me. He had to treasure that."

"But what about after?" I questioned. "What about when I found the box? There were letters there which dated as recently as two years ago."

"Yes," she sighed. "As you know, obsidian burns the divine. And since I was not one of them, I could open that box without any issue. It was a good thing that I stopped using it as a jewellery box though —any other mortal could have just as easily have opened it."

"And what about me?" I demanded. "You never worried that I would find it. The lid was really heavy, by the way. What's that about?"

Phoebe shook her head wearily. "You were a child of a god, Savannah. Hades' blood ran within your veins. I knew that you would not be able to open it. It was spell-protected against divine beings."

A wicked, awful thought manifested in my mind. I could not help it —I was still a little agitated about all of the things about Hades which she had kept from me. "Was that to purposefully keep me away from it? Or was it a deterrent against my Dad at first?"

"I was just upset," she reasoned. "It had little to do with hiding it from you. I wanted to spite him, so I made him enchant it when he left. I didn't explain why, but he didn't question it."

I bit my lip thoughtfully. "…Why did you even keep the letters, Mom?"
She looked utterly guilty this time. "Part of it was for you," she murmured.

"And the other part?" I pressed.

A faint smile tugged at the corner of her dark red painted mouth. "You know, if you truly love something, you can never really let it go. I tried to burn those letters —but time and time again, I couldn't bring myself to do it. I decided to save them for you, for when I would eventually tell you about Hades. But if I'm honest with myself, each piece of paper reminded me of him. That he was real. That what we had...had been real."

Phoebe Green was just as human as I had been.

As I was, since mortals had been shaped by the gods' experiences and antics. To hear her admit out loud —in fact, to have her realise it at all —that she had not quite grown to hate my father as she pretended to, eased some crease within me which I had not known was so misshapen.

As though it meant that it had not been all my fault.

"So...do you want to step outside and read that letter?" my mother then suggested, breathing deeply. She was exhausted from the mental drain.

I offered a small smile. "Sure."

On our way back to the balcony I spotted a flash of black, tattoos, blonde hair, and navy blue wool. I had not exactly planned to introduce them, but my mother steered us in their direction as she then noticed their stares.

"I didn't know you had a sister," Chainsaw Guy said before anyone could even exchange a hello.

He then earned a swift jab in each side from both Søren and Abigail. "That's her *mother*," the Trainer hissed.

Chainsaw Guy's eyes widened slightly before he had the sense to offer an apology. Søren extended his hand. "Nice to see you again, Mrs. Green."

"*Ms* Green, please," Phoebe corrected a little icily. "I've never been a missus in my life."

"Oh, sorry," Søren said sheepishly, flushing. "And, I apologise for Melchior —he's not usually like this."

Chainsaw Guy gave him a desperate look.

"Yeah," I agreed, giving Chainsaw Guy a crafty smile. He dithered accordingly. "He's usually gayer."

By the look that he gave me in response, I knew that he would not let me get away with it. My mother suppressed a laugh as she shook Søren's hand, then offered it to a mortified Chainsaw Guy, before greeting Abigail. "So, you must be the rest of Savannah's friends?" she guessed.

I stiffened and dubiously tried to explain exactly how we knew each other, but Abigail had apparently been showered with some kind of magical amnesia spell because she came to my rescue, "Yes we are. She couldn't have won without us."

My mother looked at me for confirmation, but I just blinked stupidly. "Well, I'm glad that she's not alone and hopeless," she told them. "Thank you for taking care of her."

Murmured welcomes filled an awkward silence.

She had made it sound as though I were a toddler who needed to be reined in on a leash. My cheeks consequently warmed.

"...*Okay*," I then blurted, grabbing Phoebe's hand, "Later," I called as I pulled her away, desperate to put as much distance between us as possible.

"Why did you drag us away so suddenly?" she asked as I marched towards the balcony.

"Mom, that was...so weird," I struggled to find the right word. "Why did you imply that I can't do anything by myself, like a child? They're my...*friends*. Sort of. They might all be over a century but they've the got the minds of teenagers, trust me."

My mother snorted. "That'd be the first time I'm hearing something like that. You have always been so insistent on your independence, but usually your escapades don't end well."

"They didn't need to know that," I grumbled.

"Ah, what? Did I embarrass you?" she cooed.

"Very much so, yes," I admitted.

"Oh, you'll get over it," she scoffed. Then she smiled fondly. "...Look, Savannah —I can see that you're perfectly capable of being on your own now. You've finally proven that. And, by the way, embarrassing you just happens to be a part of my job."

I still grumbled —but I was suppressing my own smile.

✠

My dearest Savannah,

As you can tell from the opening sentence, I changed the letter from its original draft. In the old version I realised that I was sounding too much like the man I did not want to be — the man who I used to be. But starting now, today, I plan to change. I want to be the father you deserve. I also want to the friend your mother needs as well, if she will let me be that much. Know that I never wanted to leave you — either of you. You will both always have a place in my heart.

Fate and circumstances will not allow us to be the family I am sure that each one of us wishes that we could be, but I hope that will not stop us from acting like family. Of course, I hope that your mother knows that I would take the opportunity to be with her in another life in a heartbeat. I know how unbelievably selfish that is, but that is what I feel. Do not ever tell Persephone. She is my wife, my love — and in this life we find ourselves in, I will honour that. I cannot help what my heart feels, however.

And you, Savannah, whom I love unconditionally, know that you will always have your father's heart. You will always be one of my favourites. I would and will love you no matter what reality we are in, or what Fate decrees. I know how you forgave me when I returned was well undeserved, but I am eternally grateful for your compassion. You had no obligation to forgive me at all. But thank you. I am still working towards forgiving myself. I am not sure that I will ever be able to do so. But on a lighter note: I look forward to having you around for eternity. Perhaps it will one day make up for the years I wasted being a coward.

```
      Now, if you do not read this with your mother,
    please tell her that I will always love her,
    even if she does not. Because I have come to
      realise that that is indeed what love is.
```

                            Hades.

In the end, the letter was the longest that he had ever written.

He had poured himself into the pages, bore his soul. Some parts were a little controversial, especially his feelings for Phoebe versus Persephone. But we had to give him the benefit of the doubt. My mother acted irritated, whether with the length or contents —but I could see that she was actually less upset with Hades than usual. Her gaze lingered on the last few sentences for a while; words declaring that he would love her even if she would not —and I felt for her as tears welled up in her eyes.

"If anything about him should change, *that* shouldn't be it," she had whispered, the hint of a smile tugging at the corner of her lips.

She did not tell that to his face, even when he personally saw her off by one of his portals towards the end of the celebration. I could not tell exactly what they were saying, but my mother did not look like she wanted to tear his head from his shoulders. I wondered if it would always be that way —my parents at constant odds; wrapped up with other people and responsibilities. It made me feel sick when my mother told me that she was growing quite fond of Don, and that she would not mind spending more time with him. I was happy for her —truly. But parts of me felt more torn than before; like I did not know where I fit in anymore. I was reserved though, and I swallowed the pain.

I could pretend to like Persephone.

I could pretend to like Don. I could pretend like being a part of two separate families was okay.

Maybe if I pretended for long enough it would start to become true. Then I would not feel like I was being ripped in half, like I did when I watched my mother disappear into the portal and my father walk back in the other direction, and with infinities between them. I sighed and decidedly looked away, up at the sky. It had no worries. The universe was its kin, and no one could take that away from it.

As I watched the cosmic heavens move from the balcony and clutched the letter against my chest, I still could not help it as my gaze followed the god of the Underworld in a black suit walking by a crystal blue river that marked the edge of a thick forest.

✠

I did not have to be quiet, but it felt as though I might wake the castle up with every step that I took. I was nervous. Regardless, I made my way to the meeting spot on which Thanatos and I had agreed. He looked haggard, as though he had not slept in a month. I expected him to snap at me about the hour, but it seemed that he did not even have the energy for that.

"You know, I really shouldn't be doing this. It can be seriously dangerous," Thanatos warned me again. It was dark in the castle hallway, and the only light came from the moonlight that streamed in through the burgundy curtains. "Does Hades know that you are here?"

I rolled my eyes and sighed but I could not ignore the anxiousness in his own eyes. He was actually worried about me. I fought a sly smile.

"I know," I murmured. "And no, he doesn't. But please —I need this to happen. I have to ask."

Thanatos sighed, but closed his eyes and waved his hand, summoning a soul. I inhaled sharply as a red misty form materialised before us —a stocky woman in black jeans and a torn leather jacket.

"…Nadine," I breathed.
Her glowing eyes bore into mine, not full of pain but full of dull emptiness. She did not need to ask why she was here.

And she knew exactly what I wanted to ask.

462

"For the future," she answered, and her voice seared my ears like Aaron's had, making me wince. Emotion flickered on her face for a moment at the realisation that she was the cause of discomfort. "…The future could go on without me. But not without you."

"That's why?" I asked. "That's why you died for me?"

"You're not a *total* pain," she said, tilting her head in a way that suggested amusement.

I could not repress the scoff that then came from me. "I wish that I could say the same," I said quite truthfully. Thanatos gave me a sideways look which I ended up ignoring. "…I didn't ask for you to do it," I said self-consciously through my teeth. "You didn't need to —"

"You didn't have to," she cut me off. A chill shivered through me as I flinched at her voice. "I had to. It didn't matter how we got along. It was a matter of your life…and I could not let you die."

How unfair. How could she be so selfless after the way we treated each other? And what about her brother —had she thought of him? I clenched my fists. "…Lewis ran off. He…*he* can't go on without you."

Nadine tensed at the mention of her brother's name and appeared to be a little guilty. "Tell him that I'm sorry."

"*You* should have told him," I insisted, taking a step forward. Thanatos held me back, and I did not realise that my anger had gotten the best of me until I felt the heat of fire in my hands. I paused, curling them into fists. "…You didn't even say goodbye."

"He would've tried to stop me," Nadine pointed out. "But…please tell him that I am sorry."

I lashed out. "He won't *listen* —"

"He needs to. He needs to understand that I'm gone," she urged, and my hand flew up to my ear of its own accord. I gasped, and Nadine faltered.

"My voice…is hurting you." She looked at me desperately. "Stop."
When she gave that command, her voice softened, and no screech accompanied it. I could feel it; I could see it in her eyes. A flood of compassion. Tears stung,

463

and I moved my gaze to the floor, where it was less intense. We may have clashed but ultimately Nadine felt that our relationship had not mattered when it came to the cause. She put my future and so many others like me ahead of hers, no questions asked. I knew the name for it: a hero. Nadine had died knowing it might be in vain; knowing it might not have guaranteed victory. Even with that risk, she had given her life for me. How could someone like that truly exist?

Thanatos then put a hand on my shoulder, causing me to start. His eyes told me that I needed to draw it to a close. I nodded solemnly and turned back to Nadine. "Thank you," I told her. "Really. I'll never forget."

She nodded once, before her soul's sudden disappearance, leaving a shower of red dust in its wake. It was then silent; too quiet and too cold, as though the very atmosphere understood what had happened.

"Did it help?" Thanatos murmured.

I did not know. I did not feel any better than before. Not even worse. In fact, I felt nothing. I felt numb.

"...Yes," I lied, wiping my face.

Everything in me then understood the weight of how Nadine's soul would never be able to rest in peace.

I felt it in my immortal soul.

SON

OF

DEATH

THE STORY CONTINUES
JUNE 2021

ACKNOWLEDGEMENT

'*The Daughter of Fire Saga*' started in 2017 as an idea on paper; and I never would have anticipated that the story would come this far. Along the journey, I would like to thank every single one of my first readers, for their undying support. I would like to thank my family; my mother, father and sister along with my cousins, who encouraged me every step of the way. And lastly, I want to thank the people I met along the way who always instantly loved the idea and encouraged me to follow my dreams.

ABOUT THE AUTHOR

Stacey Willis is a writer and
freelance graphic designer; born in Zimbabwe and raised
primarily in South Africa. She now lives in the UK.
She has been writing since 2015, beginning online and now
specializing in all levels of fantasy and gritty fiction.

Printed in Great Britain
by Amazon